After the Silence
Volume 1
Bree

JACQUELINE PAIGE

Published by FRP
Copyright © 2015 Roxane Kerr
Cover art by: Off the Wall Creations
Edited by: Gaele Hince

Updated 2020

ISBN (paperback): 978-1-7774387-9-1
ISBN (digital): 978-1-7774387-8-4

DEDICATION

To Abi and Lauren- what can I say?
 Both of you showed me that kindness still exist in a world of harsh realities.
I miss your smiles every day – you rocked my world right to the foundation with your generosity. I 'heart' you both.

ACKNOWLEDGMENTS

Without my beta readers and favorite editor, this story would never had made it as far as it did. As I worked through the vast world of After the Silence, the constant encouragement from all of you is the only reason I found the momentum to finish it. Thank you for pointing out what wasn't working, what did mesh together and the endless suggestions on several "next" volumes. I will try to finish them all … in this life.

CHAPTER ONE

I was nineteen when the world went crazy, nothing that
was would ever be again.

Remnants of a familiar world remained, but not enough
to instill those warm, fuzzy feelings you get when life is
comfortable and predictable.

I'm Bree Taylor. This is an account of what I remember,
how things happened when life changed forever and I
managed to survive. There is so much to tell, a thousand
pages wouldn't be enough to explain it all, but someone has
to tell it. There needs to be a record so if we, as a planet
survive, others will have the history. If we don't, then the
next species to invade earth will know what we did wrong.

It is now just a few days after my twenty-second
birthday, I'm standing looking out the window and wishing
my brother, Shawn, well in the afterlife. A seemingly small
laceration on his leg became so much more and took him
away from me, leaving me to figure out this world on my
own. If I have relatives left living, I wouldn't know. All that
I cared for are now ashes spread over the dirt and just
memories inside my head.

I am alone.

"Bree?"

I turned towards Darren, one of my adopted brothers,

and gave him a look to tell him we were done discussing my decision. He didn't heed the warning.

"Are you sure this is what you want to do?"

His voice was filled with grief and worry. *Was I? Yes, at least eighty percent certain.* "Darren, I can't stay here. Being in the city is dangerous enough as a family, never mind a single girl."

A desperate look appeared in his eyes. He was probably wishing at this point that some of the other brothers were still alive, but only Bobby and Darren were left out of my six older brothers.

"We'll move you closer to us, keep you safe."

We, being his very old mother and wheelchair bound brother. I gave him my most stern look. "I think you have enough to worry about, you don't need me to add to that list."

Darren's eyes strayed to the picture I still held. The one of my family and me before life was forever altered.

"Shawn would have wanted me to. I feel like I'm letting him down."

I offered him a smile that said I had accepted it, even though I really didn't. "Shawn is gone and I have to go and try to find my own place now. You guys did all you could to prepare and teach me to fend for myself, your job is done.'

He stuffed his hands in his pockets and leaned back against the wall. "Where will you go?"

I turned and looked out the window. "I think the mountains."

A sound came from him that told me he thought I was too much of a girl to survive that. "The crazies hide there."

I chuckled and slowly turned back, rolling my eyes at him. "And they don't in the city?" His expression pleaded with me. "Darren, I know you have always been close to my family, you're like family. So I know that Shawn probably told you I changed after the virus." The fear in his eyes confirmed my suspicions. He knew the truth. "I have to find out what I've become, before others do. I need to know if

I'm a good thing or a bad thing. And I need space and solitude to discover this."

"Bree, you could never be bad."

My heart warmed from his words. "I hope you're right."

He sighed loudly. "Fine, but you're taking Tremor and Shawn's weapons – otherwise I'm going with you."

I knew he wouldn't, we both knew it, but it was his way of feeling like he had done all he could. "I don't have to take Tremor. I can walk."

He shook his head sending his black hair scattering around his face. "We have LadyBell and her colt; we don't need any more than that. Tremor's fast and loyal and he'll get you through the bad times."

I was hoping the bad times would be few, naive I know, but I could hope. My heart strained as I fought to keep my resolve. He loved his horse and to know he was sending him out there with me meant more than I could express. "Thank you." I wanted to hug him, I really did, who knew when I'd have any friendly human contact again. If I hugged him now I knew I would fall apart, and I needed to keep my head out of the emotional whirl that was already threatening to suck me in. "I should get ready. I want to leave early enough so I can be out of the city before darkness falls."

Darren nodded, even though his entire face told me he didn't agree. "I'll go get Tremor. You get your stuff packed up." He looked at me for a long silent moment before he rushed back out the door.

I stood there looking at the door long after he'd gone. In my head I wasn't at all sure this was a good plan. I was following my heart and it was telling me to get out of town and find out where I was meant to be. Of course my head was saying that was a load of crap, but I was still going to do it. I couldn't explain why I needed to be outside and away from all the buildings and people, it just felt right.

Darren didn't know I was already packed. When I knew Shawn wasn't going to recover I started to gather up what I would need. Before Shawn was too far away from me, we had discussed my plan. He agreed I needed to leave. He had also said he was coming with me as soon as he was on his feet. I think by that point we both knew he would never recover.

I swore to follow the least traveled path. I promised to stay away from crowded places. I vowed to him I would survive and then I tucked the blanket around him and went off to cry by myself until my eyes felt like they were going to split in half.

I'm done with the crying and ready to take on what's left of this planet and the series of trials I know it will throw in my path. Tale of a colony of peaceful people live high in the mountains, it's my plan to find them. I hope the stories of the crazies that live between here and there are just that, a farfetched creation of some idiot's imagination.

Going into my room, I quickly headed to the closet to pull out the packs that had been sitting ready for me. I didn't need a lot. I could live off the land if needed, but one entire bag contained dehydrated food, just to be safe. As I swung the largest pack up onto my shoulder I caught a glimpse of myself in the mirror. Would this be the last time I saw the woman looking back at me? I looked into my now green eyes, a leftover from the virus. I stared until I saw it; determination, hidden just under the surface. Sighing, I ran a hand through my choppy red hair and debated, very briefly, if I should dye it a dull brown and tone it down. I knew that would never happen. I wouldn't trade in my brilliant hair for anything. It was a statement and if I couldn't do anything else I was definitely going to make one.

Closing my eyes, I prayed for my spirit to stay strong. When I opened them I didn't look at the mirror again, just picked up the other two bags and walked out of my home for the very last time

Darren stood outside holding the reins and crooning softly to Tremor. I couldn't see his face, which was a blessing, I didn't have to see his eyes begging me not to go again. The large horse's ears flicked as he listened attentively. No doubt he was receiving instructions to keep me safe and out of harm's way. Darren lifted his face away from the animal and looked over at me. "He's quite happy you're getting him the hell out of this city." A half hearted grin appeared on his face. With a tilt of his head he motioned to the other side of the porch. "We're going to walk with you until you're outside the city limits."

I turned and looked to see Bobby leaning against the side of the house. I couldn't help but smile when he wiggled his eyebrows at me. Bobby was the clown of the group that grew up together. I often wondered if anyone else ever sensed he was too serious inside and that was why he joked around as much as he did. Bobby was my first crush when I was thirteen. It never went anywhere, for obvious reasons, but I still had a secret place for him in my heart. I was grateful he was coming along; it would prevent Darren from pleading with me to change my mind, again. "Hey, Bobby." He pushed away from the wall and sauntered in his easy way towards me, his long leather jacket making him look like he floated.

"Hey, Brat. You didn't think you were going to sneak off without saying bye did you?"

"Wouldn't dream of it."

He pulled the bag from my shoulder. "Good to know."

Darren came over and took the bags, taking them to secure to Tremor's saddle. "I think you should walk with us for a while and then he won't be too tired to haul ass when you need him to later." He didn't look at me when he spoke.

"She'll be fine, Dare, we taught her." Bobby's tone sounded annoyed.

Silently I hoped he was right.

Stepping in front of me, he looked me over. Without a word he moved and took off the coat that I couldn't ever remember him not having. "You're going to need something to keep you dry and warm." He held the coat out to me.

I opened my mouth to say something, but nothing came out. Pulling my hands out of my pockets I took the jacket and looked up at him. Bobby was a good six inches taller than my five foot five making me wonder if the leather was going to drag on the ground when I put it on. He continued to stand there and say nothing so I put my arms quickly into the sleeves. It hung about three inches off the ground. He gave me a triumphant grin and then moved around behind me, pulling at the material muttering about straps as he did. When he was finished the coat didn't gape away from my body as much as it had.

"There's a nice custom pocket on the inside left." Leaning around me, he flipped the coat open to point to it. "And this…" Bending down to the cuff of his jeans, he pulled up the material to reveal a knife handle sticking out of his boot. "Fits in it perfectly." I knew my eyes were wide as he slipped the knife into the pocket.

He stepped back quickly and jammed his hands into his pockets like he was afraid of grabbing me if he didn't. As he looked down, just before his shaggy blonde hair covered his eyes, I thought I saw a tear running down his cheek. "Find a better place, Bree," he whispered, so softly I almost missed it.

I swallowed the lump that lodged in my throat and nodded. "Thanks."

"Let's go." Darren urged from where he stood. "I want you to have more than enough time to find somewhere to stay when it gets dark.

I wanted to take a huge breath and build the courage to take this final and first step, but I couldn't bring myself to do it in front of them.

"Mom sent a bag of things." Darren patted the small one tied to the back of the saddle. He didn't elaborate what kind of things. Running his hand to the front of it, he flipped open the small pack. "Shawn's hand-gun is in here and there's enough ammo on the other side to last a long time." He looked down at the ground and said nothing further.

I moved around to the front of Tremor and looked up into his big eyes. 'We're going to be just fine aren't we?'' I ran my hand down the blackness of his coat over his neck and picked up the reins. His ears flicked and he brought his mouth down to nibble at my shoulder. As far as encouraging signs went, that one worked for me.

I couldn't stand the looks Bobby and Darren were giving each other, so without prolonging this any further, I turned and started to lead the way down the street, thankful we weren't far from the nearest border.

~

I kept Tremor at an easy trot until we were far enough away that I wouldn't be tempted to go back. Stopping, I turned him and looked back to the two men that stood exactly where I'd left them a few minutes earlier. I waved my arm at them, silently thanked them and wished them well. Turning the animal in the opposite direction, I prodded him with my heels to get us out of here. He complied without hesitation and carried us quickly away from the city that was filled with nothing but heartache that I could no longer face.

CHAPTER TWO

The ride was long and so silent it had me on the edge of panic the entire time. Tremor's hooves hitting the dirt were the only sounds I could hear. The solitude gave me too much time to think, making me miss my brother and family more than ever.

The years leading up to my nineteenth birthday were relatively ordinary, or as ordinary as they were before. Day to day life carried on at the hectic pace, people hurried to possess every technological advance possible, filling their personal world. The news, from time to time broadcasted some tragedy or disaster. The bulk of the planet was under the belief that as long as it didn't happen to them, it wasn't important. No one took these rare instances as a sign of what was to come.

The changes at first weren't alarming, but written off by most as the natural evolution of things. Gradually over the course of a year, tragedy after tragedy grouped together started to be significant. Spiritual fanatics began harping that life was forever changed. Of course, anyone that looked out the window or read a newspaper knew this. Their 'empowered' connections weren't giving them a special kind of heads up that the run-of-the-mill sinners weren't privy to.

My own thoughts at this stage of my sheltered

immaturity were that Mother Nature had decided to fight back. I know I would be if you tore me down, used me up and polluted me at the rate the human race was with the earth. I'd be more than pissed off enough to take something back and make a very loud statement.

There was no way to escape what was happening. Nowhere was exempt from the chaos or safe to hide.

It wasn't just a few more frequent tornados and earthquakes…where there had never been any before I might add, but flash floods and landslides, fires and heat waves…any natural disaster you could think was now a reality.

Everyone began to wonder and notice the weird fluctuations in the weather. Even the skeptics, accepting the abnormalities began to admit that global warming was possible.

The news called it climate chaos when sink holes large enough to swallow whole blocks began to appear. After months of back to back chaotic climatic events everyone's warning bells were finally ringing loud and clear.

Then things got worse.

Schools and education were abandoned. Hospitals filled with refugees more than the sick or injured. It was a shutdown of society, at least the good and necessary parts of it ceased to function.

Panic hit a high when the super viruses began to develop. It was then that all who were old enough to rationalize what was happening knew there may be an end coming.

Medications no longer worked, the germs had evolved and overcome were immune to treatment. If you did survive this major ailment, you were no longer a simple human. You had mutated and as a result, were feared by all.

Diseases were no longer named or classified; there was just *the* virus. Mutated and stronger, new symptoms, same name.

I supposed it turned out to be the one thing that no one

could placate with meaningless promises, or hope to control.

I tried to feel lucky in all of this, in the fact that we lived in the part of the world that wasn't completely devastated—although sometimes it felt close.

Other countries were not lucky. Tsunamis and hurricanes ripped shorelines apart and leveled cities. The water grew so vast in some parts that new rivers were born. The earth and water did not care about who or what was there. Just as humans hadn't when they cut all the trees down and slapped pavement and concrete on any surface, a mall and parking were more important than land or trees.

The earth, the virus and even the sky seemed to work in sync to shut us down. The super moon—which had once seemed to me like a giant blow up balloon that had been taped in the dark sky—brought with it a glowing calm to the earth. Providing a false sense of calm before the threefold increase in the chaos. Fault lines began shifting, tidal waves springing up without warning; crashing entire pieces of geography into the oceans making them something from the past.

I gave up watching the news. Emergency networks ran around the clock, and stopped right around the time the virus claimed rights of survival on the evolutionary scale.

For a handful of millenniums humans were lulled into a false sense of security, believing that they were on the top of the food chain and the dominant species. The virus proved it was all just a ploy.

My feelings of being lucky ran out when the quakes started. At first the shock and awe of experiencing one was on everyone's mind, until they increased in strength to the point where the Richter scale no longer applied. At the slightest tremor you moved to safety and prayed to a god…that probably couldn't hear you, their heavens also rocked with the noise from aftershocks of angry mother earth.

By my twentieth birthday, my father and brother were the only members of my family remaining. The virus claimed my two sisters and mother in the last year. A part of me died with them. It's a piece I'll never get back. No family escaped the loss of someone. Death became a prominent part of everyday life.

In that same year I survived an attack of the virus. I don't remember much while I had it, but from what I've seen of others while ill, that's a good thing. The virus at least displayed mercy by making the victim incoherent. The doctor said I was a rare miracle because I escaped death and obvious mutation. I didn't feel like a miracle.

I survived and even though we never discussed it, I was now some sort of sub-human species. Exactly what no one knew and I didn't try to discover it, there was just something inside me now. I could feel it, but ignored it. My family feared this change in me but we all carried on pretending nothing had changed.

Our world had narrowed. You went out only when necessary, stuck to areas you knew and never spoke to strangers. My father in all his paranoia began hoarding everything that could be accumulated, we had enough clothes and supplies to last several years. At first I thought he had lost all sense of sanity. His paranoia turned out to be wisdom only a small number possessed.

If you came into contact with anyone that sneezed or looked slightly unhealthy in any way, you went in the other direction as fast as you could and then quarantined yourself for the weeks to follow.

No one was safe; none escaped the invisible killers that so far had taken ten times more human lives than the natural disasters.

With the amount of deaths, burials for those that passed onto the next life became illegal; the law now stated bodies were to be cremated. Even in death you were something to fear, your corpse would somehow still manage to infect them. Your existence was erased, not remembered.

The population was dwindling, a metropolis that once claimed millions of residents now numbered only a few thousand. It was terrifying, and it was the new reality. Births were fewer, survivors weren't able to breed and no one knew why. Even those that had always been healthy weren't having children. No one wanted to bring a child into this, with the future so unstable and unknown. Most adults at this point weren't even certain they wanted to remain living, so we accepted the declining population and tried to carry on.

As my twenty-first birthday passed, I lost my father to the virus, leaving my older brother and I on our own, not sure we knew what to do about it. Five of my brother's lifelong friends that had survived to this point, adopted me as their young sister and felt responsible for me. I can't even express my lack of enthusiasm at having six older brothers trying to rule my every move.

Eventually after a few months of my refusing to bend to *their* wishes, they relaxed and began to teach me how to survive and defend myself. It was now a world where no one walked alone in the streets. We weren't even safe from those that hadn't quite made the transition to the new times smoothly, they would attack you as you went by, trying to get you to see the truth. Many were labeled stark raving mad, even though I thought they'd just taken the easy way out and this was their way of not dealing with reality.

In the span of one month, we lost three of my adopted brothers. Only one was to the virus, which seemed to lessen the pain in my heart. His death was easier to accept than the two that were literally slaughtered when they were caught smuggling supplies into the city. When the fourth brother was attacked by the virus I began to accept than I may end up alone in the near future and a part of me shut down, so I wouldn't feel too much. I hoped I was over-reacting to all the death surrounding me, but deep down I somehow didn't think so.

The structure of society was forever changed in this time. When I think back to what some thought unjust before, I now wished that those simple injustices were all we faced.

Doctors, the small number that were brave enough to practice, no longer worked toward curing the ill or dying. Their only goal was to contain any case of illness. They now preferred natural products to help alleviate the suffering as much as they could.

Before all of this, a medical doctor would never have said he didn't know. He would have given you a long spiel of terminology that no one understood, leaving you feeling he knew what he was doing. That was no longer the case. The doctors didn't know and they were admitting it, willingly working with naturopaths and various other holistic practitioners to try to get a jump on any ailment or health issue they could. I think as this point if they thought performing ritual sacrifices would help to cure a small few, they may have tried it, regardless of jail time.

Not that there was a lot of jail time in this broken world. The newly established law enforcement wasn't exactly giving people speeding tickets and seatbelt fines. That was in the past, now they had their hands full trying to keep the few commodities any community had safe. Commodities like a grocery store, which was more important than a bank. Money was of no use to the simple layman. Bartering for goods and supplies was now the norm. The law enforcers tried to keep the innocent safe, but even that was a feat no mortal man could accomplish.

In all the population devastation, the politicians survived. I found this unfair in ways that are too frustrating to explain. They were still there to create laws and make decisions for the populous as a whole. I tried to discuss my opinions of politics with my brothers, but I'm told my thoughts are not very lady-like. To summarize my thoughts in this; briefly put, there will always be vultures to scavenge from the ones that can't stand on their own.

I feel nothing but bitterness for this group of people charged to represent our needs and look out for us. They failed us when we needed them most. How many years had they choose to ignore the signs? How long did they do nothing to prevent the planet from eventually trying to spew us into the solar system?

The new political leaders are worse than the old ones, if that's even possible. The latest idea to do to protect us leaves a bad taste in my mouth. They have, in their higher intellect and wisdom, decided that any person who had mutated should be marked or tagged visibly, to protect the general public from danger. Were they actively trying to right the world and people that lived in it? Did they pay the geniuses out there to come up with solutions for starvation and the filth we lived in? No. They paid number crunchers to research anyone that had been more than mildly ill and record them on a list. This list would track people's whereabouts, should it decided they were less than safe at a later date. In my opinion this was a complete waste of time and resources. Other than a few attention seekers, any that had been mutated stayed hidden and tried to blend in and steer clear of any kind of trouble.

I didn't even know what I was now able to do, so I sure as hell wasn't going to let some brainpans poke and prod me so they could determine my level of hazard to people.

Oddly enough we still had our advanced technology—if you could afford it. Everything went to the highest bidder. For those of us that couldn't afford it, we lived in what everyone was now calling olden times. The few elderly that had existed when life was slower and without high tech were the scholars now and reveled in being useful in society once more. It was their skills that allowed people to seek out a living, their knowledge that brought the population back.

Four months ago the entire planet shook with a quake so strong that everyone figured that was the end. She was ending our torment once and for all. I will remember that feeling for the rest of my life. There was nothing that didn't move. Every single object moved, all at once. Hearing so much motion at the same time was deafening, the loudest I have ever heard, and something I never want to experience again. No one knows how long it lasted, but it felt like hours.

I was lucky enough when it struck that my brother and his two surviving friends were at our house. I don't think I would have come through it sane if I'd been alone. The four of us huddled together, the three males placing me in the center and doing as they had always done, sheltering me from harm. I remember thinking at the time when I was desperate and trying not to panic, that if they hadn't done that, I may have fled and probably wouldn't be here now.

When it stopped, the world had never seemed so silent. So still.

The silence lasted weeks until those left began to live once more. I don't think anyone went outside unless they were given no choice. There wasn't one person that left for work in the morning and not a sound on the streets. It was as if the whole world was afraid to move.

I will always remember the first sound I heard outside of our window, two children playing. After that moment of joyous noise, life, as odd as it now was, finally resumed after the silence.

It took more than a week for our small neighborhood to clean up and clear out the debris and dead. It was the first time in a very long time that everyone worked together, no longer paranoid of being near others.

That community feeling didn't last long, a few days after the clean up was finished the guarded expressions and glancing over your shoulder resumed. It was then that I realized life was never going to recover to carry on as it had before. Fear and distrust was how the planet had decided to live. I know I was only fooling myself before this thinking that maybe somehow things would go back to normal, but I knew different. It was a sad, devastating day for me.

CHAPTER THREE

I glanced at the sky, trying to gauge how much time I had left until the sun was completely set, before turning back to look at the trees ahead. The last hour had been nothing but open space and the odd abandoned vehicle or trailer. I'd rather take my chances in the trees than stop where I had no shelter at all. It may be quiet but I wasn't going to hold false hope that this was going to be easy. I didn't know exactly how it was going to be, but I knew easy wasn't one of the words I'd use later on.

In the last few hours I'd only questioned what I was doing half a dozen times, far better than I thought I'd do. Why was I second guessing myself? In the city there were places you could try to run to, hide in and hope that what you were running from got distracted by a brighter prospect. I'm not just talking about muggings or robberies, the things I was afraid of in the city were much worse than that.

We all knew mutants existed, but not all were invisible or good in any sense of the word. Then again, I had learned there was bad in all species. I had only to see a few bad mutants transforming into something hideous, more evil than I had ever know existed, that was enough for me.

After witnessing what at first I thought was just a disagreement between some young teens, I never wanted to see anything like that again. I'd hid at home for three days afterward. They had been arguing and then one of them started to change, gradually morphing into something other than the boy he had been. I will hear that boys' screams inside my head for the rest of my life. Bobby had been the one to find me that time. He took me home and stayed by my side for two days watching over me.

Shortly after that was when my *brothers* decided I needed to know how to defend myself. Defend might be a loose description of what they taught me. After a few months of sparring with them and listening to their every instruction I could probably take down someone three times my size. I'd managed to take all of them down, and often wondered if they let me do it to build my confidence. Thinking back now, I hoped I had won by my own skill and they hadn't been placating me.

They had taught me so much. Although I never understood why they'd be so disappointed when I couldn't remember what a move was called. My thought was as long as I could perform it, did it really matter what it was called? They all had lessons for years, so maybe that was part of it. I was the ripe old age of eight when asked if I too wanted lessons. To a girl who played with dolls—kicking people and knocking them down wasn't really something I felt I had a need to know for my future. Hindsight is a nasty creature I've come to realize.

When they stopped teaching me I could fight on instinct alone; armed with a knife, I could end someone's existence. Using the gun I could hit a bull's eye dead on. The only problem with all of this—I didn't have it in me to kill anyone.

That was almost a year ago. Rigorously I'd practiced my lessons each day, and hoped the survival instinct Bobby told me I had would kick in—actually kick in and save my ass if I needed it. I hoped that my size would fool others, into thinking that little me couldn't possibly do any sort of damage.

My mind just kept racing through one thought after another as I rode in the silence. I kept coming back to realize

that the world hadn't just gone crazy, it had gone psycho—
and I was placing myself on the doorstep of insanity and
hoping like hell I had what it would take to come out on the
other side.

If I could figure out exactly what 'it' was, I'd be half way
there.

A movement caught the corner of my eye. With my heart
in my throat I looked in the fading sunlight to figure out what
it was. A large black dog ran parallel to us about fifteen feet
away. It didn't make a sound, just ran at a steady speed in the
same direction.

Dog breeds weren't my specialty; I guessed he was a mix
of shepherd and a husky. I watched it for a moment, hoping
it was going to turn and head off in another direction, but it
continued on. Tremor didn't seem to be bothered, so I
figured it was just doing as we were and relocating.

Dragging my attention back towards the trees, I scanned
along them for a spot to stop for the night. I didn't want to
admit it, but my body was starting to object to riding and it
was starting to get dark. The only stop along the way had
been when I'd found water. Not knowing when we'd see
water again, I stopped long enough to fill the extra
containers. If Tremor was going to continue to do all the leg
work, the least I could do was offer the animal a drink when
we stopped.

We walked slowly along the tree line; the dog stopped
and sat watching us. It almost looked like he was waiting for
us to check it out; make sure it was somewhere he wanted to
be. He was kind of cute in a large gangly sort of way. I rolled
my eyes and gave myself a stern internal lecture that I was not
going to start adopting every stray we came across. Animals
had always been a weakness of mine, to the absolute
distraction of my family when I'd drag home a kitten or dog
and even the bird that one time. I couldn't afford to make any
attachments right now. It was going to take everything I had
to look after myself, never mind a pet or two.

Tremor paused and stood there, waiting for me to make

the decision. It was the first sign that he was tired and I wasn't going to ignore it. "All right boy, I can take a hint." I guided him in the direction of the thickest group of trees I could see. I wanted as much protection around me as I could find.

Getting down out of the saddle was not a moment of gracefulness on my part, I slid over the one side and when I hit the ground I almost landed on my butt as my legs buckled underneath me. The horse stood patiently as I hung off the saddle and leaned against him until I had my feet under me again.

With stiff limbs, I moved to slowly take the bags and the saddle off. The large Tremor that was now my companion watched as I took my time figuring things out. Two large trees were close enough and seemed a safe enough place for me to stay for the night. Only having to worry about one side to watch seemed like a good idea to me. I certainly wasn't going to chicken out on the first night alone in the dark, making sure I was situated right was worth the extra time.

Securing a thin rope between one of the larger trees and another that was ten or so feet away, I attached Tremor's reins so he could move freely between them. I wasn't sure if I even needed to tie him, but that would not make a good first morning to wake up and find out I lost my horse. He didn't seem at all bothered by it as he moved to the far end of the line and began checking out the growth on the ground. Filing the basin with water, I set it against the tree so when he decided he might like a drink, there was one. With my back against the tree, I sat down and heaved a loud sigh.

It was dark by this time. I debated whether I wanted to light a small fire or find somewhere to go to the bathroom. My heart did this little stutter as I realized the first thing I was going to really miss was a washroom.

My body ached and despite the nerves, I was tired. Digging in the smallest bag, I found the battery free flashlight, one of my fathers' hoarded treasures, and gave it a shake to light the direction I was looking. I didn't want a giant bonfire, but a small one would give me comfort, rather than sitting here in the pitch black trying not to freak out.

I didn't remember the trees and forest making the noises this one was. Of course, all the other times I had always been with someone. That scurrying sound that I kept hearing, logically a branch or leaves brushing against each other. The not so logical girly part of me screamed giant rodent. Add that to the various creaking sounds the trees were making and I'd be lucky if I didn't have a nervous breakdown by the time daylight returned.

Ignoring the way my body objected, I got up to look for some small dry branches to light a fire with. I had paper and fire starters packed, but why waste those when I was surrounded by wood dry enough to do the same thing?

Tremor made a soft whinny and I froze where I was, listening. The snapping and crunching of branches told me something was moving through the trees. Turning the flash light off, I hunched down to be as small and invisible as possible. I listened in the darkness for anything that would let me know where the noise had come from and what had made it. Voices were carried to me in the dark, a man and a woman. I moved slowly back towards my things and sat with my back against the tree straining to see in the dark.

Time stopped as I waited to see if the voices kept moving or came closer. I wasn't sure what I'd do if they did come closer. I touched the handle of the knife inside my coat, hoping this wasn't when I find out if I could use it. Leaves rustled from behind me. I held my breath and pushed back against the tree, waiting. When I heard a low growl coming from around the tree I think my heart even paused.

I had strangers coming closer on one side of me and an animal voicing a warning behind me. Tremor shook his head and pranced a few times and the growling got louder. I sat there trying to gauge what was the most important and decided there was no way I was going to let something happen to my horse. Sliding up the tree as quietly as I could, while focusing on the voices, I tried to recall every skill instilled in me, drawing more blanks than anything useful.

Pulling the knife from the pocket, I prayed it was sharp enough to cut the rope I'd tied Tremor to. I guessed I had about fifteen seconds to cut it and get to the horse before whatever was growling took a bite off one of my legs or other body parts. Chewing my lip, I hoped I could still get on his back without the saddle. The plan was to ride like hell and come back later for my stuff—if we could find it again.

I drew a deep breath in through my nose and squatted down ready to bolt towards him. Before I could move something flew by me, close enough I felt fur against my cheek. Trying not to make any sound, I lifted the flash light; I couldn't stand the dark any longer. I shone it towards the growling, it was the dog that had been running with us; it was facing away from me growling in the direction of the fading voices. I checked on Tremor, eyes wide, he looked as shocked as I did by the dogs behavior and moved closer to me. For a brief moment of weakness I wished the horse had arms so he could hug me, I was definitely in need of one right now.

Backing up until I hit the tree again, my legs quit at that moment and I found my body sliding back down it. Tremor moved closer and stood over me. I reached up and rubbed my hand against his chest. He nuzzled my hair and then looked back over at the dog; which was sitting down, looking at us. I couldn't hear the people anymore, but now I had to figure out if this furry creature was friend or foe. Shining the light close, but not in its eyes, I tried to get a good look at it. In the darkness it looked black and big. That was all I could conclude at this point.

Tremor moved against me, almost as if he was trying to protect me. I'm the one with a knife but have an equine protector and a canine guard apparently. Neither one were really helping boost my ego. I patted Tremor, to get him to back up so I could stand again. He rubbed against me trying to prevent me from stepping out into the open. "It's okay boy. If it was planning on eating me it would have by now."

I moved, with him practically attached to my shoulder, towards the bags I'd set by the saddle. Without taking my eyes off the dog, I mentally ran through everything I'd placed in the pack and hoped I'd be able to differentiate how dehydrated fruit and dehydrated meat felt in the sealed packets. Hungry or not, I was pretty sure this creature wouldn't get a happy tail over fruit.

This was probably going to end up being the stupidest thing I'd done in my life, so far, but I moved towards the scruffy creature with my shaking hand held out. I knew it could smell the jerky I held because even I could. It lowered to crouch and moved forward a few inches. Careful and keeping my movements slow, I knelt down in front of it. The knife was in my other hand behind my back, I wasn't completely insane. Its eyes flicked from me to the fragrant meat in my hand. Holding my breath, I stayed completely still as it crept close enough that it could pull the food from my fingers. Retreating quickly ate it fast enough that I knew it had been starving.

I smiled and reached in my pocket for the package. Pulling out the second piece I tossed it over and watched it vanish in one bite. "Now you have to either go away or stop being scary," I whispered and stood up, placing one foot behind the other until my back was against Tremor again.

Sitting down, I looked over at the dog and then up to Tremor. "You two have guard duty." I didn't have any plans on actually sleeping, I just wanted to lie down and rest my sore back muscles for a few minutes. Reaching over, I pulled the saddle closer, and flipped open the small pouch that held the gun. With a gun in one hand and a knife in the other I leaned back against the saddle and rested my head in the seat.

There was a possibility I had lost part of my sanity, leaving a wild dog with my horse in the dark while I rested, but my brain just didn't want to delve into that kind of reasoning right now. Was I safer out here than I had been in the city? I honestly didn't know but there was no doubt in my mind that I was going to find out in the immediate future.

CHAPTER FOUR

Opening my eyes I looked up into the eyes of my black knight, Tremor, looking down at me with those large silent eyes telling me to get my butt up so he could relax and not have to stand above me like a giant statue. I wondered, often, what exactly Darren had whispered to him the day I left because every morning for the last week this was the first thing I saw when I opened my eyes. Did he stand over me all night?

The second thing I would see would be Kismet. Turning my head I looked over at my scruffy Kismet that was lying at my feet looking around. Yes I kept the dog, or he kept me, I'm not sure which. I figured fate had sent him to me, hence his name, so I'd better listen and keep him around. Tremor seemed to barely tolerate him, but then I've always figured the horse was a bit of a snob.

One week so far and we'd survived. I honestly had no idea how much ground we'd covered, the mountains were still a small blur in the distance. Until this point we hadn't encountered anything too life altering or terrifying. We were very good at hiding; we'd proven it each time someone got too close. I had to learn how to survive the small things before I started throwing strangers into our adventure.

Yesterday we'd stumbled on someone else's camp. There had been dead animal corpses and skins all around. The smell of death had been a little more than I wanted to deal with; Tremor had been in agreement with me. Kismet had taken one sniff and had high-tailed it in the other direction. I couldn't blame him there; a few of the coats hanging to dry resembled his.

Other than that one instance we hadn't seen anything that I would call a home. There had been a lot of things along the way that appeared to be left behind. We would slow down and walk around, looking for signs of how long it had been abandoned. Most had been in place a long time, which I found reassuring because that meant we weren't following behind anyone too closely.

Kismet came over to me, where I was still lying on the ground looking up at the trees. "I'm working on it," I mumbled and ruffled his fur. He was an interesting dog, not a cute fluffy one but with a bit of attention and food he would be quite regal looking. I still wasn't sure what breed he was, but as he watched over me and gave me another set of ears to talk to, I figured his pedigree wasn't top priority. He needed some real meat soon though and we hadn't come across any sort of animal that might be meal worthy. "Go find something to hunt; I need to stretch a bit before we pack up." As if he could understand me, he took off through the trees.

Tremor decided I was awake enough and moved off to see if there was anything for him to fill his stomach with. Darren had sent me a small bag of grain, but I was making sure to ration it as much as possible. This left me with one problem, what was I going to do when it was gone? If the planet was more stable we would have had three months until grass and growth became an issue. But since the change snow could arrive with very little warning. I looked back up at the leaves above me; they were already fading from a deep green to something more opaque and dull. Today I was going to work on coming up with a plan of survival for my animals. I seriously doubted they would want to eat dehydrated potatoes and bananas with me for the winter. I wasn't sure I wanted to eat those either come to think of it.

A yelp came from the direction Kismet had gone. Without hesitation I was up and bolting towards him. He yelped again. Pulling the knife from the jacket, I clutched it in my hand and crouched down as I went through the trees. I spotted him and slowed down, he stood struggling and biting at his foot. Pausing, I checked the area around me, there was no one in sight. Whistling softly to get his attention I moved towards him as I reached into the back of my jeans and my hand on the handle of the gun. He stood there yanking his leg trying to come to me and making the most heart wrenching noise I'd ever heard from an animal. "Shh. Just stay there boy." When I was close enough I spotted the wire snare around his leg. My skin crawled.

We were in someone's hunting space. Turning, I surveyed the entire area making sure we were still alone. Sliding towards him, I knelt down and studied the wire. If I could get him to relax I should be able to get him out of it. I pulled him into me and rubbed my hand down over his head. "Hold on, let me help." He stopped struggling and leaned into me. My heart ached that he trusted me enough to get him free. Holding the trapped leg gently I lifted it and he made a whimpering sound. As fast as I could I worked the wire loose and slipped it over his paw. He immediately started licking it.

Looking at my hands I realized how much blood there was. "Can you walk boy?" I stood up, carefully scanning the area again. Kismet stood and tried to follow but yelped with each movement of his foot. I stuffed the knife back into my coat and reached down to get him. It took me a few tries to get him lifted, cursing my short arms the whole time. For a starving dog he weighed more than I expected. In length, he was the same height I was which made the struggle to get him back to the camp more than a challenge. Half running, half stumbling I tried to get there quickly. I wasn't taking any chances on someone thinking they had dibs to my dog just because he'd tangled with one of their traps. We had to move now.

Tremor stood waiting for us as I reached the camp. I lowered Kismet to the ground and then dropped down to look at his leg. It was a mess and still bleeding heavily. Pulling one of my bags over, I dug through it until I could find something to tie off his leg with. The only thing I had was rope. "This is going to hurt, Kizzy, but it's all I can do until we find someplace safe to look after you." Leaning into his shoulder I tried to block him from getting to his leg, and so he couldn't bite my hands as I wrapped the rope around twice, cut it and tied it off. "There. Now just lie still while I pack up."

As soon as I grabbed the saddle Tremor pranced. He knew we needed to move and was more than ready to. I packed up and secured it to him in record time, not caring if everything was carefully placed back where I'd packed it the day before.

Once it was all secured to the saddle straps, I walked him over to a rock and grasped his large face between my hands. "Kismet has to ride. Stand right here so I can get up." Turning I went back over to get the dog and hoped like hell I would be able to get him up on Tremor's back. It figures I'd end up with a horse that was too tall to reach half the time. Without something to stand on I had to haul myself up high enough with the straps to get my foot near the stirrup, how I was going to do it with an injured dog that outweighed me was going to be interesting.

It was a struggle and I slipped off the rock twice with the dog half over my shoulder before I had him lying over the saddle; it worried me that he stayed there unmoving as I climbed up. Pulling him close, I rested as much of him over my legs as I could and gently prodded Tremor to go. Kismet cuddled his head into me and panted loudly as we started in the opposite direction of the trap that had hurt him.

~

My legs were numb and the arm that I held Kismet across was starting to throb unbearably before I decided we were far enough away. Stopping for any reason was a nerve wracking event and wasn't getting any easier. I had to make sure we were relatively hidden and most times that was hard to do. The trees were thick enough, which meant that I couldn't see around us to spot anyone coming. Right now I was aiming towards two large boulders and hoped nothing else laid claim to that spot as I wasn't in any sort of position to defend anything right now. "Hold on Kizzy, we're almost there." What I didn't tell the poor thing was I had no idea how I was going to get him off the tall horse and onto the ground without dropping him.

I tried to slide off Tremor holding the other animal in my arms and onto the rock, but my legs couldn't reach the rock and after several attempts of almost sliding down and being sandwiched between horse and stone I climbed off and balanced on the rock. My legs were numb and one arm tingling, which didn't help at all. Tremor looked over his shoulder at me, and his questioning glance wasn't very reassuring. I pulled on the saddle so he had to lean against the rock, hoping he didn't pull away and dump me on my head beneath him. He stood there just long enough for me to get Kismet into my arms again. When he moved away I slid down the hard surface to the ground. I knew my butt was going to complain about that move later.

Once he was safely on the ground, I pulled one of the bags from the saddle and then dropped back down to look at his leg. "You have to be okay, Kismet." I poured water over his leg to try to wash some of the blood off. It wasn't in good shape and I had no idea what to do with it. Tears started running down my face; I felt helpless and didn't know what to do to stop the bleeding. I knew I couldn't keep it tied up indefinitely, not unless I wanted a three legged dog. Grasping the injured leg gently in my hands I tried to think of a way to patch it up so he would be okay.

Kismet whimpered and I looked down when I realized my palms were getting really hot. He yelped and I pulled my hands away and looked down at them. They felt like they were pulsing as they radiated a lot of heat. I glanced quickly down at his leg and paused, the blood was dried. I'd cauterized it with my hands? That was just ridiculous. Without thinking it through I touched the injured area again with one hand and nothing happened. Now my sanity was in question.

Picking his leg up again I cupped it between both hands and stared down at them. My palms started to warm again. He didn't yelp, but he tried to pull free of my touch. I forced myself to wait a few moments before I lifted my hand and looked at the bloodied spot. It looked better. Moving the fur carefully I saw no sign of a deep slice anymore, in fact there was only a faint red mark where it had been.

Sitting down, I looked from him to his paw and then down at my own hands. I had just healed my dog with my hands. Was I freaked out? Yes. I knew mutations were bizarre and most times unbelievable but never would I have guessed that's what the nasty virus had done to me.

Closing my eyes I tried not to think, but it inevitably rushed into my head. If I'd know about this while Shawn was still alive, could I have tried to heal him? Would he still be alive?   I was a coward, too afraid to find out what I was and now it was too late. Dragging the startled dog into my arms I pushed my face into his fur and cried. Forget about food and my present surroundings, I just needed this one moment for me.

Rubbing a frustrated hand over the tears on my face, I paused and glanced down. Blood was smeared across my hand, which meant I now probably looked like an Indian warrior going off to battle with blood smears on my face. I needed water. I looked down at my pants, and clean clothes. Standing up, I looked around for Tremor and couldn't see him. Why hadn't I tied him? Grabbing the bag I glanced down at the dog that rested against the rock. "Stay. I'll be right back." He opened his eyes and looked at me briefly before closing them again.

"Tremor?" I started walking back the way we had gone,

but he wasn't anywhere in sight. I'd lost my horse! He whinnied and I squinted and looked around the other direction. In his easy stride he came out from behind the large stones. "And what did you find?" He had long grass hanging out of his mouth.

I moved toward him and spotted a creek running through the trees a short distance away. In a perfect world we could have camped out here for several days and had shelter, water and plenty of grass for Tremor.

Perfect was an illusion. The water source would attract every animal and passerby, just as it had us. I sighed and looked over my shoulder at the horse. "Fill up; we'll have to move again in an hour or so." Just long enough for me to wash and rinse out my clothes. I went back to get Kismet, even he might benefit from a bit of a bath.

The bathing part had been a bit colder than I would have liked, but my skin still thanked me for being able to breathe again. I rolled my wet clothes up and tied them so I could lay them out to dry later when we stopped for the night. Tonight, from the looks of the clouds we would definitely be aiming for something that would actually shelter us more than the trees.

I'd taken several feet of the rope and gathered up as much of the grass as I could and bundled it, feeling elated that I'd come up with at least one solution for feeding Tremor when we didn't have fresh growth for him. Now if I could just bring myself to become a hunter, Kizzy and I might survive as well.

Darren's mother had put seeds in the bag of things she'd thought I would need. I didn't know a great deal about growing vegetables, but if I found somewhere to call home I would at least try it. My mouth watered at the thought of fresh vegetables. A salad would taste wonderful after eating dried things for the past week. Shaking my head I turned and grinned at Tremor who was still grazing as I secured everything to him again. "You're going to be a fat horse if you don't slow down." He paused long enough to acknowledge I'd said something and then his head went down again.

I let Kismet ride on Tremor, as I walked along beside while we followed the creek. It was actually funny to see the dog lying half across the saddle and bracing himself. The fact that he stayed up there told me that even though my hands had managed to seal the wound closed, he didn't feel quite like himself yet.

Held loosely in my hand were the small throwing knives that had been Shawn's. Darren had packed them in with everything else. Not to brag, but I was quite good with them, always hitting my target. Of course my targets at the time had been drawn on paper, they didn't bleed or die. My plan was to have them ready in case we came across any small animals. Unfortunately I doubted they'd stand still for me to aim and I decided they'd also have to be on the ugly side for me to kill them. I just had to hold on to the fact that Kismet needed meat to survive so I would be able to do this. I could let him go hunt on his own, I'm sure he had before he met this red haired woman with beef jerky, but I didn't want to be wandering around with a wild dog filled with blood lust, so I was going to be a hunter.

Tremor paused; I turned my head and almost laughed to see a very ugly bird standing by a tree. Was fate possibly listening to me? It wasn't huge, but it looked like it would be meal sized to me. I didn't know if Kizzy liked fowl, but now was the time to find out. I stood behind Tremor and turned only my upper body—I wasn't taking a chance on making a noise and failing my very first attempt at hunting. Moving one of the knives into my dominant hand, I checked the position and then raised my arm slowly. With a well-practiced flick of my wrist the knife sailed through the air and went into the side of the bird. It hadn't felt a thing and surprisingly neither had I.

We gradually moved away from the creek and continued at a leisurely pace in search of shelter for the night. I felt more confident than I had in a long time, a bundle of grass hanging from the saddle and Kismet's and my dinner in my hand—we might just make it after all. At least for today.

When the thunder started to rumble across the sky, Kismet wanted no part of being a passenger, he was willing to limp along beside me on the ground. I hadn't thought of how bad an idea it was to be in the trees during a lightning storm until this very moment, and like the rest of the crazy weather we were now faced with, rain storms always had the potential to turn into much more.

Tremor pranced sideways when the next boom echoed across the sky. Pausing I surveyed the land around us. We had been traveling along a small ridge of hills among the trees, which meant I could go down towards the ravine we'd been avoiding or look for higher ground. I had only packed one tarp, not knowing at the time that I would have companions with me on this journey. The tarp was not big enough to shelter all three of us, and would offer no protection from the vicious winds that quite often accompanied the new storms.

Feeling that new found confidence slip, I looked down at Kismet, who didn't look impressed with the noise surrounding us. "You take the lead, boy, find us somewhere to hide." His amber eyes studied me for a long moment before he turned and limped off to the left of where we had been heading. I didn't even have to lead Tremor along behind; he turned and started after him, barely pausing long enough for me to climb up in the saddle.

We caught up to him a few minutes later as he paced along beside a large group of fallen trees. It wasn't the Hilton, but if I used the tarp right we might at least stay dry. "Pretty smart aren't you?" I slid to the ground and rubbed my hands over him in praise. The trees were big enough that nothing short of a tornado would move them. I set out to get as many branches collected to help secure the tarp in a very rough lean-to. If the rain held off long enough, I might even get a fire going and see what I could attempt to do with the bird.

When the first raindrops began to pelt off the tarp I had a small fire going and the bird over it. Cleaning my kill was now number one of the top grossest thing I'd ever done list. When I was younger I'd watched my parents do it when my father had come home from his hunting trips, but actually doing it was not something I would ever volunteer for. As the meat started to cook through, the smell was more than worth it though.

If Kismet got any closer he was going to be on fire, I ruffled his fur and pulled him back. "Rescuing you once today was enough." He turned quickly and licked my faced with excited rough kisses. "I can't eat it raw, so you're going to have to wait for a while yet." In truth without an oven I wasn't even sure how long this needed to cook. I was aiming somewhere between golden brown and charred and hoped I was right.

I wasn't.

A blur of cramps and dizziness became the next day of my life. I don't remember much other than a few vague moments of seeing Tremor look down at me and Kismet lying tight against me as I wavered between consciousness and agony. I know I threw up more times than a body should be able to, faintly I recall hoping I wasn't lying in it afterward. Not that I could have moved to do anything about it.

Clouds floated through my vision as the earth swayed beneath me. The only way to ground myself was to hug Kismet to me like a child would a stuffed animal. In a brief moment of awareness I managed to drag myself over to the pack and find some water.

A few times loud echoing thunder managed to bring me back to reality, but it didn't last long. Through it all I vowed I wasn't eating ugly bird ever again, even if I was starving and on my last breath.

At one point in my delirium, I lost track of reality. Lights were flashing and I wondered what was going on. It was night, who would be rude enough to have all those lights going. Struggling I tried to prop myself up against the headboard, only to remember through the fog that it was a tree and there were no lights, it was lightning. Kismet moved over and leaned into me, probably more for his own comfort, but it was welcome either way. I looked around to see we were still relatively sheltered. That was the length of time I was alert enough to know what was going on.

The next time I opened my eyes and looked around it was dusk and I guessed the next evening. My head pounded and my guts felt like they'd been put through a press, but I was awake and aware. Every muscle in my body hurt like I'd been working out on some crazy fitness bend, I wasn't even certain I would be able to stand.

With a shaking hand, I pulled myself up to my knees and stayed there until everything stopped spinning around. Tremor stuck his head under the tarp and looked me over before he went back out into the warm night. Kismet came creeping over and sniffed at me, I imagine I smelled like something even he wouldn't want to touch. With any luck the bags were still dry and I could get changed.

It was too late to pack up and move on, so I decided to move the shelter down further on the trees to escape the odor of my sick hours. Not that I would have been able to pack up, I felt completely drained and just moving five feet over felt like I was building a stadium with my bare hands. I should try to eat something, but my stomach squeezed shut at the thought of putting anything in it. I eyed the dog when I finally crawled to a dry spot, and wondered how it was fair that he'd eaten the same thing as I did and yet, he was perfectly fine. He lifted his head and glanced at me as if he'd heard my thoughts. Smiling, I patted the ground beside me and waited until he came over.

I managed to keep several drinks of water down, but just the small amount of moving around had me exhausted and more than ready to sleep again. I called Tremor back to the shelter, knowing he would stay close until dawn, rested my head on Kismet's shoulder and closed my eyes.

CHAPTER FIVE

The sun was bright enough this morning that I wished for sunglasses. How they had escaped being packed I wasn't sure, but the first barter stop I came upon that was the first thing I was looking for. I didn't have anything to barter with, so I made a mental note to try to collect something for trade along the way.

My body still ached from the aftermath of ugly bird, so I took turns walking and riding to try to work it out with as little discomfort as possible. For the first time since we'd begun this journey we actually wandered closer to something that might have been considered a path. I didn't feel brave enough to be right on it, but it was close enough to see through the trees. What compelled me to do this today I didn't know, but my guts told me this was where I wanted to be; so we were.

When we came to the edge of the tree line, for the first time in over a week the three of us stopped to wonder, what now. For miles there were sparse trees and nothing but open ground, with a few hills in the bare open space. Even if we hurried we couldn't make it to more trees by nightfall, because I couldn't even see any trees. Kismet was still favoring his tender leg and I was not up to any mad dashes.

I looked down at the dog and patted Tremor's neck.

"We'll be fine," I reassured them, even though it was far from the way I was feeling. Wanting to see as far as I could in front and behind us, I climbed into the saddle and looked over my shoulder. Stay in the trees or go for it? Kismet yipped getting my attention. He was already heading out into the open space. I guess we were going for it. Prodding Tremor we began to follow.

~

Two hours into our ride, I decided it was far more interesting in the trees, there was much more to look at. Kismet had vanished a few minutes before; I didn't worry when several birds flew up out of the grass like a demon was on their tails. I was fairly certain Kizzy was their demon. Something caught my eye sticking up out of the weeds, so I guided Tremor in that direction remembering that we were going to scavenge for useful things.

We circled it a few times as I whistled for the dog to come back, to make use of his sensitive smell. When he came through the grass, he glanced at us briefly and then went over to the area I was looking at. A few seconds passed and he made no sign of warning or distress, so I climbed down and followed his path to see what it was. Tremor took the opportunity to have a bite to eat, confirming there was no threat waiting for me anywhere close by.

A small trailer standing on its end was the object in the grass. I trampled the weeds to get a closer look at it. It looked like a bicycle trailer and was completely empty. A trailer would be useful, but would it slow us down? I called Tremor over so I could see if this would work. He stopped and looked at the trailer and flicked his tail a few times. If I had to guess I'd say that was his way of saying, "you're joking right?"

When I turned it over so it was on both wheels, Kismet growled a warning in time for me to turn and see a large snake coming out from under it. I was not a snake expert so all snakes as far as I was concerned were bad news. It hissed at me as it slithered closer and that was all it took. The knife was out of the pocket before I realized I'd even reached for it and I flung it straight at the reptile.

Blinking I looked to see I'd severed its head right off. The dog went over and sniffed at it and then turned to explore the trailer some more. With my nose wrinkled up at the grotesque sight, I flipped it further away with my foot and pulled my knife out of the ground. That instinct the guys had said would find me, had. I was still a little shocked at my reaction, but I'd take it over the barely able to breathe for fear moments I'd experienced in my recent past.

~

My horse was not happy with me at the moment as he turned to look behind him at the trailer now tied to him. It didn't weigh all that much, so that wasn't the issue. I'm sure he thought it beneath him to be pulling a puny faded blue bicycle trailer. He was probably right, but if I wanted to start collecting what we needed to barter or live with, I had to be able to move it. Kismet came over and stepped into the trailer and sat there looking at me. The trailer jerked back and forth as Tremor stated exactly what his opinion was to giving the other animal a ride. There would be no free-loading for Kizzy today.

I didn't actually put anything in the trailer just yet. Paranoia was very much present and if we needed to ditch the trailer and haul ass out of any situation I wasn't going to give up the few packs I had with things in it we'd need.

We had to stop several times in the next half hour to make adjustments to the way I had the trailer tied. I needed a long stick to prevent the trailer from bumping into Tremor's legs when he slowed down. Turning back I looked at the trees we had left. They were too far to go back to, so we'd have to make do until we found something else.

We had just figured out the right pace to move along without having trailer issues when I heard a loud cry. It wasn't from an animal, but a child. My heart sped up knowing we were close enough to other people. I kept moving, determined we were not going to investigate and possibly run into trouble, when the crying turned into a heart wrenching sob. I knew the sound, it was one of pain and agony and the soft part of my heart wasn't going to let me just ride in the other direction.

Spotting the source of the sound long before we reached them, I had enough time to assess the situation. It was a family of two children and their parents. The parents looked weathered, worn and in need of new clothes. The one child was probably eight and more interested in exploring something on the ground than at his much younger sibling that was making a lot of noise. I glanced down at Kismet, uncertain of how he would react to other people. His walked slowly his ear twitching each time the child wailed. He whined softly making me think his heart was softer than mine.

The man saw us coming and rounded up his other child quickly. I held up my hand, hoping they didn't have a weapon hidden. Stopping Tremor, I got down and slowly walked towards them. The mother looked at her husband once and then gathered the crying child into her arms and stumbled in my direction. She was saying something, but I had no idea what that could be it wasn't English. They were native, judging by their appearance, I thought. When she was a few feet from me she dropped down onto her knees with the moaning child in her arms. I slowed and moved over to them, kneeling down close.

My stomach lurched when she uncovered the little girls' leg. There was a long gash on it and it was oozing a very unhealthy looking substance, I swallowed trying to keep my stomach settled. Turning I glanced at Kismet over my shoulder; he was sitting beside Tremor and watching intently. I know, for fact that I healed his leg – could I do the same for this child? I didn't know but we were going to find out. Nodding to the woman I got up and went back to get some water and one of my smaller throwing knives. I knew what needed to be done in theory, I just wasn't sure if I could bring myself to do it. Digging in one of the bags I pulled out a candle and matches.

The man looked uneasy and speaking quickly at his wife and while I didn't understand the words—her tone was universal, she told him to shut up. Kneeling back down beside them, I set the candle on the ground and lit it. I'd seen this done and read about it, but the exact steps were a mystery to me. I glanced at the man, who was talking quietly to his son. Slowly he got up and came over. The other child stood there looking at me before his eyes wandered over to the animals behind me.

When the man sat down beside us, I held the knife over the candle and then offered it to him. His eyes were huge, but he nodded and took the blade. His wife held the child tightly in her arms knowing what was to come. We had to open the wound to drain as much of the puss out as possible, and I was thankful the man loved his child enough to do that. I may be able to kill ugly birds without emotion, but I wasn't nearly ready enough to slice into a small child's leg. I poured water over the leg trying to take as much dirt off of it as I could. The child's cry grew louder as if she could sense what was coming. Leaning down I touched her face softly in apology and then gave the father a look that I hoped he interpreted as do it.

I watched, fighting the bile that rose in my throat as the father cut into the festering area, the mother cried and held the child as still as she could. When he had finished there were tears streaking down his face as the blood and puss rolled down his child's limb. Taking a deep breath I put my hands around the oozing area. My fingers slipped in the vile substance and I had to swallow the nausea down again. I closed my eyes and focused on the cries coming from the small body, wanting more than anything to help ease her suffering.

I heard the man gasp right after my hands grew intensely hot but didn't open my eyes to look at what I was doing. The girl squealed with pain, breaking my focus and I had to look now to see what I had done. Lifting my lashes I looked down at my hands to see the infection pouring from the site across my fingers. I couldn't believe this much came from such a small body; how had this wee being survived it? Moving my hands I grabbed the water and washed the grossness from the leg. It looked closer to normal skin color underneath. The mother reached out suddenly and touched my cheek, speaking quickly and smiling. The touch made my heart pound, to know a woman's gentleness after so long without it.

I inhaled deeply and held her look for a few seconds before looking back down at the little one she rocked in her arms. I couldn't leave the cut open to grow another infection, this much I knew. Taking a deep breath I leaned down over the tiny leg again and lifted it to hold between my palms. My eyes flicked quickly to the man once before I closed them and thought of helping the child once more. When the vibrating heat filled my palms the man began speaking in a hushed tone. If I wasn't mistaken he was praying, hopefully for me and not against me. As the heat receded I looked quickly down at the leg and sobbed out a relieved sound to see the gash looking less painful, cleaner and close to being healed.

For the first time the little girl was silent and looking at me with the biggest brown eyes I'd ever seen. She looked tired and drained of all energy but she wasn't suffering any longer. I watched her eyes drift close as she snuggled into her mother's breast and a tear rolled down my cheek at the peacefulness of it. So many refused to bring life into this world the way it was now, yet once here I couldn't think of anything that held more hope than a young life.

Leaning back I picked up the water and rinsed off my hands, extinguished the candle and wiped the knife off on the leg of my pants. Feeling a little light headed I stayed where I was until I felt it was safe to stand up.

Picking up my things I went back over to Tremor and stuffed them back into the bag, sealing it closed again. The mother and father were close together, holding both of their children and speaking softly in the way families do at times. I took a shaky breath and glanced around at their bags lying in a pile. Kismet came over and nudged my hand with his nose, I absently patted him.

Tremor watched me with those large eyes of his and I smiled as if he were sending me a silent message. I stroked my hand down his face and leaned into him for a brief moment before moving behind him and undoing the complicated set up I'd just spent a long time coming up with. Pulling the trailer away from him I walked back over to the family and set it a few feet from them. I'd known I needed to get this trailer, but what fate hadn't said was I'd be giving it away to help someone that needed it more.

The man's eyes were wide as he looked at the trailer and then back to me. I smiled, not even bothering to say something he wouldn't understand. He bowed his head in thanks and then got up to get their bags. The older child came over and wrapped his arms tight around my legs in an over-exuberant hug only children were free enough to give. I stroked my hand lightly over his dark hair and fought the tears that were welling up in my eyes again.

Getting up slowly the mother went over and handed the sleeping girl to her father before she came over to me. She clasped my cheeks between her hands and leaned over to kiss my forehead. It was such a motherly move that my heart jerked inside my chest recognizing it as that. She spoke quickly and in broken English, but I understood enough to hear the gratitude and praise in her words.

Pausing, she reached inside her shirt, pulling a cord with a stone hanging from it. It had eight lines coming from the center with symbols on the end of each. She held it up and then slipped it over my head. "To find you - safe." She said slowly. "The spirit the eight … earth … elements guide and keep safe."

I held the stone in my hand and nodded, smiling briefly.

She said something over her shoulder to her husband and he answered her quickly, without hesitation. Bobbing her head a few times and then took my hand. "Walk ten days north – to – wards big hills." She paused and I wondered if she was translating her words into English inside her head before saying them out loud. "Follow the unused - road until the water grows silent." She stared into my eyes as she spoke. "Deep in trees - under hanging earth - a home for keep you safe in winter."

Nodding, she smiled at me again, leading me to understand that was the end of her instructions. I wasn't sure exactly what she was telling me, but I caught enough to mull it over until I did. "Thank you." I said in a whisper.

She kissed both my hands and moved back to her husband to take the child from him. The look of love she held in her expression when she looked at the small person in her arms, made a lump form in my throat. I had to go. As I turned to get on Tremor her husband came over and bowed to me. When he lifted his head he extended his arms and held a small bundle out.

Hesitantly I took and opened the dried hide to see a small hollow piece of wood. Raising my eyes back to his I knew he understood I had no idea what I held.

"Mush – room. Grow." He said in clipped English. My eyes widened and I looked back down at the piece of wood again. "In dirt. Dark. No sun." He said quickly.

I nodded and then smiled at him. Of course I didn't know the first thing about growing mushrooms, but my mouth watered at the thought of eating mushrooms. "Thank you." I wrapped it carefully and bowed my head as he had done. He looked very pleased as he backed away. Tucking the bundle into the larger pack, I tied it closed again and climbed up into the saddle. Kismet stood watching me, waiting for my choice in direction. I looked once more at the family and with my heart feeling lighter— yet heavier at the same time I nudged Tremor in the direction of the mountains once more.

~

As I rode I mulled over the instructions the woman had

given me. Ten days north. That part was easy enough; we were heading in that general direction. An unused road, most likely meant an old road. After that part it got a little less clear what she meant. Until the water grows silent – maybe there was a creek or a river near the road? If it grew silent that could mean it ended or ran into a lake … I was purely reaching for the answers, mostly to give my mind something to do as we traveled throughout the day aiming for the shelter of the trees once again.

I picked up the stone around my neck and studied it. Spirit of the eight earth elements, she had said. I looked around and laughed, as if they'd be lined up and reveal themselves to me. I didn't know what the eight were, but was hoping they did guide and keep me safe was more comfort than I'd had up to this point. The symbols at the ends of the lines on the stone didn't help in revealing any answers to me. One looked like a leaf and one looked like a mountain, which didn't really help, but once again it gave my mind something to do other than count the steps Tremor took across this empty area. So far our journey had consisted of long hours of silence, mixed with a little paranoia and a few intense moments that had me preferring the moments of silence.

Kismet yipped, drawing my attention back to him. He was standing looking towards smoke in the distance. I focused in on it and sat there waiting for my guts to tell me if I wanted to find out or if we should circle around and avoid it. Tremor pranced uneasily with our sudden stop; the open spaces bothered him as much as it did me. Biting down on my lip I watched the smoke rise, it wasn't a huge amount which led me to think it was someone's cooking fire. It was the 'who' part that worried me. I looked in the other direction, then towards the mountains. There was no cover to hide us if we went closer, so unless I wanted to lead us a day further away from our goal we were heading toward the smoke.

Running my hand down Tremor's neck I spoke softly to him. "We'll be fine, boy. Let's just give who-ever that is a nice wide berth and hope for the best." I grinned down at Kismet. "You've got the lead and I expect fair warning if your doggy intuition says bad things." His amber eyes watched me for a moment and I'd like to think he understood perfectly. Tapping my heels against Tremor's side, I started in a nice easy gait towards the smoke.

CHAPTER SIX

My heart was fluttering, my stomach knotted with nerves as we rode closer to the smoke. I told myself that since it wasn't black or ominous looking it signaled a good reason. Then again what did I know about smoke?

It was too late to circle away so they wouldn't see us. I watched Kismet more than the rising smoke, looking for any sign of apprehension. He was moving at a more cautious pace now, but still easily enough that I wasn't feeling completely tense.

I'd like to think I had my hand over the gun out of a sense of self-preservation, but in truth, I was completely paranoid and felt better keeping it within my reach.

We reached the smoke a lot sooner than I wanted to. Circling out away from it, I couldn't see as clearly as I'd like, but well enough without riding right into the scene. I could make out three people. One sat near the smoke, and two more were off to the side. The three of them all moved at the same time suddenly, standing side by side to face towards us. Gone was the world where you waved in moments like this, instead now you felt suspicion and paranoia at the possible motives of anyone you came across.

I didn't want to stop and stare back at them, so I kept Tremor moving at an easy pace. The hair on the back of

Kismet's neck was the first indication that he wasn't at all comfortable with the people in the distance. One of them moved from the group and bent down to the ground a few feet away. What I had thought to be their packs turned out to be someone with a rope tied around them.

My heart jerked in my chest. I didn't want to know any more than that. For about the same time it takes to blink I toyed with the thought of riding to the rescue of the person being dragged to their feet – and then one of them raised what looked like a stick from this view point to his shoulder. Tremor and Kismet both reacted at the same time and I trusted their sense of smell to confirm that the stick held a bullet.

Kicking my heels into Tremor we bolted as fast as we could in the direction leading away from them. I leaned down, almost resting my face in his mane. Kismet flew by us, his feet moving at speed. Unless they had a rocket hidden in among their packs, there was no way they were going to catch us. I held my breath and waited for the tell-tale echo of riffle fire. When it didn't come I glanced over my shoulder back towards them. It was hard to tell at this speed but it looked like they were packing up. Not willing to chance it, I kept Tremor at a full run until I noticed Kismet slowing down.

Easing Tremor into a slow trot, I looked around behind us once more. I couldn't even make out the smoke now so we must be safe. I walked him for another hundred feet and then we stopped and I climbed off. Kizzy came over, his tongue hanging from his mouth and his sides heaving. Glancing around I swore under my breath, I wanted the security of the trees back. Without some sort of shelter, not one of us would rest through the night.

I wasn't wrong.

We traveled as far as we could when dusk fell and clouds covered the moon, stopping us from going further. I ate dried food for dinner, not wanting to light a fire out in the open to reveal our location to anyone. Kismet had dehydrated meat. Tremor was surrounded by dinner, but wasn't in the mood to eat. He stood there looking out into the night.

I hadn't even bothered to take off the saddle or the bags attached to it. I sat on the ground with the blanket wrapped around me and the gun in my hand. It was going to be a long night. Clock watching wasn't an issue because that was also something I hadn't thought to bring. Then again what felt like hours could turn out to be ten minutes, here out in the wide open surrounded by the dark night trying not to react each time you heard a noise.

Kismet moved over and rested his head on my lap. For a second I thought he was looking for comfort, but as he watched without missing a blade of grass moving in the breeze, I realized he was offering comfort to me. The thought of his actions made me think of Bobby. When I was down or upset he would do the same thing, literally. He would flop down and put his head in my lap watching me with a comical expression in his eyes until I had no choice but to smile.

Looking up into the obscured sky I wondered how Bobby and Darren were doing. Did they wonder the same thing about me? That first morning when I woke up—from a very broken night of sleep—I half expected to see one or both of them in front of me. The fact that they accepted I was all grown up and could do this alone had been a shocking realization. With the few things I had gone through since leaving, I'm sure Darren would have hives, where Bobby would have grinned and said he knew I could do it, or something similar. I did miss them. What I didn't miss was being afraid to leave my house or look out a window. At least out here, on my own I could see what was going on and didn't have any corners to look around. And so far the population was much, much smaller.

Tremor leaned down and nudged the top of my head, bringing my attention back to the situation at hand. Realizing the moonlight was shining down on him, and I looked up to see that the clouds had moved on. Raising my chin up to the sky I saw that most of the clouds had moved on. Rubbing

Kismet's head in my lap I spoke softly. "Come on boy, there isn't going to be any sleep for us so we may as well keep going."

The shadows of a horse, dog and a woman were cast beside us as we walked in the moonlight through most of the night.

As the moon leaned down towards the horizon, someone ran in front of us almost too fast to see. I hadn't even heard him coming, neither had Kismet. There was a quick curse and then he stopped and turned back. The three of us stopped and stood there, groggily trying to decide what to do. My hand went to the gun in my pocket as the stranger walked over closer.

"Don't be alarmed, I'm quite harmless."

I still tensed, not buying a word of it.

He held his hands up beside his body to show he held nothing in them. "My name is Micah and honestly, I mean no harm to you." His hair was sticking out all over his head, whether intentional or not I wasn't sure. He stepped nervously from one foot to another. "I'm in a bit of a situation and…" he stopped and sighed loudly, "I'm a nightwalker and as you can see the sun is way too close to arriving."

"A nightwalker?"

He waved his hands around. "Mutated into one—I used to be a normal bloke before this."

He stepped closer and Kismet moved against my leg, but wasn't growling so I relied on his senses and listened.

"I can't be in the sunlight—it fries me crispy and makes me ill. Do you understand?"

I nodded.

"Could I persuade you for a quick ride on your beasty to some shelter then?"

I looked up at Tremor and then around us. "There's shelter near here?" I didn't know how there could be it was still miles and miles of flatness without so much as a silhouette of anything larger than the odd boulder.

He nodded, still paced on the spot and glancing at the sky every half second or so. "Yes. An old uh ... what-you-call-it ... bomb shelter, not far really."

There was no way I was giving anyone my horse but that soft spot in my heart started prodding me and I sighed. "How far?"

Spinning around, he pointed. "I would say a ten to fifteen-ish minute ride that way." He turned back and I pulled the gun out of my pocket and made sure he could see it in the dim light. His hands immediately flew in the air.

"I'll take you, but if you try anything you aren't going to have to worry about the sunlight."

His mouth dropped open, and then he snapped it shut and nodded. "On my word of honor, I'll do a dance if you like too, lady, just get me out of the dawn!"

I moved over to him slowly, turning Tremor. "Get up, you take the reins."

He hesitated for a few seconds and then nodded again. "You're a treasure."

As I climbed up behind him, I made sure I sat as far away from him as possible. Grabbing the strap of the bag to hold on, I kicked Tremor into a run and hoped he didn't object loudly and send us both bouncing off into the grass below.

My brain was busy digesting this new information. There was a mutation that prevented you from being in the sunlight. I had to wonder how many different kinds of left over effects the viruses had. It seemed intentional at times; the germs we had fought to suppress for so long were fighting back and changing our chemistry and structure like we had done to them over the years. A childish tit for tat rationalization I know, but still the truth.

Micah hadn't been lying. As he slowed Tremor I could see an area cleared of any growth. When he drew us to a stop, he flipped a leg over and jumped to the ground. Looking up at me he smiled and held his hand over his heart. "I thank you from the bottom of my nocturnal heart."

Quickly he glanced at the sky. "Many thanks." He flipped open the door in the ground and then paused. "I don't suppose you're a nightwalker too?"

I shook my head.

"Ah, well can't help wishing." He grinned. "A difficult feat it is to find a girlfriend that has the same night life I do." He winked at me.

I had to smile. "I'll be sure to send any female nightwalkers your way."

"Many thanks." Going down two steps he saluted. "I'd stay and chat but the day is a little too close to searing my ass." He ducked down, pulling the door closed behind him. The sound of locks sliding into place turned out to be the last noise from inside his shelter.

I sat there looking down at the door for a few minutes still not sure if I'd he had been a hallucination. Shaking my head I looked down at Kismet, my imagination wasn't that good. Sighing I turned us in the direction we had come from, if dawn was that close maybe we'd soon find some-place safe to rest as well.

Not finding anywhere safe to rest, we had to settle for another brief nap under the tarp. It was sweltering underneath, but my eyes didn't care how hot I was, they had to close for a short time.

Kismet left his head peeking out, and Tremor stood right next to us, I drifted off before I could see if he at least closed his eyes. Waking up covered in sweat and feeling like I was on fire, I shoved the hot fur coat away from my side and flipped the tarp off. The sunlight was peeking through more clouds. I looked up at them and dared them to rain down on me. They didn't listen.

Sitting up, I looked over at Tremor. "Rest well?" He flicked his tail in the way I now knew to be his way of expressing annoyance. "Yeah me either." Climbing back to my feet, I leaned against him and looked down at Kismet. He didn't look very well rested either. Bending down I rolled up the tarp quickly. "Let's keep going, there has to be water or a tree or something soon—no place is this empty."

It took me three attempts to get back up in the saddle, not a good sign. We'd only gone about three feet when Kismet growled. I had the gun in my hand before I even looked at him. When I did I started laughing and came close to falling out of the saddle again. He was dragging my leather jacket by the collar. I was so out of it I almost left it lying on the ground. Tucking the gun back into the pouch, I almost fell back off Tremor to get the coat.

~

I'm not sure how much time passed, but it felt like we were all moving in slow motion. From a distance we probably looked like a filler scene in a western movie moving slowly across the endless landscape under the sun. I'd no sooner completed the thought when the sun vanished behind the clouds and rain pelted off me with a force that was shocking. Where was the thunder? The lightning? The warning?

It stung my arms, confirming I was sporting sunburn. Tremor shook his head like he wasn't sure if he wanted this either. Kismet was energized. He was such a traitor. This would be one of those times where 'be careful what you wish for' would apply. Wiping the rain out of my eyes, I prodded Tremor to get moving. If we were going to have a reprieve from the sun, we may as well make the most of it and cover as much ground as possible.

CHAPTER SEVEN

Ten days ride—so were we on day one or two, I didn't really know but it gave me one more thing to think through as we moved across the endless fields. I was really looking forward to a shelter of any kind. At this point a hole in the ground with some shade would be a wonder. In the time since we'd left the trees we'd only seen a few. Most of those were too small to even cast a shadow in the daylight, never mind offer any sort of cover.

We did find one large tree in the open space and attempted a brief nap. However with it being the only tree in sight every bird in the area had to stop there and have a conversation after the heavy rain, making the brevity of the nap a more than we would have preferred.

I was tired, still damp and could taste nothing but dirt when we stopped to take a break. Our water supply was dwindling and I had no idea when there would be water to replenish it. If this sparseness continued for the next ten days I didn't know if we were going to make it. Tremor was the only one out of the three of us that wasn't suffering. Although considering he was surrounded by grass of all kind, he didn't eat very much.

By late afternoon I was looking forward to the night so the sun would go away again. I always loved the sunlight, but now I was seeing it from a whole new perspective. I really missed sunglasses. With a shirt tied over my head I tried to keep my brain from frying completely. When each step started to feel like I was doing it in slow motion I'd climb back on Tremor and try to speed us along, even that felt slow.

This was turning out to be one of the longest days of my life.

A few clouds started to form and I found myself almost hoping for rain. A nice cooling rain being viewed from a shelter would be very welcomed right now, but without the shelter not so much. I prayed as we crested one of the few hills we'd seen, that we'd look down over a forest or nice lake with trees nearby. Maybe a river? A few more steps, I held my breath. It whooshed out in defeat when I looked down the other side of the hill that held nothing I wanted to see. More open space.

In the distance, very far off I could just see what looked like a tree line. Maybe there was hope after all. Turning to look in all directions and my heart stopped. Moving along the base of the hill was a large group of people. Not just people, they had wagons and horses too. For a minute it was like we'd stepped into a western, well if you didn't count the U-haul trailer and truck's boxes being pulled by horses. I bit my lip and looked down at Kismet; he had the same expression I was feeling inside. There was nowhere to run and hide so they didn't see us.

Wishing I had binoculars or anything to help focus; I stood there like a statue watching the group move at a slow pace. There were many people walking along with the wagons, children included. Could this be one of the groups from the colony in the mountains? A more pertinent question was, did I want to find out? Tremor jerked on the reins, bringing my attention back to him. He just wanted a decision, standing around never sat well with him.

Taking a deep breath, I pulled the gun from the pouch on his saddle and tucked it in the back of my jeans. I had no case to put the knife in without the coat on, so I opted for a few of my throwing knives. Not having any idea what I walking into, I refused to take a chance.

As we wandered down the hill at a leisurely pace, I kept an eye on the slow moving travelers. I'd counted twenty that were within sight, only wondering what the wagons held. The old U-haul trailer made me a little more than nervous; what was sealed inside. I thought no one had noticed us until two children, pulled at an adult and pointed right toward us. The wagon procession stopped and children vanished into various covered areas.

I took a deep breath and kept walking. Kizzy moved over and paced right beside my leg. Tremor jerked on the reins again, almost pulling my arm out of the socket. I was pretty sure that was his way of telling me to get my ass in the saddle so we could move fast if we needed to. Stopping, I looked down at the dog almost shoving me under the horse. "Fine." Getting up into the saddle, I turned again and looked at the people watching me. "Now or never," I whispered.

I kept Tremor at a slow walk, and made sure my hands were loose, within sight. I couldn't see any weapons, but many of the adults had vanished along with the kids so I was fairly certain a few barrel sights were aimed at my bright hair.

"Hello." A tall man called out. He reminded me of someone from a mob movie, all he needed was the expensive suit. Who knows, maybe he had been a mobster before everything changed.

I slowly raised a hand in a friendly wave.

He looked to the woman at his right and said something I couldn't hear. "Are you alone?"

The sarcastic voice in my head wanted to ask him where I would hide anyone else, but I kept a lid on it. "Yes." I said loudly.

The woman looked worried and said something to him. "Is your wolf friendly? We have children here."

I looked down at Kismet, with his tongue flopping out of his mouth as he walked along side of us. "I'm probably more of a threat than he is." And it was the truth.

The woman stepped forward. "You've been in the open a long time." It wasn't a question and I wondered just how bad I looked. But I nodded. "Come, travel with us a while, we have shelter."

That was a word that sounded magic to my ears. "Thank you." I stopped Tremor and slid down to the ground. Kismet stood against my leg as I waited. "We'd feel a lot better if the guns aimed in our direction were lowered."

The man laughed and turned around and waved to someone I couldn't see. Turning back to me, he stepped forward and extended his hand. "My name is John. This is my wife Lily."

I shook his hand. "Bree." I patted the horse leaning over my shoulder. "This is Tremor and the fuzzy one is Kismet."

He smiled and put his arm around his wife.

Kismet growled low and I spun to see what he was growling at. A large snake was coming up beside the woman. Without thought, I flicked the knife still nestled in my palm. It landed, impaling the snake just behind the head. Kizzy sat down beside me. I looked back at the couple to see the man holding a knife in his hand and staring at the snake.

Two more women and a man started walking over towards us. I hadn't been around people I didn't know in a long time, and was starting to feel surrounded. Holding Tremor's reins I moved over slowly and pulled the knife out of the snake's body, trying to hide the *eww* expression on my face when the body convulsed as I pulled it out. Wiping it on the ground, I tucked it back into the hand holding the leather straps.

Lily came over and touched my shoulder. "Thank you. Please come and get something to drink." She ushered me towards one of the wagons. "I'm afraid you're going to be bombarded with questions any minute now." She smiled. "It's been a long while since we've seen anyone we might talk to."

As we moved, I studied her out of the corner of my eye. Anne of Green Gables came to mind, and the thought of her being with the mobster was just too funny. She continued to chatter quietly, I was only able to focus on a few words here and there, my brain was obviously mush with the garbage I was thinking, I just couldn't focus. She made a motherly *tsking* noise and that got my attention.

"We're going to keep moving until dark, or the rain comes back, which ever happens first. Why don't you lie down in our wagon and rest for a while?"

If my eyes hadn't dried up in the sun early today I might have cried at her words. To lie down and close my eyes and not worry would be wonderful. I glanced at Kismet, he showed no sign that we shouldn't be among these people. Even Tremor seemed more than fine with the situation.

With Kismet lying with his head looking out the back of the wagon and Tremor tied to it, I leaned back into the soft mattress. I almost sighed out loud from the sheer joy of it. An old saying rang true; you didn't miss what you had until it was gone. Next to a bath-tub, a mattress ranked right up there on my list of things I missed the most. To just close my eyes for a half hour would be amazing. As the wagon started to move again, I watched Tremor as he walked along behind.

~

That was the last thing I remember until I bolted up. It was now dark outside and we weren't moving anymore. I leaned down and touched Kismet still at my feet. Moving quickly to the opening, I let out a quick sigh to see Tremor standing there looking at me. I couldn't believe I'd slept that long, leaving my animals unprotected. "Hey, boy." Kismet popped up and nudged me. "Okay you're free of watch duty." He hopped over the end and vanished into the dark. I wasn't far behind him.

"Hello." A deep voice said from the shadows.

I held onto Tremor's halter and looked around.

A man stepped out into the opening. He wasn't tall like the others that seemed to be traveling together. Then again almost everyone seemed tall to me. He had long sandy hair and a very pleasant smile. "I'm Jacob." He shrugged. "I didn't get to see you when you arrived today—as it was daylight."

"You're a nightwalker?"

He tucked his hands into his pockets. "I am. You've seen my kind before?"

Nodding, I rubbed my hand down Tremor's soft coat. "Yes. He cut it a bit short getting to shelter before dawn, we gave him a lift."

"Ah, yeah dawn is scary as hell to someone like me." He motioned towards the group sitting around a fire. "Vince and I struck a deal with John. If he hauls our ass during the daylight, we watch over them at night."

"Sounds like a good deal."

He grinned. "It is for us. We're hidden from the sunlight and still traveling all day long."

I glanced at the people rocking their children and talking quietly. "Where are you heading?"

Shrugging he took a few steps closer. "Mostly in the direction of the mountains; it's been a long trip with the wagons though." He ran his down Tremor's flank. "This is a nice animal you have."

"Yes he is." Right on cue Kismet ran up beside me and sat down. "So is this one," I rubbed his head.

Jacob chuckled. "No need to fear. I heard the tale of you and your knife." He glanced at the animal at my feet. "And I'd say what you can't do with your knife your doggy can do very well." He motioned to the fire. "Come over and meet everyone."

I looked over at them and then towards the other side of the wagons. "I will in just a minute." He nodded and turned to walk over to the fire. Sighing loudly, I patted Tremor and then untied him. I needed to find somewhere that was private enough to go pee before I had to socialize.

We went to the end wagon, Tremor and Kismet stood watch for me. I grinned, knowing how odd that was over-all, but it was a routine we'd settled into and there was small comfort in things like that.

Finishing quickly I turned to head back towards the firelight when an arm wrapped around my waist and gripped me tight.

"If your hair is this bright in the dark it must be like flames during the daylight." A man whispered against the back of my neck.

I held my breath, trying not to panic and assess the situation. Releasing Tremor's reins I let them drop to the ground so I'd have both hands free. Kismet issued a low warning growl to the stranger. I didn't pull against his hold, but stood there without resistance. I'd put my knife back into the pouch on the saddle, but the gun was tucked back into the waist of my jeans, now I just had to figure out a way to get to it before he noticed it.

He was rubbing his cheek against my neck and inhaling deeply, it was a creepy feeling and one I had had more than enough of. Kismet snapped and then growled again and the stupid man still persisted.

There was a movement at the end of the wagon. "Bree… Jesus! Vince, are you stupid?" Jacob demanded.

The arm let me go and I whirled around pulling the gun out, cocking it and aiming right at the stranger's face.

"Whoa." Jacob came up beside me quickly. "Yes, he's an ass, Bree, but a harmless one. Please don't shoot him." Kismet growled again and he backed away. Jacob turned towards the shorter man. "You idiot! She doesn't know you have some stupid idea you're a vampire just because you can't go out in the sun—are you trying to get shot?"

I looked down the barrel at the odd man standing in front of me looking at the other man like he'd just betrayed him.

"It was a joke. How the hell was I supposed to know she was armed?"

Jacob walked over and smacked him in the head. I lowered the gun. "Maybe the wolf at her side and the knife story would have been a pretty good clue how well she'd take it." He glanced at me. "I'm sorry my friend is an ass. Thank you for not shooting him." He glared at Vince, "even though he deserves it."

Vince looked thoroughly chastised. "Sorry," he mumbled and then turned and walked back into the shadows.

Jacob turned around and looked at me as he rubbed the back of his neck. "I cannot even find the words to say." He shrugged. "He has all the kids believing he's a vampire and guards over them at night."

I tucked the gun back into my jeans and shook my head. "Clearly they've never seen a single vampire movie. I don't recall any that guarded humans so much as killed them."

Jacob laughed. "I know." He let out a long sigh. "He'll be off pouting for the night now. Come on, Lily sent me after you so she could feed you." He glanced down at Kismet. "If I try to pet your wolf is he going to bite my arm off?"

I looked at Kizzy sitting there without a care again. "I really don't think so. He might lick you to death though."

"Oh I don't know he was fast enough to protect you."

I rubbed Kismet's head. "Yeah, as long as there is no threat to me or Tremor he's like a puppy."

"I'll keep that in mind." He stepped closer and held out his hand to him. Kismet, confirming my every word licked his hand and then rubbed into it. "Well," Jacob muttered quietly.

~

The wagons moved out just before dawn. Jacob said good night and went into the U-haul. I never did get to see Vince again after he wandered off, so I assumed he was sulking in the trailer. Most of the adults were still sleeping with the children inside the wagons, as the few awake started in a slow line. I'd had another very short nap and felt rested enough to take my turn in the early day. John had asked if I could lead with Tremor and Kismet and keep an eye out for us, I was happy to help after having been fed and had a soft bed to rest on. It wasn't my plan to stay with these people all the way to the mountains, but for a few days, it would be nice to not be alone.

There were six children, all under the age of ten roaming around. I couldn't keep the names straight or remember exactly which parents they went with, but it was nice to see happy children. Just the laughter from them made the reality of this world seem a little less harsh, even if it was only for a short time.

By noon three of the men headed off to hunt, planning to meet up with the group later. I debated on going with them. Maybe I could learn how to do hunt, but the thought of wandering off alone with three armed men by just seemed like the wrong step to take.

Tremor ignored the other horses, which confirmed what I had thought of him for the last few years; he was a snob. I told Darren that when he had tried to use him for breeding, not that there was a lot of opportunity for it. Tremor at that time had shunned all but one of the prospects that Darren had found for him. Of course defending another male, Darren said he wasn't a snob just selective. But now, with the large beast I called companion, he ignored every look and sound the other horses made as if they weren't even there. Only I would end up with the ultimate anti-social herd animal.

The group only stopped three times throughout the day, allowing them to cover quite the distance. Just after the third stop we reached an old grown-over road and the native woman's words came back to me. I checked to see if it went in the direction of the mountains, it did. Ten days walk. Considering I'd been on horseback for most of the way, did that mean it was a shorter time? I didn't even know if I'd traveled north the whole time we were baking in the sun. I chewed on my lip and watched as the line of wagons moved over to travel on the road area. Listening, I didn't hear any water so hopefully I hadn't missed it already.

Even though the sun had tried to fry me, I knew fall wasn't far off and winter lie in wait close after that. I didn't know these people, and was trying not to as much as I could so the only thing that made sense to me was to find this shelter and learn what I could to live out here. Inside my heart I knew I couldn't take losing anyone close to me again and the only way to insure that was to be alone.

"Pretty serious thoughts."

I turned to see one of the men standing a few feet from me. Wishing I could remember his name, I smiled. "Just staying alert."

"You've been out here for a while on your own?"

In truth, no, but I wasn't telling him too much. "I haven't kept track."

"None of us do." He started to wander towards the last wagon as it moved onto the road. "Lily said to tell you it's your turn to ride and grab a nap." He motioned towards the road ahead. "You never know what lies ahead, so we try to keep well rested just in case we need our strength."

"Oh. Thanks." I moved Tremor in the direction of John and Lily's wagon. Lily waved from the back as I got closer.

"I'm just moving up front to ride with John for a few hours. The back is all yours." With that she disappeared inside.

Climbing down off Tremor, I walked along and tied him to the back. "Later we'll get that saddle off you, boy." Before I could get all the way inside Kismet was up behind me and hanging out the back again. How had I thought I could survive without him? As I closed my eyes I wondered what it would have been like without the creature lying beside my feet. Truthfully, I probably would have just died of fright without his senses to rely on.

~

The next few days were so similar; they could have been carbon copies. I was asked more questions than I had answers for; I was the one that had been in civilization most recently. I found it strange that they considered what I came from civilized in any way. I told them the city I came from and most other cities had all turned into something we would have watched years ago in a movie. I explained that they were a place where no one knows anyone else and you never go out alone. I described the abandoned areas and shattered buildings in great detail. They weren't sure what to make of it until I told them I would never go back to a place like that.

Ever.

The only one that didn't question me until I wanted to scream was Jacob. He was more interested in me, not where I came from. Had this been another time and he didn't live only in the dark, I may have wanted to get to know him better.

We sat in the hours before dawn and talked, when the rest of the group was quiet before they started their early day again.

"I get the feeling you're not telling me something, Bree. You're even more quiet than normal." He gave me a lopsided grin.

I studied the ground, not that I could see it clearly in the dark. "I'm leaving in the morning."

"Ah." He sighed. "I knew you weren't going to stick around very long."

"You did?" He had surprised me.

"Yeah, I never get my own way and I wanted very much for you to stay." He sighed again in a very dramatic way.

"Maybe I'll see you again when I reach the mountains." I was aiming for enthusiastic, but knew I fell short.

"I hope I do." Getting up, he reached down and offered me a hand up. I let him pull me to my feet.

"I think Vince will miss you," he stated in a monotone voice.

I laughed. "I haven't seen Vince since that first night."

Leaning closer until I could feel his breath on my cheek, he whispered. "It may have something to do with that gun of yours being stuck in his face. It's very intimidating."

"I'll keep that in mind for the future."

"Do that. Now run away before you break my heart."

He touched my cheek briefly and I thought for a minute he might kiss me. And I might let him. But then he stepped away and turned. "I'll break it to the others for you, to make it easier to get away." He paused and turned slowly. "If you happen across any female nightwalkers—preferably tiny ones with bright red hair, be sure to give them directions to this little wagon train."

"As odd as this sounds, the other nightwalker I met asked me to send females his way."

"I'm afraid that to my knowledge, no one has ever met a female afflicted the way we are."

"That's so sad." I answered automatically before thinking.

"Ain't it though?" Glancing towards the fire he shrugged. "I hope to see you around sometime, Bree."

"Me too. Thank you, Jacob." I felt a little disappointed that he hadn't tried to kiss me. He was so nice to me, almost like the guys used to be before everyone started dying that is. Then they were just overprotective and more than a bit annoying. It made my heart heavy to know Jacob was also searching for something that he may never find.

CHAPTER EIGHT

I waved again to the kids hanging out the back of the wagon. When I lowered my hand I watched the U-haul trailer until it was almost out of sight. Had I really expected him to try to stick a hand out and wave? I glanced at the sun above me. No, just wished he'd tried something.

Kismet whined, bringing my attention back to him. He wasn't happy we left the kids that loved to play with him, but he'd have to get over it. It dawned on me that since the planet started objecting, I'd never really been around a lot of people. After my parents died, it was just my brother and his friends. Only on a few occasions had I traveled somewhere unescorted by one of them to face strangers alone. Just being around others the last few days had shown me that I was meant to be a loner, at least when it came to humans. Animals were a different story. I loved being around them and for the most part they seemed to be okay with me.

We moved slowly along the side of where the road would have been. The sound of running water echoed through the vacant land, past the few trees that were starting to appear more frequently. I had to figure out was whether the water growing silent meant no sound at all or less. The trees weren't thick enough to worry even though; she'd said deep in the trees; there was no depth so far.

Maybe it was having slept on something that was like a bed again, or that I hadn't been out in the sun all the time but I didn't feel as listless now. Or the sun in just three days wasn't nearly as strong. That was a bad thing. At the moment of this realization I got down off of Tremor and started keeping an eye out for anything I could gather up to store as the days grew colder. Long grass, helpful herbs and even bark would all have its place in surviving my first winter without walls, a roof and a furnace.

Looking down at my feet I realized I was also going to need one more item to make it through the cold months. Furs for warmth, it wasn't as if I could stop at the next shopping center and buy some cozy boots and leg warmers. The only problem I had with getting the furs was the part where I had to take them off dead animals. Animals I killed. Killing a bird or even snake was no problem for me, but unless I wanted to walk around in feathers and snake skin all winter I had to learn how to kill to survive. Did that make me part of the new world lunacy or a survivor?

I'd had the silly notion in the first few days out here that we'd reach the mountains before winter—after the first week that dream seemed more fantasy. Pausing I looked towards the mountains in the distance, the far distance. They were still months away, even without having to stop and take shelter from the snow. I rubbed a hand down Tremor, more than thankful that I had him as it might take years on my two feet alone.

Kismet stopped and cocked his head, studying something in the distance. I watched him for a few seconds before trying to see what he did. He was alert, but not disturbed. That wasn't always a definite sign of good or safe things. When he let it go and turned back to us, I breathed a sigh of relief. Don't get me wrong, I like reacting on gut reflexes, but it wasn't something I wanted to practice often. Nudging Tremor, we continued toward the sound of water. At least if I could see it, I wouldn't miss the place where it became silent.

When I was twelve or thirteen I wanted to be a social worker. There was nothing I felt was more important than helping people and bringing peace and togetherness to any situation. Funny how I was now riding in the middle of nowhere, avoiding any contact with people and plotting to find the strength to kill my winter attire. Life may be mapped out, but I'm pretty sure it's done in pencil so it can be erased and redrawn many times over.

Being so caught up in my own thoughts, it took a few moments to realize we weren't moving. I patted Tremor's neck and wondered if he was tired, then I noticed Kismet looking off into the distance. It was a town, or what was left of one. The road led that way. Biting my lip I considered if the native woman had literally meant to follow the road or just keep it in sight. Even the group I'd left had deferred following it into the city, if the tracks we'd passed earlier were any indication.

Kismet turned his head and watched me with those amber eyes. "I don't know," I replied to his inquiry in a soft tone. Surely the shelter I'd been directed towards wouldn't be there. Tremor pranced impatiently. "Okay, we'll follow it for now and see where it goes."

We moved cautiously in the direction of remnants that once would have been large and shiny buildings. This wasn't a town, closer to the size of a city. I didn't see any signs of smoke or movement from this distance, which worked just fine for me.

As we got closer I couldn't help the twinges of depression that sparked in my mind. There were crumbled buildings, leaning helplessly in all directions. No sounds came from within, and I knew it was one of several cities that people had abandoned completely. The survivors had moved on in hopes of finding something more like the world they knew. It was probably once filled with traffic and the bustle of busy lives, and now it sat in dead silence, haunted by what was.

What had taken decades to build and establish were

erased in a few moments time. Did the planet select the areas that were extinguished and the ones that were allowed to stay? I had wondered about that since it all began. Did those that were selfish and uncaring become the target of the viruses that now ruled the direction we all went? If that were true had my integrity been in question before it permitted me to overcome it and survive? Thoughts like these were morbid to think, but I'm sure I wasn't the only one that ever thought them. At least I preferred to assume I wasn't.

The road forked off at thirty feet from the entrance to the discarded society and we didn't stop to debate on whether we'd take the turn or go into the graves of the structures. It would make sense to go in and see if there was anything of use to be found, but was the unknown risk worth a few items? I chose no.

I glanced over my shoulder too many times as we moved away from it, waiting for someone to appear. No one did.

~

By nightfall I could still hear the rushing water, but we hadn't found it. How could something loud enough to hear for miles around be so well hidden? We wouldn't have a soft bed and night sentry tonight, so finding somewhere that felt safe enough to rest became our new quest as the sun started to dip down low in the sky.

It was a full moon tonight, which was good and bad. Good because I would have the moonlight and I could see. Bad because when I was still at home, the nights of the full moon brought about strange events. I was hoping that out in nature the moon is just a giant nightlight in the sky.

Kismet came back from his scouting and stopped to give us that look. The look that meant 'come on I found something'. I didn't understand how I always figured out his looks, but was still happy that I had. We followed him into a small area with several trees and my brain immediately started sorting out what spot was good and which ones wouldn't work. As long as the wind didn't kick up we could at least use the tarp and make a small shelter of some kind.

As I set up our latest camp, I decided that if I didn't find this shelter tomorrow we were going to stop following the sound of water and start looking for a place to get organized and prepared for winter. As if on cue, a frigid breeze blew over me confirming the snow wasn't going to wait forever.

The night was long and well lit, but I was too on edge to sleep. Kismet and I sat side by side and stared out into the trees, listening for anything that disrupted the silence. My mind was compiling a list of things I needed to do before winter. There was a lot on the list that I needed to prioritize it and decide which came first.

I was tired so my mind was starting pushing doubts into my plans, altering my determination. I knew I could do this and the fact that I didn't have a choice was the only thing that kept me moving forward. Even if I were to ever attempt to go back, there was no guarantee anyone I'd known before would still be there. Nothing was permanent these days. There was now and sometimes a tomorrow, beyond that was pure luck or fantasy. I could plan for the winter and cling to the hope that I would see another spring in my life, but putting too much value into those thoughts led to heartache.

~

For three hours we had followed the sound of the water. Did this sound ever fade or was it never ending? I'd lost track of my calculations in how many days walk we were on. The wagons and horseback had made the equation too complex for me to even attempt. This was the last day we would be led by nothing but a sound, a sound that seemed to me like it was getting louder instead of growing even slightly silent. It would be my luck to have completely misinterpreted the directions given in some way.

The trees were getting denser and all three of us seemed to be more at ease traveling in them, I held onto that thought as we went. Tremor was getting moody and I knew he had reached his limit on how long he was comfortable with the saddle on, so I walked along following Kismet's turns as we made our way towards the sound of rushing water. I couldn't really blame him; I didn't want to be in my jacket or boots at this point either.

To pass the time I tested my knowledge of the plants we went by, attempting to name those I could remember. I didn't have a book in my hand to check my answers, just my instinct that let me know when all the various keys fit in place. I paused in my thoughts and could have sworn the water seemed less angry sounding, then again I'd thought that at least a dozen times in the last hour.

Kismet yipped loudly and startled me out of my internal place. I turned to take him to task for almost scaring me half dead but he wasn't there. All I caught was his bushy tail heading through the trees. Glancing around at Tremor to get his take on our companion's sudden exit, I was surprised to see him looking very alert in the direction Kizzy had gone. Was my horse even hoping the canine would find some place to stop?

Rubbing his large face with one hand I smiled up at him. "Okay, we'll go see what he's up to this time." His ears danced around as he nuzzled my hair. Turning we moved to follow him. Tremor jerked hard on the reins. I shook my head and pulled the knife out of my coat. "Worry wart," I teased.

Before we could see where he'd gone, he was back. He ran around us and then barreled back in the same direction. Something had him excited and playful. I moved faster to follow him this time up a small knoll into a thicket of many aged trees. We crested the top and looked down to see Kismet sitting at the bottom patiently waiting for us to catch up. Twenty or so feet from where he sat appeared to be another knoll.

Pausing, I dropped Tremor's reins and walked slowly towards the mound of dirt, it seemed so out of place in the middle of trees. There was a small hill off to the side, but that still didn't explain it. Kismet was at my side as I slowly walked around it. We both stopped at the same time and then looked at each other. The other side resembled a clam shell that was open. Weeds and saplings grew out from it at odd angles, the hanging earth… We'd found the shelter.

Moving slowly towards it, I let Kismet take the lead. He knew when things needed investigating and when they didn't. Ducking down to peer in, I gripped the knife in my hand. I wasn't in a snake mood today and the first thing that moved was going to be vacated from the premises. Kismet sat down after he'd sniffed all around it so the chances of anything that creeps, crawls or slithers was highly unlikely.

It wasn't as big as I'd pictured when the woman had said it would keep me safe, then again only my imagination was wishing for walls, a door and a roof. Tremor ducked under and came up behind me; he apparently needed to check this out too. Like me he didn't seem all that excited. I sighed, it was better than just a tarp, so I should take a deep breath and see what I could do with it. Going over I ran my hand down the far wall, it was mostly stone. The earth and vegetation must have grown over the rock creating this little spot. It was pretty interesting when I stopped and thought about how long it would take for that to happen.

Digging around in my bag, I found the flashlight. The back corner went back far enough that I needed to see all of it. Shining the light into every little corner, I shrugged. It would be a good place to store everything out of the elements. It was deep enough to be well out of the elements and with only one way in, it was less area to watch at night.

A soft whinny from right behind me made me smile. That was Tremor's way of asking if we were staying, most likely wanting all the bags and extra bundles taken off of him. "We're staying and I promise you saddle free for at least a week." He nuzzled my hair. "I thought you'd agree."

~

By the time I got everything piled into the corners, I was ready for a rest. I knew there were things I should be doing, but just having found the shelter removed that worry, I could sit and do nothing for a short time. Tremor was out of the cave and checking out the growth out front, he shook his coat every few minutes as if he was trying to get the feeling of the saddle off it.

Kismet sat in his usual observation mode looking all around us as if he was waiting for something interesting to happen. He whined in a peculiar way that I'd never heard and the hair on the back of my neck stood up. Tremor pranced on the earth in an uneasy way. At the same moment I moved cautiously to the edge of the opening birds flew up out of the trees scattering in every direction. It was suddenly so quiet; not even the slightest noise could be heard.

With the knife already in my hand I went and stood just under the lowest part of the overhang, scanning the area around us trying to pick up on whatever they were sensing. I was just taking a breath to speak and calm them when the ground beneath my feet quivered. A nauseous feeling flooded through me, one that I knew all too well. My heart pumped triple time and my brain flashed back to last huge quake we'd had.

I had a few seconds, only enough to decide if I wanted to take the chance outside of the shelter with the tall trees very nearby or risk being suffocated under it if it collapsed. The dirt under my boots rocked again, more noticeably this time. Tremor reared up and called out his fear. Racing towards him, I grabbed his halter and pulled him back closer to the cover. Kismet whined again, almost an agonizing plea making me wonder if they knew something I didn't. In a building I knew the rules; stand in a doorway but out here there was an absence of doorways leaving me at a loss of what to do.

The next movement was not a warning but a full scale shift. The trees around us protested with loud cracks and sounds that came to me like moans of pain. I couldn't say how long this went on, but it felt like hours. Clinging to the halter, I tried to keep Tremor from bolting, I couldn't help thinking if he really wanted to leave I wouldn't offer much of an obstacle with my size.

There were no dishes breaking or paintings banging

against the wall. The sound of glass shattering wasn't one I missed. All of nature was silent as the earth bucked below in a cry of rage.

I was panicking inside, but trying to stay calm to reassure my animals to lessen the panic they were feeling. The earth behind me slid down from its perch and would have knocked me off my feet if I weren't hanging onto the horse with all the strength I had. A deafening crack was the only warning we had, I don't know what made me look up but when I saw an older tree leaning towards us, I released Tremor's halter and smacked his neck to get him to move. He didn't hesitate as he bolted in the opposite direction. I stumbled behind him and landed on my knees when the grassy floor distorted taking my balance away. Uncertain what else to do I flipped onto my side and covered my head, hoping the tree fell far enough away I'd survive it.

~

I don't know how long I was lying there, but as soon as I realized all I could hear was my own labored breathing I opened my eyes. Without moving I waited for the ground the heave again. When several seconds passed and it didn't I uncurled and stretched out looking at the sky. There wasn't a sound to be heard, all animals seemed to be waiting like I was.

Holding my breath, I was almost afraid to look around, not sure what I would find. Pushing up onto my knees I slowly looked in every direction except the shelter. Preparing myself for the worst, I fully expected the dirt awning to be caved in trapping all of my things under it.

Tremor stood thirty feet away, his ears flicking back and forth as if he were trying to calm himself down. My throat seized just at the sight of him, whole and uninjured. Kneeling there I turned and looked at where we had been standing, at least I tried to see around the tree now blocking it. It was much larger lying on the ground then it had looked when it was coming towards us. Panic washed through me again to think what would have happened if we hadn't moved in time.

Getting to my feet, I walked carefully towards it, not trusting for one second the earth was finished with us. My legs were like jelly and my heart was still skipping far too fast. I didn't see Kismet anywhere and hesitated to call him. I knew he wasn't mine really, but he was all the same and I was terrified to think something may have happened to him.

"Kizzy?" My throat was dried out so it came out more of a croak then a word. He didn't answer. "Kismet!" Walking back towards the shelter as fast as my wobbling knees would allow I climbed over the tree and looked at the entrance I had been standing in. Most of the loose earth was now on the ground, I would have been buried beneath it if I hadn't moved. Turning, I looked in every direction. "Kismet, come on," I encouraged. He needed to be okay.

I stopped and listened hoping if he were hurt he'd let me know. When there were no whines of distress, panic filled my entire body. Tremor came up after going around the tree and stopped to look at the opening of what all of us had hoped was going to be home. Just as I was trying to persuade my feet to move towards it Kismet came out from inside it and looked at me. I wanted to chastise him for scaring me, but instead I lurched to him and dropped to my knees pulling him into my chest.

He licked my face enthusiastically; apparently relieved we were alright and then he pulled out of my arms and turned towards the back of the shelter.

Staring in disbelief, I couldn't move. It had collapsed on top of all of my stuff. There would be no sitting and just taking a few minutes of not watching over my shoulder. I had to try to salvage what I could. Getting up, I dropped my coat onto the ground, prepared to dig everything out. As I reached the pile of branches and dirt I realized I could still see my bags beneath it.

Kismet pushed by me and went right over the top of the pieces of wood, he disappeared. I know my jaw dropped, but it was one of those moments when that was the only thing you were able to do.

Stepping onto the wood, I moved carefully so I wouldn't crush my things. Kismet sat in the middle of a cave, or that's the only description I could come up with. This cave had been lived in, recently. There was a fire pit in the middle and a large cone made from bark above it, leading me to think it was a chimney in very rough form. There were benches by the one wall and a small stack of wood a few feet away from them. The walls were covered with something, dried mud perhaps. I ran my hand along where I stood. It was rock underneath. Later I would wonder more about how there came to be a hollow cave in the middle of trees, but I was just so happy it was there, I didn't want to question how it came to be.

Stepping down off the wobbling pile I moved to stand in the middle and look around. We had a home, and it was much more than I had thought we'd have. Yes I'd wanted walls and doors, but this was nestled into the earth and would offer more protection than anything that sat out in the elements. More than that, it had survived the quakes and I was fairly confident it would survive the next one.

Turning back to my crushed belongings, I lifted the nearest branch only to find out it was attached to several more branches that turned out to be a door. It was not just a door, but one that had hid the inside from even me seeing it while I'd piled all my bags of possessions against it. At this point I didn't know whether to laugh or cry in relief, which I would be sure to fit in later I'm sure but right now I had a home to set up.

CHAPTER NINE

The following week was full of hard work and
exploration for all three of us, but we welcomed it. The clock
was ticking—when it ran out winter would be here. Along
the one wall of our little cave I had bundles of the longest
grass we could find hanging and drying. At night when I
closed my eyes it seemed like I was sleeping in a hay field.

The fact that I slept for the first time by myself since
leaving the city was amazing. My little space only had one
way in or one way out, so trying to listen in all directions was
not a problem now.

Tremor didn't come inside the first two nights, but on
the third one he just decided he didn't want to be left out
there alone and stood by the door. The fact that I'd gone
from sitting under a tarp with no sides to having real shelter
that all three of us could fit in was something I thanked all
the gods for several times a day.

The wood pile was much larger now, as was the wind
break wall I'd made outside the opening. I knew it wasn't
enough wood to get me through the entire winter, but it was
a good beginning to having warmth. If I'd only brought
more than a little hand saw, that tree that hid the opening to
our cave would be a huge pile of wood right now. I didn't
know how to chop wood, but I'd have figured it out.

Each day we went in a different direction through the trees to see what was beyond our new home. In one direction there was a large pond that I hoped didn't freeze over completely being the only source I knew of for water, and possibly fish that we had. I wasn't fond of fish, but I was pretty sure I would stomach it better than ugly bird. Two nights before I was finally brave enough to try eating foul again, but with each bite I waited for it to turn on me. It hadn't in the end which led me to believe I might get over my aversion of it eventually. Then again if I didn't get over it, I might end up starving.

I'd found yams growing wild, after tasting to be sure, in an area near the swamp that was close enough we'd spent a whole day there to forage. Figuring out how to store them took longer than actually gathering them. After hours of digging with mostly large sticks and a rock I finally made a hole deep enough to be a root cellar, cool but not freeze. At least I guessed that four feet would be deep enough. I placed the yams into a bag and lowered it down. I was proud of coming up with the idea and if my precious vegetables survived the frost it would be worth getting all grimy to come up with it.

Along with the yams I'd brought back more reeds than I could fit on Tremors back, so he'd had to suffer the insult of dragging them along behind his large body. It was my plan that they would be soft enough to weave into some style of mattress and a barrier to keep me off the cold ground in the winter. The closest thing I could come to padding for a mattress were miles of cat tails and hoped I wasn't allergic to them once they were dried out.

Today we were going to try fishing. I didn't have hooks, so I was still working on the actual catching part. I'd once watched a movie where a native had stood motionless in the water with a spear and had no problem catching his meal. I didn't have a spear handy, but I did have throwing knives and a stick. How hard could it be?

Famous last words. Soaked up to my butt and frustrated

after twenty failed attempts, I glanced at Kismet sitting on the bank of the pond. He didn't seem all that encouraged that I was going to succeed as he stared off in every direction but at me. Tremor wasn't very inspiring either as he grazed near a huge maple tree a few feet away.

The only thing I had managed to do was scare any fish that might come close enough for me to try to spear. Now I stood here like a wet statue, my arm going numb from being in the air waiting for a fish to swim by. A bird's shrill startled me out of my pose. I looked around at the tree to find it sitting on a limb hanging over the water. It stared back at me like I was in its territory or something. Sighing, I decided I was wet and my feet cold enough for one fishing trip and started back towards the bank.

I sat beside Kismet, watching out over the pond, hoping for some brilliant plan to fill my head. I could shoot them, but that wasn't exactly wise conservation of bullets I couldn't replace. Flopping back I stared up at the leaves covering the vast limbs on the tree above me. It was probably one of the largest trees I'd seen in a long time. Very few had been left to grow old. Of course the fact that it had a private water source probably helped a lot. A squirrel skittered across one of the branches and disappeared around the other side.

Sitting up, I grabbed my homemade spear and studied it. If I could somehow use the knives without the branch I'd have a better chance of actually hitting something. Getting up, I grimaced at the feel of the cold wet denim clinging to my legs. Going back and changing would have been a good idea, but I had something to prove and wasn't leaving until I had a fish or two.

Wrapping my legs around the large branch, I looked down at Kismet sitting there watching me with a puzzled look on his face. I could have reassured him, if I'd felt that way but I didn't. I was really reaching for success now. Shimmying out across the bark, until I was lying across two of the rough barked limbs I looked down at the water. If the cord I'd tied into the handle was long enough this might work. Of course I needed to hit the fish as well.

What felt like an hour later and six attempts later I starred at the knife swinging in the air a few feet over the water, surrounding the knife was a nice sized fish. It had worked and I couldn't have been more surprised.

~

I'd left both animals back at our camp and practically ran to the rolling area that was alive with green foliage of every variety I could name. It didn't take me long to locate the lemon thyme we'd come across the day before. Inhaling the scent of it I tucked it into the little bag I'd brought. I moved slowly up the one side of a steep hill, keeping my eyes down and picking a few different things that caught my interest. Weeds, or wild herbs were tricky and I wasn't going to eat anything I wasn't sure of. This required a little research in one of the few books I did bring. The thyme I knew for sure and couldn't wait to try it with the fish.

Tucking the fourth possibility into the bag, I turned to head back. My heart lodged in my throat as I stopped where I stood and held my breath. Through the trees were four hulking men. It wasn't their size that had me afraid to breathe it was the way they looked. I couldn't even come up with an adequate description of them. I was far away from them yet their aura reached me and swamped me with panic like I'd never felt before.

Two of them dragged something along behind them but I didn't attempt to conclude what. The other two walked at the sides and carried large blades; one blade as wide as my leg and very sharp looking. Crouching down, I slowly picked up the bag I'd dropped and looked over my shoulder at the small knoll I'd just come over. My breathing was shallow as the adrenalin kicked in and I waited for the chance to move unheard. Moving my eyes only, I watched their progress in through the small clearing at the bottom of the hill. They were loud and uncaring if anyone heard them. One of them said something and the other three burst out laughing, sucking in a breath I stood up quickly and bolted back up the knoll.

Spotting a large tree, I headed towards it as fast as my feet could move to duck behind it. Something grabbed me tightly and before I could react I found my face coming to a sudden stop against a hard chest. I tried to struggle but the arm that held me tightly wasn't going to move.

"Don't make a sound." The man whispered softly against my ear. Shivers ran over my skin. "One of them is mutated and can hear a sound as quiet as a heart-beat a mile away." His hold loosened enough that I could move my face away from him.

His large hand grasped my arm and pulled me down towards the dirt. I moved with him, not having much choice, and watched out of the corner of my eye as he got down on his stomach and looked back towards the men moving noisily away from us. Lowering myself all the way down, I turned to see for myself. The men had stopped and were doing something with whatever they had been dragging.

When something suddenly touched my head and I jerked sideways thinking it was a bug or something much larger and worse. Turning my head I watched the man touch his finger to his lips as he lowered a piece of material over my bright hair. I hadn't thought of my hair being a beacon in the green surroundings. Letting out a slow breath I watched as he turned back towards the men.

He had to be as big as the scary ones I was hoping to not meet, but there was something about his aura that said he was peaceful. Black hair, almost as dark as Tremor's midnight shade touched around the edges of his face and coat. Dark glasses hid his eyes and all I could see from my view were long lashes moving beneath them. The structure of his face looked like it was carved out of stone, weathered lines feathered around his eyes and mouth. I glanced back to his hair, not spotting any signs of age there. If I had to guess I'd say he was a survivor like I was, but then again wasn't everyone that was left?

A loud noise from the men below had me jumping

again, I turned my attention back towards them. They had changed directions and it looked like they were heading in our direction. Had the man beside me been right? Was there a mutated one that could hear me? I didn't know how, when I was scarcely breathing and my heart was beating so fast it probably sounded more like a hum than any recognizable rhythm.

There was movement again. Before I could turn to see what, his big arm wrapped around my waist and pulled me over closer to him. He was now lying on his side and brought me tight against his body. If it hadn't been for the fact that I was afraid I was living my last moments, I might have appreciated the hard form of his body a little more. He cradled me tight in both arms and moved his mouth to rest against my ear again.

"We have to go."

I nodded, more than agreeing with getting the hell out of here. The branches breaking from the feet of the four seemed to be coming closer. "I'm going to slide us back to the trees and then we can get up." I wasn't sure how he planned to do that, but I was all for any plan at the moment— because I had none. "Hang onto me." His lips brushed against my ear once more. Rolling onto his back, bringing me to rest on top of his long body, he stroked a hand over my back before dropping it away.

Moving my hands slowly up to his shoulders, I turned my face and rested my cheek against his chest feeling small comfort in hearing his heart-beat was almost as fast as my own. As he started to move, I reached down and tucked the edge of the bag between us so I could use both hands to hold on. He lifted our weight by reaching out with his arms and we inched along the ground. With each movement he made I could feel his muscles tighten against my body. There was no sound as he slowly brought us closer to the trees, I didn't know how he was doing it but was glad that he could. I kept my eyes on them and counted each heartbeat to distract from the intimate feelings his body flexing into mine brought.

Now was not the time for hormonal urges of any kind, I told myself.

The large tree I had been trying to reach when I ran was only a few feet away when he stopped. He moved his hand slowly until his fingers rested under my chin and tilted my head up to look at him. "Go." He motioned with his head towards the trees.

Letting go, I moved down off of him until I was on my stomach on the ground again. With careful motion I crawled on my belly towards the tree. I waited until I was almost by the tree to come to my knees and then stand.

"Hey!" One of the men called.

I stopped and hugged my body against the tree. Had they seen me? I closed my eyes and took a deep breath before peaking around far enough to see the dark haired man sitting up slowly.

"Could you make any more noise?" My black haired savior bellowed back at them. "I was trying to catch a nap."

"Ah. It's only you." Another voice shouted. "Serves you right, sleeping in the middle of the day out in the open."

"I'll keep that in mind." He stood up and I know my eyes widened to see him at his full height. I couldn't even guess his height from where I stood cowering against the bark. He took two steps back towards me and moved his body close to the tree. I watched him salute the men and then he turned into the tree, pulling my arm so I stood in front of him.

Reaching down he picked up a backpack and gave me a gentle shove to start walking, making sure to keep me shadowed by his size with each step. I wanted to turn around and look behind us, but he didn't slow enough for me to even have the chance.

When we made it down the knoll, he steered me to the left and kept us in the thickest part of the trees. Lowering his head close to the back of mine, he spoke softly again. "Do you have shelter nearby?"

His breath against my neck sent shivering down my

spine. I nodded.

"Let's head there."

I glanced over my shoulder and pointed in the direction. Taking him there may or may not turn out to be the best idea. But so far he hadn't done anything to make me think he was insane or unsafe, so I kept going. Deep down I admitted I just wanted some human company for a while. Silently, I prayed it wouldn't be a mistake.

Inside my head I was having a conversation with him; well I was asking him questions at the very least. Neither of us spoke, he walked a step behind me the whole way and didn't say a word. I slowed down when we were almost to my hidden spot, feeling leery now about taking him there. No one had found the cave beneath the land that sheltered me and kept me safe since the last occupants had lived there and I had second and third doubts about showing him.

I whistled softly to warn Tremor and Kismet that I was close. Were my companions safe from the giant behind me?

"Who are you warning?"

His voice breaking the silence made me jump. I paused and looked up at him, wishing I could see the eyes hid behind the dark lenses. "I have a dog and horse, I don't want to startle either." Continuing to stand there I tried to gauge his reaction, he didn't say a word or make a move, just stood there looking down at me.

Sighing, I turned back towards the darkened area hidden beneath the over growing plants. I whistled again and listened for the soft whine. Kismet's head popped out of the hole beside the overhanging rock. He gave one soft yip and then ran towards me.

Before he reached us, he stopped and crouched down, his ears flattening and teeth showing. "Kismet, it's okay." The dog didn't seem reassured. I stepped back beside the tall stranger and placed my hand on his arm, trying to show Kismet that it was okay. He straightened and sat right where he stood. More or less saying, he can come to me, but I'm not going to him.

"That's your dog?" He sounded amused.

I nodded and looked at him. "Yes. I'm not sure what kind though."

He grinned at me and his smile was both predator and charming. "I'm pretty sure there's a lot of wolf in there." He squatted down and whistled softly without reaching out towards him.

Kismet sat there for a moment before moving cautiously forward, he crept along almost on his belly for the last few feet. I stood there and watched the man wait for the animal to come to him, to scent him and hopefully accept him. I had no instances to compare it to, as we hadn't been around many people since Kismet decided to adopt us. He seemed uncertain, but still went to him and sniffed his hand. I know my eyes must have bulged when Kismet dropped down and rolled over on his back with his legs in the air. Patting his stomach the big man laughed.

"A tough beast you are." Shaking his head he stood up and looked down at me.

My heart was doing something strange that it hadn't done since I was seven and thought I was in love with Bobby. I swallowed. "I'm Bree, by the way."

He stood there for a few seconds and I wasn't sure if he'd heard me. Slowly he reached up and lowered his glasses to look over the top of them at me. The pupils of his eyes were a color that I could only say was silver. Even though my heart sped up to beat ten times faster than it should, I wasn't afraid—I probably should have been. "There's power in a name, Red. Be careful who you give that power to." His eyes continued to move over my face and for a few more seconds, shivers moved over my skin. "Kane," he said in such a low voice I barely made out what he said. With that he pushed the glasses back up and then turned and headed towards my shelter. Kismet, my little trader trotted along beside him.

I took a deep breath and tried to regain control of my heart that felt like it was flowing through my veins as my blood should have been. Every instinct in my body told me Kane was dangerous but seemingly my brain wasn't going to listen as I followed along behind them.

Tremor stepped out of the trees near the opening and I immediately went in his direction to give me a bit more space until I could get a handle on my own body again. I was sure my reaction was only because of the scare from those other men—at least this is what told myself. Anything other than that wasn't something I wanted to be dealing with.

Tremor's ears twitched as he watched the stranger with Kismet. I rested my hand against his soft coat and felt the muscles beneath quivering as Kane walked closer.

"He's a beautiful animal. Where did you get him?"

Tremor stood perfectly still and let him come right up to him. "He was given to me."

One black eyebrow raised above the glasses as he glanced at me, but he didn't comment. He motioned with his head to the bag I'd forgot I even had clutched in my hand. "Do you want to tell me what was so important to keep that you dragged it along with us?"

I looked down at it. "Herbs."

He paused in stroking his hand over Tremor. "Herbs? You risked your neck for herbs?"

I nodded, realizing it was more than silly now considering the men that I'd almost ran right into. "For dinner—to go with the fish." I looked down at the ground, not sure what else to add. "I don't like fish all that much so I'm going to try to hide the flavor."

His deep chuckle brought my eyes back to him. "Show me this fish and I'll show you how to cook it so it doesn't need herbs."

I knew the surprise was on my face for him to see but I nodded and turned back towards the entrance. I paused after a few feet, not wanting to take him inside. I didn't know this man. He may have just dragged me out of a bad situation, but that didn't mean he was friend-worthy. Glancing behind me, I saw he was still with Tremor and quickly moved inside to get the fish. Grabbing a pan and few other things I reached up to unhook the fish and found an empty cord dangling where my three fish had been. Grabbing the empty cord, forgetting about the door or anything else, I stomped back out.

"Kismet!" I shook the cord in his direction and stared at him, putting my hands on my hips. "You ate our dinner!" He lowered his head and then dropped down and rested his chin on his paws looking repent. "Bad!" I hissed. His ears flicked as he began to move slowly towards me, his belly only inches from the ground. By the time he reached me and looked up at me with those sad amber eyes I sighed. "You get to stay here while I get more." I tried to sound angry still, but failed miserably.

Kane walked over and looked down at the animal that all but pleaded at my feet. "You do know that's a wolf you're chastising, right?"

I glanced at him and then back down at Kizzy. "He's a dog, just a little wild looking."

Kane hissed out a breath. "Okay we'll say he's a dog." He shrugged out of his faded denim jacket. "Point me in the direction you caught the fish and I'll go get dinner."

My eyes flew to him, my brain only pausing for a second to take in the overall size of him that had been hidden under his jacket. Before he noticed my face flushed, I turned to go back inside. "I'll take you there." I went in, grabbed my throwing knives and the cord I'd used earlier.

Going back out, I whistled over to Tremor. "Come on, boy. We have to go fishing again."

"We're taking the horse?"

I smirked at the odd note in his voice. "It's faster. Do you ride?"

He stepped up beside me, his face looking stern. "Not since I was a child."

I grabbed Tremor's bridle and motioned to his back. "It's like riding a bike, without moving your feet."

He frowned and placed his hand on the horse's back.

Beside him, Tremor looked like an average size horse even though I knew he was a larger than normal horse. "No saddle?"

"It's his day off, so no." I rubbed my hand against Tremor's jaw trying not to laugh at the hesitation the very large man was having about getting on a horse. "Come on, he won't bite I promise."

Scowling at me, he looked back at the animal under his hand. "I'm not worried about biting; it's the landing on my head part that has me a little apprehensive." Taking a deep breath, he squatted down and more or less vaulted on.

Tremor pranced for a few seconds, adjusting to a much heavier body than he was used to carrying. When he'd settled down, I flipped the reins over and looked up realizing I couldn't get up with him sitting there. I held out my hand. He looked at it and then leaned down and grasped my waist, lifting me up as if I weighed no more than a child.

Settling between his thighs I tried not to think about the fact that I'd just put myself in a very vulnerable position.

"Can we just walk for a minute so I can remember this?"

His breath brushed against the back of my neck sending shivers down my spine like it had earlier. I nodded and turned Tremor in the right direction. Kane gripped my hips and squeezed, making me smile that he was really that uncomfortable to ride be on a horse. "Are you okay?"

His hold loosened a bit, "Yeah. Just don't tell anyone if I cling to you like a scared child."

Laughing, I realized it had been a long time since I had. "I think your secret is safe with me." Kismet came running over. I glared down at him. "You stay, bad dog!" With his tail between his legs he went back over to the shelter and dropped to the ground.

"You're kind of scary, Red."

I didn't say anything, just kicked the horses' side and held on as he broke into a fast canter. A strong arm wrapped around my waist, crushing me back against his hard chest. I could feel his heart beating wildly against my shoulder blade.

"I take that back," he whispered in a low voice under my ear. "You're not scary. You're nasty."

I laughed again and let Tremor have his head so he could run at his own preferred speed. Kane's thighs tightened against my hips as did his arm around me, but he didn't say another word as we traveled through the trees towards the little pond a few minutes away.

I hadn't had anyone to share anything with since I'd left Darren and Bobby standing on the city limits. This man behind may be a complete stranger, but there was something sad inside him that drew that soft heart of mine to him. I'd only had a brief glimpse of his unique eyes, yet I could still see the emptiness that haunted him and kept him going.

As we neared the pond, Tremor slowed down without prompting until he was walking slowly towards the big tree I had taken him to earlier that day. When he stopped, Kane's arm was gone and he was standing on the ground before I could drop the reins. His big hands circled my waist and lifted me down, slowing until my feet hit the ground. He didn't move his hands right away, just continued to look down at me.

I swallowed, not sure what to make of the moment. Reaching up, I put my hand against the side of his glasses and slowly slipped them off. He blinked and then silver eyes looked down at me. I offered him a smile, trying to ignore the way they moved over my face. "I like to see someone when they're looking at me."

His hands let me go and dropped to his sides. "You may not always like what you see, Red." He backed away until he was a few feet away.

Frowning I folded up his glasses and walked back over to him. I tucked them into the neck of his shirt and hung them there. "Maybe, but I won't know if I can't see." Making sure the pouch was tucked into the waist of my jeans; I went over to the tree and started to climb up it.

When I was out on the wide limb I'd used earlier I

looked back down at him. He stood there watching me with his hands on his hips and the oddest expression on his face. I grinned at him and moved out to lie on the bark so I was out over the pond. Looping the cord through one of the knives I leaned back down and watched the water below. I wanted to look at him again, but I was having enough trouble focusing on what I was doing and it seemed like every time I did look at him my body forgot how to function properly.

It didn't take me even half the time to have three fish hanging from the cord once more. Shimmying back towards the main branch, I pushed myself up to straddle the wide limb. Looking around for Kane, I found him sitting, leaning against the trunk of the tree. "Catch." I swung the fish towards him and let go. They dropped down right beside him.

He picked up the cord and dangled them to look at them and then shook his head and looked up to watch me working my way back down. "Do you always fish this way?"

I concentrated on making sure my foot found the groove in the trunk before I answered. "Today is the first day I've fished. It took me half the day to figure out they can't see me if I'm in the tree, so it's much easier than my earlier attempts." I worked my way slowly down to the lower branch, sitting on it to catch my breath for a second.

He stood up and then reached up and tugged on my ankles, making me slip from the branch down far enough that he could reach my hips and lift me down out of the tree. "You're a constant surprise, Red. Makes me glad I wandered in your direction today."

I grinned as my feet touched the dirt once more. "Me too, but you need to stop picking me up and grabbing me. I'm not used to it." I brushed the bark off the front of my shirt, not wanting to look at him.

Kane threw his head back and laughed. "Then you need to stop fitting so easily into my hands."

My jaw dropped open, I'd been teased about my small size all of my life. I looked at his hands and then glared at him. "Those are hands? They look like giant paws to me." He continued to laugh as he turned his hand over and looked at it.

Shrugging he followed me over to Tremor and then grasped me by the waist again and set me up on his back. I scowled down at him, but couldn't hold it when his silver eyes looked at me and seemed lighter and less desolate than then had earlier. "Are you coming? You have fish to cook."

Smirking, he patted my leg and then swung up behind me. His arm wrapped around my waist again as he fit me between his to rest tight against his chest. Reaching around me, he took the reins from my hands. "I think I'll steer this time."

I turned my head to look straight ahead and closed my eyes for a moment, relaxing into the feel of being against him. A feeling of being safe for the first time since Shawn had died flood through me.

~

I watched him clean the fish, silently noting everything he did so I could do it that way. He made it look easy, which told me it probably wasn't. As he got the fire ready, his back was to me and I again found myself studying the size of him. I had never seen shoulders that wide before and the muscles on his back did a dance with each movement he made. When he placed the pan over the fire, he turned and smirked. "What kind of herbs did you find?"

I smiled, wondering now if he wasn't sick of plain fish too. "Lemon thyme and it should make it taste … less fishy."

"I'd like to try that."

I nodded and went back in to get the herbs. He hadn't gone inside when we got back, only glanced in the door. Maybe he felt more at ease out in the open with his size, I wasn't sure. I took the herbs back out and squatted down beside him, breaking them up in my hand. "Just sprinkle this over the top while it's cooking, that should work—I've never tried it with fish though so we'll see."

Nodding, he leaned back away from the fire. "How

long have you been out here?"

I shrugged. "Overall, I'm not sure. One day seems to blend in with the next after a while." I bit my lip. "Do you know the date today?"

He shook his head. "No idea, there's not much need to keep track of day or time out here."

"Yeah." I dusted off my palms on my jeans and then moved over to sit against the wall again. "How long have you been out here?"

He gave me an odd look. "How do you know I have been?"

I tilted my head and studied him. "You carry a worn backpack. Your face is weather…" He raised an eyebrow and dared me to continue. "You're tanned and your jacket is faded from the sun."

There was a long silence. "She has reasonable logic as well," he mused with a teasing tone. "Since it began, I've been out here that long." He paused and looked over at the fish. "I was quickly left with nothing comforting or familiar." Reaching over he poked the fish around I the pan. "So I headed out to see what I could find."

When I realized he wasn't going to continue, I spoke softly. "So you wander around helping people like you did me?" I honestly wanted to know.

His silver eyes flicked over my face before he looked back down at the pan. "Don't paint me a hero—Bree."

The way he said my name struck a chord deep inside me and I understood what he had meant when he'd said there was power in a name. My heart was thrumming steadily behind my ribs now. I didn't want him to know. "I'm fresh out of paint, sorry."

He laughed quietly. "You have a smart mouth too."

I wiggled my eyebrows at him. "Maybe."

~

In the darkness of the night, I sat there trying to reason out why the fish had tasted better than anything I'd eaten since I left. The only thing I could conclude was I'd had someone to share it with, and distract me while I ate. I was leaning back against the wall, my jacket wrapped around me as we sat there silently watching the fire die down. It had been a good day. For once my heart was light and my brain wasn't worrying about the future.

Sensing, rather than seeing him moving, I realized I was drifting off to sleep out here in the open. He touched my head softly and then I found myself in his arms being carried inside the shelter. I felt my body touch my blanket. Opening my eyes as best I could I watched him put the other blanket over me. He tucked it around me and then just knelt there.

"I have to go," he whispered.

I searched his eyes and saw that the haunted look had returned. I didn't understand it, but thought that maybe it wasn't my place. "Keep *you* safe, Kane," I said softly, my voice heavy with sleep.

Large fingers touched my cheek gently. "You as well, Bree." He stood up and looked down at me for a few seconds before moving back to the door.

I felt Kismet lie down beside me and heard the door moving into place. I could hear him speak softly to Tremor and then I heard nothing.

CHAPTER TEN

The day was warmer than it had been in many days, so
I thought we'd go exploring a little further. We followed the
sound of the water again; this time I was determined to find
out where that water actually was. Neither animal seemed to
mind. Kismet was always up for exploration and Tremor just
seemed happy that I wasn't making him drag or haul
anything.

A week had passed since our encounter with Kane and
we'd worked hard gathering. Even Kismet pulled bundles of
grass and bark for our cause now. There wouldn't be many
more trips like this before winter, the leaves were turning and
earlier that morning I'd noticed Kismet's coat was thickening.
I wished for a coat that naturally thickened as I still hadn't
been able to bring myself to kill anything furry.

When we finally discovered the river, it was quite wide
and curiously appeared out of nowhere. Tremor lost the
prance in his step when I hit the ground to search for
anything useful. Trial and error had shown me that only
certain stones created enough spark to light a fire and I
wanted to have plenty stored for when the matches ran out.

After I filled a bag with stones, we wandered near the
shore. It was too pretty to hurry away from it. The water
rushed over the rocks, echoing for miles. I didn't know what

it led to, but we still had a few hours that we could investigate further before we started heading back.

We sat under the shade of a tree for a quick snack of dried jerky and some water.

Afterward I was leaning back just watching the water when a strange mewling sound traveled to me. Kismet sat up and looked around. I wasn't sure what was making the noise but I knew it was young and terrified. Sitting up, I tried to block out the sound of the water to see where it was coming from.

Kismet found the animal in distress before I did. A tree a little further up the river held a small feline cub, its wide dark eyes huge with terror. Tremor pawed at the ground as I looked around for the parent the cat belonged to. We sat there for several more minutes watching, waiting for the mother to come looking for her lost child. When the minutes ticked on and there was no sign of one, my heart began to ache for the tiny creature.

As I started to move up the river bank, Kismet gave me a look that clearly said 'are you crazy?' I patted his head and kept going. The cub, a mountain lion if I wasn't mistaken, had managed to get out on a limb hanging over the water and now didn't know how to turn to go back. If it went out any further it was going to tumble into the rushing water. I didn't know much about an animal like this or if they could swim, but the water beneath it was deep and rough enough it might drown before it had a chance to live.

Kismet sat in my path and looked up at me. Shaking my head I stepped around him. Tremor inserted his large body between mine and the tree I was heading towards. "You two work as a team now?" I rubbed a hand down his neck. "I'm just going to help it get down and then we'll head in the other direction." I studied the tree as I moved towards it. Getting up wasn't going to be too difficult, there were more than enough knots to climb up. Once I reached the first large branch it would be simple to shimmy out and help the little guy turn around so he was heading in the right direction.

Flipping my coat over the horses back, I rolled up my sleeves and looked up at the cub. It had stopped making that heartbreaking sound and watched me intently. "I'll get you down," I crooned to it as I moved towards the trunk of the tree.

I straddled the limb and tried not to look down at the water rushing beneath the branch I was on. It had seemed like a great plan, but the water didn't look nearly as daunting when you were level with it as it did when you hung over it. No wonder the animal was frightened.

Planning as I went, I knew I couldn't sit astride the tree all the way out to where it was, but if I did this right I figured I'd be able to reach it and get it turned around. Of course I hoped like hell those little claws that gouged into the bark would leave me unscathed. Kismet yipped at me from below scaring the little thing even more. I sent him a glare that he must have understood because he sat down immediately.

I managed to get within a few inches of the cubs' side before my plan went wrong in a blink. I heard the sound of the branch cracking and grabbed the animal with both hands, trying to throw my weight back away from the weak spot.

Claws dug into me as it climbed to my neck at the same moment ice cold water swallowed me. My breath left my body so quickly it felt like my lungs were going to burst. The intense pain from the incisions the animal was making across my chest brought me the strength to kick as hard as I could towards the surface. I wasn't the strongest swimmer by far, but I had more than enough will to live to try for both of us.

In the brief glimpses I managed to keep my head above the water, I didn't spot the shore once. We were being sucked into the middle. Through the white choppy water that blurred my vision I was only able to catch a quick look each time before we were dragged under again. I could feel the rocks rake over my back and hoped there would be enough flesh left to survive it.

The cat was practically wrapped around my neck and

holding several layers of skin and flesh captive in its young claws as we swirled around again in a deep pit of rushing water. Each time we surfaced, I gulped as much air into my lungs as I could before water filled my mouth again. The undercurrent calmed just long enough for me to find the direction of shore and with every ounce of strength I could find I kicked and paddled with my arms trying to shove us in that direction. I could make out a tree that was floating near the bank just seconds before I was inhaling water again.

Hitting the bottom I shoved as hard as I could and tried to aim to the calmer water near the shore, not even knowing if I was going in the right direction until air hit my face once more. The tree was still in sight and I somehow knew if we didn't reach it we wouldn't be on land after that. Releasing my hold on the animal that was anchored to me so deeply that no way was it going to jump off and float away I swam towards the tree and prayed I'd reach the limbs lying in the water before we were dragged beyond them.

I kicked something with my foot and quickly shoved against it reaching out to the waterlogged wood that was visible. My pants snagged on something, but I didn't slow down as I felt the fabric tear and it gouge my leg. Grabbing the slippery branch, my hand slid off twice more before I used all limbs to propel us towards it again. Holding it with an iron grip I pulled my heavy body closer and flipped one leg up to rest over the branch nearest to the one I held.

The cats' razor claws left my flesh as it scrambled over my head and onto the branch. Resting my chin on the rank smelling bark I watched it look at me for no more than a few seconds before it teetered along the lifesaving limb and reached the shore. "You're welcome … ungrateful brat…"

Hooking my elbow over close to my chin, I continued to lie there floating between the two branches, trying to gather the strength to pull myself out of the cold water. Barking registered and I opened my eyes again to see Kismet pacing along the shore. "Gonna rest for a few … s'okay …" I tried to reassure him. The cold was numbing the stinging which I was more than happy for, between the claws and rocks I felt what hamburger would and was in no hurry to assess the damage.

I thought about the things I'd been through in the last few weeks and would have laughed if I'd had the energy, as I realized I'd put myself through more out here than I would have encountered in the city. The only difference, in a good way, was the peace I felt out in the wild. I did chuckle at that, deciding that maybe the peaceful part didn't as I bobbed in a river that had just tried to swallow me whole.

The cooling air over my face told me it was getting closer to dusk, and I needed to get out of the water. Floating around in the dark wouldn't win me any safety awards, but I couldn't find the thought in my dulled brain to make my muscles move.

I heard movement and tried to turn my head to see if some large creature was scoping me out for dinner, but even my neck had given up on me.

"Red?"

The voice registered but I decided I'd just answer later, there was no rush, I wasn't going anywhere. I felt like I was moving and knew I must be dreaming now, as I didn't have the strength to move my eyelids at this point.

There was splashing and barking, and I really hoped Kismet wasn't taking a swim in this, hadn't he learned from my mistakes? Even from his canine's eye what I had been doing out in the water could not have looked fun or refreshing. I'd give him hell for it later; I was just going to rest now.

Opening my eyes, I squinted in the dark, unsure of where I was for a moment. I felt dryer and had to wonder if there was a point where you just couldn't feel wet and water logged anymore. Vaguely it registered that I wasn't on my face any longer and gave myself a mental pat on the back for finally moving. The warmth I was imagining was a welcomed feeling, so I closed my eyes again and just let it wrap around my numbness.

~

When I opened my eyes again the only thing I could see were two large concerned amber ones looking right back at me. "Kizzy," I croaked. I tried to move my hand to touch him, but they felt like they were molded against my side. I wanted to scold him for coming out on the branch, but in truth I was happy for the company.

"It's about time you came around."

Moving my burning eyes I looked for the source of the voice. It took several seconds to focus in on Kane. What was he doing out on the branch with me? I squinted at him and then it registered that he was squatted down beside a fire. Even in my state I knew you couldn't light a fire on the water.

He came over and I felt him lift my head and place a cup against my lips. I really hoped he wasn't giving me water to drink, because I'd had my fill, thank you. Whatever it was I tried to swallow was awful and my throat burned as I gagged it down. Lowering my head back to the blanket he gave me an odd look.

"Felt like taking a swim did you?"

"Cat."

He frowned. "Let me guess you were saving a kitten?"

I wanted to roll my eyes but they were so gritty I was afraid to. "Cub," I whispered.

The look of surprised mixed with a bit of anger appeared in his silver eyes. "You risked your ass to save a mountain lion?"

"I think so." I wasn't happy that he made me sound stupid for helping something in trouble. Of course I came close to drowning for the unappreciative creature, but that wasn't the point.

"That explains the chunks missing out of you." He moved the blanket and I felt the air on my arms he'd had cocooned to my sides. When the air hit my skin, I panicked to realize he'd taken my clothes off. "Relax; shredded woman isn't exactly to my taste."

I scowled at him. "My back?"

"Is a mess as well." He leaned back on his heels. "Jesus, Red, you scared the hell out of me when I rode up and saw you floating face down."

My head was pounding, but I still caught what he'd said. "Rode up?"

He grinned. "I was on the other side and I saw you go by—I high-tailed it back around and headed down river …"

I tried hard to focus on his words but his voice was fading in and out.

"Your pets came and got me, more or less—which is how I knew it was you swirling past riding the river."

I didn't know what to say. I was exhausted but hurt like I'd been kicked repeatedly, and my head was throbbing so loudly each time I tried to move it, my stomach rebelled. "Where are we?"

Kane sat down beside me and brushed his hand over my forehead gently. "Still about an hour from your cave, you were shivering so bad I had to stop and see if I could warm you up a bit first." He tucked the blanket back around my neck. "I need take a closer look at your injuries someplace warmer."

I shrugged around inside the blanket that was holding me prisoner until I managed to get one hand free. "Thanks." Knowing I didn't have the strength to sit up left me no choice but to lie there and look up at him.

His glasses were off, but it was too dark to see his eyes clearly. I didn't know why I wanted to see them as much as I did but I reached out and grabbed his jacket with a weak hand and pulled at it until he brought his face closer to mine. Just the shift in his position made the firelight reflect off his silver stare. I could see he was worried and that shook me a little. "How bad am I banged up?"

He looked at me, his eyes wandering over my face for several seconds before he took a deep breath. "I'm not sure."

Not the answer I had hoped for. "Okay."

Straightening up, he kicked dirt onto the fire. "It's going to hurt something terrible to get you back up on the horse for the rest of the ride."

I knew he wasn't exaggerating, every inch of me hurt lying on the ground without moving so I could only imagine what upright was going to feel like while jostling around on top of Tremor.

~

I was wrong, I couldn't have imagined this. Kane had me sideways in front of him, wrapped in a blanket that I didn't know where he'd gotten; I had no choice in position. If I leaned back against his arm my back burned like someone was placing hot coals against it, but sitting upright only caused my back muscles to spasm and threaten to knock me to the ground.

"You're killing me with that hissing noise you're making," he rumbled quietly near my ear. "Turn into me and let me support your weight." I tried to turn my head enough to look at him, but even that hurt. "Come on, Red, I promise not to bite you. Snuggle in and try to find a position that doesn't hurt as much."

As I moved, Tremor paused in his stride and stood there while I shifted towards Kane's large chest. The moment my face touched it, he scooped my legs so they lie over his and wrapped the blanket around my feet. With a gentle arm he held me close to him. Tremor took a few steps and I sighed when it didn't hurt as much. "Why are you doing this?"

His chin brushed my head as he looked down at me. "Maybe I have past sins to repent for so I'm doing all the good deeds I can."

I made a pathetic noise that was meant to be a laugh. "You believe in a God?"

There was silence for a few moments. "Not anymore." He pulled the blanket up higher on my neck. "Do you?"

"I believe there's something out there—I just don't know what." I mumbled against his chest.

"Then let's hope your something comes back from vacation soon, because we could use a little help down here."

Wrapping his other hand around my hip, he nudged Tremor with his knees.

With that I felt like he was ending conversation, so I just lay there and tried to stay as coherent as I could. I didn't want to pass out in his arms and make the trip more difficult but as I listened to his heart beating I felt myself fading with each thump until I felt like I was floating again only this time without water.

Vaguely I was aware of lying down again, I wasn't sure if it was a dream or really happening but it felt so damn good I went with it for as long as I could. I felt light touches against my skin and the result cooled the tight burning and made me want to sigh. I may have sighed out loud, but there was no way to distinguish what was just inside my head from things that were reality.

Struggling to find consciousness I finally managed to get my eyes to almost open. They were still gritty and painful to move. Recognizing enough of what I looked at I knew we were back in the cave and that was relief enough. In the dim light from the fire I could make out Kismet's form lying by my feet, he watched me without movement. It took three more attempts to get my eyes to open far enough to look around, even in my groggy state I realized I was looking to see if Kane had stayed or if I was alone.

When I focused in on him, he sat beside the fire with his head down watching it. Part of me wanted to get up and go to him, even though physically that wasn't going to happen. Deep inside I caught the fact that he wouldn't want me to see him like that, almost vulnerable. His silver eyes flicked up and looked at me as he somehow sensed I was awake.

A weak smile spread over his face. "Get some sleep, Red. I'll be here in the morning."

It was all I needed to hear. My heavy eyes drifted closed and I heard myself sigh loudly as I let the exhaustion wash over me.

~

The next time I woke, I was shaking and shivering to the point that I could hear my teeth chattering. It was like I'd lost control of every muscle in my body at the same time. Kismet moved against my legs and whined loudly. I could hear movement, but wasn't able to open my eyes to see what. When the blankets weighing me down lifted, I jumped.

"Easy, it's me." Kane whispered near my head.

I felt him move beneath the blanket with me and sighed to feel his warm body press up against mine as he pulled me into his arms. He tucked the blanket tight behind me and lowered his head down onto my pillow. If the heat from him wasn't so welcomed, I would have objected to the feel of his bare chest and arms against my skin. I'd never slept with anyone before but thought that in this instance it wouldn't be a bad thing.

"Try to go back to sleep, I'll keep you warm." His voice was so deep and soft it was soothing to hear.

Once the shaking stopped and my body settled down I started to drift off again. The last thought that crossed my mind before I faded was me wondering if he did this sort of thing often for strangers.

~

The burning radiated through my back, bringing me fully awake before I'd taken a breath.

"I'd hoped you'd sleep longer."

I blinked up at Kane. "My back—it's on fire."

A frown filled his face. "I'll put some more ointment on it. If you can deal with the smell, it works fast for healing."

Smell wasn't anything I cared about, just so long as the burning was gone. "Okay." Moving in what probably looked like slow motion, I rolled as far onto my stomach as the cuts on the front of me comfortably allowed. Watching out of the corner of my eye, he took something out of his backpack and then knelt down beside me. "Where did you get the ointment?"

The cool air hit my back as he pulled the blanket down.

"There's a small settlement about a day away from here—one of the women make medicinal salves and ointments."

A weird feeling went through me, I'd like to say it wasn't jealousy but that was the only thing I could label it. Of course Kane knew other people — other women. "Is that where you live?" I clenched my teeth as the mixture hit the scrapes near my spine.

He made a noise, which I could only figure to be a sigh. "No."

Something in his tone told me that was all I was getting for a reply on that topic. "I guess I'm lucky you were in the neighborhood."

He made another quiet noise under his breath. "I left some things I need to go pick up I dropped them when you went rushing past—hopefully they're still there, I didn't take the time to hide them."

Guilt washed over me. "You should go get it."

Kane sat back, wiping his hand on his jeans. "Just let the air at that for a while, and then we'll put some on the front." He cleared his throat. "I'd like to go get that stuff. I found an abandoned camp..." We both felt the tension from those words, not saying out loud that abandoned didn't mean the people left on their own or lived to actually leave. "I went through it and bundled up anything useful."

Tucking the blanket under my chest, I lifted my aching body up onto my elbows and looked at him. "You should go get your things, Kane."

"I will, once we get you up and moving a bit."

Did that mean he was leaving and not coming back? With shaking arms, I pushed until I was kneeling. Clutching the blanket close to me, I sat there waiting until my head wasn't floating. "I'll be okay," I whispered in a breathless voice.

He chuckled. "Tell that to the walls flying past your head." Kane moved quickly and scooped me up, setting me upright near the wall. "Just sit there and let the earth settle a bit. I'll get you something to eat." I was able to focus a little better as I watched him move around. He stopped and picked up one of the dehydrated pouches of food. "You prepared for this long before you left didn't you?"

"Yes. I knew I was going to have to eventually, so I worked and saved and got things a bit at a time."

"Worked at what?"

His expression was harsh and I didn't know why. Not wanting to see him look like that, I looked down at the dirt floor for a few seconds. "My brother and his friends all worked for the distribution center—they got me a job in the receiving department—they used to joke I was better guarded than Fort Knox with all the merchandise that came in." Glancing up, I was surprised to see a look that was close to relief on his face. I could see he had questions, but he didn't comment.

Tossing the package back where the rest were piled. "As tasty as those probably are, I thought I'd make some of those vegetables and leeks you have instead." Without waiting for a reply he turned away.

"You said something about a settlement not far from here?" Did I hope it was the sanctuary I was looking for? I wasn't sure.

Pausing, he looked at me. "Yeah, it would be about a day's ride north of here. You'd do good to go there for trading."

"I don't have much to trade."

He kept his head down as he sliced up the leeks. "You'd be surprised. That homemade mattress of yours is quite ingenious—many would be interested in sleeping on something soft again." He smiled, his eyes shining. "I know I enjoyed it after sleeping on dirt for too long." Picking up the pan he moved over to the fire pit. "Just a few of those mushrooms you have growing would be a treat for anyone as well." He shrugged. "The flint stone is also valuable."

I listened as he rhymed off a few other things that I would never have thought to be valuable and had to wonder at how odd it was. A few years ago a cell phone, computer and the flash of your car were an important thing—was it sad that cattails for mattress padding were not considered wealth? When I looked up again he was sitting there looking at me. "Sorry, my brain wandered."

"I was just saying you should definitely go there and see if you can barter an axe or hatchet." He smirked. "You have a lot of wood stored, but no way to cut it up."

I sighed. "I know. I sawed my arms numb with my little saw just getting it small enough to drag here."

"I can imagine." When he looked back at me, his silver eyes were very sincere. "You've done a hell of a job though."

I don't know why his praise made me feel giddy, but it did. "Thanks."

~

I listened to Tremor's hooves hitting the ground as they rode away. I was shocked and happy that Kane agreed to take Tremor considering his earlier fears of riding. He wouldn't be gone as long with the horses help, and the fact that I didn't want him to be bothered me a lot. I knew I couldn't get attached to this man—knew it right to the bottom of my soul, but that still didn't make a difference.

It took me what felt like hours to get up and put on some clothes to go outside to go to the bathroom. I added another thing to my list of things to figure out while I moved in slow motion, what was I going to do about going to the bathroom when I was waist deep in snow? That thought occupied my mind the entire time it took me to get outside and back again. When I finally lowered my throbbing body back to my blankets, I was exhausted and decided I'd solve that issue later on.

Kismet settled just outside the door, my wonderful sentry. I closed my eyes and inhaled deeply thinking a short nap wouldn't be such a bad thing. Considering there was nothing I could do today that might fall into the work spectrum, I settled on my side into my cattail mattress and pulled the blanket up to my neck.

~

When I opened them again, the fire was stoked up and crackling. How long had I slept? Kane's smile was the first thing I saw as my eyes started to focus.

"Good nap?"

I swallowed trying to get my voice to work. "Yeah."

He grinned again as he squatted down with a cup. "You were deep asleep when we got back, so I just left you." Motioning with his free hand, he drew my attention to things lying out all over my little space. "I managed to get it all here."

I accepted the cup from him and took a sip as my eyes assessed all of the stuff spread out. There were furs, blankets, dishes and many more things I wasn't quite sure what to label. "That's a lot of stuff."

"Yeah. It's yours to do with whatever you want." My eyes must have bulged because he chuckled again. "I was heading here to give it to you when I caught your water act." He shrugged. "There are only a few things that are useful to me, so the rest is yours."

I didn't know what to say. What do you say when someone solves most of your problems with one generous action. "Don't you need it?"

Kane sat down and leaned against the bench behind my pillow. "No. I stay on the move all the time, so the less I have to carry the better. I don't need much."

There was so much in what he said that it made my heart ache. I didn't dare look at him. "I —uh, thank you." Pushing the blanket off I slowly started to stand. Before I could rise to one knee, he was there gently pulling me up without a word.

Once standing I surveyed it all silently for a few moments. "Are you staying tonight?" It hadn't been what I'd planned to say, but it was the only thing my mind wanted to center on.

He moved over and picked up a dark fur, holding it up and examining it. "Tonight for sure, we'll see how you're doing tomorrow."

I could see the worry in his eyes from his words as he moved around looking at things without making eye contact again. Did he worry about me or about some other thing, I wondered.

~

Kane did stay the following day and left the morning after that. Again, it was nice to have someone to talk to and as it was only one person so I didn't feel overwhelmed. Once he was gone, I took the time to go through everything he'd given me and set aside what I didn't need. Eventually I would be moving on, I shouldn't keep more than I could carry. I already knew Tremor's opinion about dragging things behind him.

I spent the day taking it easy and feeling guilty for it, even though I still hurt too much to do anything. I tried to heal the scratches on the areas I could reach, but found out other than taking the angry look of the wounds away my own hands weren't very helpful on injuries that were mine. Considering how I'd gotten them I figured just being alive to put up with the slow process of recovery was worth it.

CHAPTER ELEVEN

It was only a little past midday and I was exhausted. Not having the stress over bringing myself to kill something fuzzy to keep warm this winter, my new focus was spent foraging to find and store everything possible to help us survive the winter. Tremor was tired of hauling branches for wood and I had to agree with him there, it was a hard and tedious job. We hauled first thing, when we were fresh, and then started the search for food. I had plenty of the dehydrated packs so I wasn't panicking, but winter could last from one month to eight, so the more edible things we had, the better for all of us. After the snow arrived I planned to build an igloo freezer to store fish. I had no idea how to dry meat to store, so my options were pretty limited at this point.

Between the hard labor and the food storage each day I took a little time to write in the journal we'd found among the abandoned bags. Kane was right that someone should record this time or some of it at least. I couldn't write of what was happening all over the world, but I could jot down what we'd seen so far and what we'd left behind. Up to this point things weren't written in any detail, but it wasn't like I'd forget those if I ever had the desire to expand on my notes.

For the last few days I'd been trying to figure out how much time had passed since I left the city. My birthday was in the middle of June so I knew the starting point. I couldn't count each day that had passed but I was able to guesstimate within a few days. If it had been ten years ago I could have looked around at the plants and leaves and know it was October, but signs like that didn't work anymore. The date from my best guessing was the start of September. That alone threw me more than it should have. I'd survived not only that first night alone, but close to three months. In most ways it seemed like only a few weeks, but in others it felt like forever.

I promised myself I would mark each day in the front of the notebook from now on, so I could pretend to know when it was. Without keeping track of the marks I knew enough signs to tell me the season even if the date wasn't accurate. The ground was now damp and cold, as if the winter was starting on the inside of the earth and working its way out. I was out of time. Each morning and night I could see my own breath, telling me winter had already begun.

We were going to collect the things I didn't need and take them to the settlement to trade. I was pretty certain Kane wouldn't send me somewhere I shouldn't go, so the only real worry I had was closing up the cave for a few days so no one would know it was here. The wood was well hidden under the branches from the tree that had tried to flatten me in the quake—so the only thing I had to figure out was how to hide the inner entrance.

~

Making sure everything was hidden well enough to sate my paranoia, we finally headed in what I hoped was north. I was getting better at finding directions, but without a compass or road signs I could only do so much. The laws in nature were all broken, or changed because of the ever-changing climate and everything related to it, so as we moved out of the sight of our camp I prayed I wasn't sending us out to get lost—or worse.

I was just wondering if I hadn't followed Kane's directions properly, when I saw the settlement, it was so well hidden I was almost to it before I saw it. Nestled in a sheltered ravine, you wouldn't see it when the trees were filled with leaves. After looking around, I realized it was designed to be easily hidden and defended with only one safe entrance.

Tremor had only taken three steps toward the shacks hidden in the rocks and trees when two people appeared from behind the shrubs in front of us. I rested my hand nonchalantly on the horn of the saddle, hiding a knife in my palm.

The tall man with long shaggy hair stepped forward. "What business do you have here?"

I noted the slightly overweight man standing a few feet from him had one hand behind his back. Kismet crouched down, his dark fur standing on end. "I was told you traded."

"Told by who?"

A few other men appeared from shadowed trees, no weapons were visible but that didn't mean they didn't have any. "A man I know."

"What man?"

A low growl came from Kismet. "Kane." I grasped the reins tight and was trying to see how I could get back out the way we'd started without giving my back to them. The two in front of me looked at each other for a long second.

"Get down and walk." Kismet inched forward. "And control your animal—please."

Keeping the knife hidden in my palm, I climbed down. "Kizzy," I said quiet enough for only him to hear. He sat and looked up at me. "It's okay." I tried to reassure him, not even knowing how I was feeling about this situation.

"You know Kane?" Another man to my left asked.

I kept my shoulder against Tremor and nodded.

"You have to meet with Maisy before we'll make any trades with you."

My heart was racing as fast as my mind. Kane wouldn't have sent me here if it wasn't safe; at least I was trying to hold onto that thought. I didn't know who Maisy was, but I nodded again and motioned in front of Tremor. "Take me to Maisy then."

I felt surrounded as we moved slowly down the incline to the small buildings along the sides of the ravine. With each step I cursed inside my head, deciding that coming here was a huge mistake. I was slightly miffed with Kane as well; he could have warned me there would be hoops to jump through when he told me about it. Sweat trickled down my back as I followed behind; my nerves were strung tight, ready to jump if I needed them.

We were moving towards a large shack that was centered among the rest. An old woman appeared in the doorway, she looked like the sweet grandmotherly type, all soft and loving—but in the times we now lived judging a book by its cover was a dangerous thing to do. A younger woman with long brown hair stood at her side. I could see she spoke quietly to the elder as we approached.

"Who have you brought to see me, Donald?" Her voice was soft and caring.

The last man that had spoken to me looked over his shoulder at me for a second before answering her. "She says Kane told her we were here."

The old woman turned her head and looked at something beside the shack. "That's quite interesting. Bring her to see me, please."

Not once did she look right at me. My eyes were darting back and forth from her and trying to see what she was looking at. Wrapping the reins around my hand I stepped closer to where she stood. When she finally faced me, it was then I noticed her eyes. They were void—she was blind.

She smiled in my direction. "What does Kane call you?"

I found it odd that she didn't ask me my name, but what he called me. "He calls me Red." Her smile widened.

"You have a black horse and wolf with you?"

"Uh—yes." I looked down at Kismet, who had his

tongue hanging out of his mouth and showed no sign of feeling threatened whatsoever.

She reached out a weathered hand. "I'm Maisy. Please tie your horse and come inside."

I tucked the blade in my pocket and took her hand to shake it. She clasped her other one around it and stood there without movement. Inside I panicked and wanted my hand back, but I also didn't want to jerk it out of the hand of a blind woman.

"Oh," she whispered. "She is one of us." Her voice was loud enough that anyone within hearing could have heard her.

It was an odd thing to say, but so far nothing about coming here was fitting into my normal, so I offered no comment. Once I got over the weirdness of it, I studied her smile and face; it was a genuine one that made me feel welcome. Something inside made me feel a kinship with this older lady. Were they all survivors, is that what she meant?

"Come inside and have some tea, you can do your trade and barter later on."

I tied Tremor's reins to a small tree near the door and glanced down at Kismet. He sat beside the horse, as if he knew I wanted him to keep watch while I was inside. Going through the door, I was surprised to see it looked like a normal home inside, complete with a floor.

The young woman spoke softly into Maisy's ear. "The floors were Kane's idea, if there are heavy rains it washes under them—leaving my feet dry. It worked wonderfully during last spring's thaw." She smiled and made her way over to a rocking chair in the corner. "Please sit. I can feel the questions floating around in the air surrounding you."

They had been here that long. I sat on a handmade kitchen chair. "You know Kane?"

"Oh yes, dear. He's the reason all of us here are alive and surviving." She motioned towards the younger woman. "This is Rosy. Would you like some tea?"

I shrugged. "Uh, yes. Please."

"You are being so polite for someone that has more questions than you know how to ask."

"I'm just—I don't know Kane very well but he seemed to be a loner, so I am…"

"A little surprised that he's helped so many people?"

I nodded only to remember she couldn't see me. "Yes."

"I am so pleased he sent you here to us." She leaned towards me and whispered. "I suspect you're different—for him."

"I don't know what you mean."

She sat back and with a secretive smile on her wrinkled face. "Kane doesn't send people to us, he brings them."

"Oh." I still didn't know what she meant.

"I find it curious that he didn't bring you himself." She made a clicking noise with her tongue.

"I don't think he's much for staying around people."

She laughed. "Oh we know that. He's never once stayed with us—and he helped build most of the things around here. Kane has too many demons chasing him, or he thinks he does. The man never stops long enough for them to catch him."

I realized how well she knew him, having thought something similar where Kane was concerned. "So he helped everyone here?"

She nodded and accepted the cup Rosy placed in her hands. "I suspect he has helped set up settlements all over the new country but he never speaks of it." She sipped the tea.

I accepted the cup from and sniffed it. It smelled like real tea. Taking a sip I closed my eyes and savored it. It was real tea. Where did they get real tea from?

"You haven't been out here long have you?"

Opening my eyes I studied the woman. She may look like a sweet little granny, but there was something about the way her eyes never stopped moving that told me she was much more than she seemed. "No. Not quite three months."

"And you've been avoiding the Red Bands?"

"Red Bands?"

Her expression changed without pause. "How is it you're out here on your own and don't know who the Red Bands are? Where are your people?"

"My brother died. I left the city…"

"Ah. I take it the Red Bands are hidden well within the cities." She took another drink. "The Red Bands—called that for the red line tattooed on the left side of their face, are supposed government representatives. They are gathering information, statistics and said to be the peace keepers in the new country." She hissed a loud breath. "We know the truth out here though. They are henchmen, plain and simple. They steal anything they can, rape and kill anyone that gets in their way." She shook her head a few times, a frustrated expression on her face. "They take those of us survivors that have useful skills to the leaders or the rich, whichever is the most profitable for them and then auction the rest into slavery."

I was too shocked to say anything. How could this group of people exist and we hadn't known in the city? Yes there were government groups, but they certainly hadn't had any tattoos on their face and even though I didn't agree with some—well, all of what they were doing I didn't think they were as bad as what she was saying.

"I'm so happy Kane sent you to me. Most likely he wants you to stay with us, but I suspect you're not going to."

Was that the real reason he sent me? "No. I'm not. I have to …"

"I know dear. I have to believe you're going to make it, you have a strong aura and it would break my heart if you didn't." She smiled at me again and lifted her cup.

Setting down the cup, I leaned forward.

"Miss Maisy!" Someone called from outside. Rosy went over to her quickly and took her elbow to help her up.

"So much excitement in one day," Maisy muttered as

she moved to the door. Just before she reached it, a young boy came running through it.

"Miss Maisy…" he gasped to catch his breath, "it's mama, she fell…" he swallowed, "Sissy says the baby's in danger."

Rosy helped Maisy move through the door as the young boy took off running. I stood there and watched as people came out of what looked like trees. There were so many of them, I was momentarily stupefied.

"Red."

I snapped back to look at Maisy as she paused on the worn path. "You need to come with us."

The way she said it made me think I needed to, so I hurried to catch up to them. Kismet stood up beside Tremor as I moved by him. "Stay here boy; I don't know what's going on."

When we stepped inside another shack similar to Maisy's, I paused on the door step. There were three women hovering over a very pregnant woman lying on the floor. Maisy moved over and two of the women helped her kneel down beside the woman. "I'm here, Trina." The pregnant woman grasped the old woman's hand.

"Maisy, the baby it's kicking violently. I fell outside and crawled back in…" she panted and squeezed her eyes shut. "It's too early. It's too early," she said out of breath.

Maisy reached out and rubbed a hand over the woman's belly. "Sissy? Is Leif on his way?"

One of the women kneeling on the other side of the fallen woman nodded. "Yes, he was out hunting but they've gone to get him."

Maisy clucked her tongue. "We'll wait for him." She leaned down close to Trina. "You need to move onto your side and work on relaxing, we have to wait for Leif so he can tell us what's going on inside." She sniffed. "Are you bleeding? I smell blood." The concern was obvious in her voice.

"My hip…"

I stood back watching as they worked to get her onto her side and ease the clothes off her hip. A long gash across her flesh bled onto the white skin surrounding it.

Maisy turned her head towards me. "You're in luck Trina; I've brought the first aid kit with me." She smiled. "Unless I'm losing my sight, Red, could you come and help her please?"

All eyes snapped to me, my mouth dropped open. I stood there looking at the grin on Maisy's face. "I-I can try." Flipping my coat off, I set it on the floor and moved over to kneel behind the woman. "I don't know if this will work, but I'll try." I rubbed my palms together and took a deep breath.

"You'll do fine child," Maisy said softly.

My hands were shaking when I held them over the gushing injury. I honestly didn't know if I could do this in front so many people, but I had to at least try. The woman was so scared and tense. Taking a few slow breaths I lowered my hands to touch the slippery cut. As I closed my eyes I focused on the feel of her skin under my hands, she was so cold. My palms tingled only slightly and I was afraid it wasn't going to work then that strange sensation began to move down my arms until my palms heated.

Taking deep relaxing breaths I thought of nothing but helping this scared woman. She moaned and I opened my eyes and looked down at my hands. They were coated with her blood. Lifting them slowly I looked at the red skin of her hip. Blood was covering it, but it seemed to have stopped flowing. "I need a cloth." As soon as I spoke a hand moved in front of me and dabbed at the injured area. There were several gasps as the last of the blood was wiped off to reveal a long red mark that was freshly healed closed. Taking a shaky breath I looked up at the amazed faces leaning over us.

"See. You did fine." Maisy smiled at me.

Someone handed me a wet cloth to wipe off my hands. I was shaking; my emotions were all over the place. I moved back to give the woman's friends room to tend to her.

"Trina?" A large blond man bolted through the door.

He dropped to his knees and slid to her.

"Leif, I'm afraid." She touched his face as he brought his cheek to hers.

"Let me take a look and see how she's doing, okay? Just relax and take some deep breaths." He straightened up and then looked down at her hip. His eyes darted to my hands I was trying to wipe clean and then to her hip again. I was waiting for the questions, but instead he lowered his hands to her stomach and ran them slowly over it.

He sat there with his eyes closed, without saying a word for the longest time. "She's frightened. Something has happened with your heart beating so fast, it's upsetting her." He frowned and then opened his eyes. "There's a small tear in the placenta wall."

Trina grasped his hands. "Will she be alright? It's too soon, Leif."

He ran a gentle hand over her dark curls. "I can't fix it, I can only see it."

The pregnant woman's eyes locked on mine. "Please, can you try to help?"

My own heart started beating too fast. "I don't know anything about babies."

Maisy reached over her and touched my arm. "You can try, child. Just think of the baby being safe. I know you can do it."

I was humbled by this woman's belief in me. My hands were vibrating, I looked down at them. Could I do it this soon? "I'll give it a try," I whispered as I moved over beside the man. "Can you give me a general area to aim for? Usually I can see and touch what I'm trying to heal."

He nodded and moved to give me more space. "I'll watch as you're doing it."

I hesitated with my hands hovering several inches over her body. "I don't know if your hands will affect what I do—or if it's safe."

He shrugged. "A chance I'm willing to take."

I nodded and took a deep breath, letting it out slowly.

"Show me." I watched the area he moved his hand over and then closed my eyes as I lowered my hands to touch her rounded belly. I could feel the movement of the little one inside as soon as my palms connected and it threw me for a few seconds, but also motivated me to try as hard as I could so it would survive.

With the infant bumping up against my palms, I continued to breathe slowly as they grew warm. I couldn't let myself think of this not working.

"It's working. She's doing fine."

That was the confirmation I needed to focus on the inside of Trina's tummy and the area that surrounded the baby. Trina let out a slow loud breath and I almost lifted my hands until she spoke.

"It's calming me. Leif is she okay?"

I lifted my hands slowly and then opened my eyes to look at him. He was smiling, a single tear rolling down his cheek.

"It worked and she's all settled down now." He leaned down and kissed Trina's cheek and then straightened up and turned to me. "You're a miracle. Thank you."

Miracle? That was the last word I'd ever expected to be tagged with as the result of surviving the virus. A lump was in my throat and there was no way I was going to be able to form anything close to a reply, so I smiled and lowered my eyes to the swollen tummy that held the tiny being I'd just helped. My mind hovered over the word saved for a second, but after the miracle tag I was sticking with helped. Saved was just too much to digest.

"Someone help Trina get up from the floor, and then we'll need to celebrate." Maisy held up a hand and Rosy moved over and helped her stand. She smiled down in my direction. "I don't think anyone here is going to have a problem trading with you, Red. Get cleaned up and then we'll eat. You'll stay the night."

My heart was still thumping loudly in my throat as I stood up. My head was a little light feeling, and I didn't know if it was from the surprise of the last few minutes or healing twice in so short a time. "I need to check on my animals." I offered a polite smile around the room and rushed out the door.

Outside I hurried back to Tremor and Kismet. They were familiar and grounding for me and I needed that right now. Kizzy stood up and watched me approach, his ears forward as if he was trying to figure out if me coming at him at this speed was a good or bad thing. "Hey guys," I said in a weak voice.

Running my hand over his head, I knelt down to him. I wanted to hug him, but wasn't sure how he'd interpret that without an obvious reason so I settled for rubbing his fur under my hands as his amber eyes assessed my face trying to get a feel for what was wrong. Tremor kicked at the ground with a hoof and lowered his head to sniff at my hair. I grinned. "I'm good, just a little out of my zone right now."

"With good reason."

I jumped up and spun around to see a teen boy standing there. "Sorry, I didn't hear you."

He gave me a lopsided grin. "S'okay, most people don't until I'm right on them." With a quick motion he shuffled sideways and if I hadn't seen it with my own eyes I would have never dreamed what I saw. The boy—blurred, was the only description I could grasp for a moment and then was standing there again. My jaw must have dropped, because I closed my mouth and studied him. He looked like a normal average boy, thin, uncombed hair all over the place. All seemed to be the norm except he had one grey eye and one green.

I frowned, not believing I just put the pieces together. Anyone I knew to be virus survivors or more bluntly put mutants all had something different with their eyes. Mine were a washed out green, Kane's silver, Maisy's were a void white…

"I know my eyes are freaky," the boy mumbled.

I snapped back to the now. "Oh. No that's not what I

was thinking." I sighed loudly. "I just now realized that all survivors' eyes are altered."

He chuckled and gave me a 'well duh!' look. "Don't get out much do you?"

I rolled my eyes. "I guess not."

"I'm Tanner. I saw you dash from Trina and Leif's and thought I'd come see if you're okay."

I was touched that he would think to do that. "Yeah, I just needed a little space after that."

Tanner glanced down at Kismet before he looked back up at me. "Pretty cool what you can do with just your hands." He looked back at the animal.

I guess to a kid it would seem cool, and then again it did to me too. "What you did was pretty awesome too."

He shrugged. "Yeah, maybe. I still don't know what it would be good for though. I have to keep moving my whole body for it to happen." Tucking his hands in his pockets he hunched over into what I believe was the posture of all teens.

"Well, if you needed to check something out for everyone you could do it undetected or I guess unseen."

He nodded his head slowly in thought. "Didn't think of that." He motioned towards Kismet. "Can I touch your wolf?"

I looked down at Kizzy. "He's just a dog." Tanner made a sound that sounded like a snort— translated, he thought I was an idiot, which I ignored. "But he's friendly enough."

"Cool." Stepping towards Kismet he held out his hand. I was proud of Kizzy when he sniffed it for a second and then pushed his head into Tanner's palm. "He's awesome," Tanner whispered.

"Tanner, why don't you take Red to the dinner hut?" A tall woman called out as she went by carrying a large basket.

"Yeah, okay." Straightening up, he sighed and then looked at me. "Come on, its group social hour."

I grinned at his tone. World climate chaos and

upheaval or not, the teen's attitude still remained consistently bored with life and all the trivial things in it.

CHAPTER TWELVE

I did stay the night, it would have been dark long before I got back. I needed to ask questions and learn from these people. They knew things I had to find out in order to survive the winter and beyond it. After helping Trina's baby they were more than willing to show me what I needed to know.

The gifts didn't stop either. Between them knowing I was sent by Kane, the fact that I helped the baby and I was a mutant as they were I ended up hauling a lot more away than I had originally planned to trade. I'd insisted they take the things I'd brought to trade but I still felt like I owed them more.

Bundled up and tied to Tremor were so many useful items I was a little overwhelmed by their generosity. I had an axe now; I was so relieved I could barely hide it when Leif had given it to me. I had insisted he take the cloth I'd brought with me for it—for the baby I'd told him. The others had given me dried fruit; I had to stop myself from eating it all that night. I missed fruit.

We had wheat now, which Tremor was going to be unhappy about when he realized it wasn't all for him. They had also given us dried beef; I can't express how much I missed red meat and some corn. A few other things I hadn't planned on were now attached to Tremor like pails, containers and a snare. The snare might actually help me kill something to survive the winter, either that or I'd better get used to the taste of dried grass and cattails.

As we headed to our home I thought about everything they'd taught me in one day's time. I now knew how to make jerky, which would help when there wasn't any snow to keep meat cold. I'd helped make rough grain bread the last morning before we headed out and surprisingly enough had ground much of the wheat and corn into flour myself. If I found any fruit I'd be able to dry it out as well. All in all my chances of survival were looking up, and I couldn't be happier about that.

I'd even decided if we did see spring I was going to stop there when we were on the move again to see everyone. It was heart lifting to know that there were still a few people left in this vast world that were caring.

Besides my learning about the eye alterations of mutants, I realized that the myth about mutated people not being able to breed was wrong. Unless the community I'd just come from had normal non-virus survivors hidden away among them to create the baby Trina carried and the other young children I'd met—then those with the eye changes could most definitely procreate still—at least some of them.

Riding time always equated to thinking time and I was doing it in spades today with all this new information to digest and file. Inside my head I was calling the community Maisy's villiage, and I had taken the time to learn something about those who befriended me that day. Maisy, despite her blindness was able to sense and know everything around her, better than just seeing. Aside from her I'd met young Tanner and Rosy, who turned out to be Tanner's sister and had never had the virus so she was a rarity in that village being completely human and normal. Leif had his x-ray thing going on and his wife Trina was able to see further than manmade binoculars could.

I'd also met Dan and his wife Cassy who were

nightwalkers—proving females did exist in that particular mutation. If I ever ran across Micah, Jacob or Vince I'd be sure to let them know their fondest wish was out there somewhere. As far as nightwalkers went I wasn't sure what the plus to their ability was but up until this point I found something good in everyone's added skill, I suppose it just depended on the actual person's internal make-up as to whether they used it in a good or bad way.

Renee, a very tall lady from among them had this very cool change that I almost felt envious of, with just looking into your eyes she could tell if you were a survivor and almost pinpoint the exact mutation you were left with. Wouldn't that come in handy when you ran into strangers? Having something like that would make traveling out here a lot safer than most other abilities to have.

The downside was I now possessed a fact I almost wished I was still ignorant to the existence of the Red Bands. Just knowing they were out there gifted me with more paranoia to carry around on my shoulders, which I really didn't need but now I knew there were people I had to avoid at all costs.

I knew what I could do with my hands would fall under the useful skill department and there was no way on this earth or any other planet for that matter would I ever work for a government system that only looked out for themselves and their own benefit.

Nope, if I came across any of these mercenary political employees I would tell them to go to hell and wish for the cloud they floated on to dissipate into thin air and drop them on their self-serving asses. Okay, so maybe I would run the other way but I'd be thinking the cloud scenario the entire time.

On the way back I had to really keep alert, in just the time we'd been gone the look of the trail had changed. Trees were almost completely bare and fewer patches of grass were showing. I kept Tremor moving at a fast pace, not wanting to see winter arrive on top of our heads on the way back.

The sky even looked like winter, the dull hue of fall hung over us. Kismet seemed driven to stay on task today as well, which made me more nervous of running into a storm before we reached the cave. I'd never seen him run without distraction before, his nose to the ground more often than not.

We were probably an hour from home when he stopped and stood looking through the trees, the hair on his back ruffled up. I slowed Tremor and we stood back, scanning the space beyond the trunks surrounding both sides of us. He was prancing now and Kizzy was standing still, the hair on his body not even daring to move. My heart sunk and the worst possible scenarios starting flashing through my mind—the foremost one being of another quake hitting.

I almost wished for a quake when Kismet started to growl in a way that I'd never heard before, a deep warning being issued. Following the direction he was looking I finally saw why and our chances of surviving a quake seemed much more likely. A pack of wolves, probably six but I wasn't going to take the time to count, was headed slowly toward us. Tremor jerked on the reins and I knew we were on the same page—to get the hell out of here, but there was no way I was leaving without the growling beast that was my friend.

Pulling the gun out, I paused only long enough to make sure the safety was off and then prodded Tremor gently so he'd go over closer to Kismet. He didn't like it, but he complied with jerky movements. We stopped right behind the hunched over snarling creature, hoping he appreciated how much nerve it was taking for both of us to offer some back-up.

As the pack cleared the trees, my heart did this strange little stumble. I was looking at several different versions of the animal I called my *dog*. To realize the joke was on me and I had a wolf as a close companion was more than a little startling. Kismet growled again in a way that made the hair on the back of *my* neck stand up. The pack stopped and hovered less than twenty feet away, I thought for sure we were going to be chew toys when the large one in the front growled back. I wanted to understand wolf, so I knew if we should be high-tailing in the other direction or growling back.

Kismet paced back and forth in front of us, his back straight and tail swatting back and forth in an agitated manner. Another one of the pack responded by lunging forward a few feet and before I could take a breath I had the gun up and pointed in its direction. Did I have an aversion to killing cute and fuzzy, yes, this wasn't cute it was lethal and threatening my animal.

"Get!" As soon as I said it I realized how lame it was to say, but I didn't do growl and snarl.

The pack assessed me briefly and then turned their attention back to the snapping animal in front of us. I'd never seen Kismet look so aggressive and I can honestly say I didn't want to see it again; it was downright terrifying. I was proud of him. One of the smaller wolves took a few steps towards him but paused when the largest one made a strange noise that was between a bark and growl. My guess was he had just told the punk to stand down—at least I hoped so because my hand was shaking as I plotted how fast I could make fatal hits with the number of rounds in the gun. I wasn't a quick draw, but I figured I could take out at least three before teeth were sinking into me or Kizzy.

Tremor threw his head back and whinnied, Kismet answered with another warning growl. The large wolf looked at him for a moment and then backed up a few feet and turned to go back towards the trees. Kizzy didn't stop growling in his new menacing voice until the last tail had turned and was heading away from us. He paused for about thirty seconds and watched them and then started heading back in the way that lead us home. We wasted no time in following him.

I watched over my shoulder almost constantly, as did Kismet; we were taking no chances on a repeat. I don't know why they walked away, and I really didn't care, just so long as they did. I guessed the reason being I had a strong alpha wolf for a buddy and left it at that. Of course I couldn't help wondering why he chose to be with a horse and woman as opposed to his own kind, but I'd never complain either. My furry alpha had just earned himself a whole bird dinner to himself tonight.

CHAPTER THIRTEEN

Each morning for the past week I fully expected to look outside in the morning and see nothing but deep snow as far as my eyes could see. Strangely enough, there had only been a light snowfall a few days back, and nothing since. There were still patches of snow here and there but not enough to have me ready to hibernate. It did make me nervous, winter in the last few years had arrived all at once and gotten worse while months had passed and you were only at the point of dreaming of green grass and flowers. Who knew what the earth was up to this time—which was the problem. I didn't know.

At least I was thankful that I'd always had snow and a winter to cope with. As the climate started to shift and change, areas of the world that had always been warm and without a real winter had gotten snow. I couldn't imagine going from a grass skirt to a snowsuit, then having to learn what snow was all about.

Taking advantage of the co-operative weather we headed out this morning to try to find somewhere close by— but not too close, to set the snare. It had taken me the entire week to talk myself into it. The final verdict was if an animal was trapped in it and suffering, it was okay to kill it. Of course I changed the subject every time my conscience reminded me that I'd be the reason the animal was hurt in the first place. My stomach, having loved the taste of the cured meat was the deciding vote. Having something other than fowl and fish for the months to come was too appealing to wimp out.

I watched the ground for signs that small animals had passed, trying to gauge where would be a good place and where I'd be wasting my time.

I heard voices and slowed. Tremor stopped without complaint, I didn't need to come face to face with anyone and not be prepared. Watching Kismet, he turned and started to prowl slowly towards a small valley at the other side of the hill. I reined Tremor in so we could move along the trees and not be seen by whoever was on the other side. I could make out three distinct voices as they cursed and made snide remarks. They didn't sound like anyone I needed to meet. I was a heartbeat away from turning and heading back in the other direction when I heard what sounded like flesh being beaten. Clenching my jaw, I knew I had to at least look now, what if it was a woman that needed help?

I climbed off Tremor and crept low to the ground to look around the tree. My heart jumped up into my throat as I saw what was going on thirty feet away. Three large men were beating the hell out of Kane. From the way he staggered with each blow they must have been doing it for some time. He dropped down to one knee and his head fell forward. I bit my lip and prayed for help I knew wasn't going to come.

I was the help.

Touching Kismet lightly I leaned down to close to his ear. "That's Kane. We're going to help." He crouched down and looked back towards them. Backing up slowly I got back onto Tremor and pulled the gun out of the pouch attached to his saddle. With my other hand I got out one of my throwing knives and hoped like hell I wouldn't have to use either.

Taking a deep breath I dug my heels into Tremor's side and bolted out from the protection of the trees, heading straight towards them. Kismet kept pace with us until we were ten feet away from them, then he moved around to my left and stood their growling.

Two of the men turned and looked at him; the other one released Kane's hair and stared at me. My heart jumped up into my throat when I saw the red tattoo's on each of their faces. Red Bands were real. Pure self preservation had me aiming the gun at him and cocking it slowly. "Leave him be." I tried not to sound as scared as I felt.

One of them snorted. "You're being rescued by a tiny red head, her horse and dog, Kane." He laughed.

Kane rested one hand on the ground and lifted his head to look up at me. One of his eyes was already swollen shut, but the other silver eye watched me without faltering. There was something in that look that said for me to put them in their place. So I listened. "Back away from him. Now."

Only one of them moved, which started Kismet snarling and snapping at them as he moved closer. I didn't see any weapons, which made me feel a little braver. "Now!" I repeated louder than the first time, with a little more conviction.

The blonde haired one that was behind Kane started to move back towards him, without pause I flicked the knife in his direction and watched as it passed right over Kane and landed in the ground right at the toe of the man's boot. He froze and looked down.

I couldn't look at Kane to see if he was moving, I just had to hope he had the strength to get to me. Two of the men now had their hands up in surrender and were backing away. Kismet snapped at the third one. He looked from me to the toothy snarling animal in front of him and began to back away with his friends.

Kismet quickly inserted himself between Kane and the men, enabling me to be able to look down at Kane. I spotted his bag on the ground a few feet away. Pulling out another knife I kicked one leg over the saddle and slid to the ground, without taking my eyes of the men. Going over I picked up the bag and tossed it over beside Tremor's feet before going to Kane. He was standing leaning over his knees by that time, but the way he was breathing wasn't good.

I could either let go of one of my weapons or help him, and I didn't want to give up the weapons. I whistled softly and Tremor moved closer. Kane glanced at me briefly with one eye and grasped hold of the saddle. Trusting Tremor to keep him standing I grabbed the bag and tied it to the saddle and then turned and looked back towards the men. I aimed the gun at one of them. "You should run." I said softly not thinking for a second they would listen. Kismet growled once more and all three of them turned and started running towards the trees. I stood there shocked they had done it. Going over, I grabbed the knife I'd thrown and tucked it into my pocket.

I shoved the gun into the back of my pants and leaned down to Kane. "Can you get up there?" He didn't answer, just leaned against the horse. I bit my lip and checked to make sure they weren't coming back. "I can't lift you, Kane." He nodded slightly and pulled himself to stand taller. I shoved and he pulled until he was finally on the horse's back. I had no idea how I was going to keep him there, but it was a start.

Part of me wanted to get up there and kick Tremor into a run to get us away from here, but Kane was a big man and by the time he slumped forward over the horse's neck, there was no space up there for me. I grabbed the reins and started to lead the way back up the hill. Kismet fell in behind, checking every few feet that we were still alone. Kane didn't speak; he just lay there panting like he couldn't breathe.

~

Getting Kane off the horse proved to be more difficult than getting him up there. He was barely conscious by the time I got us back to the cave. I couldn't get him into the back area either, Tremor struggled to fit through the opening without a body and saddle, so I had to settle for getting him as close to the entrance as possible.

I pulled him, trying to carry as much of his weight as I

could, but he outweighed me by too much, and almost crushed me to the ground beneath him. In the end he hit the ground with a groan and I bit my lip feeling low for hurting him further.

The trip back had taken a lot longer than I'd planned. I'd been afraid of jarring Kane so we'd walked slow the whole way. With only an hour of daylight left, I quickly got some water and rags together so I could clean his cuts and see how bad he was hurt. Kismet and Tremor moved to the outside of the opening, staying out of my way. I gently wiped off his face and cringed when I saw how bruised and swollen it was. I washed the blood off his hands and felt better knowing he must have gotten a few blows in of his own before he was out-numbered.

Descent clothes were hard to come by so I didn't want to cut his shirt off of him. I pushed it up on his body and sucked in a breath when I saw his ribs. They were red and already bruising. I didn't need an x-ray to tell me one, or more were probably broken. I felt tears form in my eyes at how badly he must be hurting. Looking down at my hands, I took a deep breath reached out to rest them over his ribs. I didn't know if what I could do would work on something this bad, but I had to try. He moved as my hands connected with his bare skin. Closing my eyes I focused on how much pain he must be in and tried to find whatever it was inside me that reacted to this.

I felt my palms getting warmer and pushed them a little harder against him, I had to reach inside his body and not just the surface. He moaned, but I refused to stop. The hotter my hands became the more he moved around. "I'm sorry," I whispered without opening my eyes. Hoping I was helping, I slid my hands over to another area, I could feel the swelling without looking. He hissed out a breath, but I didn't let up.

After I'd covered the worst areas on his ribs, I opened my eyes and realized I was swaying and a little dizzy. Taking a deep breath I looked up to see his eyes open and him looking at me through the swollen flesh surrounding them. I didn't know what to say, so I just offered him a weak smile and slid closer to his face. With a slow movement I pressed my hands over his eyes. His own hands came up to lightly circle my wrists when my hands began to grow warm, but he didn't try to pull me away or make a sound. I could feel the swelling going down right under my touch and it made me smile to know I was able to do this to ease his suffering.

After a few minutes I lowered my hands, he didn't let go of them. When he opened his eyes, he was able to see out of both of them. Gently he lifted my hands and looked at them for a moment before letting go of them and taking a deep breath. "You better keep that a secret..." his breathing was still labored, "Lest someone finds out and sells you to the highest bidder." His voice was hoarse. Silver eyes moved all over my face and my heart skipped a few beats before he closed his eyes again.

Leaning over I got the water and touched his face gently. "Here." I lifted his head and helped him take a few sips. When he closed his eyes again his breathing relaxed and I knew he was sleeping.

Getting up I stood there and studied him for a long time. Why did this man keep appearing in my life? I didn't know, but as every other time I wanted to know more about him. Why of all colors were his eyes silver? What mutation had he been given? I knew given probably wasn't the word to use, but it was less intrusive than any other I could come up with.

Kismet moved over to lie down beside him, which made me even more curious to know more about the man that had won my *dog's* loyalty with barely a word or action.

I covered him up, instructed the animal to stay with him and took Tremor out to hopefully find something to make for dinner.

~

Serious silver eyes watched me as I entered the opening. They moved over me so slowly I thought I might melt right there in front of him. "You're awake. How are you feeling?"

"I've had better moments." He shifted slowly until his back was against the rocks and pulled himself to a half sitting position. He held his ribs. "Thanks, for everything."

I shrugged. "I figured I owed you a few."

A smile appeared on his face. "I thought I was hallucinating when I looked up and there you were on your horse, red hair blazing in the sunlight." He coughed and grabbed his ribs again.

I squatted down in front of him. "I'd like to try to ease the pain some more, after we eat though." I sighed. "I've been a little shaky since the first session."

His serious look was back again. "Later, when I can talk without pain, I want to know *what* you did."

I leaned back. "I honestly have no idea, it just happens." Standing up, I moved over to the hidden entrance and pulled the tied branches out of the way. "Are you up to coming inside? If you don't you might wake up covered in a snow blanket."

"Inside," he said softly.

I nodded. "Just let me put this down and I'll help." I went in and set the birds down and quickly went back out to get him. He'd managed to get to his knees and was leaning against the wall panting.

Reaching under his arms I tried to pull him up, but he didn't budge at all. "You're too big." He reached up and wrapped one hand behind my neck and pulled my face down close to his.

"You're just small." He gave me a lopsided grin and dropped his hand away. "I'll crawl; I don't think I can walk."

If he wasn't in so much pain I might have found it funny to see a man his size crawling. When he stumbled a few times and came close to landing on his face, I forgot about it and went to help him. "Before you lay down, I want you to take off your coat and shirt." His breathing had sounded strained again.

~

Kane just lay there on my blankets watching me silently as I moved around to get some food ready. I felt funny being watched and figured it just hurt him too much to talk. Too often I found myself looking at him out of the corner of my eye as he sprawled there with no shirt on. I'd seen men's chests before, and even as bruised as his was I'd never seen one like his.

"What are you making?"

I jumped when his voice broke the silence. "Uh, I killed two birds and I'm going to add some herbs and try to come up with something edible."

"I didn't hear a gun."

I glanced at him over my shoulder. "I don't use the gun for hunting. I use my knives."

"Handy with them are you?"

"Yes."

"I'll have to keep that in mind." He coughed and then gasped in pain.

Tossing the meat into the old pan, I placed it over the fire and went over to him. "I'm going to try to heal that a bit more." I bit my bottom lip for a moment and looked down at the marks on his body. "I don't know how much I can do at one time to help, we might have to do a bit now and more in the morning."

He winced and tried to take a deep breath, but then just nodded.

Moving closer until my leg was against his hip, I rubbed my hands together in a nervous gesture. "Just relax," I whispered as I placed my hands close together against his inflamed skin. He didn't move or make a sound as the warmth began to spread into my hands. I couldn't focus with his eyes holding mine, so I let out a slow breath and closed my eyes as the heat grew more intense.

I did this all over his ribs again, until my head felt light. When I opened my eyes, he caught me by the shoulders to steady me.

"You over-did it." He winced as he lowered his arms.

"Mmm. I guess I did. This is the first time I've tried it on so many injuries at once." I leaned into his hands until I felt the room settle down.

"Don't try that again until you've rested. I can deal with the pain."

Leaning back I looked down at his bare skin. "Did it help at all?"

"Breathing is better now."

"Good." I smiled at him feeling very pleased with myself.

He grinned up at me briefly before his eyes grew serious again. "Thanks, Red."

There was no more conversation. He ate and then went to sleep. I sat up and watched him for a long time, imaging all sorts of scenarios that explained his life. As I was closing up the door for the night, he started shaking. I debated on waking him, not sure if it was a night mare or something left over from his ordeal that day. Not knowing what else to do, I grabbed my other blanket and lay down beside him, curling my body carefully into his so he would know he wasn't alone.

CHAPTER FOURTEEN

The sounds of dawn came to me, lifting the sleepy haze I was surrounded in. My heart paused when I realized there was a heavy arm around my waist and hot breath against my neck. His large body was formed to fit into my back and for a few seconds I wondered if he knew he was holding me against him. Before I could decide what to do about it, my body heated, startling me with sensations I'd never had before. This was too new to choose whether I liked it or not.

I didn't want to jar him, but I had to find a way to get out from under his arm. Moving slowly, I turned onto my back and looked over at him. His hand splayed across my stomach, causing it to tighten and soften at the same time. He looked peaceful in sleep and not at all like his face was made from stone. Long black eyelashes formed half moons on his face, his lips looked soft. I studied his lips a little longer than I should, when I looked back up his eyes were half open and watching me as I examined him.

"You keep looking at my mouth with that longing in your eyes, Red and it's going to have to oblige you." His silver eyes burned into mine with a heat that made them appear like they were smoldering, "and I'm afraid the rest of my body isn't up to a tumble with you just yet."

I felt my face flush hot and started to move away

quickly. His hand held me down so I couldn't get away from him.

"Take it easy." His breath was hot against my cheek. "I do not use women. You're safe with me."

My heart was still in my throat as I turned to look at his face. His eyes had lost their appealing softness and serious eyes were looking back at me. "Sorry. I'm not used to being around anyone anymore." It was a partial truth; I couldn't bring myself to say that I'd never been with anyone before in any sort of intimate fashion.

A gentle smile softened his mouth. "I understand."

His hand moved lightly over my stomach before he slid from me and I felt lonelier for it, which was silly really. "I need to check on the animals and go to the bathroom."

He closed his eyes and turned slowly onto his back. "I won't be too far away."

I stumbled to my feet and stood there for a minute before exiting as gracefully as I could. The cool dawn air hit me once I was outside. Tremor was a few yards away nuzzling the new snow looking for edible grass beneath it. He paused and looked over at me for a second, assured that all was well he lowered his head again. Kismet sat, posed like a statue looking out into the trees. "All clear, boy?"

He glanced at me and then got up and ran through the trees. I watched him until he was out of sight before going off to find somewhere private.

~

Most of my days were usually spent wandering and exploring the areas I could reach and get back to by dark, but today I stayed close to home. Kane spent much of the day drifting in and out of sleep and was determined he was going to be back on his feet by the next day. He hadn't let me try to heal him any further. Each time he got up and moved around for a few minutes, I had to bite my own lip seeing the pain etched on his face. It worried me that my healing didn't reach inside and there was more wrong than I could repair.

He'd been outside for a few minutes before he dragged

his feet on the way back. Using one hand to brace himself, he practically fell to his knees near the blanket. As he sat down he hissed out a sharp breath and something inside of me snapped.

I went over and knelt down in front of him. "This is ridiculous. Take off your shirt and let me take a look."

Leaning back, he looked at me with that hard look in his eyes. "It's not necessary."

I snorted. "Yes it is. I'm worried that there might be…"

"Don't be."

He was more infuriating than my brother had been with that final-word male attitude. I leaned closer to his face, feeling very serious myself. "I can do this at gun point if that would work better for you."

Kane looked down at the dirt we were on and then a lopsided smirk appeared on his face before his eyes met mine again. "I think you would do it too."

"Yes I would." I sighed and reached for the hem of his shirt. "Stop being a he-man and let me help you, Kane."

Grasping my wrists lightly, he stopped my hands from dragging the shirt any higher. "The way you touch me…"

I leaned back and watched the way his eyes moved over my face. There was something in that look that should have warned me that he could hurt me if he chose to, but I ignored it. "Does it hurt badly?"

Shaking his head he turned my hands over and looked down at them. "It burns, but that's not the problem I'm having." Releasing one of my hands he held his palm to mine. My hand almost fit in his palm, showing me how large he was. He studied my hand in his, sandwiching it gently between his two large palms. "You touch me with such tenderness…" Releasing my hand he dropped his away and looked back at me. I could see pain in his eyes, pain I didn't know how to ease. "It makes me want things I can never have again, Red."

I swallowed, having no clue how to respond to that.

Searching for the words that would take that look out of his eyes I finally tilted my head to the side and smirked. "I could smack them against your bruised flesh if that would help?"

He sighed. "I think we'll pass on that, but thanks for the offer." Clearing his throat he leaned back. "Go ahead, I'm going to be down longer than I can afford if I don't let you speed this up."

Feeling like I'd just won an argument I didn't understand; I nodded and leaned down to pull his shirt up. "It would be easier if you took it off."

He moved awkwardly back up again. "You are always trying to take my shirt off, Red."

I kept quiet, knowing he needed to make light of the confession made a few minutes early. I grew up with six males surrounding me; I'd learned a few universal truths about men. I bit my lip as soon as he had the shirt off and leaned back. The bruising looked red in several areas; it wasn't a neon sign, but it was close enough. "I think there's some internal damage that I didn't get to last night." I didn't wait for a response. Straddling one of his large thighs I took a few deep breaths and leaned down placing my hands lightly over the spot that looked angrier than the rest.

Closing my eyes, I focused on my own hands until the heat flooded into them. He hissed out a breath, but didn't move.

'What's your real name, Bree?" He whispered hoarsely.

I kept my eyes closed not wanting to see if he was looking at me. "Breenna," I whispered so I wouldn't lose focus with what I was doing. He shifted under my touch.

"Stop for a second." His voice crackled with pain.

I lifted my hands away and opened my eyes.

He breathed out a long sigh. "I think you're right, there's more inside going on than we thought." He took a few steadying breaths with his eyes closed. When he opened them I gasped to see the color of his eyes, far closer to black than the silver I was used to. "Kanen," he whispered. He trusted me with the power of his name; I felt a twinge at that realization. He watched me for a few seconds, expressionless yet waiting for judgment.

"Let's try again." I encouraged, ignoring the look on his face for both our sake. He nodded and closed his eyes again. Placing my palms against his heated flesh again I took a deep breath and then let it out slowly, determined I was going to be able to help the only person I really knew in this new muddled world.

How often we stopped and started, I couldn't say since I was focused on controlling the power that sprang from my body. I knew my hands were shaking and sweat covered my forehead, but I continued until I had covered every inch of his chest and abdomen. When I was taking a deep breath to move my hands and refocus on another place, he grasped my wrists lightly and stopped my hands from touching him.

"Enough."

Opening my eyes, I looked down at him and was startled to see he was covered in sweat as I was. His now black eyes watched me. "You've done enough for now, Breenna." The exhaustion in his voice gave away how much this had taken out of him.

Dropping my weight off his leg, I sat beside him. His big arm wrapped around me and pulled me down to rest my head on his shoulder.

"Do my eyes scare you?" He asked softly against my hair.

There was a vulnerable note in his voice. I didn't answer right away, examining how they did make me feel. Even though I should have screamed and run the as fast possible in the other direction when his silver eyes had turned to midnight black, I hadn't felt one bit of fear of them or him. "No." I answered honestly.

Kane squeezed me in his arm. "I am in danger when I'm near you."

Turning I looked up at his face, his eyes were not quite as black but slowly swirling back to silver. "You are?" I honestly didn't see how a man a big as he was felt any sort of danger from little me.

He smiled as his eyes caressed over my face. "Yes I am, Red. I'm too tired to explain the why." Exhaling loudly he closed his eyes. "That is some vicious power your petite hands hold, I'm as weak as a baby."

"Give me two minutes and I'll get us something to drink. I've been experimenting and I think I have a weak version of tea all figured out."

"Tea." He chuckled. "It's been so long since I had it, I may not even know what it tastes like anymore."

"That's good then you won't know if I failed miserably or not."

He was silent for a long time; I thought maybe he'd drifted off to sleep. "You know I'm not staying don't you?"

I turned onto my side so I could look at his serious silver eyes. "I know." I tried to ignore the feeling of panic that crept into my chest at the thought. "The next time we meet though, you're going to tell me why." His eyes focused on my mouth as I spoke and caused my stomach to suddenly be filled with butterflies.

"I am?"

I watched him lick his lips and felt a jolt run through me when I had the notion I wanted to lick them as well. Strange things were happening that I knew I should avoid, but couldn't. "Yes, you are. It would be the only polite thing to do on our fourth meeting."

He reached up and brushed the hair away from my forehead with gentle fingers. "This is the third time our paths have crossed?" My heart pained that he didn't know and that made me feel silly for thinking he would. "It seemed like several more." He grinned and I wanted to smack him. With a lazy movement he leaned his head back from mine. "Go make your tea, Red. I need a few minutes here to assess what you've done inside me." Moving his hand over his ribs he closed his eyes.

I got up on shaky legs to light the fire and get the water boiling..

CHAPTER FIFTEEN

By the third morning I didn't even question waking up wrapped in Kane's warm body. It was the only time I'd felt safe since I'd left my home behind. I wasn't even sure how long ago that was now. I managed to get his heavy arm off me without disturbing him too much. Before I could reach the entrance he was moving. I turned to watch and he managed to sit up without grimacing. My heart knew what my head was saying was true. He would be leaving soon. I didn't say a word, just went out into the foggy morning.

I ran my hands down over Tremor's coat; it was getting thicker with each day. I may not know when winter was going to hit, but he did. Kismet yipped and came running over and rubbed up against my leg, making me feel guilty that I hadn't spent much time with them in the past few days. Rubbing his neck I realized his fur had also gotten thicker. Kizzy turned his head and then bolted away. I didn't need to turn to know that Kane was coming towards us.

Despite telling myself I wasn't going to look, I did. I watched the way he moved, like a predator. Long graceful strides appearing relaxed, but the way the muscles flexed with each movement said he was alert and ready for anything. The way his eyes moved over me, made my heart flip in my chest.

That childhood crush on Bobby hadn't prepared me for the onslaught of feelings this man in front of me was creating.

"Winter isn't long off." My voice sounded strange to my own ear.

He glanced at the trees and then back to me. "No, it's not." He came over and stood beside me, his hand automatically stroking over Tremor's flank. "You are staying put for it?"

"I think we should." I avoided looking at his eyes, not knowing if I would say something I'd regret. Focusing on his hand that moved over the coat the same color as his own hair I cleared my throat. "I wanted to reach the mountains before winter, but they seem like they're moving further away with each day."

"It's a good four more months ride to reach them." He paused and looked at me for a moment. "I had hoped you'd stay with Maisy."

I wasn't surprised that he knew how far the mountains were—or his wishes of me staying in a community. Of course he'd probably been to the mountains. "Well now I know how far I need to travel." Finally I looked up at him. "I needed to be alone for a while before I learn to live with people again." He studied me without comment before he nodded. I really had to change the subject so I blurted out the thing that had been bugging me since we'd found him with those other men. "I didn't want to pry, but it's driving me crazy not knowing how you ended up in the predicament I found you in."

"Stupidity."

"I thought you were sensible." I tried to keep my voice teasing and light.

"I'd like to think I am most of the time." He rubbed a hand over his shadowed jaw. "I pissed those guys off a few weeks ago when I liberated their slaves" My eyebrows shot up. "They were keeping a family to do their every bidding…" He shrugged. "I let my guard down thinking I was far enough away. I was wrong."

"And the family?"

He grinned. "Long gone and safe out of their reach."

"Good." I started to turn back, but he reached out and grasped my shoulder lightly.

"I owe you for what you did, Red."

I looked into his hard serious eyes. "No you don't. You've saved my butt a few more times than I have yours."

He shook his head and stepped closer to me, his hand still gently circling my arm. "I wouldn't have made it without your touch and we both know it." I didn't want to think about that. "Thank you." I stood there feeling like I was in some sort of a dream as I watched his eyes watch mine as he lowered his face towards mine. His lips brushed the corner of my mouth and then moved up to feather across my cheek.

My knees started to shake right around the same time my insides melted. I had to grasp his forearm to keep from slipping right to the ground at his feet. He lifted his head and pulled me gently into his chest. I rested my head against the warmth of him, listening to his heart beat quickly in his chest, I could have happily stayed right there until the day floated by.

Kane leaned back and grasped my chin to tilt my head up so I would look at him. There must have been something in my eyes that gave me away, because he cursed quietly and stepped back. He stood there looking down at me with his hands on his hips and anger in his eyes. "Have you ever been with a man?"

I swallowed and shook my head.

He let out a long stream of ugly curses and paced a few feet away. When he turned back towards me his eyes bore into me. "What the hell are you doing out here on your own?"

I frowned and opened my mouth to answer, but anger flashed into me and I snapped it shut and turned to go back inside.

He jerked my arm and spun me around to face him. "Do you know what would happen to you if anyone found out?" His voice was low and filled with anguish. "You'd be put on the market and auctioned off to the highest bidder." He cursed again and dropped my arm. "I can't afford any attachments in this life now…"

My head snapped up. "Did I ask you to babysit me?" I took two steps away and then stopped and turned back to face him, my chin held high. "Do you think if I had a choice I'd be out here alone? I have no one left, Kane. No one!" With that I walked quickly back to my shelter and went inside before he could see the tears running down my face.

If anyone could call what I was doing, cleaning, then I was cleaning—vigorously when he came back inside. I organized my bags and rearranged everything that was inside this space—anything to avoid turning around and facing him. I could hear him digging around in his own pack and was curious, but still didn't give into the urge to look at him.

"I'll go rustle up something to eat. Can I borrow your knives?" His voice was cool and distant, like we hadn't just spent three days curled up close together.

I'd fought it all my life, the redhead's stereotypical temper—it wasn't until right now I believed there might be some sort of truth to it. Stomping over to my pack, I pulled out the pouch that held the knives. Common sense would have dictated that I hand him the pouch, but I wasn't feeling sensible at the moment. I was hurt and angry and possibly feeling slightly demonstrative. Reaching in, I pulled out the knives and turned and flicked them one right after the other until they lined up in the ground in front of his feet. With that I tossed the pouch onto the ground beside them. Finally looking up at his face, I felt the anger fade and defeat take its place. Covering his intriguing eyes were the dark glasses I once thought were a part of him. The Kane with steel in place of his heart had returned.

He bent down slowly and pulled the knives out of the ground one at a time and dropped them into the pouch. Grasping it in his hand, he looked at me, his jaw twitching. "I'll be back shortly."

I wanted to scream in rage, but was not going to give him the satisfaction of hearing me do something so out of control. The knives had illustrated that I was a *bit* aggravated.

~

The rest of the day was the most uncomfortable one I could remember. It was cold out, but the anger simmering in my veins was better than warm clothes to repel the chill. I spent time with Tremor, checking his coat for burrs and his hooves for anything that shouldn't be in them.

Kismet got attention that he was more than thrilled with as we played for an hour or more. I had accepted that everyone thought that my dog was really a wolf, but was still determined that a wolf could learn how to play fetch. I was raising my arm to toss the hundredth stick in hopes that Kizzy would catch onto the plan when he dropped onto his belly and looked up at me. I lowered my arm and frowned down at him, as the feeling crawled over my skin that told me we weren't alone.

Dropping the stick, I turned to see Kane standing a foot away. "He's not a very smart wolf at all. The game of fetch just isn't doing it for him."

Kane stood there looking iron hard and unapproachable. "The fact that you adopted a wolf and tamed him like a dog should be enough."

I glanced at the animal flopped over onto his side in front of me. "I think he adopted me." I shrugged, "he just decided I was who he needed to be with."

He crossed his arms over his chest, the nerve twitching in his jaw. "I can't even feel shocked by that right now." The silence made me nervous when he just stood there looking at me from behind his dark glasses. "I made some food." He turned and went back towards the shelter.

Watching him walk away, I decided that was probably as close to an apology I would ever get from him. I knew he would be gone by morning, the way he carried himself told me. Did I want to spend the last few hours being mad at the only person I'd get to see for what might be months? Taking a deep breath I followed him.

~

"That was great." I patted my tummy. "Then again I didn't have to make it, so that makes it twice as good."

He smirked, the first sign that he had relaxed again. "I don't have your flair with adding weeds, but I get by."

I leaned back against the wall and watched as he cleaned up. "Do you play cards?"

Stopping, he looked over his shoulder. "Cards?"

I nodded. "Yeah."

"Not very well."

I laughed. "Even better." Getting up quickly I went over and pulled a deck out of my pack. "What game don't you play well?"

He put the tossed the scraps to Kismet and set the dish down. "All of them."

I sat down crossed legged and started to shuffle the deck.

"You want to play cards?"

I stopped shuffling and looked up at him, feeling even smaller with him towering over me. "Yes. It may be months before I see a person again, Kizzy isn't into card games or conversation."

"All right—but don't say I didn't warn you. The wolf probably plays better than I do." He lowered his large frame down onto the floor and leaned on one elbow, stretching his legs out.

Reaching over, I pulled the glasses off his face and set them beside me. "Wearing dark glasses and playing cards would be cheating."

He raised one eyebrow up giving me a suspicious look. "How is that?"

"My brother wore them and I could see his cards reflected in them." He laughed. "I didn't say it was you cheating," I confessed in an innocent tone.

~

"You cheated!" I tossed my cards down and glared at

146

him.

"I said I didn't play well, I didn't say how." He grinned at me.

My jaw dropped open and then I snapped it shut. Picking up the cards again I flipped them at him, scattering them all over him.

He chuckled and began to gather them up. "Well at least it wasn't knives this time."

I flushed, feeling regret for doing that earlier. "I wouldn't have hit you."

His eyes looked over me briefly. "I'm glad to hear that. You can be one scary woman when you want to be."

"It's the hair—or so I've been told."

Kane just shook his head and picked up the rest of the cards. Sitting up he set them in a neat pile in front of me.

"Kane, were you serious when you said if anyone found out that I was—that I haven't—I'd be auctioned off?"

He rubbed his hand over his jaw and looked down for a few seconds before he answered. "Yes. I'm sorry to admit it but my gender mostly keeps their brains in their pants and don't think beyond that."

"Oh." I didn't know what else to say to that admission from the most masculine man I'd ever met. He got up to get a drink. "Then help me."

He glanced over his shoulder and gave me a puzzled look. "Help you what?"

Getting to my feet, I grasped my hands and continued before I could change my mind. It was one of those now or never moments in my life again. "Make it so I'm not such an appealing find."

I knew the second what I was asking him sunk in, he clenched his jaw and then unclenched it and cursed. "I can't…" He shook his head and went out through the door before I could stop him.

I chewed on the inside of my cheek and stood there with my hands on my hips. As far as propositions went it failed miserably. Taking a deep breath I went out after him, more determined than I had been when my brain had come up with this ridiculous plan. He was standing right outside the shelter, his hands on his hips staring out into the darkness of the night. I moved cautiously towards him. Placing my hand lightly on his arm hoping he would turn to look at me, he didn't. "I'd rather give it to someone I choose than have it taken…"

The muscle hardened under my hand. "You don't know what you're asking from me."

"Yes I do." He still didn't turn or look at me and then it hit me, what if he wasn't as drawn to me as I was him? I felt an embarrassed flush come into my cheeks. "Oh." I dropped my hand. "That's okay. I just thought you felt…" I couldn't say it now feeling like a fool. I turned to go back inside when he wrapped his arm around my waist and pulled me back into his body.

"Don't for one second think I don't want you," he whispered against my ear. He pushed his hips into my back letting me feel his obvious arousal. His hold loosened and then I was spun around to face him. He picked me up into his body as his mouth found mine.

I didn't know what I was expecting but I got much more. His kiss wasn't gentle and hesitant. His mouth ravished mine with an intensity that would have had me sliding bonelessly to the ground if he hadn't been holding me up. Wrapping my arms around his neck I wove my fingers into his hair and pulled so he wouldn't stop what he was doing.

His hands slid down over my back, he grasped my legs and lifted me higher, wrapping them around him. Holding me he slid me up and down over the hard bulge in his jeans. I moaned against his mouth, dizzy with the need he was creating in me. He dropped down onto his knees making me straddle him as we hit the ground. Pulling his mouth from mine his lips and teeth traveled down my throat making me gasp with each touch. Holding his hair I leaned my head back so he could move down further.

He was rocking back on his heels, riding me over him and making me so wet I wasn't sure I could keep going like this without having some sort of melt-down. He lifted his head, shoved my jacket down my arms and reached to pull my shirt over my head, catching my waist in his hands as I untangled the sleeves and lowered my arms. I should have felt the cold air, but my whole body was overheating. Rocking his body into mine his mouth moved over my exposed flesh, I gasped when his teeth found one hard nipple and bit it gently. Dropping my feet down I rubbed into him harder, needing to be closer to him.

Lifting his mouth away from my body he held my hips in a tight grip and helped me by thrusting between my legs as I rode him. His eyes found mine; they were black and filled with the dark need that was swamping both of us. Lifting me away, he stood me in front of him. My knees threatened to give out as his hands ripped open my zipper and yanked my jeans down off my body. The cold air hit my body, but I couldn't have cared if it was snowing on me at the time. I was trying to kick my feet free when he hissed out a breath and bit gently into my thigh.

Holding his hair, I clung to him not knowing what else to expect as he licked his way up my thigh and over one hip. I looked down to see him watching me as he lowered his mouth and held open my thighs and ran his tongue over the throbbing tip of my center. I groaned and almost collapsed onto the ground in front of him. Reaching around me, he hooked my legs over his biceps and supported my weight as his tongue tasted me again.

I was completely helpless as I straddled his arms, my legs held apart and open to his mouth. He bit me tenderly and then kissed the sting until it turned into one spasm after another as his tongue drove in and out of me. My whole body was quivering when I cried out, trying to breathe through the wave of feelings shocking my entire being. I leaned over him, my hands twisted in his hair.

When he lowered my feet to the ground and my legs

shook, threatening to dump me on my ass if he moved too far away. I looked down at him as he pulled his shirt over his head and lifted his hips so he could pull his jeans down and free his body. When his hands wrapped around my waist again, I balanced myself on his shoulders, not knowing what he wanted me to do. His lips closed around a sensitive nipple and I stopped worrying about what he might expect from me.

His mouth brought me back up to that excited point again. Hands tightened on my waist as he lowered to kneel once more, taking me down with him. He slid my sensitive folds down the length of him and I had to catch my breath when I felt how hard he was. Dropping my head down I bit at his neck and tasted him. Kane growled deep in his throat and pulled my hair to take my mouth off him.

With his black eyes burning into mine he lifted my hips until the heated tip of his erection rubbed over the wet heat between my legs. He clenched his jaw and lowered me an inch at a time, watching and waiting as my body adjusted to him slipping inside me. When he came to the barrier I tensed up, unsure what to expect. He lowered his mouth to my breast once more and sucked hard on the nipple, while holding still. I moaned from the pleasure his tongue created. Lifting his head he grasped my hair and brought my mouth to his. He growled against my mouth and attacked it with a frenzied passion that threatened to consume me. I felt the brief pain as he thrust up into me, but his mouth erased the discomfort quickly.

He filled me completely, bringing me to a new awareness of spasms inside my body. Lowering my legs I lifted and matched his thrusts, wanting to make him feel as good as he was making me feel. When his hands moved from my hips to grasp under the back of my thighs, it was the only warning I was given as he thrust up into me in one hard stroke. As our bodies connected I felt heat gathering inside again and cried out. All I could do was hold on, his mouth attacked my neck as I tried to ride the furious drive of his body slapping into mine.

I cried out as an orgasm suddenly washed over me, my whole body shook with the force. He groaned and thrust into me once more and I could feel him pulsing deep inside me. Dropping my head down to rest on his shoulder I tried to remember how to bring air into my body. He rocked us gently, sending aftershocks trembling through me until I was sure I would pass out from the feeling.

I could feel his heart hammering against his chest and softly kissed his neck. His hand stroked up and down my back in a lazy caress. "Did I hurt you?" He whispered breathlessly against my ear.

I found the energy to lift my head and looked into his swirling silver eyes. "I don't think so, but I can't feel anything right now." He grinned and kissed me gently.

"Let's go inside where it's warm." He licked down my throat, "I still want you."

CHAPTER SIXTEEN

"Breenna."

I opened my eyes at the soft whisper of my name. Kane lay behind me, his hand running up over my bare hip and waist lightly. "It's morning?"

His lips brushed over my shoulder in soft teasing kisses. "Yes."

My heart thudded to a stop; at least it felt like it did. "You're leaving," I whispered, hoping I was wrong.

"I have to." His voice was so soft he barely spoke out loud. His mouth brushed down over my neck a few times. "I am mutated too." He rested his head against my shoulder. "I can't be around anyone too long."

I rolled in his arms so I was facing him, needing to see his face right now.

"I become something not pretty. I'm not safe to be around." His eyes were silver now but I could see the pain hidden from the words he spoke. I was thankful for any explanation he was willing to offer.

"I understand," I said still watching his eyes move over my face. He lowered his mouth and kissed my lips tenderly. I knew he meant it as a soft good bye kiss, but I wasn't ready yet. Wrapping my arms around his neck, I pulled his mouth back towards mine as I slid tight up against his body. "Kiss me, Kanen."

He hissed out a breath and brought his lips to mine. The tender kiss grew into something hot and demanding. Rolling onto his back, he brought me up to rest on top of him as his tongue danced with mine. I straddled him and slid the wet junction between my legs against his already hard need. I was sore from the many times the night before but I didn't know when or if I would see him again, so I was saying good bye in my way, not with words.

Lifting my mouth from his, I pushed until I was sitting on him. His eyes were swirling between silver and black and I found both appealed to me, the dark and the gentle Kanen. I slowly lowered my body to take him inside of me. He sucked in a breath when our bodies connected and he was buried deep. Leaning back, I moved up again, rocking our bodies together, I had no idea how to move but I didn't hear him complain so I hoped it felt as good for him. Grasping my hips he helped balance me so I could ride him faster.

With a force I didn't know I had I drove myself onto him, slapping our flesh together. Kane's black eyes watched me as his breath grew more ragged. My legs were shaking when the first inkling of spasms started to spread through me, sucking him in deeper. He groaned and gripped my waist, picking me up and impaling me as he thrust hard into me. I gasped and then was taken over the edge with a satisfied growl from him.

Flipping me onto my back without missing a stroke, he continued to thrust harder until I was gasping for air, not caring if I could breathe at the same time.

Holding my legs open I lay there unable to move as he drove into me, slamming his body against mine. His eyes were a brilliant black looking down at me, the intensity and possession in them sent me flying over the edge again, taking him with me. He cried out and then collapsed on top of me.

Regaining my breath, I tried to find something I could say to make this hard moment pass faster, but there was nothing. Neither of us knew what the future held and we weren't about to make promises that would grow into blatant lies.

Kane pulled his body from mine and I felt lonely already. He sat up, his breath still uneven. I reached over and ran my hand down over his back. "Keep you safe, Kanen," I whispered.

Lowering his head, he didn't move for a few seconds then he rolled, dropping a quick kiss on my lips as he stood all in one fluid motion. "You as well, Breenna."

I watched in silence as he got dressed and gathered up his pack. He swung it over his shoulder and paused in the door. His eyes held mine for a frozen moment. I offered a smile, even though I know it didn't reach my eyes. Slipping his dark glasses on, he turned and walked out the door.

"Be safe." I whispered to the empty air and then stayed there fighting tears that I would not let fall.

I don't know how long I just laid there looking at the door, but Kismet had inched his way up to my face and licked my cheek a few times before I responded. I hugged his head into my shoulder. "I'm okay. Just—I don't know." I turned to look at the fire pit, the heat long gone from it. Sighing, I shoved the blanket and fur back and sat up. The cold air hit me immediately making me want to curl back up under the covers again. Of course if I did that it would never get warm inside—and I had to go to the bathroom, so there would be no more lounging right now.

My body was sore in places I never dreamed I could be, not that I was going to complain. Compared to the fantasy I'd created when thinking of losing my virginity—Kane has surpassed each one, setting a new standard for my dreams.

Shrugging into my clothes, I moved over to the door and stepped out. The chilled air hit me immediately and I was momentarily surprised. Going back in, I grabbed a sweater and reluctantly went through the door. Kismet sat just under the opening, doing his usual morning scan—the snow falling onto his coat was something new though. I peeked out and rolled my eyes, the snow fell at a steady speed. Winter had finally made up its mind. Tremor wandered over and shook his long mane a few inches away from me, scattering all over my sweater. "And so it begins, boys. Keep your paws and hooves crossed that we know what the hell we're doing."

After getting the fire going, I pondered what I needed to do first over a cup of my homemade tea. It wasn't as good as Maisy's real tea, but it was pretty close to the real thing, I decided. I stared at the wood stacked against the one wall and knew I should be outside chopping as much as I could before it was long buried in a white blanket.

I had managed to cut quite a bit and had the sore hands to prove it. The first several attempts were not what I'd call successful. I had no idea chopping wood involved as many body parts as it did. The first few times the blade bounced off the wood I dropped it and swore loud enough, I would have rivaled my father when he was alive and pissed off. When it did actually go into the wood, it hurt almost as much. I also learned after only a few hours that the most difficult part was getting the axe out of the wood if it got stuck. At the rate I was going I'd have muscles the size of Kane's just from having to beat the holy hell out of the logs to free the blade from it.

Once I decided to start with the smallest and waiting to try the larger pieces—as my level of skill increased, it got easier. I wouldn't be lumberjack of the year by any means, but we'd be warm and should have enough wood to keep us alive for the winter. With breaks, I managed to get enough cut to not be chopping for every moment of the next few days.

I stepped back outside with my tea cupped between my palms and watched the snow fall. It was beautiful to watch as it covered all within its reach in a pristine white coat. Then again the start of winter was always a pretty sight—the beauty of it faded when you were tired of cold feet and a chapped nose. I gave myself a month before I reached that 'bring on spring' moment.

The stack of uncut wood caught my attention and I heaved a loud sigh as it reminded me it was still there. What I wouldn't give for a chain saw right now. Not that I knew how to work one or could afford the gas to run one. Gas was one of those things that only the very wealthy could afford to use. They still had cars too, no idea why because they never went anywhere in them. Few ventured out from their safe and sterile environments.

I had only ever driven a few times before my father had decided the car was going to be a luxury we didn't need. He hadn't been alone in that thought, shortly after many families gave up their cars and opted for other means of transportation that didn't involve fuel or power. It was right around this time we all thought Darren's father lost his mind and built a huge fence around their large city lawn and then bought horses. Horses in the city—seemed ridiculous at the time. I turned and looked at Tremor and had to say a silent thank you to Darren's dad.

Kismet rubbed up against my leg, bringing me back to the present—and the wood that still waited for me. With a moan I went back in to grab the axe.

~

By that night winter was well under way and seemed to be making up for a stalled arrival. The snow was up past my ankles as I went out to bring Tremor in. If it got as bad as I thought it might, he was better off inside with Kismet and I for the night—and the extra heat his large body created was never a bad thing on a cold night. I rubbed him down to dry his coat before I offered him a handful of dried grass as a reward for putting up with my mothering him. He accepted the offering and backed up near the door to stand where he preferred to be whenever he was inside. I didn't know why he practically liked his hind end pressed up against the door, but he did. Maybe it was the fire that bothered him, even though it was the furthest from the door than anything else, other than my bed area.

I went about my nightly ritual of a brief sponge bath as

both animals looked at me with their usual disinterest in the human things I did. I'd accepted I may never lounge in a tub again, but that didn't mean I had to smell or feel unclean. I did this each night—it seemed to wash away any melancholy that was trying to take over.

In truth I was lonely, and still very unsure out here on my own. I missed Darren and Bobby almost daily and it seemed each night I spent the last of my energy in wondering if they were alright. Not that I could ever do anything if they weren't—even when I was there, but I could still think of them and hope.

What I attempted not to think about was Kane and whether I'd see him again. I still didn't know much about the silver-eyed giant of a man, yet from the first time I looked up at him—while lying on the ground hoping I lived through the upcoming minutes—there was something about him that made me feel at peace. To pass the long hours of the night I'd guess at what his mutation could possibly be. The only hint he'd ever given was he became something not pretty. This told me nothing. I'd pieced together his eyes changing somehow involved this not pretty part, but beyond that I had no idea what he could mean. For a few fleeting moments I had wondered if exuding that peaceful feeling I felt was his mutation. I discarded that hypothesis after I added in the eyes going black and not being able to be around people.

Kismet jumped up and brought me out of my thoughts. I paused in fixing the fire and watched him. I didn't need to see what was bothering him when I heard the howling outside. Paranoia kicked in, which I liked to tell myself was really the instinct to survive and I went over to the door and began propping the long branches I'd cut just for that purpose. I may not have a dead bolt out here but I could make it damn difficult to open my branch door from the outside. Kismet came over and stood at the door, his ears back waiting for any sign of trouble.

When the howling sounded again Tremor decided being further inside our little space wasn't such a bad idea after all. When he moved from the door Kizzy moved over and lay down in front of it, watching. I stoked the fire and crawled under the blankets with the gun in my hand. Setting it beside my pillow I turned to watch the door.

Curling up beneath the warm fur I kept my eyes on the door, or more to the point Kismet. He had relaxed which was my cue to sleep while I could. It had been a long day for me and I worried that I had many more long days coming my way in the very near future.

My last thought for that night was hoping we reached the other side of winter. For me the cold months of snow were the final test. I'm not sure what graduating would bring. Maybe just prove I was a survivor or possibly I would be one of those who emerged after the silence. The pioneers those generations many years from being born would talk about. I'd like to think what I was doing would count for something in the end.

CHAPTER SEVENTEEN

Feeling the cold air on my face was not much incentive to open my eyes. I knew it was morning and the longer I burrowed under the blankets the colder it would be without the fire. Opening my eyes, I blinked looking at the rough ceiling above me. It seemed darker than it should —once again moving my wish for a watch to the top of my list. A wet tongue brushed over my cheek making me suppress the 'yuck' feeling from the animal trying to get my attention. "I'm getting up." Kismet was a great guard, but he wasn't the most patient when it came to being freed from the enclosed space each morning. I considered myself lucky though that he hadn't yet relieved himself inside our home.

Stumbling in the direction of the door, I still couldn't figure out why it was this dark inside. The door wasn't exactly solid and light should be filtering through it. I was just about to voice my thoughts when I found my ankles surrounded by what could only be snow. Groaning loud enough to bring Kismet to my side, I turned around and headed back to the bed to get the flashlight. Did I really want to see why there was snow inside my little space? No, but at the same time I couldn't just pretend it wasn't there.

Turning on the flashlight I aimed it towards the door and could do nothing but groan again. A drift led from the door to three feet inside. With only a sparse amount of light by the one corner it didn't take deep thought to understand that outside was buried under snow. I paused for a few seconds to decide which was higher on the priority list, clearing the snow to find a way out or heat and light. I stood thinking and shivering and heat won.

Kismet whined. "You're going to have to put that on hold for a few, Kizzy— I have to find outside before we can go there."

Just as I was about to light the fire, I paused and twisted so I could look up into the cone shaped chimney that led outside. There was no light whatsoever coming from the top. Biting my lip I looked down at my strategically placed kindling and logs. Either I took it all apart or found a way to cover it up.

With the fire pit covered I straddled it and bent in an almost impossible position so I could poke a long branch up into the chimney and not bring all the snow down on top of my head. It was probably one of those crazy picture moments with my butt stuck out and feet spread as I reached to stab at the snow covering the top without tipping over onto my face, I was thankful I was alone for it. On the third jab of the stick the snow let loose and fell down with a *thunk*. My sleeves were filled with it and for the second time in the few hours winter had been present I was dreading it.

Dragging the tarp off the logs, I tried to aim for the door to dump most of the snow, but succeeded in leaving a nice icy trail of it instead. With numb fingers I worked to get the fire going and create enough of a blaze that it would rise and thaw the rest of the snow coating the tubing to the outside. It sizzled for a few minutes I wondered if more was going to come down and put out the flames or if the snow would melt.

As I warmed my hands to a useable temperature I studied the entrance and wondered just how deep the path that I was going to have to cut would be to see outside again. The very next thought was did I even want to see outside? It was doubtful. I had a long day ahead of me for once I found the white outdoors; I'd have to find a way to block the snow from doing this every day for the next several months.

Grabbing the water pot, I filled it with the fresh snow and placed it by the fire to melt. Might as well have some tea while I dug my way out—with a bucket, the only thing I possessed that could possibly be used to move snow. A new list would have to be started of things I didn't have but would want for the next winter season.

When I finally moved the door I just stood there and looked at the wall of snow. We were snowed in—literally. This brought me to the new obstacle with my plan to dig out, where was I going to put that much snow to clear room for an opening? I was not going to fill our dry area with melting snow.

As I bundled up in extra layers and wiggled my three-pairs-of-socks-thick feet into the used boots, I looked around trying to find something that I could use to bulldoze the opening and speed up the task. Coming up empty on that thought I walked over and stood studying the snow. I could see no way around it all from winding up inside. Jamming the hat on my head I scowled and dove into the white wall with my whole body.

I now knew that it was much thicker than a thin drift and my hopes of getting outside to go to the bathroom was not going to be happening as quickly as I'd like. I refused to give into the nagging thought that we might be stuck in here for a long time. Growling much like Kismet would I began pawing my way into the snow bank and knocking it down onto my feet. Shaking the snow from my face I caught sight of the animals; they stood side by side and both were looking at me with 'she's losing it' expressions. I had no choice but to laugh when I realized it could be worse.

If you ever get the opportunity to move snow by the pail full, I'd suggest you decline. The process took far longer than any shovel would have. With snow overflowing the tarp I was using to contain it, I finally wrestled it thought the narrow path to dump outside the shelter. Kismet was gone as soon as daylight appeared; Tremor checked it out and decided he had nothing pressing to go out for at that point.

I stood there squinting from the brightness of the sun glaring off the snow and wondered how it was possible for this much snow to appear in such a short time. The drift on the outer part of the shelter was up past my waist and for as far as I could see it appeared the snow was that deep everywhere. Tremor nudged me in the back; he'd decided he needed to check things out finally too. With a loud sigh, I stepped out into winter.

For the most part the snow was fluffy enough I could walk through it, but after moving only twenty feet from the shelter entrance I knew I was going to have figure out how to make some sort of snowshoe or it was going to be a very long confined winter.

~

The sun was close to setting by the time I had a wide path cleared into the doorway. The tarp was now used like a curtain inside the tunnel at the opening. It didn't exactly blend in with the white snow, as it was a very bright blue, but if anyone thought to step into what looked like a hole in the snow then they had far too much time on their hands to begin with.

Dinner was going to have to be dehydrated packets tonight. Digging out had consumed too much daylight to head towards the river to see if it was frozen over and no birds were flying. The snowfall that had started the day before was showing no sign of stopping. I didn't look forward to stepping outside in the morning.

The idea of spending the winter with snow deeper than I was tall was very deflating. I needed to figure out how to make snowshoes. I'd been toying with possible items to make them with since I'd stepped outside this morning. I could use some of the cord and thinner hide Kane had brought me, but the wooden frame left me clueless. The tools I had at hand, aside from eating utensils, consisted of an axe, a small handsaw, knives and a gun. I wasn't a MacGyver so I didn't have the slightest idea how I was going to accomplish this with so little. Of course if I'd only thought of this before the planet's natural supplies were buried under the snow, it would have been better.

Sorting through the longer branches I'd kept for kindling I attempted to bend some of the thinner ones into a curve. With a few I managed to gain a few inches of angle, but found I was not as strong from wood splitting as I thought I was. Added to this morning's list was to find some young saplings that might co-operate for my new project.

Kismet and Tremor watched me with their usual indifference and I had to laugh—they most likely stuck with me because they thought I was addled and needed watching over, this time they weren't far off. Giving up, I went out and got some snow to melt for my bathing water. At least winter was good for one thing; I didn't have to haul water.

~

Refreshed, I hung up my wet clothes to dry for the next day. I may be roughing it, but I still couldn't deal with dirty clothes on my skin. With a hot cup of tea, I sat down on my bedding to write in the journal. I had to prioritize what was important to jot down, as this was the only paper I had.

I couldn't write about the temperature, as I had no thermometer to gauge it with. The snowfall was measured by my body and whatever body part it reached. The times of day were approximated by morning, day and night. Was it better to not have the conveniences that were taken granted for? My own feeling was if I had a thermometer, watch and the rest of modern gadgets I would spend more time agonizing over what was lost instead of focusing on what I needed to do to see days in the future. Then again I talked to a wolf and horse and believed I understood their responses so I could just be falling into my own special delusional state.

It wasn't quite dark yet when Kismet jumped up and darted to the door I hadn't closed completely yet. Before I could call him, his disappeared out through it. Gritting my teeth I got up and grabbed my coat once again. I was moving it aside when the hair on the back of my neck stood up, without questioning it I turned around and grabbed the gun. Being out here had taught me is to listen to those little signals all your senses gave you.

Peeking out through the tarp I saw Kizzy hunched down in the snow watching something in the falling light. He didn't move or make a sound. As quietly as I could manage I slid past the tarp and squatted down beside him. The sounds that had gotten his attention finally came to me. Voices. Male voices. I had a brief flash back of the large scary men I'd almost run into the day I met Kane and that alone had me dropping down onto my elbows beside the animal. It was dark enough we couldn't see where they were, but we could hear their conversation clear enough to know they must almost be on top of us.

"How the fuck did we get selected for this?"

Just from the sound of the voice I knew I didn't want to see or meet the male it came from. A shiver traveled over my skin at the harshness of it.

"I'm guilty by association and being the ass that calls you friend. You are the reason my ass is numb and my feet have icicles on them." Another more civilized voice growled.

"How the hell was I supposed to know the Captain wanted the little mutant slave bitch for himself? He didn't say squat!"

I stopped breathing at that point; not wanting to make any sort of sound that would draw their attention in our direction.

"Just fix your damn boot so we can get moving, I don't want to stand out here all night."

I placed a hand lightly on Kismet so he would stay with me and hopefully he knew to be quiet.

"There. Let's go."

Long after their voices faded away from us we waited in the snow until my legs were numb and arms were shaking. When Kismet stood up, I knew we were in the clear but my heart still didn't slow down. Moving stiffly back into the shelter, I pulled the door closed tightly, and shoved the bracing up against it again. I didn't for a minute think the branches would stop anyone of adequate size, but it would at least bring my attention to company arriving.

Keeping my coat on, I stood by the fire until the shivering stopped. Shivering from the cold was soon under control, but the fear wasn't going away anytime soon. Had those men been Red Bands? I was fairly certain the Captain reference didn't have anything to do with a real army of any sort. How had the world reverted back to slavery? Once again making the same mistakes from the history books—any found to be different were to be feared and enslaved to make others feel better.

I wished for a larger notebook, somewhere I could vent all of the feelings crashing through my system. Anguish surrounded me as I felt for the girl they spoke of and her fate. The fear rocking me had me questioning being here alone, which did nothing but make me angry. I'd accomplished a lot to be proud of since I'd rode away from the people that were familiar to me, to have the faith in my own abilities was hard to feel positive about.

Peeling off the coat, I hung it back up and moved over to get more wood to put on the fire. Sleep wouldn't come anytime soon tonight, not with the turmoil inside me. Yanking off my jeans, I tucked them under the end of the covers so they'd be warm in the morning. As I crawled in, with the gun still clutched in my hand, I looked around at everything inside the home I'd made. It may not have smooth walls and a shingled roof, but it was a far cry from that first night in the bush when I'd been unsure of everything.

Setting the gun beside the pillow, I pulled the covers up to my chin. Kismet moved along my legs until he found the position he took most nights. Tremor was standing in his usual spot. This was now my life, my world. I didn't remember the feel of my old bed, or the sounds I listened to then before I feel asleep. I'd remember some of it, the parts that I needed or wanted, the rest was already fading. I had no idea what the next day held for us—or year but I knew one thing I wasn't going to hide in fear.

We'd been through more than I would have ever thought possible out here and we'd come out of it relatively unscathed. So what if there were brutal people out there, they had always been. The only difference was now they didn't attempt to stay hidden. If the noisy men that had passed by were any indication they made no attempts to conceal themselves, making avoiding them much easier.

I don't usually dream but that night I did. I dreamt of an army of the survivors joining together and stopping the Red Bands from terrorizing everyone in their path. When I woke up I could only shake my head at the sheer silliness of the scenes my unconscious mind created. But sleepy dreams sometimes are there to put you at ease even if you don't realize it then.

~

You would think after two weeks of maneuvering with my crude snowshoes I'd be some sort of pro, but no such luck. I still got tangled up more often than not and landed in the snow. The problem was my legs were too short or the shoes were too wide. If it hadn't been sheer luck that I'd managed to make them at all I'd try a second time and make them longer and not as wide. Dusting the snow off my butt for the fourth time during this outing I picked up the string of fish and moved more carefully back towards camp. Fish again. The very thought didn't stir even the slightest twinges of hunger inside me—since winter had arrived not one bird had been within throwing distance to go after. I'd woken up determined to swallow my apprehension and set the snare, which turned out to be a complete farce the moment I grabbed the cord I used for fishing.

As I crested the small hill I stopped and crouched down. There were two people outside the shelter.

Keeping down and out of sight, I studied the way

Tremor just stood there not overly concerned with the two people outside our home. Kismet wasn't too bothered by them when one of them knelt down and rubbed their hands over his shaggy coat. Standing slowly, I moved down the slope towards them. Just because the animals seemed okay with the guests didn't mean I was going to go hug them. Shifting the fish to my left hand I pulled off my glove and reached for a knife.

When I was close enough the taller one turned and a boyish grin greeted me. It wasn't until he pulled his hood down I recognized him. It was Tanner and his sister, Rosy. A thousand questions went through my mind at the same time. The most important one I blurted out. "What are you two doing this far away from home?"

Tanner closed the distance between us. "Kane gave us directions. It's Maisy—she fell and hasn't been up since."

My heart stumbled. "When did this happen?"

Rosy stepped beside her brother. "Three days ago, she slipped on some ice." I could see the worry on her face. "Kane came yesterday and sent us to get you."

Just the mention of his name made my pulse race. "You made it here in a day?" Tanner nodded. I wanted to ask why Kane didn't come and get me, but didn't when I noticed how tired they looked. "Come inside and rest for a bit." I waved them to the entrance. As they moved inside I glanced up at the sky. If those clouds kept their distance we might make it back to their village before morning.

I put the water on to boil and began peeling off layers of clothes. "We'll take Tremor and should be there by morning." I didn't voice that I had no idea if I could help Maisy. "You two stretch out for an hour and I'll get some supplies ready." I didn't have to persuade them any further than that. They dropped their packs onto the ground and just as quickly flopped down on top of the furs covering my bed.

As I gathered up anything we might need, and a few things we probably wouldn't, I tried not to dwell on the reason Kane would have for not coming himself. Telling yourself not to read too much into an action and actually doing it are two different things.

With the fish stashed in the snow fridge I'd carved out of a snow bank and my pack stuffed full of supplies, I checked the sky again before I woke up the kids. Tremor stood by the entrance, knowing something was going on. "Up to a bit of exercise big guy?" I rubbed my hand down over his jaw. I wasn't going to bother with the saddle; we could keep our packs on our backs and give Tremor the lightest load possible. Using my snowshoes, we could take turns and only ride two at a time. On ground that wasn't deep with snow I had no doubt Tremor could carry all three of us, but I didn't want him hurt as he trudged through the deeper snow.

Turning, I went back in to wake them. The muscles in my neck and shoulders had tightened the moment they'd told me what happened. The adrenalin alone would drive me to get there as quickly as possible to help. I didn't want to think what would happen if I couldn't help her—or what it would do to the people that lived there if I failed.

~

Thankfully the snowshoes weren't needed at the start of the trip—I couldn't imagine being strapped in them for that distance. The kids led me through the trees on the path they had traveled where the snow was sparse in several areas. After their nap, they felt up to walking again to save Tremor's strength. Kismet just seemed happy that we were going somewhere, and the added company to pay attention to him was welcomed.

The clouds held at bay, allowing the moonlight to illuminate a path for us. I had brought the forever flashlight but hadn't needed to use it yet. It was the eeriest feeling walking through the trees, with patches lit up by the light filtering through them. The only sounds were my feet and Tremor's hooves. Had it been summer the sound that would have crawled up and down my skin would have been crickets, but tonight there was nothing.

Kismet would bolt ahead and then eventually circle back.

He was like my own furry black scout, clearing the path for us. With each step my legs began to complain. A midnight hike hadn't been on my agenda or I wouldn't have gone out for three hours on the snowshoes. A few times I stumbled and Tremor would move closer so he was right along with me. Maybe he thought he could catch me if I took a tumble. I just had to keep going; my conscience wouldn't have it any other way.

Kismet paused to look back at us, I knew I was walking slower and slower with each step, but couldn't shake the lethargic feeling. I'd had to abandon the snow shoes when the moon sat the highest in the sky, not having the energy to lift them high enough to keep going.

"I can walk the rest of the way; you should ride for a while." Tanner said in a tired voice behind me.

I refused to make the teen that had been up for over a day walk so I could rest. "We don't have much further to go," I said over my shoulder. Inside I just prayed I was right because with each step through the snow my muscles protested more.

Kismet paused and stared into the trees. Reaching into my pocket I pulled out the gun and held it down my side. Tremor jerked on the reigns and stopped moving. In the silence of the bright night I heard movement in the trees. Whether from exhaustion or the fact I had young people with me, I raised the gun towards the sound and waited.

"Easy, Bree." A familiar voice from the dark shadow of the trees said.

"Kane?" I lowered the gun and waited. As he stepped out of the darkness I was already moving towards him. In two strides his long legs closed the space between us. I didn't know what kind of greeting to expect so I stopped right in front of him.

He looked down at me for a few seconds and then leaned down and wrapped his arms around me, lifting me into his hard body. I could feel the cold plastic of his glasses against the side of my neck as I wrapped my arms tightly around his. "You got here fast." His lips brushed against my skin briefly before he set me back on the ground.

"How is she?" I glanced behind us to see identical looks on Tanner and Rosy's faces. Just seeing Kane lifted the veil of weariness that had been covering me moments before.

"The same. She's awake most of the time, but doesn't say much." He wrapped an arm around my shoulders and went over to grab Tremor's reigns. "I didn't want to leave her." He nodded at the two sitting on Tremor giving him an odd look. "You two must have run the whole way."

Tanner shrugged. "We stuck to the trees like you said so the snow wasn't too deep." He gave me a lopsided grin.

"They need sleep." Kane leaned down and nuzzled my hair. I tried not to sigh out loud from his gesture.

"We're only ten minutes away; they can sleep all day tomorrow if they need it."

~

I wasn't sure what I expected when we walked into Maisy's little home, but it was beyond what I could have imagined. The small sitting area I'd once had tea in now was full of chairs, wall to wall, most holding people—exhaustion and concern etched on their faces. The small fireplace was crackling throwing enough heat that a coat was unnecessary. I turned and saw Maisy lying on a small wooden platform, with furs and cushioning so abundant they dwarfed her body. She looked fragile, her skin was pale and breathing shallow. My heart kicked a few times as I studied her.

"Thanks for coming." Leif got up from where he'd been kneeling beside her and came over. He gave Kane an odd look over my head. I wasn't sure why. "There's been no improvement, but we did manage to get some broth into her a few times in the last few hours."

All at once it struck me; I had no business being here. I wasn't a doctor, what did I know? Without realizing I backed into Kane's chest and stood there looking at the man in front of me. "We got here as fast as we could." I glanced again to Maisy and my heart actually began to hurt. "I don't know if I can do anything."

Leif shook his head. "As far as I can tell there are no bones broken, but she has torn a few muscles and ligaments in one leg. There is so much bruising and swelling in her lower back I can't be sure if there is more damage hidden behind it." He looked at me with pain in his eyes. "She fell a good six feet."

I took a shaky breath and fought to breathe through the anxiety threatening to swamp me. "Where do you think I should start?" Kane helped me ease out of my jacket and extra layers. The entire time I looked at the old woman lying there. Leif had gone back over to her, waiting for me to join him. Panic gripped my insides so tight I wasn't sure if I could move. Looking through the room at all the eyes watching me I felt surrounded.

Kane's hands tightened on my shoulder briefly as he turned me to face him. I stared at his chest, unable to think. With a gentle touch he lifted my chin so our eyes met. "You've got this." He rubbed a hand over his own chest. "You fixed me up and you'll do what you can for Maisy."

With a shaking hand I reached up and slid his glasses down the bridge of his nose, so I could see his eyes. I needed to see if his words reached them, if his belief in me was there. For timeless moments his silver eyes didn't falter from mine. He stood there looking down at me, his hands kneading my shoulders in a silent encouragement. I took a deep breath and then nodded slowly before I pushed the glasses back up to cover his eyes. I could do this. As I turned I didn't look at anyone else in the room, I looked as Maisy as I walked towards her. Maisy, the woman that had held my hand and declared her faith in me, the woman that believed in me as much as Kane did.

Kneeling down beside her, I pulled off my gloves and ran a hand over her hair lightly. "Maisy, its Red." She took a ragged breath but her eyes didn't open. "I'm here to help you." I glanced down her frail looking body as I slid the blanket covering her back. "It might hurt like hell—I'm sorry." Taking a calming breath I looked finally at Leif. "Where do I start?"

He was silent for a moment. "Do you want to do her leg first or start on the worst of it?"

I wanted to tell him I had no idea because I didn't, but that wouldn't reassure the people behind me that I knew what I was doing—which I didn't. "Let's tackle the hardest part first. I'll get weak so I want to do it first while I'm not shaking."

He nodded abruptly and slid his hands over her lower back. When he closed his eyes I realized he was pinpointing the area with the most damage. "I can't get a clear picture above her hip, her kidney area is so engorged with bruising— it worries me."

I couldn't focus on his worry, only on wanting to take the pain away for Maisy. When I'd helped Kane I'd been able to take the swelling away with sheer determination to ease his pain. Closing my eyes I took a few deep breaths and then lifted the shirt away from her back. I didn't need Leif to show me where, I could see the reddened area and lowered my hands to it. "Talk to her, tell her what I'm doing," I whispered as I placed my hands against her skin.

The area was warm to my touch, assuring me I was in the right spot. Leaning down I closed my eyes and concentrated on my touch taking the pain out of Maisy's body. Forcing my mind to forget about the people that were present, I leaned gently on my hands when I felt my palms heat. The buzz, that now was familiar to me, began traveling down into my palms. I didn't stop when Maisy moaned, I didn't stop when I heard someone gasp and move behind me. When the heat in my touch lessened I moved my hands over and started again in another area on her body.

When I finally reached her injured leg, even my spine was tingling—I knew I'd over-done it, but I wasn't stopping until I brought her a measure of relief and healing rest. My stomach churned and I knew I was at my limit. Lifting my numb hands away from her body I opened my eyes and looked up to see hers watching me—or her eyes were in my direction, a quiet understanding in them. Her mouth curved into one of her motherly smiles, and then sighing softly she closed her eyes and drifted off to sleep. My heart filled with pride to see her skin tone was better and her breathing was stress free.

Leaning back onto my heels, I took a few seconds to steady myself before trying to get up. I swayed as I got to my feet and quickly stepped back before I tipped over and landed on her. Strong hands gripped my shoulders when the room began to spin.

"She needs to rest." Kane scooped me up into his arms and moved quickly to the only other door in Maisy's home. When he closed the door I realized it was a bedroom. He stopped and shifted me long enough to light a single candle and then stood there and looked down at me.

Reaching up I pulled the dark glasses from his face and smiled up into his silver eyes. "Hey." A slow smile appeared on his face.

"Hey," he whispered with a hoarse voice. "Do you need a drink or anything?" I shook my head.

I found myself sitting on the bed, with him kneeling and pulling off my boots. I couldn't even lift a hand to help him. I should have tried to eat or drink, but I was quivering inside and out, and didn't want to take the chance of throwing up.

Pushing my jacket off my arms, he stopped and grasped my face between his large hands. Before I could ask what was wrong, his mouth covered mine in a crushing kiss that stole the breath from my body. With my head spinning I gave him a dreamy look when he finally lifted his warm lips from mine.

He sighed and rested his forehead against mine. "I've been worried about you." Lifting his head he finished taking my coat from my arms and pulled the blanket back. "Climb in, you look ready to drop."

Shuffling under the blankets, he started to pull them over me. I caught his arm to stop him. "Stay." He looked back towards the closed door. "No one is going to care."

Getting up off his knees, he peeled off his jacket and shirts and tossed them onto the floor, his boots followed quickly. The entire time he looked at me without speaking, his silver eyes caressed over my face and the lines around them relaxed. Leaning over he blew out the candle and climbed under the covers.

Shifting to make room for him in the small bed, I reached over and wrapped my arm around his bare waist. His big arm hugged me against him, his face rested in my hair. I could feel his heart crashing against his chest. "Are you alright?"

He snorted softly. "No. I have no idea how I'm going to lay here with you and behave myself." To demonstrate his words he reached down and pulled me on top of him. I could feel the bulge in his jeans and had to smile.

"I've missed you as well," I whispered with my lips brushing against his chest.

Hissing out a breath he gently grasped my hair and moved my face away from his skin, tilting it up towards his. "Don't touch me or move and I might be able to pull it off."

I was giddy knowing this, I wasn't sure if it was just the exhaustion or that chance to tease him, and I didn't care as I stretched up towards his face. I nipped at his chin. "I'm sure you have more control then I do."

His big hand covered the back of my head, as he rolled me onto my back. "You're wrong. Control is something I fight with every single day—and with you I seem to have to fight ten times harder." I could feel his breath brushing over my lips as he spoke. "You destroy me with a single touch."

I opened my mouth to tell him it was okay, that I understood, even though I didn't but his mouth crushed down on mine again and took all thought of speaking away. I drank in the emotion and reveled in the feelings he stirred inside me. I was out of breath and gasping before he lifted his head again. If I could see in the dark I know I'd be looking into coal black eyes that wanted to consume me.

"It's okay, Kane." Reaching up I rested my shaking palm against his cheek, I wasn't sure if it was from the healing or the emotions in his kiss swamping me.

I felt his chest expand and he let out a slow breath. "You're shaking." He lifted his head and looked down at me. Shifting again, he rolled onto his side and brought me up against his chest. One strong arm wrapped around my waist. "You need rest more than anything right now." He kissed the top of my head.

I wanted to ask about what he meant when he said I destroyed him, but my eyes didn't want to stay open. The warmth from his body and protection of his arm gave me a sense of peace and safety I didn't often feel lately. Resting my cheek against the rhythmic rise and fall of his chest I let myself drift off.

~

In the morning, the door opened slowly, I looked over the top of Kane to see Rosy's head sticking in. Kane tensed, telling me he was awake.

"Maisy's awake and asking for you both," she said softly before closing the door again.

With his hand caressing my back, he nuzzled into my hair. "Not the wake up I'd like, but we'd better get up."

My body protested as he dropped a light kiss on my mouth and rolled out of the bed. I stretched and watched him locate his shirt and pull it on to cover up his skin. I still hadn't moved when he sat down to put his boots on. With the warmth of his body missing, the cold air hit me. "It's colder out."

He finished tying his boots and then turned to study me. "You should stay here with Maisy for a while."

I could see the concern in his sleepy eyes, but just the thought of not going back to our secluded little cave hidden in the earth made my chest tighten. "I will today and see how she's doing." Wrestling the blankets off my legs I sat up.

He reached over and gently grabbed by chin in his big hand. "That's not what I meant."

"I know." I smirked at him. "If you were to stay—I might think about it."

He sighed loud and released my chin, standing up quickly. "I can't."

Scrambling up, I stood on the bed and looked down at him. "Hey." He turned and looked up at me. "I know." I wobbled from getting up so quickly and grabbed onto his shoulders to steady myself. "I'm not ready to be part of anything yet."

Big warm hands wrapped around my waist as he leaned closer and rubbed his face into my chest. I hugged his head. "I worry about you out there alone, Bree."

I could barely hear the words he spoke. "Then it gives you something to think about while you're out there doing your lone ranger thing…" His head snapped up, almost lifting me from the bed in the motion.

"Lone ranger?" His tone was serious, but his eyes held amusement in them.

I shrugged. "You got a better name for it?"

He grinned and shook his head. "I am so far from the lone ranger." Grasping my waist I was lifted free of the bed and held against his chest.

"Fine. Robin Hood—Tarzan, I could go on…" His mouth brushing over mine in the gentlest kiss cut off any words I was about to say—and any thought of saying anything. Wrapping my arms around his wide shoulders I held on and enjoyed the teasing movements of his lips.

When he lifted his head, he lowered me to the floor. "I'll go get you some tea and something to eat."

I watched the door close, and for about two seconds debated on staying for a while. As weird as it was I missed my little piece of the world. Sighing, I looked around for my boots so I could go out and see how Maisy was doing. Today I'd stay just to be sure, but I was going home tomorrow.

CHAPTER EIGHTEEN

I counted the marks once more. Twenty-One. Three weeks. It had been that long since I'd left Maisy's little village. I'd made everyone promise to come and get me if she'd taken a bad turn again, so I could only assume she was up and running things again.

Other than brief—very brief—trips outside to see how it was or go to the bathroom that wasn't really all the way outside, Kismet, Tremor and I had been holed up in the shelter for the last four days. It was bitterly cold with no relief from the constant wind. Scanning the wood pile, I knew I'd have to bring in a few tarps full of wood today, or we were going to be living with icicles soon. Tremor was restless and would spend hours standing in the narrow tunnel to the outside, breathing in the frigid fresh air. Even Kismet spent more time lying by the door looking out through the opening with longing in his eyes than he did anything else. I too wanted to go outside, move around—even to chop wood at this point. There wasn't a great deal one could do for this long in a space this size, alone. Neither animal thought much of watching me play solitaire—or my explaining the rules as I played and frankly the card game had lost the appeal it had to me after a few hundred games.

Our little home was clean though, as clean as dirt and

stone could be. I'd re-arranged things at least twice now trying out different arrangements, only to eventually put it all back the way we had it. Again the animals didn't seem too enthralled by the details of housekeeping.

I could have written an entire book if I'd had the paper to spare. It hadn't been easy to limit myself to just jotting down a few things here and there. Paper was on my trade list the next time we had the opportunity. Right now going to trade sounded like a great idea, not missing people and interaction, but I now understood what stir crazy felt like. I'd say cabin fever, but it didn't seem to fit.

Kismet whined at the door once more. Sighing I put the cards down and looked at him. I knew what he wanted and it was the same thing he'd requested about six other times so far this morning. "We can look, but I don't think it's going to be warm and balmy out there." My nostrils had almost frozen when we'd ventured out a whole ten feet earlier that morning. Getting up I began to pull on my extra layers, figuring I may as well get the wood while we were all wanting a numbing breath of air. The only real protection I had from the wind or wet was the coat Bobby had given me. If I added three to four sweaters underneath, it still wasn't too tight to move. Today was definitely a four sweater, four pairs of socks kind of day. The gloves Kane had found weren't exactly hot paws brand, so I'd been forced to wear my fingerless ones underneath and a thick pair of socks over top, just for extra warmth. After the under layers were all put together I'd jam my hat down to my jaw and wrap the long scarf—the only newish item I had—around my mouth, head and face imitating a woolen turban with chin strap. I probably looked like an ad for a second hand clothing store when I was done, but as long as nothing went numb, turned blue or fell off I really didn't care. I grabbed the tarp and shuffled my over-wrapped body towards the door.

Opening it, I ushered the animals out and quickly closed it behind us. The heat inside only stayed if I kept it as draft free as possible, which I accomplished by tying bundles of dried grass to the inside and sacrificing one of the blankets to cover over that. It wasn't perfect but so far it had kept the icy wind from moving in.

When I moved the outer tarp out of the way it crinkled like it was made of paper. I somehow doubted it was going to make it through the entire winter, but hoped it lasted for the worst of things to come. The first blast of arctic wind that smashed against my face had my eyes watering. So much for Kismet's animal instinct, if anything I think it was colder out now than it had been. This was going to be some fun, trying to get the wood without suffering from hypothermia.

Patting Tremor's neck, I left him to decide if he was venturing out and stepped by him into the frosty air. Without stopping to admire the scenery I moved in a straight path to the wood pile. If I didn't freeze to death I knew two tarps of the rough cut wood was enough to keep up warm for three days and decided stir crazy or not I'd rather chance insanity than have to come back out in this weather for the next few days.

Our fish store was getting low and we hadn't had any fresh kills in almost a week. It was as if the animals had been warned what was coming and nothing was out moving any time we'd ventured far enough to see. Part of me hoped nothing had been caught in the snare and left to suffer and freeze to death. Then there was the small part of me that figured if anything had, we had some fresh frozen meat waiting for us. I'd make an attempt to get to it tomorrow.

Kismet began digging in the snow surrounding the wood pile; apparently he didn't want to be out here any longer than to get what we needed either. I couldn't speak to him, it was enough to keep my head down and breathe into my scarf without the wind stealing my air. Holding the tarp, I laid it out on the ground— fighting with the wind with each movement until I could get one foot to hold it down and get some wood onto it.

It felt like it took an hour to fill it, dragging it back had me walking right into the wind and each step was a fight. My throat hurt and eyes were so painful I kept them closed more than open and prayed I was going in the right direction. When the blue tarp hanging over the opening appeared a foot in front of my face, I wanted to run through it and forget the wood entirely. Struggling to open the one tarp and drag the other one inside at the same time proved to be the last challenge I was up to today as tears threatened to freeze in my eyes.

Ushering Tremor back into the shelter, I dragged the wood in and pulled the door closed just as Kismet's tail cleared it. Falling back against the door, I reached up with numb arms and pulled the scarf free from my face. The air was warmer and welcoming as I stood there panting, trying to catch my breath. Taking the socks off my hands I looked down at how much wood I'd managed to get. At most it would last a day and a half and frankly it was going to have to do. I was *not* going back out there today.

Kismet went over and dropped down beside the fire pit. I raised my iced over eyebrows at him. "Seemed like a good idea at the time huh?"

~

Thawing out took longer than freezing did, why was that? I didn't know, but I sat beside the fire looking at the wood still sitting on the tarp. Sighing, I got up. It wasn't going the thaw out sitting over by the door covered in snow. I began moving it where I'd discovered worked best. If I piled in it in a small row a few feet from the fire, and also blocking the breeze from the doorway, it worked great. This was just one more thing I'd found out by mistake when I had brought in too much wood a few weeks ago and ran out of space to pile it. It wasn't like I needed the entire area to be open; I wouldn't be hosting any parties any time soon.

Kismet jumped up and bolted over in front of the door. I stopped all movement, including breathing and watched him. He hunkered down in front of the blanket covered door, ears forward, listening. Careful to keep my body facing the door I moved over to the bed and got my gun and knife.

Had someone found our little hidden spot? Who would be out in this insane weather?

Those and about ten other thoughts went through my mind as I nudged Tremor to the back of the corner, not wanting him to get in between whatever was outside and me. Inching closer I stood behind Kismet and looked down at him. He turned, sensing I was there and looked up at me. Without prodding he moved over and inched closer to the door.

I tried to listen and hear what had gotten his attention, but all I could make out was the wind whistling.

The door shook like someone was trying to get in. I cursed silently at myself for not putting the braces back up against it. Kismet crouched down and growled so softly, standing right beside him I could barely hear him. The door moved a few inches, whoever was out there was figuring out how it opened.

Bracing myself, I tucked the knife into my front pocket for quick access and raised the gun towards the door. My brother had made me practice for hours at holding it steady so I knew I could stand in this position for as long as it took without fatigue getting me.

Cold air hit me as the door began to open. I could have leaned into it and stopped the opening, but that wouldn't have gotten rid of whoever was out there pushing on it—and I didn't exactly have any heft to my weight so it would have been a wasted attempt. My gun was the best bet I had at deterring our intruder.

When the door opened wide enough a large figure stepped in. I couldn't make out a face in the clothes, so I wasn't sure if they had one of those tattoos or not. "That's far enough." Kismet backed me up with another growl.

The intruder raised both hands slowly and made no move to do anymore than that for several seconds. In slow motion they moved one hand towards their face and pulled at the wrap covering it. Skin almost raw from the wind was slowly revealed, as if it hurt them to uncover it. It only took one silver eye to be revealed before I lowered the gun and rushed forward to pull Kane inside and shut the door letting all my heat out.

"Kane. What are you doing out in this crap weather?" I shoved until the door was completely closed and then turned to look at him. He just stood there looking at me. He looked half frozen. Pulling the scarf down off of his mouth, I grimaced at how chafed his lips were.

"I was worried about you," his voice sounded worse than he looked.

Tucking the gun into my jeans, I moved over to him and started to work the ice covered scarf off. With it finally removed I tossed it on top of the wood I'd just piled and began working the jacket open. The zipper was frozen closed. "You're going to have to thaw out a bit before this opens." Stopping I looked up at him, he was still standing there looking at me. "Are you okay?"

Amusement filled his eyes. "I'm fine now." He huffed out a breath, "a little numb in places," he mumbled.

Pulling on his sleeve, I guided him over closer to the fire. "Aside from freezing, you came close to getting shot by going for a winter stroll…" I tugged on one of his gloves until it finally came off his hand. His fingers were red as well. "You're insane," I more or less whispered.

His large cold hand cupped my chin, tilting my face back up towards his. "I had to make sure you were still here."

"Where on earth would I go in this weather?" His eyes were swirling, with that mix of black and silver letting me know that emotions were strong inside him right now. "Tell me." Taking his icy hand I held it between my own and tried to warm it up for a few moments before I began working at the zipper again.

"I was holed up in a less than savory spot waiting for this freeze to run its course—going stir crazy—and I overheard a conversation…"

When he stopped I looked up at him, a pained look had entered his eyes as he stood there touching my hair softly.

"Kane?"

He dropped his hand and continued. "There were four or five Red Bands waiting out the weather as well. They were mostly keeping to themselves, but after a few drinks their tongues forgot they weren't alone. They were talking about the latest slaves they'd rounded up—how the tiny redhead had given them all a run for their money and cut up one of them pretty bad…"

He reached out and grabbed me so fast I almost tripped over my own feet as he crushed me into his frigid coat.

"I thought they got you," he finished quickly with a shaky voice.

I didn't know what to say. The very thought of it made my stomach tighten. "How long have you been out in this?" I pushed away from him so I could see his face again.

"Two days," he stated very quietly.

Two days in the wind I couldn't do for more than a few minutes. "You are insane." Moving out of his arms, I began tugging on the zipper again. "You'll be lucky if you don't lose a few body parts from this." The coat finally opened. Reaching down I tugged off his other glove and then began pulling on the sleeve to get him out of it.

"My body temperature is higher than normal." When his arm was freed from the sleeve, he reached out again and touched my hair. "It's longer."

Moving around him, I pulled his backpack off and then the stiff material from his body. "I didn't cut it—thought I could use the extra hair for warmth."

"I wondered if you colored it somehow—it's really this color."

Tossing his coat onto the wood, I set his backpack down and turned back to grin at him. "Yep, it's always been this odd shade."

"I like it."

This was not the Kane I was used to. "Are you okay? Did you eat or drink anything in the last few days?"

He shook his head. "I didn't stop, couldn't, it would

have been too hard to get going again." He gripped his own hands, trying to get the circulation going again. "As long as I kept moving fast I created enough body heat to not freeze."

"Go over and sit down, there's enough heat by the bed to warm you back up fast enough." He moved with slow awkward steps over to my pile of bedding.

When he got down onto the furs, I squatted down and began to work the frozen laces loose. "What do you want first? Food or drink?"

He leaned back onto his elbows and looked down his body at me. "Some of your dehydrated soup broth would be great. I don't think I could chew anything just yet."

Glancing away from the stiff lace I was wrestling with I looked up at him. His eyes were once again silver, but he was still giving me the oddest look. "If you keep looking at me like that I'm going to develop a complex."

"I just spent the last few days thinking you were at the mercy of some lunatics—you'll have to forgive me if I just want to look at you now that I know you're safe and warm."

When he put it that way I felt like a twit, so I smiled and looked back at what I was trying to do. Kismet crept up onto the furs and shuffled over to Kane, lying across his chest. Kane looked into the wolf's eyes and then gave me an amused look before he dropped back and ruffled the animals' fur.

~

After he'd gotten some liquid into him and warmed up a bit, I finally voiced my thoughts. "So, if I hadn't been here when you'd arrived—what were you planning on doing?"

Kane looked from the fire he'd been watching for several minutes to me. "I would have run back to those Red Bands and beat your location out of them."

His voice was hard and deadly causing a shiver to go down my spine. "Oh." Not the most brilliant response, but aside from believing he would have done just that I didn't know what else to say. I played with the invisible lint on my pant leg. "Have you been to see Maisy?" What I really wanted to ask was why he'd been gone without a word the morning I was leaving to come back here.

"She's doing fine."

This was the Kane I knew, the one that didn't say very much unless you prompted each word. "I missed saying good bye to you the morning I left..." I squeaked in a complete girly way when I found myself pulled from where I sat a few feet from him to beside him. As his mouth crushed mine in a hard breathless kiss, his arms wrapped around me in a vise-like grip holding me against his body.

When he lifted his mouth from mine, he buried his face in my neck and held me. Wrapping my arms around his neck I lie there holding him against me.

"I had to leave," his voice was a whisper beneath my ear. "I woke in the middle of the night ..." his lips brushed against my throat. "You were so soft in my arms, so tempting lying there against me." His hands molded my body to his. "My emotions spiked—which is not a good thing—I had to get out of there before anyone got hurt."

I waited as his mouth brushed lightly against my entire throat, wondering if he was going to continue. Each movement of his lips on my skin caused the heat to start traveling through my veins. "You could have got me up," I whispered against his mouth when it finally brushed over mine.

He opened his swirling eyes and studied mine. "No." He kissed me in a way that made me feel the emotions going through him. "It came up fast, usually I get warning but I didn't have enough time—or control."

"Maybe I could have helped..."

He hissed out a frustrated breath. "I won't take the chance, Bree."

I didn't know what exactly he was talking about, but it shook him to speak about it, so I decided not to push further.

His mouth was wandering down my throat again.

"I think if you took off some more clothes you'd warm up faster."

Lifting his head, he looked down at me with amusement in his multi-colored eyes. "I definitely need to be warmer." He glanced over at the animals on the other side of the shelter. "I don't suppose you'd agree to send them out for some fresh air."

Peeking out from under his huge mass covering me I looked over at Kismet who slept curled up in a ball and Tremor who seemed to be off in his own space. "I think they're fine where they are." I smirked up at him. "They won't give us funny looks in the morning either."

He grinned. "Yeah I caught those too from Rosy and everyone else." Leaning to the side he began to pull my shirts up, his cool palms running over the skin as he exposed it. "It was very unnerving considering we behaved completely."

"But we're not this time," I prompted.

"Not this time." Raising up to his knees, he grasped the bottom of my shirt and pulled it up over my body.

I watched him as his eyes moved over me. Reaching down I undid my jeans and noticed he followed every move I made. When they slipped over my hips, he grabbed the legs and slid them the rest of the way. His eyes were getting darker the longer he looked at me, just the way he looked at me made me wet and more than ready for him. With fast jerky movements he removed his own shirts and tossed them to the side. As he worked his jeans off, I slid under the covers and memorized each muscle of his chest and abdomen.

When he was as naked as I was, he flipped the cover back and began to slowly crawl up my body. Leaning down he gently nipped the sensitive skin of my stomach with his teeth, I inhaled deeply. When he raised his eyes to mine, they were black. My blood boiled seeing the possessiveness in his eyes. With slow movements he nibbled his way up to my breasts.

I almost jumped off the blankets when his mouth latched onto my hard nipple. Hissing out a breath I grasped his head in my hands and held him there. His rough hand slid up over my hip to my other breast. I moaned softly, my hands running down over his shoulders and seeking out any skin of his I could reach.

Lifting his head he moved his mouth up my throat. "You are so responsive to my every touch— it almost undoes me."

Lifting my body as much I could, I slid my bare flesh against his. "I don't want it to almost undo you—I want you undone." Hooking one leg around his waist I pulled him back down with me as my teeth were busy leaving a trail of little bites down his neck and chest.

He growled and flipped me onto my side, pulling me until my back was against his chest. One big hand held squeezed my hip tightly as his other one moved up to cup my cheek and turn my face towards his. His mouth brushed over mine lightly, "It has to be like this so I don't hurt you," he voice was rough.

I tried to speak, but his mouth covered mine again in a desperate kiss. The way his mouth demanded complete submission made me quiver inside.

When he lifted his head, his black eyes searched mine. "Are you okay with this?"

I felt my cheeks flush. I had no knowledge of what *this* was going to be. "I won't know until you show me."

He moaned and buried his face between my jaw and shoulder. "I still can't believe I'm the only man to ever touch you, Breenna."

Not knowing if he was looking for reassurance or if I should just stay silent, I pushed back into the hardness of his body. "Show me," I whispered.

CHAPTER NINETEEN

A few days later the cold finally broke, the wind had died down to a tolerable strength. Kane had stayed until the middle of the next day and then once again he had to go. I could probably fill what was left of my notebook with questions I wanted to ask him. Why did he *have* to go? Where did he go to?

Shaking myself out of that space—again—I got up and started to get motivated. I didn't know how long the break in the weather was going to last, I needed to go get food when the weather was good. Fish, bunnies, birds—anything at this point to stock up again in case the unbearable cold returned. Yesterday I'd gone and found the snare buried in iced over snow and reset it. Checking it was my first stop today.

Kismet ran back and forth in front of me as I tucked the cord into my pack and put it on. I shook my head at him. "I need you to stay here, boy. The snow is too deep to take Tremor and I'm not leaving him alone when he can't outrun anything that comes along." He stopped in front of me and sat down. I could almost see him analyzing my words putting together what I was telling him. His amber eyes pleaded briefly with me, then he took off to sit on top of the snow mound that covered out home, maintain his dignity in silence. Nodding to him, I turned and started towards the snare. My agenda was to check that, circle around to the river and see if any fish were catchable and then head into the thick treed area and hopefully scout out a few birds.

The snare was empty, the fish were nowhere to be found so I tucked my pack into a snow bank I'd be able to find again and headed into the trees with my throwing knives and gun. There had to be something out here moving and I was determined to stay out here until I found it.

With shaking hands I buried the rabbit in the snow beside my pack. My first non-feathered kill. I'd learned two things, first rabbit were damn sight harder to aim for with a knife than birds and second, I had been right when I'd thought it would hurt me to kill something fluffy. If my stomach hadn't reminded me of hunger, there was a good chance I would have placed it deep in the snow and left it there. Cleaning it was going to be a whole new trauma for me. Leif had shown me how, that part I knew—it was the actual doing it that was going to be a struggle.

Brushing the snow off my jeans, I headed back into the trees hoping a bit further in I would find some birds. The trees were thick for quite a distance, but I knew they thinned out into an opening fifteen or twenty minutes from where I'd left my pack. Not being a bird I really couldn't figure out where they'd be but I was hoping

As the trees started to thin out, I wished for my snowshoes. The snow just seemed to be getting deeper and deeper. If I continued much further I'd be waist deep in it and then the numbness would start and I'd lose all ambition to locate dinner.

The sound of wings flapping had my undivided attention; I stopped and held my breath trying to locate the direction it was coming from. The moment I honed in on the area the bird had been I wished I hadn't. Here I was half way to the middle of the clearing in snow up past my knees and coming out of the trees roughly thirty feet from me were two very rough, huge men. I had twenty seconds grace before they spotted me, just enough time to turn in the snow and take the first step in what would likely end up being the most difficult run of my life.

Running in snow this deep was like running through water. If your feet didn't clear it you got nowhere. I hadn't stopped long enough to measure the height of the men quickly gaining on me, but I was fairly certain their long legs would move through this snow faster than my own.

As I hit the tree line again, I hesitated long enough to pick a direction. Kismet and I had been through this area enough times I knew most of it without thinking now. Slipping in the snow I changed directions and headed towards the hill that led to the river bed. If I could out-maneuver them in the densest part of the trees I might just be able to put a big enough gap between us that they'd give up.

Chancing a glance over my shoulder I noted one thing. They were large enough it would take four of me to make this anywhere near equal. My heart was thrumming, pumping blood through my veins in a chaotic beat. A part of me knew I couldn't outrun them, but I had to try. Turning, I bolted back towards a tight grouping of trees. I could hear the pounding of their feet hitting the ground behind me and had one second to regret the one time I didn't let Kismet come with me. He would have evened the odds.

One of them was close enough I could hear his heavy breathing over my own as I dodged between two trees I knew he wouldn't be able to go through. My coat was actually slowing me down, but it held the knife and gun and there was no way I was dropping either of those right now. I heard him curse behind me and knew I only had seconds before he would have me. Ducking left, I stopped and spun around at the same time. My knife was now in my hand held down against my side as I gasped to settle my breathing. He stood a foot away from me and looked really pissed with the fact that I had made him run after me.

I wanted to look around for the other one, but didn't dare take my eyes off of him. A familiar flick sound brought my attention to his hand to see a blade slide smoothly from the handle it had been folded into. There was nothing I could say that was going to change this man's plans. His eyes were wide and bored into mine with a look of craziness. A branch snapping behind me was the only warning I got before a big arm wrapped around my waist and pulled me back into a hard chest.

They spoke to each other and it wasn't in any language I understood, then again I only knew English. The tone the man in front of me used and the sudden smirk on his face told me I was in deep shit. There was no way, no how this was happening to me. I refused to be a victim. The one behind me tightened his hold, making breathing hard. He rubbed his face against my neck making my skin crawl. The other one waved the knife in front of me a few times and then used it to push open my coat. He grinned and said something to the one that was breathing on my neck.

The adrenaline was pumping so fast through my body I didn't know how I was able to not vibrate. *Now or never!* Lowering my head, I relaxed my body as much as I could. Taking a deep breath, I threw my head back and brought my hand with the knife up at the same time, aiming for the arm around me. The loud crack and sudden pain in my head told me I'd connected hard with the face behind me. He cursed and let me go just as the other one lunged towards me. I felt the sting across my cheek as I brought the knife down and across his chest. He yelped.

A low hair-raising growl came from the trees, a sound I knew like my own voice. I backed towards it, keeping the men in my sight until I felt fur brush against my hand. Shaking my head I tried to clear it, I'd connected a little harder with that face then I'd intended. Kismet growled and snapped at the men and their eyes bulged from their faces. The one tossed his knife to the ground. He stood there holding the slash across his chest. Briefly I enjoyed the knowledge of knowing I scored a blow on him. I took two steps back and glanced out of the corner of my eye at the dog. "Come on boy," I whispered.

Kismet snarled and growled at them again and then circled me only to face them again. I started walking backwards in the opposite direction of our hideout, not wanting to lead them there. One of them dropped to the ground to lean against a tree and the other one was wrapping his arm. Turning I began to run as fast as I could, knowing Kismet would be right on my heels. I didn't stop until I knew we were safe. Then I dropped down on my knees and hugged the panting animal to my chest. "Good boy."

When I realized how close I'd just come to being raped or worse, the tears started rolling down my face. With them was a sharp sting, then I remembered the knife grazing my cheek. I touched it gently, it didn't feel too severe, but either way I needed to get back to the camp and get it cleaned up. Kismet licked my face and gave me a concerned look. "I'm good. Let's get back to Tremor." Getting up I headed down through the gully that would allow us to bypass the men and head back to the camp. After all of this I wasn't leaving my kill in the snow to go to waste. Getting back to it and then home would take twice as long from our present location, but it had to be done. It would be dark by the time we reached it. As long as we arrived in one piece that was fine by me.

~

I was still in a state of shock from the whole scene as I cleaned the rabbit for dinner. Being distraught and emotionally exhausted served me well—I cleaned the rabbit without feelings of guilt. Kismet hadn't stood down from his guard post by the door the whole time I prepared dinner. I'll never know how he knew I needed him, but he would be rewarded for not listening to me. Even Tremor was agitated when we'd gotten back. Although, if I'd been left standing in the snow, alone in the dark and unable to get back inside I probably would have been the same.

Our stomachs were full, the door was braced for the night and the animals were ready for rest. That was when it hit me. What had almost happened. No one would have known either, I'd just stop existing and that would be the end. A shiver went through me, kind of a mix of anxiety and fear. I lightly touched the inflamed mark across my cheek bone.   As if it cued something from deep inside me, the tears began to fall.

In all the months I'd been out here, I'd never stopped and let every trauma catch up to me. Sure I'd had long moments of lying in the dark thinking, anticipating and even planning but the emotions I'd buried inside, always putting off came flowing to the surface. Kismet inched up on the bed to offer some comfort.

I didn't want comfort this time. I wanted it all to go away. The constant paranoia and fear that surrounded everything I did from the time I woke until I slept—probably even while I slept. I wanted serenity back. Of course as I lie there with the tears flowing down my face I knew it was never going to happen. Serenity and safety hadn't been a part of this world in more than five years and deep down there was the realization that it would never be again. Did this stop the shaking and weeping? Did it lessen the weight of the burden I could feel coming from my very soul?

No.

I had to let it out so I could move beyond it again. At this moment though, it didn't feel like that would be possible. I'd survived alone and frightened this long —a small part of my brain knew this but I couldn't find the way to make it go away. Tremor hovered over the bed and leaned down to push his nose into my hair. I stroked a shaking hand across his jaw, hoping it would assure him I was going to be fine.

I was.

I had to be.

Shoving the covers back, I crawled out of the bed and got up. The tears blurred my vision so I stood staring at the fire taking deep breaths trying to calm down before I moved around anymore. The last thing I needed was to twist an ankle or fall into the fire pit.

As I stood there I remembered the people I'd met in the time I'd been on my own, so many with the same thing on their mind as I did—survival. That's what every person and creature alike on this planet had in common. We all wanted to survive.

I pictured Micah, out there completely alone living in his bomb shelter in the middle of nothing, always on the look out— Vince and Jacob living in a U-haul trailer, fearing daylight more than anything else—the children from the wagon train as well as Maisy's village, always having to look over their shoulders. I also thought of Kane. He called nowhere home and was driven to constantly be on the move, never settling long enough to be at ease.

Taking a ragged breath, I exhaled slow releasing all the piteous emotions with it. I had more than most did out here—I was one of the few, the lucky, that wandered the new country and I knew it. At least I understood that now. At this very moment I didn't know if I would ever reach the mountains—if I would even last through the next season. All I did know was I wouldn't stop trying until there was no other choice. My mind could create a lengthy list of the reasons why I couldn't make it, but logic was starting to return and I wasn't going to give doubt the opportunity to make me falter.

I tossed another log into the fire pit and turned back to get into the bed. In the morning I'd start coming up with a method to move everything inside this space so when the thaw came we'd be ready to move on again.

I wasn't quitting.

~

Never put off what you need to do no matter what gets in the way. This is what played through my mind like a recording the next day as I fought the cold and ice trying to bring wood inside. I knew the day before we would be out but I was too busy enjoying the warmer day to be bothered by doing it right then. Now as each breath bit into my throat and my hands no longer had feeling I was thinking hindsight was a nasty thing.

It took most of the morning to bring in enough wood to

get us through the next few days. I had to stop after each trip and thaw out completely before heading back out again. By the time I was finished I had didn't even have enough strength to pile it completely so I settled for dumping it near enough to the fire pit it would dry.

With just about every piece of clothing I had dripping as the ice melted from it, I sat on the bed wearing every blanket and fur that we had. I was still cold. Kismet under normal circumstances would have curled near me to help warm me, but this time he wasn't leaving the warmth of the fire. Tremor wasn't in a cuddling mood either as he stood as far from the door that his large self could go.

Despite the packing and blanket over the door, cold air still filtered through making the cozy space we were used to damp and more cave like than usual. Gone were any ideas I'd had of taking stock of all of the things we needed to haul out of here in the spring. The very thought of spring was nothing more than a fantasy at this moment with the sound of ice beating against the earth outside.

I'd never seen weather like this and my nerves were buzzing with the morbid possibilities that came to mind. What was going on out there was more than a snow storm, exactly what, I wasn't sure. I hadn't been able to see anything except white when I did manage to open my eyes long enough to look. My face still felt the sting from the pellets hitting my skin.

A clump of frozen snow fell down the chimney tube causing the fire to sizzle and part of it to go out. I hadn't thought to check the tube to make sure it was clear and half a fire or not I wasn't going to do it wrapped in blankets. As soon as I could feel my feet again I'd have to go and see what I could do about it, but for the time being I wasn't moving from the bed.

~

My lungs burned as I woke up coughing. Rolling over I opened dry eyes to look around. The entire area was filling up with smoke. Wrestling with the blankets I jumped up out of the bed, pausing long enough to wrap one blanket around me like a towel so I wasn't darting around the shelter naked.

More ice and snow had fallen into the fire. I could feel the draft coming down the tube so I knew it wasn't blocked. With a log I shoved the smoking coals around until they were out of the wet area. My only problem was getting the fire going again away from the wet wood while trying to inhale smoke instead of oxygen into my lungs.

By the time I had flames again my eyes were burning and tears running down my face. I crawled over to the bed again and pulled more of the blankets around me. With blurred sight I looked over at the animals as they stood close to the door-way. Getting up, I shuffled inside the blankets to go over and check on them. Tremor shivered under my touch letting me know he was less than impressed with being trapped inside with the smoke. I couldn't blame him, but what was outside was worse.

Kismet wasn't in the mood for reassurances as he briefly allowed me to touch him and then moved away from my hand to lie down by the edge of the door. Stating loudly enough he'd rather have a cold back than be near the smoking fire.

I could still hear the wind whipping the sleet around outside but I didn't have a choice, I had to crack the door to clear out the lingering smoke. We'd have to live with it, breathing was as important as heat was at this point.

Shivering, I propped the braces back against the door and sealed it as best as I could. We could breathe again, but the heat was gone.

Tossing a few more logs onto the flames, I grabbed the pail of melted snow from beside the fire; I stumbled back over to the bed and climbed in once more. With chilled fingers I filled a cup with water and drank it to put out the fire in my throat. Lying back again I watched the fire, almost afraid to close my eyes and wake to the same.

I didn't wake up again until the fire was burned down to few coals. Not knowing how long I'd been asleep, I sat up slowly and tried to figure out what time of day or night it was. With the door sealed like it was there wasn't enough light coming through to determine. I felt nauseous and achy, wanting nothing more than to curl back up and go to sleep, but I'd wake up a popsicle if I didn't build the fire back up again. With as hoarse chuckle I got up, thinking of the time when all I needed to do when I felt a chill was turn up a thermostat.

While I was up I got dressed in cold, but dry clothes. Every muscle in my body complained with each movement. Maybe it was the cold or from being out in the cold—the only thing I really wanted to do was get back in the bed and wake up somewhere near spring. If it wasn't for the two animals stalking me with their eyes I may have done just that. They wanted outside and until I opened the door and granted them leave, they would haunt me with stares. Dragging myself to the door I pressed my ear against it to see if I could gauge what the weather was doing outside. I couldn't hear the ice beating against the tarp outside, so with hope that the wind had died down enough that all the heat wasn't going to be erased I moved the props and pulled the door open a few inches. It was cold, but it didn't blast me like it had the last time it had been opened.

Kismet pushed past my legs and nosed his way through the door, Tremor wasn't far behind. I knew I needed to go out and at least check out the tubing near the chimney, convincing my body I needed to was going to be a harder task. Grumbling the entire time I bundled up and finally went out behind them.

The entire outdoors was glistening with a polished sheet of ice, if I didn't know how it had felt beating off my skin I would have said it was beautiful to see. Each tree and branch was frozen in time with the thick glass covering. Walking proved difficult as I slipped three steps sideways to each one I tried to take. Kismet was trying to move faster than the ground would allow and his claws scratched along the glazed surface of the snow. Tremor was heavy enough it didn't seem to hinder him much, although he sniffed a few icy spots and looked completely indifferent to the pretty scene laid out before him.

Giving up, I just stood and breathed in the cool air. It wasn't warm, but it was several degrees less freezing then the last time I'd been outside. Glancing around I zeroed in on the wood pile, the one covered in inches of ice—I'd be lucky if the axe would chip through it, it was that thick. Mentally I took stock of the pile still left inside and prayed it was enough to last until the ice began to melt. Kismet moved to run toward me and ended up sliding to a stop and bumping off my leg. With a defeated look, he lay down at my feet.

Having surveyed enough of the view, Tremor turned around and headed back into the shelter. I was with him, as pretty as it all seemed it was still winter and until the sun melted the landscape around us there was nothing to do out here right now.

CHAPTER TWENTY

The marks that represented days increased by many rows inside my little journal. Winter was still with us and showed no signs of receding. Either I was just getting accustomed to it or better at dealing, but I managed to fill each day with something to keep me busy. Our wood pile was getting closer and closer to the ground and that worried me more than the sparse food supply. We'd been snowed in three more times that had lasted two or more days each time. I didn't panic with each storm now, just buckled down the door and held out for it to break.

To kill time, I honed my pelt drying skills and came to the conclusion that much more practice was needed before I could even refer to it as a skill. Ice fishing, was not a task that I faced with enthusiasm—the tediousness was more than I could bear to face the few times I'd tried it. We weren't starving as I'd finally managed to work the snare so it fulfilled its purpose. I wasn't proud of the fact, but killing our dinner had become something I just did without thinking anymore.

The only real worry I had after so long confined by the endless season was Tremor's grain and grass was nearing the end. I'd kept back enough grain to try my hand at growing it in the spring—not that I had a clue if it would but I could try. The dried grass now took up very little space in our home. If a break in the weather didn't happen soon, I'd be digging in snow banks to see if I could find something he would eat.

If the weather remained constant, as in no ice pellets or wild snow, we were going to try trekking back through the thick trees and see if we could find an area where the snow hadn't obliterated all things living in hopes of finding some remnants of overgrowth for Tremor to tide him over a bit longer. I knew the chances were close to nil and even less likely was he'd actually eat anything we found. The last resort would be to go see Maisy's people and hope they had some to spare for trade, or find another village that traded. I had my fingers crossed on Maisy as the idea of traveling into somewhere unknown in such an unpredictable season didn't sit high on my safe-things-to-do list.

By last count, a month and a half had passed and there had been no contact with anyone. It was lonely having only creatures to talk to, that only answered me with silent looks and animal sighs. More than once a day I wondered about Kane, and knew I should stop, but did it anyway. I couldn't keep hoping that he'd walk in tomorrow or the next day—for all I knew he had got caught in the storms and wouldn't be coming back. It was a hard fact to swallow but I continued to struggle with it each day. Someday it would sink in and I'd feel something more peaceful about it.

During the long solitary moments I had sorted through everything I could call a possession, setting aside anything we could live without and that would be useful or valuable to someone else. Other than food for Tremor, there wasn't much else we needed at this point, and he was worth it all if someone had food to spare for him.

My collection for trade wasn't anything spectacular—I still had a lot of the flint stones and hoped it would have value as all the rocks were frozen under a few feet of snow and ice right now. I'd perfected drying out mushrooms, after deciding a person could only eat so many of them before the excitement of having them wore off. I had three furs that I wouldn't need soon, assuming that my pelt drying skills were perfected by the next winter season. Many of the clothes Kane had brought from his find were not things I required and others would have use for them. After coming to the realization I wouldn't be entertaining in the near or distant future, I went through the pans and dishes in my possession and cut it back to the bare minimum. As odd as it seemed I had a whole bag of dried bark and cattails, which I'd found were useful as stuffing, and for lighting fires but also for added warmth if you stuffed it in your boots on cold days. With these and a few other things to barter, I should be able to get enough food for my horse until new growth began in the spring—assuming that spring wasn't too long off.

~

Our trek to find surviving growth in the thick of the trees was a slow and tedious one the next day. The snow was deeper in more areas than not. I was soaked almost to my hips and the thought of going back to the fire was becoming more and more appealing. It was cold, but not too cold to breathe so that was a plus, yet I was huffing despite the temperature. Sitting idle inside the shelter had left me more out of shape than was good for me. Tremor didn't seemed deterred by the long walk, as he'd been left behind for so long he was probably just happy to be included again. Once we were through most of the deep snow I finally got on to ride, hoping the warmth from the animal beneath me would at least dry out the parts of my clothes that rested against him. After climbing up and feeling how much his body had thinned beneath his thick winter coat, I was more determined than ever to find some means of food for him. Losing Tremor to starvation was not an option.

Watching Tremor nose through the dried grass, only eating the bits that I'd attempted to disguise the frozen in, I came to the decision that in the morning we would pack up our barter items and head to Maisy's. They had to know where I could go to trade if they didn't have ample supplies to trade with—with everything I'd seen during my stays I knew someone had to travel and bring back most of their possessions. After all people didn't move through this country carrying things like their favorite cast iron wood-stove on their back as they relocated. So now we were going to begin our wander in their direction.

I used the tarp to wrap and secure everything we were taking with us and crossed my fingers that on our return trip it would be filled with food for my animal and maybe a new pair of gloves for me.

Dragging the last branch into the entrance, I positioned it along with the others and then stood back to appraise my work. The door wasn't visible now; our little home would be safe. With Tremor I rigged the rope to his saddle and attached it to the tarp and hoped we'd no run into ground he couldn't pull it across. A few times while getting packed I felt twinges of guilt for making him pull things, but it would take days and many rest stops if I tried to drag it myself. He may have lost weight, but he still had twenty times the strength I did.

Kismet knew we were going on one of our little excursions and he was anxiously prancing around checking in every direction.

I strapped on my own harness made from the small hides that I'd managed not to ruin and secured my knives and gun in it. If I had to ever outrun someone again, dropping my coat so it wouldn't slow me down wasn't going to be an issue.

With one last look around our area we headed towards the trees that led in the direction of Maisy's village.

It was only a few hours into our trip when all three of us were ready to admit that the lounging inside for the last few months had left all of us a little less than fit. Twice Tremor had stopped completely and just stood there looking around, Kismet and I were more than willing at those times to stand and rest as well. Maybe not having excess food was a good thing, otherwise we'd be fat and out of shape—not a good combination in our new world.

Either I was more paranoid than when we'd traveled in

the fall, or I'd learned my lesson of what happens when you relax too much because one hand didn't stray from the my weapon harness the entire time we walked. I designed it so I could easily reach the gun, big knife or my throwing knives without moving my wrist one way or the other more than and a few inches. I was not going to be caught off guard again.

As we reached the point where we'd have to leave the shelter of the trees for quite some distance, Kismet stopped and began sniffing the air and looking around. The hair on the back of my neck stood up. Going over to him I squatted down beside him to see if I could get a direction it was then I saw the prints in the snow. Someone had come this way not too long before us. Standing back up I followed the path of footprints with my eyes only, the butt of the gun grasped in my hand. They'd come from a different direction, but unless they were walking backwards they were heading the same way we were. Three, maybe four different set of prints wandered through the snow. Judging by the size of them, they weren't kids or small people—and they too were dragging something along with them. I wanted to assure my nerves that it was probably just a few folks taking advantage of the calmer weather and heading off to trade as we were, but my mind kept wandering—no, jolting back to the Red Bands. An encounter with them I did not need.

Tremor moved slowly up behind me, I could feel his breath on my hair as I stood there looking in the direction the tracks went trying to decide if we followed—at a distance, or attempted another route. Logic or possibly paranoia told me to take the other route yet my guts were saying to stay behind them and keep track of where they were going and if they stayed together. For several minutes I tried to recall the trail and remember if there were any large areas that were in the open, I wasn't one hundred percent sure but I didn't recall any.

Trying not to hold my breath, I began to lead following the same path at their footprints. Kismet didn't need any encouragement and quickly moved by me to scout as we went. Looking over my shoulder I saw that Tremor stood where he had been. Checking ahead of us again, I stopped and stared at him. I could almost see the indecision in his eyes and he looked around us and then began taking slow steps toward me.

I waited until he was almost beside me before I began walking once more. I felt better having him near me. Worst case scenario, I could cut the ropes dragging the tarp and get on him without so much as pausing. He increased his step and butted me with his nose in the back as a reprimand for putting him through the stress of this situation. I grinned around at him but kept moving. I could never say he was without personality—at times I swear he must have been a snobby butler in a past life, because he certainly had the attitude of one.

~

I had one of those moments a short time later, where I hated being right. Two of the sets of prints veered off in another direction and the rest stayed on the path we were taking. Now I had to worry about where those tracks were headed and watch ahead of us as well. I made a quiet sound to get Kismet's attention and bring him back closer to us, he listened without complaint. Having his senses closer to us upped the odds in our favor.

Every muscle in my body was tense and ready; a nervous sweat was running down the back of my neck as we continued to move cautiously along the path. The only sound heard was the soft *woosh* of the tarp dragging along the snow behind Tremor.

A sound echoed through the silence and it only took half a breath for me to know it had been gunfire. Gun in my hand ready, I knelt down. Reaching up I grabbed the reigns and steadied Tremor. With slow soundless movements I looked around us in all directions. It could have come from any direction, I couldn't be sure. Kismet crept over to me and it wouldn't be until later that I realized he'd been a little too close to gunfire at some point in his life.

A second shot rang out. Closing my eyes briefly I focused and then opened them and looked through the trees in the direction I thought it had come from. No trees were close enough to get to without being seen if I was wrong. Kismet's head snapped to the side and he began his soft growl. He knew where they were.

Watching in that direction I pulled Tremor around so we were facing them when they cleared the trees. Inside my head I did a silent chant hoping they would go in the other direction. Out of the corner of my eye I looked at the tarp, there was no time to do anything about it. Gritting my teeth I fought the anguish that climbed through me at the thought of losing my chance to get more food.

I could hear them moving back towards us. Kismet rumbled again deep in his throat. I'll never know what spurred my sudden inspiration, but I'd never doubt my quick wit again. Stuffing the gun into the waist of my jeans where I could get it easily but it would be hidden under my coat. Reaching down I grabbed a handful of snow and rubbed it all over my face and throat quickly. Kismet paused in watching the tree line to look at me. "Go," I hissed softly to him and pointed to the trees. He stood up and looked at me again before he took off in the direction of the men. I hoped he understood to circle them and not attack them, but I couldn't pause to doubt his instincts at this moment. Using more snow I soaked my hair and face a second time.

As the men came into my vision, I took a deep breath and tried to settle the knot in my chest. I'd never been that good in plays at school, or even faking so much as a cough, so I used the last moments I had before they spotted me telling myself I could do this. This would work. It had to.

I almost lost my nerve the moment I knew the men walking toward me saw me. Across both of their faces was a thick red band tattoo. My heart jerked in my chest, adding some real sweat to the line of my brow. One of them carried a shot-gun and the other held two rabbits dripping a trail of blood. I could see them appraising the situation—a tiny woman alone with nothing but her skinny horse. I didn't take a chance in looking around them to see where Kismet was. He was my ace in the hole and I wasn't revealing him until I had no other options.

The tall black haired one with the gun grinned a toothless smile and said something quietly to the other one. I couldn't hear what it was but when the second one grinned I knew it wasn't in my favor whatever was said.

I held my breath as they moved closer; they weren't intimidated in the slightest if their leisurely steps were any indication. Continuing not to breathe, I waited for them to make the first move—hoping it didn't take too long or I'd end up gasping for air instead of being able to pull this off. In a slow movement the one set the rabbits down and sent a look to his partner. The homely one with the gun walked towards the tarp.

"Leave my brother alone," I wheezed out in a huffed breath.

They both paused and eyed me before looking at the tarp. "Your brother?" The closest one asked.

Letting my breath out again I nodded. "I'm burying him at the ravine." I sucked in another breath. "The virus took him."

Toothless stepped back from the tarp like it was going to reach out and grab him. "He's dead?"

"The virus?" The gun was lowered from his shoulder and swung it out in front of him. "You've been exposed to the virus?"

I nodded once more and released my breath so it would gasp out of me. "I feel fine."

Reaching back down the man picked up the rabbits and stepped back. The other one stood there looking me up and down. With a shake of his head he looked to the other, looking like he was one second from running in the other direction. "Get away from us," he growled at me when he turned his head back.

I stepped sideways, trying to appear like I was dizzy.

Letting another breath escape I grasped Tremor's reign tightly and started to wobble my way in the direction we'd been heading. I was grinning like I hadn't remembered doing in a very long time. Chastising myself briefly for the silent celebration, I wiped it from my face and glanced over my shoulder. They were gone. I had to force my legs to keep moving, even though they were shaking so hard each step took focus. My brain tried to digest what I'd just done, even though I still couldn't believe it. My acting was just fine, with the help of a few small visual aids and the ingenious idea of wheezing.

Kismet came flying out of the trees ahead of us and loped over to me with his tongue hanging out of his mouth. It was the closest thing to applause I would get.

Now we just had to make it to Maisy's without meeting up with them again, if the weather held up and the skies were clear, we'd be there just around dawn. Unless I fell asleep and landed in the snow I wasn't stopping to rest until we were safely inside Maisy's walls.

CHAPTER TWENTY-ONE

The scissors in Rosy's hand clicked away at my hair. Maisy was sitting in the rocker holding Hope—Leif and Trina's beautiful baby girl. Leif leaned over by the door; it was clear he had something on his mind that he was trying to sort out how to say.

"Have you considered staying here for a bit?" He continued to look at the floor.

I smirked; having figured his inner turmoil was something like that. "I'm fine on my own, Leif."

He shook his head. "You've just had a very real and close call with the Red Bands, how can you say you're fine."

"I'm sitting here aren't I?" I noticed out of the corner of my eye that Maisy had stopped rocking.

"What if next time you don't stumble on two that aren't so gullible?" I could see the nerve twitching as he ground his teeth together in frustration.

"I'll handle it." I tried not to feel the same aggravation towards him that I had for years against my brother and friends, but it wasn't working.

"Leif," Maisy said quietly, "it's not your place."

Leif snorted in objection. "I didn't say it was—I'm just…" He sighed and straightened away from the door. "I'm glad you're okay, Red." He turned towards the door.

"I'll send Trina to get Hope in a while."

Maisy began to rock again. "He'll be fine."

Rosy moved away and then came back and handed me a mirror. "I hope it's all right the way I cut it." She started to brush my bright red hair into a small make shift dust pan. "Leif is just worried about you, we all are." Straightening up she gave me a shy smile. "We say a prayer for you each night at dinner."

My heart did something I could only call a flutter inside my chest. "You do?"

"Oh, yes. Kane even joined in last time he was here—until he ran out..." She stopped and looked down at the floor.

Forgetting the mirror, I glanced from Maisy to her. "Why did he run out?" *When had Kane been here?*

Maisy clicked her tongue softly. "I'd hoped his heart had won when he did that, but if you're here and he's not then I need to hope harder."

I played with the edge of the mirror, trying to seem calmer than I felt. "I don't understand."

Maisy smiled in my direction. "You're different for him." She shifted Hope in her arms before she lifted her head again. "Oh don't get me wrong, he worries about every living being he cares for, but with you it's more than that and he can't just admit it yet."

"Maisy's right. He looks in your direction constantly—and I don't think anyone has gotten to see his eyes unless it's accidentally—much less taking his glasses right off his face." Rosy added in quickly.

I didn't know what to say to that.

"He told me you saved him—before that first time we met you. There was something different about him after that and I think it's you, Red."

"He was in pretty rough shape when I got him away from those..."

Maisy chuckled, "I don't think it was actually the healing parts that changed him. You got through that cage he keeps around his heart."

I couldn't look at Rosy or Maisy at that moment; I felt my cheeks heat remembering that time with Kane. Lifting the mirror I looked at my reflection and my heart did another one of those flutters. The woman looking back at me was not the same one that had hugged her childhood friends good bye. This woman had hollowed out cheekbones that made her strangely shaded eyes look exotic and almost beautiful. The scar running across her cheek made her look untouchable and experienced in some odd way. The haircut Rosy had given me made my red hair look choppy, but in a good way, it completely went with the new face looking back at me.

"Is it okay?" Rosy asked from the other side of the mirror.

"It's great, Rosy. Thanks." I studied the reflection for a few more seconds, before holding the mirror out to her. "I need to check on the animals." I stood up and brushed the hair from my jeans.

"Kane asked Leif to try to get you stay with us—but he had the best intentions in mind when he did it." Maisy uttered in a nonchalant way.

I paused in my steps toward the door and looked back at her. "Really?"

Maisy nodded in her casual way. "Yes. If anything were to happen to you, no one would be safe from what he becomes."

Again the words stored inside my brain stopped forming. "Oh." I paused to find words, "I'll be back in a few minutes." Grabbing my coat, I shrugged into it and stepped out into the cold air.

I didn't make it three steps outside the door before Kismet met me and Tremor paused in his eating of dried grass to study me. They knew when something was off inside me, even before I was ready to admit it to myself. I knelt down to burrow my hands in Kizzy's warm fur. "I'm fine— just wrestling with some awkward thoughts." *Because a wolf was going to understand this.* I wanted so much to go back inside and ask Maisy to explain what she meant. *What he becomes? What was that exactly?* I knew Kane had a hard side to him, an unreachable part, but what that was precisely I wasn't sure I really wanted to know.

"Walls closing in on you?"

I jolted and turned to see Tanner standing there leaning in his teenage slumping way against a tree a few feet away. "Yeah, I guess they were."

He shrugged. "I used to have the same problem after we settled here."

"You weren't here from the start?"

He snorted. "No. Far from it!" He made a face that was half cringe, half disgust. "My old man kept moving us without ever stopping —even for a day."

"That's not uncommon now." I knew the feeling too well and I'd only done it for a short time.

"I would have given anything for your pimped out little cave, even if it was only for a week."

I smirked at his description. "It's all right." I stood up and tucked my hands in my pockets. "Where is your dad now?"

A look of regret flashed across his face. "The virus took him. It was fast."

"I'm sorry."

He shrugged again, but I noticed it wasn't as carefree as before. "I figure everyone has lost at least one person in all of this, so why should I be different."

I wanted to hug him, but somehow knew he thought he was beyond such gestures. "It still hurts. I lost my whole family one at a time." Sharing my tragedy seemed to take the hurt look out of his eyes.

"You're all alone."

I just nodded slowly. I watched him run his hand through his already messy hair. "How did you end up here?"

He smirked. "Same way as everyone else I guess— Kane." A look of adoration crossed his face briefly. "He's like some kind of hero, finding all the lost ones and putting them together to watch each other."

"Don't ever tell him he's a hero."

"I know. He just shrugs it all off like it's nothing big to wander around out there all the time and save people." He was quiet for a moment. "I think that's the part that makes him a hero—that he doesn't think it's a big deal."

"I think your right."

He moved away from the tree and came closer. It was then I realized how much he'd grown. At this rate he'd be a foot taller than me by summer. "Leif said you're moving out in the morning and heading to the other traders."

I sighed, hoping this wasn't some scheme to get me to stay, by using a boy. "Yes. I don't want people to trade away needed supplies, so I think it's best if I go to this other camp."

Tanner rubbed the side of his neck, his mismatched eyes studying me. "If I asked to come along, would you say yes?"

Eyebrows quirked I just looked back at him.

He smirked. "I figured. S'okay, I just wanted to get away for a few days."

As he stood there looking down at me—which I was still having trouble accepting—I wondered if he truly just felt the wanderlust or if there was another reason. "And babysitting me for Kane's sake has nothing to do with it?'

Narrowing his eyes he studied me. "Not entirely—but that might be a bit of the reason." Jamming his hands into his coat pocket he rocked back on his feet and looked around. "There's nothing to do here all winter and I feel— stuck."

I waited for him to continue, somehow knowing there was more.

"Leif told us about how you handled the Red Bands…" A loud shriek coming from the other side of the village stopped him.

We both spun around to see where it came from. Everyone was running towards the path, glancing at Tanner, I took off running just as he disappeared from my sight. When I reached the others they were crowded around a little boy, whose name I couldn't remember, Leif was kneeling down in front of him talking to him quietly. At first I thought he might be hurt, but there wasn't a tear in his eye or pain on his face.

Rosie led Maisy to stand beside me. "What is it?" She asked, all heads turned to her, confirming once more in my mind that this woman without vision was their alpha regardless of her handicap.

Leif turned, but didn't get up. "Mia has wandered off. She was playing on the trail with Dustin when she took off running. He can't find her."

Gasps of panic went through the group. Maisy stood there for a moment before speaking. "Dustin, do you remember where you were playing."

"Yes Maisy," the little boy said in a quiet voice.

Maisy smiled in his direction. "You take Leif, your father and mother and show them and then you come back with your mother." She turned in my direction, "Red, does Kismet have any tracking ability?"

Her question startled me. "He can find tracks well enough, so I guess he does."

She nodded her head abruptly. "Maybe you should take your horse and him along—to speed things up a bit."

I wondered briefly if this was some sort of ploy to keep me here longer, to show me that I was needed here—and I'd be damned if it wasn't working. I made eye contact with Tanner a few feet away from me, something in his expression had me answering without further thought. "We can try." With that everyone was spurred into motion, people running to grab things for those leaving. Turning back I looked at Tanner. "You want to come with me?"

He nodded, a big grin on his face.

"Then we need to untie the tarp from Tremor so he can move faster." Without replying he took off in the direction of my horse, disappearing from my sight a few feet later.

~

We were led to where the children had been playing, so many tracks to sort through slowed things down, but once we found the missing child's foot prints everyone was spurred into action. Then Dustin's mother, Sissy, was frantic and took no time in whisking him back to their home. By this time the little girl's father was on the scene, complete with older brother and guns, they had just returned from hunting. I didn't ask where Mia's mother was, the equation was all too familiar at this point, her mother was gone like so many others.

Tanner led Tremor at the back of the group as Kismet and I walked at the front. My heart sank when we found the other, much larger tracks that crossed Mia's— and then hers were gone. A mixture of grief, worry and rage filled me. Precious time was wasted as the men all decided on the game plan. Through their speculation and worry I stood beside Tanner, Kismet sitting at my feet. His ears were flicking, sniffing the air constantly. Leif was right there with me on the 'we're wasting time' page and looked relieved when I finally stepped forward and spoke loud enough to stop the useless chatter.

"Tanner and I will take the animals and stay on the tracks; you can follow further behind in case they branch off." Mia's dad looked like he was about to make some sort of 'just a girl' comment so I continued. "I can get the hell out of any situation faster than you with Tremor, Tanner can vanish if needed and Kismet is the best warning system available." He still didn't look convinced. "Or we can stand here all day and waste daylight trying to decide what to do."

Leif actually smirked. "Get going, Red." He glanced at Tanner with one of those 'just between males' looks and nodded. "We'll cover this area one more time, just in case those tracks are wrong and she's hiding somewhere nearby."

I wasn't sure if he'd just taken the emotional father and brother out of the equation on purpose, but it seemed that way to me. Moving over to Tremor, I patted his neck and motioned for Tanner to get on him. Reaching into my coat I pulled out my gun and handed it butt first to Tanner. "Safety is on." Pulling my throwing knives out of their little pocket, I turned back to the worried relatives. "We'll be back."   I didn't wait for any words, just went over and knelt by the large foot prints. "Kizzy." He came over and sniffed where I pointed. "Find Mia." He gave me one long look and then took off in the direction the tracks went.

~

I don't know how long we followed Kismet through the trees, but I was getting tired jogging along behind him. When he stopped and sat looking off into the darkened area, my heart hitched in my chest. I motioned at Tanner behind me to stop and wait, then went up quietly behind Kizzy.

He crouched down and stared into the trees. I couldn't see anything, but he whined softly and I knew we must be right on top of them. Tanner knelt down beside me. "Think you can go check it out and not be seen or heard?"

Tanner handed me my gun and before I could say anything else he became a blur and vanished right before me. Sighing I leaned back down beside Kismet and strained to see if I could hear anything. I kept the gun in my hand and ready while I waited.

Tanner returned, without me seeing him and was squatting down beside me before I knew it. I heaved a sigh and glared at him. "You love startling people don't you?"

"Yes." He turned and pointed through the trees. "They stopped just over there. Mia is fine, scared but okay so far."

I chewed my lip and looked all around us. It would be hard to get back through here quickly with all the tight clusters of trees. "Did you see any weapons?"

Apprehension crossed his face. "Just one rifle, but I'm willing to bet even I can't outrun bullets."

I didn't want to admit I was going to need his help on this one, if anything happened to him—well, I would never forgive myself. "I'm sure they'll have knives also. Can you get to Mia and out without slowing long enough to be seen?"

"I don't know. I've played with the kids a few times where I swoop them up and make the game of hide and seek more interesting—but no one had a gun on me at the time."

His honesty was surprising, something I'm sure he would lose as he got older and the maleness developed fully inside him. Men just didn't do fear easily. "I'll be the distraction…"

"They have her tied to a rope, that's tied to a tree."

I glanced up, wishing for some sort of break. Pulling my knife out of its holder, I handed it to him. "I can buy you about ten seconds, if that—so cut it and get out of there." Straightening, I looked all around us, trying to track a clear path. "We'll leave Tremor there; you get back to him and head out of here as fast as you can."

"But…"

"Just do it. Kismet will have my back and I'll follow when I'm sure they won't." Which way will you come back?" I didn't want to be in his way at any point. He pointed. "Okay. Take Tremor over there and when I'm out of sight, you head in and get Mia." He sighed a loudly as he stood up to take hold of the reins.

With each careful step toward where Tanner had pointed I checked my own resolve. Killing something for food was one thing, that I was barely managing, but if I had to kill a person—regardless of their rank on the scum scale—could I? I could throw my knives with great accuracy with both hands, but as far as shooting went only the right hand was steady enough to hit the mark. Twisting the harness, I made sure the knives were dead center on my chest so I could reach them fast. As I took the gun in my right hand I was taking calming breaths and mentally giving myself a pep talk. I can do this. I *had* to do this.

When the two men came into sight, I ducked behind a tree and slid down the side of it so I could take a closer look. They were sitting on a downed tree, one smoking the other one eating. The Red Bands on their faces were more than visible even from this distance. I tried to remember if it were the same two I'd encountered, but in all honesty I wasn't memorizing their features during our brief meeting. It was when I spotted Mia; I decided I could shoot human beings in this case. They had gagged her and her hands were tied. A longer rope was tied a tree, like a chain for a dog, and knotted around the ropes on her wrists. The scared look on her tearstained face made me seethe with rage and revenge. The need for revenge skirted its way to the top of my emotional scale at that moment.

Kismet stopped beside me and rubbed his head into my shoulder. I knew he could sense what I was feeling without needing to turn and look into those amber eyes. Placing my mouth near his ear, I whispered. "You're my back up, boy. Lets help Tanner get in unnoticed." He crouched down beside me and looked between the trees.

Standing back up behind the tree, I looked back to see if I could spot Tremor. I couldn't. Tanner wasn't too far away from where we stood. I knew he would be ready to move as soon as I got the men's attention. With a brief nod at him, I turned back and headed in their direction. I had no plan; really, I was just going to follow my instincts as I got closer.

When I was less than twenty feet from them, Kismet took off into the trees heading around the other side of them. I didn't know what his plan was either and hoped when it came down to it we were on the same page of the adventure in the end.

A branch snapping had both men jumping up to turn in that direction, the rifle was aimed and a long blade appeared in the hand of the other. Did everyone out here have blades as long as my arms? I glanced down at the throwing knife in my hand. I liked it better; I didn't have to be up close and personal with mine. When I heard the growl coming from the direction of the noise, I knew Kismet was in place and giving me the space I needed to get things going. Moving over a few more feet, I made sure most of me was behind the largest tree within range.

I looked at Mia once more, she crouched down beside

the tree she was tied to and was watching the men whose attention was not on her. Kneeling down on one knee, I aimed for the ground five feet in front of where they were looking. My objective was simple, keep their backs to the child as long as possible—even if that meant Kismet and I were targets. Without further thought I pulled the trigger and leaned around the tree long enough that they would catch a glimpse of my hair. Immediately following the echo of my shot, their riffle rang out, the bullet grazing the tree off to my right.

I had their attention.

Kismet growled louder and even though he wasn't visible there was no mistaking where the sound came from. The one with the gun dropped to his knees and scanned the trees slowly.

"Come out now." The other one called out.

Not likely. I glanced at Mia to see she was looking at the tree instead of the men. Tanner had gotten to her. Taking a deep breath I held it and fired again, making it hit the ground closer this time.

Both men dove behind the tree they'd been sitting on. The only thing visible to me now was the barrel of the gun. Then I found out their rifle was better at repetition then my handgun as they sprayed shots into the trees surrounding me. Bark hit the side of my face and I gasped, not wanting to know just how close they had come to hitting me. Sliding back through the cold snow, I headed towards where I'd heard Kizzy. We had to leave and we had to make sure they followed.

"What the hell?"

That could only mean one thing. Tanner had Mia and they knew it. Taking a deep breath I stood up behind the closest tree. Exhaling slowly I leaned around it and shot at the tree in front of them. Paused, counted to three silently and then I stuck my head out from around the tree checking before I took off running through the trees. I wasn't trying for stealth, so I hit every branch that would make a sound as

I slid through the snow. By the time the sound of the rifle firing reached my ears, the bullet was already grazing by my shoulder and embedded into the tree I just passed with a soft *thunk* noise. I didn't turn to see if they followed, their bullets were and that was good enough for me.

As I zigzagged between the trees, I glanced to my left to see Kismet was following along beside me a few feet away. He yipped loudly and my heart jerked in my chest hoping it was just him creating a distraction and he wasn't hit.

The men were following and briefly I had to wonder what the hell I'd been thinking. Hadn't I already done this chase game with bodies larger and faster than my own and almost lost? Stumbling I tried to control my slide to land behind a tree. I listened to the heavy footsteps behind me and began to wonder if I was going to come out of this one. Kismet flew past me and didn't even spare me a moment's glance. Gritting my teeth I stood up against the tree and pulled one of the knives back out of its holder. Closing my eyes I listened to the noise, focusing on the direction it was coming from. It was far too close for my liking, but I had to try to buy myself a few more seconds.

Shoulder against the tree, I took a deep breath and raised my arm. The knife was flying from my hand before my eyes even landed on the target. There was a groan and then a curse and I knew I hit something fleshy enough to get their attention. The pounding footsteps stopped. I waited long enough to hear a loud hiss and a loud "What the…" and I was off again running as fast as I could manage.

I kept running, even when I couldn't hear anything from behind me, my chest hurt, the sweat ran down my forehead and I just pushed further straight ahead. As I rounded a small group of snow covered trees, I spotted Kismet sitting like a statue in the snow. Which only meant one thing, we were in the clear.

Dropping down beside him, I sprawled in the dampness of the snow, not caring if I ended up soaked. Kismet leaned over and licked my face. "Yeah we're good." It was when he nuzzled my arm near my shoulder the stinging registered through the adrenalin pumping at top speed through my veins. Turning my head I saw the blood covering my jacket. Sitting up quickly, I pulled the material down to see the outside of my shirt covered in blood. Further investigating showed me the ugly red line that was slowly bleeding down my arm. The bullet that had gone by my shoulder had gotten really close. I wouldn't die from it, I doubted there would be much of scar—I was lucky and I knew it. Later though I'd be pissed about the rip in my coat sleeve, but for now we were okay and that was all that mattered.

Hugging Kismet, I surveyed the area around us. As brilliant as our rescue had gone, we'd forgotten one thing—I didn't know this part of the bush and presently had no idea where we were. Turning around I studied where I had just run from. There was no way we were going back in that direction. Sighing loudly I stood up and ruffled the top of Kismet's head. "Guess we get to take a long stroll, boy." He looked at me, his tongue hanging out of his mouth. "Let's go find Tremor." He started off without looking to see if I was following. I hoped at this point Tremor, Tanner and Mia were almost back to the village.

Eyes peeled, constantly scanning the trees around us we walked without sound in the direction I prayed would lead us back to the main trail at some point.

~

I was tired, thirsty and starting to wonder if we were completely lost. The sun was starting to settle in the sky when we finally saw something that looked familiar. Of course the tall boy leaning against my pretty horse was the only part of this area I recognized.

Tanner straightened and grinned at me, "took you long enough." He held out a jug of water.

"Mia all right?" I took it and wasted no time draining half of down my throat.

"Yeah. I took her back to her dad and then we headed back to wait for you." His eyes focused on my shoulder.

"You okay?"

I nodded while I tried to catch my breath from drinking too quickly. "Bullet grazed me," I touched the hole in my jacket, "they messed up my coat." Tremor came over and nuzzled into my neck, I rubbed my hand down over his big face. "I lost one of my knives too—left it stuck in some body part of one them."

He reached down and rubbed the top of Kismet's head. "We better get back, they were all starting to freak out and plan some sort of search and rescue when Tremor and I decided we'd come wait for you.

I paused and leaned against the warmth of my horse. "Thanks, Tanner."

"No problem—thank *you* for not treating me like a kid and letting me help."

I accepted his hand up and got onto Tremor's back. "Don't try to grow up too fast. The result isn't as much fun as it might seem."

He smirked. "I move fast enough that growing up is optional." Leaning down, he cupped his hands together to boost me up onto Tremor. "So, how many Red Bands have you managed to evade or scare the hell out of now?"

I dragged my tired body up into the saddle and shifted forward to make room for him. "I guess eight, but I'm not planning on going for any kind of record." He climbed up behind me. "I'd be quite happy if I never saw another one again."

Tanner snickered. "Yeah, like that will happen."

We rode back without talking, silently reviewing the day's events knowing we were useful and lucky.

CHAPTER TWENTY-TWO

By the next morning the weather had shifted again, it was raining, and lots of it. I debated on not heading for the other traders, and then decided I had to at least try. Most of the trip, according to Leif, was under the cover of the trees. My heart slammed in my chest when I thought of the part of the trip that would take us right alongside the river banks—I didn't like rivers since one had tried to swallow me.

Tremor seemed more himself after eating enough for two horses in the last day, so I chose to ride rather than walk once we were heading out of the valley. The climb up the other side had been more of a challenge than I would have liked, my shoulder was throbbing despite the harmless looking scratch it was now adorned with.

The rain was working on polishing the hard snow to a nice sheet of ice. Tremor's weight worked in his favor and Kismet had claws—once again I was the helpless human and the only one of three that had hands, which weren't of much use in this case.

I had to sit down after almost crawling up and catch my breath once we reached the top. I promised myself that I would get my butt back into shape and keep it that way. I wasn't sure how horses aged or if wolves followed the dog year's thing, but a little simple math had me at the youngest in our group and it was just spite that made me want to stay in better shape than I was. When I'd set out on this journey of discovery I'd been in top form after all the hours of practicing my *brothers* had put me through. Now less than a year later I was in sad form for sure.

Sitting and looking back down the trail we'd just climbed I was in awe. A glacial winter scene lay out in front of me, so breathtaking that I felt a small twinge of guilt for cursing it just a few moments ago. The irony of it wasn't lost on me, something so beautiful was deadly, more so with Mother Nature trying to wipe us out of existence. I wasn't sure if I should admire the view or run from it.

An hour after that I was trembling in my boots as I guided Tremor along the riverbank, wishing we didn't have to be as close to it as we were, afraid the tarp of treasures he dragged might get caught and pull us in. If any animals found themselves stranded or marooned along the way, they were on their own this time. I may not always learn from my mistakes, but my swim with the cat had taught me a lesson I would never forget.

In some areas the water looked frozen solid then would give way to sections of the river that rushed along sending chunks of ice bobbing up out of the current to slide across the hardened surface only to have them disappear under the polished ice once more. Through all of it, I was hoping the breaks in the ice meant spring was coming, but I knew it wasn't a sign I could rely on. The weather, like the river, did whatever it wanted. I glanced from where I was stepping when the river grew silent for a few steps. Overall it was fascinating and frightening at the same time. If someone were to fall in—well, that was a thought better left unformed.

When the unmarked trail finally began to lead us away from the rushing water, we stopped and looked back at it for a long moment, taking in the vicious action without the fear of falling in. I was just about to turn when something green went rushing by. I followed it with my eyes and my throat tightened as I came to understand what I was looking at. It was body, frozen if the way it bobbed through the current was any indication. A shiver went down my spine when I remembered the feeling of being at the mercy of the untamable water. I had been lucky.

Further away from the river, we stopped to take a needed break. I was sweating in my jacket and hoped it was from the warm rain and exertion and not from an infection from the bullet. Leif's wife had assured me more than once that it was clean and should be fine in a few days. With the way it ached I wasn't agreeing with her. Taking off my coat I tucked it up onto the saddle and then stood there with my face lifted into the rain. If felt like a spring rain on my face, no icy chill of winter. I didn't waste much time thinking about how it could go from frigid winter to spring in only a day as it had taken weeks when I was a child—the earth did what she wanted now, not following any schedule but her own.

Kismet and Tremor had no issues with walking along in this rain, I guess it would feel like the first bath in months to them, refreshing and renewing. The snow was nowhere near gone, but with the air breathable and the winds sweeter I couldn't help but feel more energized then I had in more weeks than I could remember.

Water rushed over the path we were taking, little streams of it along the sides, all of it flowing in the direction of the river we had just left. It was almost as if the river was calling it and so it ran back to its mother. We encountered the first of what was close to mud, or at least frozen dirt that would be mud with more warmth. I'd never been so happy to see dirt before, but it was the first possible confirmation of one thing to me.

I'd survived the winter.

~

Maybe it was the warmer weather or just the ability to relax and not be cold, but we took our time heading towards this trading place, stopping often to look at things along the way. As the afternoon leaned into the evening we stood staring off at what appeared to be the abandoned city we had passed months before in the search for our shelter. Even though I wasn't sure of where exactly we were, I was pretty sure we were on the other side of it this time, but it was definitely the same crumbling shell of that city. I felt the loneliness and couldn't help but wonder why someone hadn't taken advantage of shelter and buildings large enough to house many. As soon as I'd finished the thought, the answer came to me; the large manmade structures were just a trap leading to death when the earth decided to shift again.

Shaking off the melancholy, we turned to head in the direction we'd been instructed. The rain had slowed and was a quiet rhythmic noise against the tarp Tremor dragged. If my directions were correct, and my guesstimation accurate, we didn't have much further to go and should make it before dark. I had strict instructions to ask for Lindy when we did reach the edge of this community and she would give me a place to stay and guide me through their process of trading.

Kismet began darting ahead of us and then rushing back, a game of sorts I'd learned after all these months that let me know there was something ahead that he wanted us to see.

As we moved through the trees, a village unfolded. We'd found it. Before I'd moved ten steps into the largest opening a man and a woman appeared out of behind the tree. Kismet bolted back to my side.

"Leif sent me here to trade."

A tall woman looked at me for a long moment, taking in the animals with me. "Unless I'm mistaken you know Kane as well."

I should have been surprised by this, but I was coming to learn that everyone knew Kane. 'Yes."

She smiled. "You're welcome to trade among us." Stepping over slowly she watched Kismet. "I'm Lindy. Is he friendly?" She motioned to the tail wagging animal leaning against my leg.

"Just bordering on spoiled, actually."

Reaching down she rubbed Kismet's head. "I'll show

you where you can stay tonight."

~

I was still in awe as I wandered through the street of vendors the next morning, each having their own unique products to barter and trade. I had already managed to find the grain I'd hoped for, as well as paper—more than I had hoped for and traded the pans for it. Just knowing I could write what and when I chose gave me something to look forward to; I could fill long empty periods with my thoughts and words.

With the snow leaving as suddenly as it had appeared months before, my list was shorter because I didn't have to worry about finding as many winter weight clothes just yet, but I kept a mental list of goods on offer to know what was and wasn't available to me.

There were more people here than I would have imagined. Many pulled small wagons along behind them as they moved through the rows of vendors. It was almost encouraging to know this many people were survivors and getting along. Lindy waved at me through the crowd as she was walking along listening intently to another woman that walked quickly with her.

Several times when I'd stop and paused, I noticed a man that seemed to be looking at me each time. It was an eerie feeling and I would have felt threatened if several of the people along the way hadn't smiled at him and spoke to him as if he were a friend. Still he was unknown to me.

As I walked into a large group of people, Kismet pulled gently on the cord I'd loosely tired around his neck—one of the rules explained to me when I'd reached the village—he'd been very accepting of my being able to control his wanderings up until this point. I looked in the direction he was tugging only to see a young puppy also pulling on his leash and wagging his tail as he looked at Kismet. Leaning down I rested my hand on his head. "I don't think everyone would be pleased for you to start a game of chase among all of their stuff, Kizzy."

He studied me for a moment and then turned back in time to see a young woman scoop the puppy up and disappear into the crowd. Kismet watched until they were gone before he looked back up at me and turned to continue along the path.

~

When the last items I'd brought to trade were handed over to the man with the hay, I smiled and turned around to watch his son securing the crude bale of hay into the tarp. Tremor seemed to have no problems with the extra weight being added to his load, of course knowing it was of the dry crisp grass I'd given him a sample of probably had something to do with it. Once the tarp was secured, I stood back and looked to see if there were any gaps that would soak the load when it rained—I glanced up at the dark sky and knew it was definitely coming back.

The hair on the back of neck suddenly tingled; I turned and looked around to see that I was again being watched, although this time it wasn't a stranger. Across the small crowd a tall man stood listening to another. Even though I couldn't see his eyes through the dark glasses, I knew they were on me. Grinning, I patted the side of Tremor's neck and continued along the path between the vendors. Inside I may have wanted to run over and greet Kane, but on the outside I knew he'd prefer to keep his distance in front of others.

We had just reached the end of the small shelters when the man that had been following me came up to me.

"That's a lovely animal you have there."

I offered what might be interpreted as a smile. "Thank you." Kismet moved back over to stand beside me. The man moved to stand right in front of me, his hand reaching out to Tremor. Tremor jerked his head back away from his touch.

"What can I trade ya for him?"

My eyebrow eyes shot up. "He's not for trade."

He chuckled. "Everything's for trade at some point," he

said quietly.

Shaking my head, I grabbed the reins tighter in my hand, the other one reaching under my coat for my knife. "He's not." I could see Kane heading in our direction; his jaw clenched and knew I needed to get rid of this man before he reached us.

"Aw come on, an animal like this is meant for more than a pet to be led around…"

I unsheathed my blade and held it between us, leaning closer and looking up at him. "He. Is. Not. For. Trade."

His eyes flicked to the knife I held as he looked down at me. Raising his hands in surrender he backed away. "I got it. No harm meant." I stood there and watched as he backed up several steps more before he turned and walked away.

Kane reached us as the man quickly walked in the other direction. Tucking the knife away I grinned at him. "Hello."

He didn't say anything, but did smile as he stepped over beside me and wrapped one of his big arms around me and hugged me to him. I was surprised that he had with so many people around. Releasing me, he stood there and looked down at me. With a gentle touch he ran a finger over the scar on my cheek. "Got a little too close?"

Of course he'd know it was from a knife, so I couldn't deny anything. I shrugged. "Very briefly."

A rumbling noise came from him, it resembled a growl. "And the knife's owner?"

"Will probably not have much strength in one arm ever again."

This he grinned to. "Walk with me?" Kismet shoved against his leg suddenly feeling neglected because his large friend hadn't acknowledged him. Reaching down Kane rubbed a hand down over the Kizzy's muzzle. "I should be surprised he let you tie him, but I'm not because it's you."

Turning Tremor I walked around behind the shelters, Kane followed along beside me. "I don't know what that means."

He chuckled. "I'll explain later." With a slow touch he

ran his hand over my hair to rest on the back of my neck as we walked. "How long has it been since I saw you last? Two months or more?"

"Around that."

"Hmm."

I stopped and looked up at him. "What does hmm mean?"

"It would explain why I'm so tired. More than two months—and you've disrupted every single night of rest since I left you that last time. I close my eyes and see yours—I can still taste you—"

I felt my cheeks heat at his words. He grasped my chin and lowered his glasses, leaning towards me. "Will you leave with me?"

If it had been anyone else left alive on this planet I would have probably asked where, but this was Kane and that secure, safe feeling flooded into me—that and a good rush of hormones. I nodded.

"We'll find Lindy and say our good-byes'." Reaching over he took the reins from my hand and took my hand in his other one.

CHAPTER TWENTY-THREE

We walked in silence for a long time, our hands clasped, his hand engulfing mine. The look on Lindy's face when we had said good-bye was so similar at Maisy's village; surprise that Kane was with me. I chewed the inside of my cheek for several minutes after we left, wanting to ask him a long list of questions but I remained silent not wanting to break the peaceful feeling that always came with his company.

"Are you still in the same place?"

I turned to look at him, watching my own reflection in his dark glasses. Dropping his hand I reached up and pulled the glasses off his face and tucked them into his shirt collar. "Yes."

He stopped and stood there giving me the oddest look. "What?"

Shaking his head he smirked. "I keep trying to figure out why I let you get away with things." He shook his head again. "Never mind. I know a shorter route back to your little cave."

My jaw dropped. "Shorter by how much?"

"A day." He took my hand and started walking again.

"Does Leif know about this short cut?" I wasn't sure if I would be really impressed if I found out now there was a way to get here without going by the river's edge.

Shrugging, he pulled me closer to him but kept moving forward. "I don't know. I think I spend more time wandering the land than he does."

"I think you spend more time wandering than everyone left on the planet, Kane," I said quietly.

"It's the only option for me."

All my reserves of asking him questions flew right out with the next words. "*Why* is it?"

"I'm sure you've figured out enough that I don't have to say it." His voice had dropped.

"Maybe I have, but I'd still like to hear about it."

He stopped walking and looked down at me. "You want to hear it right now?"

"It's a long walk, lots of time." I wasn't going to back down, even though he was giving me a hard look. I expected him to argue or just stop talking; like he normally did, but instead his big hand cupped the back of my head and pulled me in when his mouth crushed mine in a kiss I could only describe as desperate. My head was spinning when he finally lifted his head and rested his forehead against mine.

"You have zero self-preservation instinct, Breenna," he said hoarsely.

No words would form in my mind so I just stood there clinging to his sleeve and looking up at him.

Sighing loudly, he lifted his head and took my hand again. When he turned and started walking I thought he was going to leave it there.

"I'm not just a man anymore, Bree. My mutation is ugly and vile." I kept silent and waited to see if there was more. "When I contracted the virus, so did my wife and daughter. I survived, they didn't." His body was ridged with tension now. "The first time I turned into this thing that was a result of being a survivor, I destroyed my entire home and almost killed my neighbors."

My heart began thudding in my chest, partially from what he was saying but more from the pain I could feel in his tone. I squeezed his hand and leaned into his arm as we walked. "Can you control it? When you . . ." *Change? Mutate?* I didn't know how to label it.

"Most of the time—unless my emotions are running high and then I struggle."

"Your eyes . . ."

"The silver eyes belong to the man, the black belong to the beast."

I took a few minutes to digest this, maybe it was a bad idea, but I knew when his eyes went black and I had to reach deep inside to see if that scared the hell right out of me. It didn't.

"You don't have to fear me."

"I don't." I stepped around a rock sticking out of the mud and then moved so my shoulder was tight against his arm. "Can you change when you want to?" He turned and looked down at me, a surprised expression on his face. I wasn't sure if it was from my answer or my question.

"If I need to, I can."

That stopped me right there in mid-stride. I dropped his hand and stood there with my hands on my hips. "You let those men be the holy hell out of you and you could have stopped it?" My voice squeaked with the emotions that still surfaced when I thought of how he'd been when I'd found him.

"They wouldn't have survived."

"Like I care. *You* almost didn't survive!" I paced a few feet away from him and stared off at—nothing, I just needed a minute. Kismet came running over and stood in front of me, curiosity in his eyes.

His hand touched my shoulder; his breath brushed the back of my neck when he spoke. "You don't understand, it's not something I would ever use against anyone."

"Will you show me? I need to see…"

Moving the hand from my shoulder he stepped in front of me and lifted my chin to hold my attention. *"Never."*

That tone I knew immediately. The discussion was finished, whether I wanted it to be or not.

"That's why I leave. When I start to feel restless inside I move on, keeping everyone around me safe from what I become." He lowered his face closer to mine, his eyes swirling with mixed color. "Promise me if it ever happens when I'm with you—you will leave, hide or even shoot me if necessary."

I couldn't speak with the knot in my throat.

"Promise me." He demanded.

Slowly I nodded. I didn't know if I lied, but I did what he wanted me to do—for now.

Kane's warm lips brushed over mine. "We need to get moving."

Before I could reply he grasped me around the waist and stepped over to Tremor, depositing me on the animals back. Without pause he was up behind me and prodding the horse's side. I glanced at Kismet to see if Kane had sensed something, but he didn't look concerned in the least. "Whats wrong?"

Pulling me back tight into his chest, his warm breath brushed against my ear when he spoke. "I've missed you."

Just his tone spread a heat through my whole body. "Oh." Is all that came out of my mouth as I felt the flush move over my skin.

"Talk to me about, anything to pass the time."

~

I couldn't say what I babbled about until we stopped. Kane being so close to me was more than distracting. His breath was against my neck, his lips lightly brushing over my skin for long moments of our journey. By the time dusk arrived and we decided on a fairly sheltered spot to stop, I was dizzy from hormones dancing in my system. The only comfort was his eyes were closer to black than silver, so I knew he was suffering the same as I was.

As I was setting up the tarp in hopes it would keep us dry if the rain came back, I watched him free Tremor from all of his gear. The way he moved always struck me as fascinating, for such a large man he barely made a sound on the ground littered with branches and mud. He didn't just live in nature he was part of it.

Lighting the fire, I tossed some dehydrated meat into a pan with water and sparingly added a touch of the remaining herbs I had. I was mixing some crude flour to make fried biscuits when he finally came over and sat down. He sat there leaning on his knees; his shoulders hunched and stared at the fire. It was the first time I'd even seen him like that.

"Breenna . . ." he finally looked at me. I stopped moving, the look on his face startling me. "Are you still planning to head towards the mountains?"

I nodded, feeling anxious by the quiet tone he was using.

He sighed loudly. "I'd hoped to sit down and persuade you to move to Maisy's area or even Lindy's…" Shaking his head, he leaned forward and picked up the pan with the meat and gave it a shake. "While I was holed up during that ice storm this winter I caught wind of something I had to go check out, before I spread the word."

"So that's where you've been?"

He nodded slowly and set the pan back down. "It took me almost three weeks to get there—I'd like you to consider traveling with someone or at least settling closer to others when you do."

The hair on the back of my neck tingled. "What's going on, Kane?"

"Some big changes are coming. The Red Bands numbers have grown." Standing up with sudden tension he paced over to look into the trees. "They have taken over part of an abandoned city and are rounding up virus survivors…" Turning, he looked at me again. "They're testing them and any that have useful *skills* are kept under guard so those in power can use them when needed." The last part was spit out.

"And I'd be useful," I whispered out loud even though we both knew it.

He knelt down in front of me. "Yes." With a shaking hand he cupped the side of my face so I would have to look right at him. "I don't want to see…"

I put my hand over his mouth, not wanting to hear it. "I'll be careful." I snorted. "I *am* careful and I'm not helpless either."

Pulling my hand away from his mouth, he clasped it tightly in his. "I know. You know my heart stopped a few times when you told me about your recent encounters. I can't believe you purposely went after them—"

"I had to. I wasn't going to ride off into the sunset and leave a little girl in their hands."

Leaning back, he studied me for a moment. "You amaze me, yet frustrate the hell out of me at the same time."

I smirked at his distress.

"I'd travel with you if I could—at least try…" he leaned back away from me, thoughts crossing his face faster than I could keep up with. "I've been moving around warning others."

Clasping his face in my hands, I kissed his mouth softly. "You need to warn as many as you can. I won't be leaving for a few weeks yet—" I stopped, not wanting to go any further. Traveling with Kane would be too much to hope for, but I didn't want to hear any promises he'd regret later. "I'll stick to a route of sorts and if you need to check up on me you can just follow it until you find me."

He sighed. "I'm sorry. I wished I could be different then I am…"

"Don't!" I got up and moved back over to the fire, kneeling down. "I won't ask for anything."

I jumped when his arm circled my waist, drawing me back against him. "Maybe you should," he whispered against my neck.

Taking the food off the fire, I kept kneeling, still in his arms. "I lost everyone once. I won't go through that again."

We stayed there, my back tight against him, his cheek resting against mine for several moments. "I understand that, I just feel like I should do better by you than I am." He kissed my cheek in a light caress. "You're so young —"

Laughing softly I turned in his arms and looked up at him. "Only in age." I touched the wrinkles around his eyes. "You've never asked me how old I am, why?"

He shrugged and then shook his head. "I was afraid to. I might have to shoot myself if you are as young as you look."

"And how old do I look?"

Leaning back, he looked down at me, his eyes moving over my face, "about seventeen."

I grinned.

He groaned, "ah, Red, *please* tell me you're not."

I chuckled seeing the stress on his face. "No I'm not. I don't know the exact date but I'm close to twenty-three."

He groaned again. "That's not much better."

Stretching up, I kissed him on the mouth. "And how old are you?"

"Feeling ancient at this moment," he cleared his throat. "Too old for you, that much I know."

"I think I'll be the judge of that—how old?"

Dropping his hands away from me, he got up and ran his hands through his hair making him look wild. "I don't know exactly either—the months blend together out here…" He sat down by the fire and picked up the pan with the meat in it. "I'd have to be pushing forty by now or close to it."

Sitting down beside him I looked at him carefully. "You don't look it."

His eyes flicked to mine and then back to the pan in his hand. "I feel it when I'm near you."

Testing the temperature of a biscuit, I picked one up and offered it to him. "I always thought old people would be all wrinkled—everywhere." I took a small bite. "You are not wrinkled *anywhere*." I felt my cheeks heat.

Grinning, he leaned over and rested his forehead against mine. "Be sure to let me know when I start to wrinkle then, we'll get me a nice rocker to sit in."

"And a quilt to cover you with…" Without warning he scooped me up and dumped me into his lap, laughing as he did.

"What am I going to do with you?"

I bit my lip and looked up at his serious eyes. "Anything you want?"

He groaned and leaned down and nibbled at my lip. "Not here, not tonight. I don't like being out in the open with you like this."

I glanced over at Kismet, where he sprawled by the other side of the fire. "I have an early warning system, we'll be fine."

His mouth crushed mine under his, his tongue invading my mouth before I could even adjust to the sudden kiss, without warning his pulled his mouth away. "No, not out here in the open like this." A gentle kiss was placed on my mouth. "I lose myself when I'm near you." He grinned. "The whole fucking Red Band army could be standing behind us when I'm inside you and I'd never notice—" He kissed me again and then helped me sit up.

My head was spinning from his kiss and his confession. My skin was flushed, my heart beating fast and my breath was uneven as he set me away from him and picked up the pan. "Then we should get back to my place quickly tomorrow."

"We'll run the whole way." His silver eyes bore into mine, causing my heart to skip around again.

CHAPTER TWENTY-FOUR

I couldn't even follow the trail we took if I'd wanted to. He hadn't been kidding when he said we'd run the whole way, I'd never traveled this fast. We ate as we walked instead of stopping for lunch. The whole time I was constantly distracted by the looks he kept sending me, his eyes devouring me. By the time we finally came into an area that was looking vaguely familiar I was ready to tackle him to the ground. It was the weirdest thing I'd ever felt, and not entirely bad.

Stopping Tremor, he reached over and pulled my arm so I was standing in front of him. "It's not far now." Grasping my waist he set me up on the horse and followed me up to sit behind me before I could even speak. Kismet paused for a moment and then took off into the trees, as if he sensed how close we were as well.

When Tremor began to move again, Kane pulled me tight into his body, his lips against the side of my neck. "I've missed you," he whispered near my ear. "Thought about you more than I should have..." his hands moved up my thighs, fitting me in between his legs. "I've been losing my mind since we left the traders—can't wait much longer."

My head was spinning as his hands moved over my body; they seemed to be touching me everywhere, all at the same time. His mouth was burning a trail from my shoulder up my neck as he worked my jacket and shirt off enough to reveal skin.

"You have to be ready for me, Breenna; I may take you like a starving animal." His teeth gently bit into my neck to emphasize his words.

I shivered with anticipation, any more ready and I'd be a puddle I thought, then he pulled the reins from my hands and lifted me to turn me around to face him, my legs over his. Reaching up I pulled the glasses from his face and slipped them into the pocket of his coat, his black eyes moved over my face.

"You should be afraid of me—" his hand moved up over my hip pulling me into his body.

I could feel how hard he was through our jeans and I shivered again. "I'm not."

Growling, his large hand palmed the back of my head as his mouth connected with mine. Wrapping my arms around his neck, I clung to him as he assaulted me with a deep passionate kiss. I was breathless as he moved his mouth down over my throat. Leaning me back in his arm, I should have feared tumbling off the horse as we moved over the uneven ground but it was the furthest thing from my mind. I didn't even know if we were going in the right direction or if he still held the reins when he pushed up my shirt and lowered his mouth to touch against my bare skin.

A light rain began to fall that should have felt cool, but I hardly noticed it. If anyone had passed by and seen us it would have been an interesting sight, he stretched me out in front of him on the horse's back, tasting any skin he could access. Lifting my legs I wrapped them around his waist and pulled our bodies tight together. He hissed out a breath and tugged me back up to kiss me, reaching between us and undoing my jeans as he did.

With a frustrated noise from deep in his throat I found myself turned in his arms again, his hand moving down into the material he struggled to free me from. When his hand stroked over my wet flesh I moaned and dropped my head back on his shoulder. He growled against my ear when he slid a finger deep inside me. "Fuck! I'm ready to take you right here in the mud like a wild animal."

I wouldn't have cared at that point where; I was trembling and trying to focus on breathing with each movement of his hand. I barely noticed when Tremor stopped moving, so caught up in Kane's touch and his rough breathing against my neck. When he grasped me around the waist and swung us to the ground, my knees buckled for a moment before I turned and held onto him. With a quick motion I was up in his arms and being carried, his mouth devouring my neck as he walked.

When I opened my eyes I was surprised to see we were back at my shelter. Sliding me down his body, he hugged me against his side as he made fast work out of the branches I'd hid the door with. Pulling the door open, he ducked down and stepped inside with me under his arm. As he placed the door back in place, my heart began to beat a crazy tattoo. The look he was giving me made my legs tremble, I was about to be consumed and couldn't find one reason to object. My only thought was *please hurry*.

Slipping the jacket from my arms, I watched from under my lashes as he began to shed his own clothes, all while moving closer to me. By the time I reached to pull my jeans off my body he was standing in front of me kicking off his boots and peeling his own pants away from his body. My breath caught in my throat when he stood before me, naked. I licked my lips, my hands trembling as I slipped the material over my hips. He dropped to his knees and pulled the denim down my legs, his eyes staying on mine the whole time.

I think I stopped breathing all-together as his lips and teeth moved down my leg when he pulled my feet free of the material to stand in front of me again. My naked body was pulled against his, my feet lifted off the ground. Clutching his shoulders I could feel him trembling beneath my touch. I knew then he was holding back, afraid he would hurt me.

His hands gripped my hips tightly when I touched my lips against his chest, when I took his nipple between my teeth I was rewarded with a growl.

When he lifted me, I wrapped my legs around his waist and bit his neck. He held my waist tight, preventing me from impaling my body on his as his mouth devoured my shoulders. With a frustrated noise I couldn't believe came from my own throat, I slid the wetness between my legs against him trying again to slip him inside me.

Kane hissed out a breath and grasped the back of my head with one hand. His mouth crushed mine in a bruising kiss. "I'm trying . . ." his teeth pulled at my bottom lip, "…not to hurt you." Holding the back of my neck he looked at me. "I want you in the worst way, Bree, if I don't control it I could split your dainty little body right in two."

Lifting my body again, I balanced on his shoulders and slid down over the hard length of him again. "You won't hurt me…" His mouth closed around an aching nipple, making me forget the words. Moaning I rubbed over him again. "Kane, I need…" He bit the flesh under his mouth and I gasped in pleasure.

Gripping the back of my thighs, he slowly lifted me over his heated flesh. "Take what you need." He moved over to the wall and braced one hand against it, his teeth scraping along my throat. When I tried to slide onto him again, he didn't stop me just tensed and huffed out a breath as I took him inside me.

He felt so good; I moaned and dropped my head onto his shoulder.

"You're too tight, I can't…" his jaw tensed against the side of my head. Wrapping my arms around his neck I pulled the weight of my body back up the length of him. Watching him I lowered myself back down again. He stood there, one hand gripping my hip the other braced on the wall, his teeth clenched together and those black eyes devouring me, but he made no move to help.

Unable to sit with him filling me, waiting for him to

move, I found a slow rhythm on my own, taking him deep inside me over and over. When my body began to tremble, I fought to catch my breath and keep moving. It was then his hands gripped both hips and he lifted me, thrusting into me as he slammed me against his body. I cried out, biting into his neck when he did it again. My whole body began to clench and shake with the intensity each connection of our flesh brought.

After a few more thrusts I wasn't able to move when my body crashed over the top and I was left gasping for air, trying to hold onto him. When I opened my eyes, his were burning into mine, his whole body vibrating. "Kane…"

Hard hands pulled me away from his sweat covered body, his mouth crushing mine beneath a violent kiss. He jerked his head up and looked down at me. "You destroy me…" he growled. "I can't…" He turned me quickly and placed my hands against the wall, holding them there under one of his. Moving against me, he wrapped the other arm around my waist and pulled me back, bending me over. My legs were shaking when he moved between them.

I could hear his uneven breathing behind me, but wasn't able to turn to look at him when his arm moved down between my legs. He lifted me that way, by one leg and held me upright with one forearm across my waist. The other foot barely touched the ground when a strong leg nudged it aside. My head dropped onto the arm bracing our weight against the wall as he plunged inside me, filling me completely.

With a groan he dropped his head against my shoulder and slowly withdrew, only to thrust into me again. If it were in any other position it probably would have hurt, and he'd known that. My body rubbed over the arm holding me in the air with each powerful movement of his hips, causing my head to spin all over again.

Barely breathing, I gasped each time his violent thrusts brought our bodies into contact, my head was spinning and somewhere it registered the whimpering noises were coming from my own throat. With each movement shocks of pleasure were sent jolting through me and I wasn't sure if I would survive if they got much more intense. I felt so completely possessed by him I was sure I was floating in mid-air, nowhere near the floor beneath us.

His breathing was ragged as he kept forcing his body into my quivering flesh. Quakes of pleasure began moving through me with such intensity I couldn't catch my breath. I heard him growl loud against my ear and knew he was right there with me. As his flesh slapped against mine again a slight pain registered near my neck, but even that turned into a pleasing feeling when I cried out calling his name in a breathless voice.

I could feel my pulse through my entire body, his too when he rested his heavy body into mine. Both of us were breathing like we'd just run a mile as fast as we could. I wasn't able to make any sound but gasping noises. I may never walk again and at that moment I didn't care either. Grinning I panted out a breath and rubbed my cheek against his shaking arm that still held me so I didn't smack my face against the wall.

With no warning at all he pulled out of my body and stepped back. I barely caught myself before I hit the floor. Squatting on quivering legs, I pushed one hand to stop my face from connecting with the rough stone and turned to look at him. He stood several steps away from me, his whole body shaking as he covered his mouth, fear in his black eyes.

"Kane?" I shoved hard against the wall to find my feet and stand. He dropped his hand and then I saw the blood coming from his mouth. With wobbling steps I went towards him, he backed away from me, stumbling as he did.

It was then the pain registered. Lifting my hand I touched the back of my shoulder, just below my neck and then looked at my hand with blood on it.

"I'm so sorry," he whispered with an anguish filled voice that made my heart ache.

Stepping closer I grabbed his arm and held him so he wouldn't move away. I leaned into him and looked up into his black eyes. Carefully I touched his face and then his lips gently. He hissed out a breath and opened his mouth enough that I was able to see the sharp teeth inside, teeth that were more animal then man. I knew I should be startled, but for a reason I couldn't explain I wasn't. "I'm okay," I said softly in a soothing tone. "You didn't hurt me."

"I fucking took a bite out of you." He groaned.

With a gentle touch I touched his mouth again and pulled so he would open it again. He did. I looked into his eyes to see they were still as black as ever. "Did you hear me complain?" I took a deep breath and tried to steady my own breathing. I ran a finger lightly over the jagged teeth in his mouth, more fascinated by them then afraid. With a lingering touch I moved my hand down to touch the side of his neck. "I bit you too."

Finally with shaking hands he gripped my waist. "You didn't take a piece out of me."

I shrugged and turned so he could see where his teeth had sunk into me. "Are there any pieces missing?" With a hiss, he touched his bite and then dropped his face down into my neck.

"I can't believe I lost control like that—with you." His voice was pure agony.

I pulled back and looked up at him. "I was having some sort of out of body experience myself, so stop it."

"Breenna . . ."

I whirled away from him and stood there, hands on hips hoping I looked sterner then I felt standing there glaring at him naked. "Kane, it happened. We were both a little caught up in the moment."

"I have never lost control like that!"

I raised both eyebrows at him and studied him for a moment. "You mean during sex?"

He growled and stocked towards me. "No, that's not what I meant. I meant without notice, just half turned without even knowing it was going to happen."

"I think you were a little pre-occupied to pick up any

warnings."

Picking me up, he crushed me into his body and held me. "I knew it was dangerous, the way I wanted you but I never thought I'd do this." He kissed the area around where he'd bitten me. "And just to clarify on that question, I've only ever had *sex* with you since all of this began." He tightened his grip on me. "Not that what we just did can be classified as sex, it was something entirely different."

My heart jumped around in my chest at his words. I was stunned and not even capable of speaking for several seconds. "Then to be on the safe side, you shouldn't stay away so long next time."

He stiffened and set me on the ground, but didn't release me completely. Shaking his head he looked down at me, with silver eyes once more. "Is that your way of saying it's my own fault?" He smirked.

I shrugged. "Maybe," and then grinned up at him.

His hand connected with my bare butt, hard enough to get my attention, gentle enough it wouldn't hurt me. "You are unbelievable. No self-preservation whatsoever. . ."

I laughed and pulled out of his reach. "So you keep saying." Looking around for my pants, I motioned towards the door. "We should really go unhook poor Tremor and get everything brought inside."

He moved up behind me. "In a minute." With a gentle touch he dabbed at the bite mark he'd left in my skin. "It's stopped bleeding, but we should put something on it—who knows what germs I carry."

I looked over my shoulder at him. "I heal pretty quickly. The bullet graze only hurt for a day."

His movement froze. "Bullet graze?"

I bit my lip, remembering I'd left that detail out of the account of the rescue. Turning, I pointed to the small scar on my shoulder. "See its fine."

Hissing out a breath he ran his finger over the still red scar on my shoulder. "I'm going to hire you a damn bodyguard, Bree."

I moved away from his touch and picked up my pants. "You could do it."

"I think I just proved I can't be trusted."

With jerky movements I yanked on my shirt and jeans. "Don't start. I'm fine and I'll continue to be fine." Slipping my boots on as fast as I could, I hurried outside to look after the animals unable to stand there and listen to all the reasons again Kane thought he was some sort of beast that couldn't be near people.

I had the ropes off of Tremor and the saddle resting on the ground when Kane came up behind me. Without a word he moved in behind me and pulled me to rest against his chest. "I'm sorry." His breath brushed against my cheek. "You turn me inside out, Bree—I don't know what to do half the time when I'm around you."

His confession was making me feel better. "I don't have any answers either. I like being with you and I try not to pry or complain when you take off."

"I know," warm lips brushed over my neck, "if I thought there was a chance I would be able to control the change all the time, I'd stay."

Tears filled my eyes, which angered me all over again that he could do that to me. "Then I'd feel selfish. Others out there need you, Kane." Sighing, I leaned back against him. "I left because I didn't feel safe in the city alone, after my brother died. I came out here to find out where I belong—I can't explain it. My brothers' friends thought I was crazy to set off alone…"

"And they should be shot for letting your innocent ass go, exposing you to men like me."

I turned my head and glared at him. "I needed to. I didn't even know what the virus had done to me until we were out here alone—I just have to find that place, Kane. Do you know what I mean?"

Sighing he turned so I was looking at him. "Yes I do, it's not much different than the reasons I'm out here."

"You've never found that place either?"

His eyes roamed all over my face for several seconds before he answered. "Being with you is the closest I've come, but…"

I reached up and placed my hand over his mouth. "Leave it there." Taking a deep breath I exhaled slowly. "You try to come back from time to time and I'll try to stay safe until we decide differently at some point." I could see the uncomfortable emotions swirling around in his mixed eyes. "Okay?"

Closing his eyes, he nodded.

Stretching up I moved my hand away and kissed him. "Now help me get this done, I'm starving and I have traps to check."

His eyebrows raised but he didn't comment as he released me and bent down to grasp the ropes holding the tarps together.

CHAPTER TWENTY-FIVE

I wanted to say spring was here, but somehow that felt like a challenge to prove me wrong. The days were longer and warmer, at least after the cold of the winter. The rain seemed endless as it flooded ground and surfaces, washing away any sign that winter had been long and snowy. I knew I had to move soon, try to get closer to the mountains. It was hard to stand in our little home and think about leaving, it had everything we needed. The possibility of staying permanently kept creeping into my thoughts. I reminded myself the longer I stayed out on my own, tempting fate, the lesser my chances were of surviving.

I refused to be the wheezing two legged being in our traveling trio and spent the next three weeks pushing my lax muscles back into shape. The animals watched with that look, 'the here she goes again doing some odd human thing' as I ran and reminded my body how to flip and bend. They observed from the earth overhang when I was insane enough to slip and slide in the rain and mud to make sure I got the hours in that my body really needed.

For at least a millisecond I thought of swimming to increase my strength but the cold water combined with the bad memories of the last involuntary swim did not make that a choice. I decided climbing trees would be just as beneficial for my workout, and perhaps adding it as a skill that would come in handy at some point. The tree climbing only occurred after trying to climb a rope hanging from the tree. That, I discovered required more muscle than I had available. It was pretty much a whole body work-out, and I discovered rope burn too.

The sun was shining, one of those glorious spring days where everything smelled new and fresh. I spent half the day fiddling with the new tarps I'd traded children's clothes for, trying to find a way to create a shelter. Kismet lounged in the warm sun observing as I tried tying them together and propping them up several different ways. My plan was to use long poles to make a litter to pull behind Tremor and haul our things. The poles could double as supports for a shelter when I couldn't find any tree cover. The solution was eluding me, as the tarps and poles fell on me for the third time. I had to rethink this plan; two poles would not do the job. Tremor occasionally looked up from his foraging the new growth on the ground to give me a quick curious glance; he was making up for eating dried goods all winter.

He was still eating as I sprawled out on the now dead tree, the one that had tried to crush us in the fall, and began to sketch out my rough map of where we'd been. When I say rough, it looked like something a young child would draw. As long as I knew what it all meant and where we'd been, that was good enough. I had no way of knowing how far we had actually gone in the months since we'd left, but just from the areas I jotted down, estimating the number of days it had taken us to move from one spot to the next I was sure it was more than far enough to feel like we had traveled quite a distance after all.

I compared where we had been to the penciled map Kane had done for me. Just looking at it I realized that no one knew the new country as well as he did. He had to have done nothing but spend his time wandering back and forth along the trails he'd marked. I hadn't even been out here a year and I knew several local trails and landmarks, the knowledge he had meant he had been out in the open space since everything went to hell, several years ago. He had told me I wouldn't reach the mountains before the next winter and I had no choice but to believe him, so I plotted our course along his map so we would be heading towards the network of caves and caverns marked in front of me. It looked like a long distance to aim for in the next four or five months, but I felt confident we'd make it that far. Then again if winter decided to make a comeback without any announcement, as spring had just suddenly sprung, life was going to get frantic. I couldn't think negatively right now, I had to stay focused on getting us out of here and prepared for the long journey ahead.

When I was lying in the cave that night, unrealistically and briefly wishing I could haul my mattress with the stuff we needed to give some semblance of comfort, I realized I could hear the crickets singing outside. Why didn't that sound seem eerie now? I remembered last year lying in the dark and dreading the sound of the crickets and other night noises. I wasn't sure if I felt more at ease because of the walls surrounding me or if I was actually getting used to it, but either way it became a soothing sound to listen to.

~

I stood inside the empty cave that had been home and was sad that we were leaving. All that remained inside was my mattress and a small pile of wood. I'd leave it as we found it and cover the doorway to keep it safe for the next person to use. For a few minutes I had the urge to sign my name on wall or something, anything to show that I'd been here and still survived, but in the end I remembered what Kane had told me about the power of a name and did nothing. So much had happened during the space of time that we'd been here. I stood outside to look around the area, clutching the stone the native woman had given me, wearing it like a traveling talisman for the first time since we'd set up home here. I still didn't know what the markings meant, but I held onto the belief that it had somehow made sure we'd found this spot and would hopefully lead us to the next.

I touched the bite scar on my shoulder, as I caught myself doing too often, feeling a slight connection with Kane each time I did. I realized then that his not knowing where to find me when he chose was the only thread keeping me here. I had to believe that Kane could and always would find me.

Kismet pranced as I checked to make sure everything was tied down and in place. Tremor seemed to have accepted he was going to be doing the bulk of the work hauling the litter and carrying in the packs. I could still fit on him if needed but I was determined that I'd only ride if absolutely necessary. Just as I had determined to use the furs and sleep outside whenever possible, the fewer times I had to unpack and repack the faster this journey would proceed.

~

During the long trek towards the mountains I didn't stop to write, I kept count of the days that passed and tried to add new trails to my map but by dusk time was short and I was too tired to write long notes. We made it further than anticipated, in the almost three months travel. Trading camps were few and far between, the largest settlements had less than a dozen people, temporary camps to stock up on food, supplies and rest for all who passed. I still couldn't bring myself to stay more than a day near people and I wondered if I was turning into some sort of recluse that was just too paranoid to be around others.

I had thought I'd cross paths with Kane somewhere on this part of the journey, but so far we hadn't. I held onto the thought that he was out moving from one cluster of people to the next warning or helping where needed, and that he would find us at some point.

The weather would be sweltering hot for days at a time, making traveling slower and shorter. When I decided to up camp under the larger trees for shade and rest, the rain would come. It wasn't a light summer rain, either, but a flood generating rain, even with the land parched from the constant heat. Moving through valleys or ravines had to be done in the middle of the heat, fortunately the animals didn't mind moving in the rain— I think all three of us were becoming accustomed to being wet.

Finally after a five day stint of pushing and covering as much ground as possible we came across a small shack that had possibly been used for hunting. It was on a hill with a breathtaking view of a small river. It was too good to keep going; we'd earned a short break. It took no time to unpack and fill up the little structure. The door had long ago fallen off, but after months of sleeping under trees and a tarp I wasn't going to turn into a snob about something so trivial. There was a small wood stove in it and for a few seconds I had some fantasy of trying to pack it up when we left— crushed when I tried to see if I could lift it. Only Mother Nature herself would move that chunk of metal.

It felt good to sit outside it and not have to plan dinner and how far we should try to go before the weather changed again. The few stops I'd made along the way I'd heard many unsettling things. News from one settlement to the next had been passed along from the cities where communications were still possible. The climate chaos was not settling it was even more unpredictable and dangerous. Fires consumed large areas, with inhabitants limited to using buckets without the planes and helicopters that used to battle the blazes from above. Rumors of tornados in areas that had never experienced since history began were everywhere. Countries that had not once stepped into the cold of snow were now covered in deep snow. The equator had moved and the unwritten laws of the climate had been changed without notice. Overall it was scary as hell to not know what could or would happen next.

I had to believe I would adapt to whatever came our way, if I couldn't you would find me curled up in the nearest corner. I wasn't ready to give up yet.

Kismet ran along the edge of the river, stopping every few feet and looking up at me. I shook my head knowing he was trying to invite me to go for swim. I still had issues with immersing my body entirely into water that didn't follow any rules but its own, so I tossed a stick at him and watched as he leapt into the water to chase after it. I had always thought wolves didn't like water, but Kismet wasn't exactly a normal wolf, having a horse and woman as his companions. Stringing a line across some trees, I decided it would be a good time to air everything out. After months of being packed up when damp all of my stuff was starting to smell like a goodwill drop box. If I was lucky I could get everything washed and dried before the next rain arrived. It was hot enough to wear an old worn tank top that had long ago frayed at the bottom and a pair of shorts that also had seen better days. I even left off my boots for a change to let my feet relax.

~

I had just gathered up everything and set it inside when Kismet jumped up and ran back out the door. The hair on the back of my neck stood up as I moved quickly over to my gun and knives and stepped closer to the door. Squinting against the setting sun as I squatted down to look out the door, I heard Tremor whinny and every nerve in my body tightened.

Stepping out without thinking, I was not about to let something happen to him. Someone stood beside my horse, their hand on his halter. I moved around so I could aim at the intruder without hitting my cherished companion. "If you want to keep both legs you better let go of my horse." I called out. They froze and started to turn. Widening my stance I aimed low enough on their body that Tremor wouldn't be at risk.

"You'd take a shot at me, Brat?"

My heart landed in my throat when I heard his voice. "Bobby?" I lowered the gun and stumbled towards him as he turned and I could see his face.

Running, I dropped the knives and gun and pounced into his arms with such force we both landed at Tremor's feet. Pushing myself up, I looked down at him grinning. "I can't believe it's you—what are you doing out here?"

He grinned. "I was just hiking along minding my own business until I spotted a tall dark horse that looked really familiar." Kismet came running over, his ears back.

I held up my hand and sat up. "Kizzy, it's okay." Leaning down I hugged Bobby. "He's a friend."

"Is that a wolf?" Bobby's voiced squeaked.

I sat up again and looked down at him. "I'm pretty sure he is."

Bobby sat up to rest on his elbows and looked at the black furry animal crawling towards him. "Where the hell did you get a wolf?" He kept looking at it. "Is it going to bite me? I have a fear of being eaten alive."

I chuckled. "No he's more likely to lick you until you're covered in drool." I reached out and ruffled his fur. "He found me that first night and has been with us ever since."

"Wow—here we were all worried about you and you've got a wild animal guardian."

I looked down at the man I was still sitting on. "I can't believe you're here. Why are you here?" I looked all around us, "Where's Darren? Did he come too?" I realized I sounded like the little girl he thought I was, bubbling with excitement.

Bobby reached up and grasped my jaw lightly. "I'll answer as soon as you get off me," he shook the shaggy blonde hair back from his eyes. "I'm having a little bit of a struggle at this moment remembering you're Shawn's baby sister when you're straddling me like this."

I scrambled up off him and stood there brushing the dirt from my knees. "Sorry. I was just surprised to see you."

"That makes two of us." He stood there, his eyes traveling over me. "You are not that same quiet sweetling I watched ride away on a horse."

I felt a blush cover me when he continued to look at me in the way I'd done nothing but wish for when I was still a little girl inside and out. "Probably not."

He moved over and ran a finger down over the scar on

my cheek.

I covered it with my hand. "Got a little too close to a knife."

"Hmm, anything else before I try to settle my heart down?" He turned me around completely until I was facing him again. "All body parts still attached…"

I laughed. "All present and accounted for." His finger skimmed over the scar on my arm. "Bullet grazed me," I whispered.

"Don't even tell me anymore. Knife scars, dodging bullets—" He held a hand over his heart. "I can't hear anymore."

Bending down, I picked up the gun and pouch of knives and looked up at him grinning. "You might not survive the rest of the explanations."

He whooshed out a loud breath. "Jesus, Bree—it's so good to see you."

I moved under his arm and we turned to walk back to the little shack. "How long have you been out here?"

He shrugged in that nonchalant Bobby fashion. "Just after Christmas—when all hell broke loose, I hit the road." Stopping, he let me go into through the small door first. "I hitched a ride with an odd crew heading out, otherwise I'd only be about half as far as I am—but they stayed at some roughneck settlement about a month ago so I've been high-tailing it alone since then." His eyes moved over the items that filled the small space. "You've made it a lot further than I'd imagined you would have."

I moved to the stove and opened it. "It was a long winter, but we've made up for lost time since then." Lighting the fire, I waited and made sure the flames didn't die down before closing it. "I've got fresh rabbit for dinner."

Bobby groaned. "Anything that resembles food works for me. I'm half starving." He cleared his throat. "You killed the rabbit yourself?"

I grinned at him over my shoulder. "Yes I did and tomorrow I'll stretch the skin and prepare it to wait until I have enough pelts to make something useful."

"Wow—that's—you've done all right, baby Bree."

I smiled at the childhood nickname. "I'm hanging in there." I began cutting the meat into strips, "so tell me what's going on, Bobby. I'm a little out of touch here."

He moved over and slid down the wall, letting Kismet rest his chin on his leg. "All hell broke loose last fall. The fucking Red Bands started moving through our turf and rounding up anyone that had been rumored to have been sick at any point." I looked over at him when he stopped abruptly. "They took Darren's brother, he didn't come back."

My chest tightened. "He was never sick…"

Shaking his head, took a deep breath. "I know, but they wouldn't listen. Darren and his mom hid me for weeks, but I couldn't stay cooped up forever."

"You? Why?" I dropped the meat into the pan and set it at the back of the stove.

He cleared his throat. "I'm a survivor, Bree."

I went over and sat in front of him. "I didn't even know you were sick."

Flicking the hair back from his eyes, he smiled a sad smile. "We hid it from you, just in case I didn't pull through. You'd already lost so many…"

Reaching out I grabbed his forearm. "Are you okay?"

"Yeah. I'm not some nasty mutant, but they still want to tag me anyways." He shrugged. "I have my own built in spidey-senses now—I can sense anyone that's mutated."

My jaw dropped.

He grinned. "Yeah, I knew the day you came out of your fever."

"Did you know what?"

He shook his head, sending his blonde locks dancing around. "No, I don't know *what* people can do, just that they've picked up something extra."

"Oh." I sat back again, letting my hand drop. "I heal."

"What?"

"That's what I picked up—I can heal others—inside and out."

Leaning forward he gave me an odd look. "Really?" I nodded. "That's kind of cool."

Getting up, I went back over to the stove. "Yeah it is, especially when people are suffering."

He stood up and came up behind me, turning me slowly to face him. "You've been using it around others?"

I knew why he was so concerned, but for once I knew more about something in life than he did. "Yes. Around others that are like us—survivors." I thought briefly of Maisy and tried not to be sad knowing that I was several weeks travel away from her and the settlement. "There are whole communities of mutated survivors out here, Bobby."

He hissed out a breath. "I guess that makes sense, with all the people fleeing from the cities."

I moved out of his grasp and went over to get the water pail to make some tea. "I've seen a lot since that day I rode away—not all of it good."

"I realize that, why haven't you settled in one of those communities?"

I rolled my eyes, feeling the 'you should be safe and protected' spiel coming. "I will, when I reach the mountains."

"Bree, there are Red Bands moving around the whole country side collecting up people…"

I wanted to growl at him, but didn't. "I know. I've encountered them more than once." He spun me around to face him as water sloshed out of the pail all over my feet.

"Did they hurt you?" His pale eyes were moving all over me again.

I touched his cheek softly and shook my head. "No, if anything I did some damage to them."

His hands squeezed my arms tightly, dragging me against him. "Why the hell did we just let you walk away without us?"

I stood there crushed in his arms, holding the pail of

water away from us so I didn't soak us further. "I've done fine on my own," I mumbled into his shirt that was pressing into my face.

For a long time he stood there breathing into my hair. "I worried a lot after you left—stood near the city edge, watching to see if you came back."

I pushed against him until I could see his face again. "Did you think I would?"

"No, but I hoped. It wasn't the same after you left."

"Bobby, it wasn't the same long before I left—we were dwindling away, dying one by one—I couldn't wait and watch it happen again."

Dropping his hands away, he paced over to the door. "I get that. I still wish—" He just stood there. "I'm going to go rinse off in the river, I'll be back."

I watched him walk down to the water's edge, realizing he had changed since I'd been gone. The joker was gone, and the serious side had finally come out.

~

We spent the evening talking about the oddities we'd seen since leaving the city, neither really saying much about the city or what life had once been like.

Sitting in the door, we watched the sun going down. "I'm glad you stumbled upon us, Bobby. It's been a few months since I really had anyone to talk to."

"Made a few friends along the way?"

I sighed and looked across the river. "Yeah, but they're way back from where we were in the spring so it's been kind of lonely."

"I get that. I've caught myself talking out loud to no one more than often than I'd like to admit.

I laughed, "at least I can pretend I'm talking to the animals." I stood up and stretched. "I'm going foraging for herbs tomorrow, so I need to get some sleep."

He stood up beside me and looked down at me, the smile on his face fading. "I can't tell you how happy I am that you're okay, Bree." One warm hand cupped the back of my neck.

If it had been any other male than Bobby, I may have panicked, but he would always feel safe.
I knew the way he was looking at me that he was going to kiss me and the girl I used to be, that longed for his kiss for years, was going to let him. His lips brushed over mine briefly before he covered them completely. I leaned into his kiss and returned it, sad that I didn't feel any excitement.

Lifting his head, he smiled down at me as his hand played with my hair. "Missed my chance, didn't I?"

I offered a soft smile.

He sighed. "I blame your brother and the rest of them. I was afraid if I made a move on you those five would pound me into the pavement."

I felt sadness fill my heart. "I'm sorry. If you had of made a move then, I would have given you my heart—I've changed now."

Sighing in a dramatic way, he hugged me against him. "That doesn't make me feel better, brat. If I had though, you wouldn't have left and we'd both be caged in some mutant camp." Ruffling my hair, he stepped back from me. "So, there's been someone?"

I felt a blush cover me, not sure how to tell him. "Yes."

"Where is he now?"

There was no way I could explain Kane in a simple bedtime conversation. "He has things he has to take care of out there."

"I see." He moved into the small shack and picked up his sleeping bag to unroll. "I won't lie, I'm suffering a bit of heartache right now…" Flipping it out, he sat down on it and pulled off his boots. "When I saw Tremor, and you running towards me—well it's amazing the fantasies one can have in a few seconds time."

"I'm sorry."

He snorted, "Don't be, baby Bree." He exhaled loudly. "You're safe, whole and seemingly happy—that's good enough for me."

Going over I leaned down and kissed his cheek, "and happier knowing you're okay too."

"Get some sleep," he mumbled and then lied down on top of the material. "Tomorrow you can impart some of your survival knowledge upon me—I'm sick of being hungry all the time!"

CHAPTER TWENTY-SIX

The next day was picture perfect—gorgeous summer weather and someone to laugh with. I'd spent the morning dragging Bobby along the riverbanks, showing him plants and what to use them for. He complained about the bugs, pretending he was a city guy and couldn't deal with the filth in the outdoors. I hadn't laughed like this is a while. I didn't know if his joking was him falling into his safe zone after our discussion, but it was nice to spend time with him again.

I finished stretching the hide and hanging it high in the tree and turned to get the other one. Kismet barked, dragging my attention over to where he sat—beside him stood Kane, smiling at me.

"Someone found me." He leaned down and rubbed the top of Kizzy's head.

"I swear, Bree, there isn't an inch of me without a bug bite..." Bobby stepped out of the door and then stopped.

I glanced at him and then looked at Kane, who wasn't smiling now.

"Holy shit, brat—you hooked up with the terminator," Bobby whispered.

I grinned at him and then started to walk over to Kane. I couldn't see his eyes behind the glasses, but I knew they were on me as I tingled from head to toe. "I suppose I'll have to give Kizzy a whole rabbit tonight for tracking you down."

"At least one." Kane's voice sounded strained.

I moved until I was standing almost on his feet. Reaching up, I pulled the glasses off his face so I could see those silver irises' looking at me. Wrapping my arms around his waist, I wanted to climb right inside of him. "I've been worried."

His big arm squeezed me tight, lifting me off the ground as his mouth covered mine and crushed it with a desperate kiss, letting me know how much he'd missed me too. When he lifted his head, he didn't look down at me, or put me back on the ground. I turned to see that Bobby held his attention.

Bobby raised both of his hands, looking solemn. "I'm just an old childhood friend, buddy. I grew up with her brother." Bobby shrugged in his nonchalant way, "ever see how handy she is with a knife? I taught her that skill."

I wasn't sure if he was telling Kane that to let him know he was a friend, or to state he knew how to take care of himself, but I felt the tension drain from the arms that held me tight. Kane finally looked down at me and smiled again, the hard look in his eyes fading. Dropping a brief kiss on my mouth, he hiked me up into his arms and started walking towards Bobby. "Ever had her toss those knives at you when she's pissed?"

Bobby quirked and eyebrow and shook his head.

Kane chuckled. "Try not to piss her off then—I can vouch it's a frightening thing." I leaned into Kane and let him continue to hold me.

Bobby grinned at me and then shook his head. "She always was a brat."

Kane didn't set me down until we were inside the shack. He looked around and smiled at me. "You always find the best shelters, Red—how is that?"

I pulled his pack from his shoulder and set it by the door. "I have no idea. Maybe I just have good karma."

He chuckled and pulled his shirt over his head, wiping

his brow with it before tossing it on top of the pack. "Wouldn't surprise me." He turned back to look at Bobby leaning in the door way. Reaching out he offered his hand. "Kane."

I stood back and watched Bobby staring at the hand for a second before taking it.

"Bobby." They shook hands. "So, she really tossed the knives at you? And missed?"

Kane grinned. "Yeah and I hope she missed on purpose."

"How the hell did you piss her off?"

Kane looked over at me. My face went red when I remember that day. Kane hissed out a breath. "I think I'll just keep that to myself or she might not miss the next time."

Both of them laughed. My heart swelled to hear Kane laugh and to know Bobby was a part of it. I looked at Kane and I'm sure my heart was visible at that point, and then I noticed the bruises across his ribs. I went over and touched his side. "Have you been letting people beat on you again?"

His big hand moved over my hair as I continued to run my hands along his skin. "I don't intentionally *let* them beat on me." He hissed when I pushed harder against a reddened area.

"What other damage did they do?"

Kane clasped my hand and raised it to his lips. "My ribs are just a little tender, nothing like before."

"Rescuing damsels in distress again?"

"No, they throw knives at me…" I frowned at him. "A couple young boys thought they'd strike out on their own."

I gasped. "They're okay?"

"Yes, I left them with Maisy."

I let out the breath I'd been holding. "Good." I pointed to the furs on the floor. "Go lay down and I'll see what I can do to help you."

Kane moved over and stretched out on the furs. I went over and straddled him, rubbing my hands together. Kane grinned up at me. "I think you should clue your friend in, he's looking a little concerned."

Turning, I looked over at Bobby and smiled. "Sorry. Um—I don't know how to even explain. I'll touch him and some sort of heat travels through my hands and heals him."

"Burns like nothing I've ever felt before," Kane added quietly.

"That's freaky, Bree— in a cool way." Bobby moved over closer. "Do you need me to do anything?"

I shook my head and looked back down at Kane. "No he's not as badly damaged as the last time, so it should be fairly simple." I looked back down at Kane, who was still smiling at me. "You better stop grinning away at me or I'm going to think you did this so I'd have to touch you."

Kane laughed and gripped my hips tightly. "I don't think I need to be bruised to get that."

Ignoring his comment and the chuckle from behind me, I closed my eyes and rubbed my hands together lightly. When I opened my eyes I looked only at the flushed skin and the areas that were starting to turn shades of blue and purple. Lowering my hands I pushed them against the skin and held them there. Kane hissed, telling me my touch was doing whatever it did that helped.

I continued to move them over his skin until I'd touched each area that looked damaged. When I was finished my head was a little light, but nothing like I'd experienced before. I sat there on him and watched as he opened his eyes, they were as black as I'd expected them to be.

"Whoa," Bobby whispered from behind me.

Kane smiled up at me, giving me only a seconds warning before he grasped my waist and had me flipped off him and half under his body.

"Uh—I'll be outside."

I heard Bobby walk out, but couldn't take my eyes off the man hovering over me. "Feeling better?"

"Much." He skimmed his hand down my side and over my hip. "No close encounters with danger I should know about before I find any scars or gashes?'

I bit my lip to keep from grinning at his way of asking if I was alright. "I've practically been invisible."

"Good to hear." When his mouth moved close enough to mine I could feel his breath, I moved my hand up into his hair and grasped it. "I've missed you," he whispered and then licked my lower lip.

My insides started quivering from the slight contact. "It's been months, Kane." I looked up into his eyes that were so black they reflected my own image right back at me.

"I know it. I've felt every second crawl by." He moved his hand over my cheek, brushing lightly at the scar. "I don't think I can touch you right now—not with someone nearby…" I pulled his hair so he'd lower his mouth back to mine. "Breenna—" Growling he brushed his lips over mine and then went to move away, but I wouldn't let go of his hair.

"Just kiss me." I stretched up and nipped at his chin with my teeth.

"Jesus, why can't I seem to resist you?" He looked distressed when he opened his eyes.

"I like that you can't—come on, just one kiss."

He snorted and glared at me. "I'm starving for you—if I can't stop and you start moaning and crying out and your friend comes in and stabs me in the ass or something I'm going to be pissed."

I laughed, unable to hold it in with way he enunciated each word softly. "I'll accept full responsibility."

He growled again just before he began to devour my mouth. His tongue plunged in and tangled with my own, our teeth scraping together. Moaning deep in his throat, he pulled me into the hardness of his body as his free hand moved over mine in a rough caress. My head started spinning when the kiss became frantic. I was clinging to him—suddenly starving for the contact with him. Wrapping my leg around him, I pulled my body into his and then he lifted his head and rolled away from me.

"Get up," he hissed out a long deep breath.

Pushing up on my elbow I leaned over him.

"Don't even touch me, just get out and I'll be there in a minute." He covered his eyes with his forearm and stayed that way, panting.

I got up off the furs and moved over to the door, stopping to look back at him.

"Breenna!"

Grinning, I went outside and looked around for Bobby. He was sitting over by the river with Kismet beside him. My legs were shaking as I walked over to him, but in a good way. "Feel like fish for dinner?"

He turned and gave me a surprised look. "Uh, sure." He looked over towards the shack.

"He'll be out in a minute," I said quietly as I sat down beside him.

Bobby looked over his shoulder again before he let out a long sigh. "I'm feeling a little insignificant right now."

I frowned. "What do you mean?"

He motioned with his head towards the shack. "I find out last night you could have been mine—hey that's cool I screwed up that chance years ago and then…" He gave a strangled laugh. "Then I see where your tastes lie—holy shit, Bree—my heart stopped when I came out to see him standing there—and do I even *want* to know about the funky eye thing with him?"

I laughed. "He can be a little intimidating."

"A little?" He squeaked. "That's the understatement of the century! That's like saying the weather has *slight* changes occasionally."

It made me laugh again when I saw the look on his face as he said that. "You can be intimidating too."

Bobby rolled his eyes at me. "Yeah to an ant—maybe a small bird…"

"But you've got *skills* no one can compete with, and there's your charm—"

"This is true." He nodded.

I stood up, and brushed off my hands. "Come on, we'll put your skills to work on catching some fish." I turned to see Kane striding towards us. "Fish work for dinner?"

"Only if you promise not to fall out of the tree into the river." He smiled.

"Tree?" Bobby looked up at me.

"Don't ask." I smiled at Kane.

CHAPTER TWENTY-SEVEN

As I snuggled against Kane's warm body, I couldn't help but feel immensely pleased. The day had been perfect—as close to perfect as I'd felt in a very long time. Seeing Bobby and knowing he had survived, then to have Kane show up— it didn't get any better than that. The only thing that would make it spectacular was if a bath tub full of hot water and bubbles appeared on my doorstep.

Exhaling, I snuggled back into the warmth and closed my eyes again. Bobby was snoring softly from the other side of the small room, it wasn't the usual night noise but I didn't object to it either. I was just starting to drift off when I felt Kane move, I thought he was just getting comfortable but then he got up completely and left.

Trying not to trip over anything I moved outside after him. The air was cool, but the light from the moon lit a path for me so I could see his outline near the river's edge. Careful of where I was stepping I went up behind him and slid my arms around his waist. "You okay?"

He rubbed his hand over my arms and let out a long shaky breath. "Yeah, just being a man."

Moving around to stand in front of him, I ran my hands from his the jeans at his waist up over his bare chest. "I don't understand what that means."

Gripping my hips he pulled me into his body, grinding his pelvis against me so I could feel exactly what he meant. "Ah," I whispered against his chest.

"Mmm." He lowered his mouth to brush against my ear. "We don't exactly do soft, quiet love making so I thought I'd just lie with you—be happy with having you close to me knowing you're safe would be enough."

I looked up at him. "Not working, huh?"

"No. Not at all."

"Maybe we could do something about that." I moved away to slide down his body, but his strong hands grasped my waist and stopped me.

"Not a chance. With the way you affect me I'm liable to howl at the fucking moon if you touch me with your mouth."

I grinned at the frustration in his voice. "There has to be something we can do." Stretching up I nibbled at his neck. He growled but didn't move away from me. "Take off your jeans and lie down."

"Breenna, it's been too long."

I touched my hand to his mouth. "For both of us. Let me get on top and be in control for a change."

Lowering his mouth he kissed me softly, tasting me carefully before he answered. "I don't want to hurt you—again."

"I'll stay clear of your teeth." Taking his hand I lowered to the ground and pulled him with me. I ran my hands over his chest as he undid his jeans and pushed them over his hips. As soon as he was free, I straddled him.

"You're naked under that t-shirt?"

Leaning over I kissed him. "Yes."

He groaned as I slid my body over his hard length. "I can't resist you…"

"Then stop trying." I was more than happy to bypass foreplay, just seeing him worked well enough when my body had missed him for this long. Grasping his shoulders I maneuvered myself over him and then slowly slid him inside me. I almost cried out as he filled me, sending jolts of pleasure through me. Firm hands gripped my waist and helped lift me up again. When I slid back down slowly he growled.

His hands moved up under my shirt and cupped both breasts, tugging gently on my hard nipples. My insides quivered from the touch. "Don't stop." He hissed when I dropped my weight onto him.

Grinning down at him, I used his hands to raise my body up. Strong fingers closed around my own as he let me find my rhythm and set the pace. After a few movements my body began to tighten in anticipation and I knew I wasn't going to last as long as I'd wanted. His hips jerked towards me as I quickened the pace, his breathing as rough as my own.

Releasing my hands he took a hold of my hips again and began thrusting me down onto him with twice the force I could have managed on my own. I moaned and held onto his shoulders when my legs started to tremble. Leaning back I rested my hands on his hard thighs to keep from tipping over completely.

Kane growled deep in his throat and that sound alone traveled right to my core, igniting it in flames. When I heard myself start to whimper, I leaned forward and pressed my mouth into his throat, trying to keep from crying out. His thrusts increased and everything shattered inside me. My muscles clenched against him as he buried himself deep in me until I felt him swell and burst just as I bit into his shoulder and tried not to cry out in pleasure.

With slow movements he rocked into me, sending me swimming with one after shock after another. I could taste his blood in my mouth and smiled against his flesh. My breathing was impossible to slow as long as he kept moving into me. His breathing wasn't much better as he hissed out a breath each time he pushed into the heat that covered both of us.

Unable to control my own body a moment longer, I collapsed onto his chest. "Mmm—feel better now?"

His lips moved slowly across my cheek towards my mouth. "A little—I could do this all night with you." He bit my chin.

I was seriously debating on that when Kismet came running out of the dark and dropped something next to our shoulders.

"Tell me it's not something dead," Kane said in a breathless tone.

I sniffed before reaching for it. "It doesn't smell dead." Squinting in the dark, I picked it up and sat up, still straddling him. "It's a hat."

"Wonder where he went shopping at this hour."

I grinned, not expecting humor from Kane at that moment. He took it from my hands and turned it around to look at it. Even in the dim lighting I could see the expression on his face change.

He patted my side. "Get up and wake up Bobby—bring Tremor around to the side and get back inside."

I scrambled up so quick I almost tipped over. My heart was lodged in my throat as I headed towards the shack. I'd never heard that tone from Kane, even when I thought he should sound deadly, he never had. The urgency in his voice had my nerves tense and limbs quaking as I stumbled to the small building. On the way by Tremor, I grabbed his halter and pulled him to the side of the shelter with the trees. Unhooking the strap that hung loosely around his neck I secured it to the tree and hurried inside.

In the dark it took me longer than I wanted to find my jeans, pulling them up numb legs I moved over and nudged Bobby with my foot.

"What?" He mumbled.

"Bobby," I whispered. "Get up, something is going on."

He bolted upright and kicked the blankets off his legs. "What's happening?"

Squatting down, I leaned closer to him. "I don't know. Kismet came back with a hat and Kane told me to get you up and stay in here."

Nodding, he reached under his pillow and pulled out a small bag. Reaching in he pulled out his knives and began to stuff them into the leather strap along his hip.

Getting up, I went over and picked up my handmade harness and pulled it over my shoulder. In even less time I had my knives and gun secured and was tying the bag with more ammunition to it. Kane still hadn't come in, so I moved over to the door and slid down it to look around outside. If anyone wanted to they could just look right in, with the door leaning against the wall outside.

Bobby came over and dropped to one knee beside me and looked out the other way. "Where did Kane go?"

"I don't know. I don't see Kizzy either so maybe he's trying to find out where the hat came from."

Bobby moved to sit half way out the door so he could see both ways. "He sounded the alarm over a hat?" His voice was filled with doubt.

"I don't think it was just any hat. He recognized it from somewhere."

"That's not good then is it?"

I shook my head and leaned out to be sure Tremor was staying hidden. "No." I saw something move out of the trees the furthest away from us. My breath hitched until I spotted Kismet running alongside Kane.

Jogging right to us, he stopped and leaned down to pet the furry head that stopped right beside him. "I took the hat back." He pointed to the trail through the trees. "There's six of them camped out in that little clearing through the bush."

"You know who they are?" Bobby asked checking his knives again.

Kane nodded. "I know the captain."

"Captain? They're Red Bands?" I moved further out the door.

"Yeah," Kane answered softly with hesitance in his voice.

"Shit!" Bobby stood up and turned back to his gear. He started to roll it up and stuff his things inside it.

I got up. "You can't take off in the dark, Bobby." I looked at Kane for back-up. "We know where they are, we can watch and see which way they go in the morning and then we'll decide what to do."

"She's right." Kane turned and started to look around. "As long as we keep Tremor out of sight, they'll never even know we're here."

Bobby stopped and then tossed his bag into the corner. "I'll take first watch." He reached went over and looked at Kismet. "Come on vicious animal you get to do watch duty too."

We watched him walk back towards the trees with the Kizzy beside him. "Where would they be heading?"

Kane wrapped his arm around me and pulled me into his side. "There's a settlement about a day's travel up this trail, my guess is that way."

"Will the people there be prepared?"

Rubbing his jaw he was silent for a moment. "They usually are." Kissing the top of my head, he squeezed me against his side. "I want you to pack up in the morning, I'll write down a new route for you to take."

I nodded even though I really didn't want to move on just yet. I'd hoped for more time to rest but if Kane felt I needed to move, I knew I should follow his instinct and knowledge. "Where are you going?"

He stiffened. "In the same direction as you—for a while then I'm going to head around and see what damage they're doing."

"So you're following them?"

"Indirectly."

Wrapping my arms around him, I held him tight for a moment. "Your hero tights are showing again."

He snorted. "You are a brat."

Leaning back I looked up at him. "We could go with you."

"Not in this life-time."

Moving away, I looked out the door, trying to remember

to keep my voice down. "I can be of use. If there are injured people—"

He closed the distance in less than a stride and gripped my arms tightly. "I don't know what they're doing but if it's what I think, *you* are staying as far the hell away as possible." He grasped my chin with a firm hand. "Breenna—your mutation would be a gold mine, I won't take a chance—not with you."

I stared into his eyes, wishing I could find a reason to convince him to let me stay with him. "Fine. So I'll just continue on and be left wondering where you are and if you're ever going to show up again…"

Kane straightened away from me and ran a hand through his hair. "I'm not having this discussion again. You know why I can't stay."

"I know why you think you can't stay—I have no evidence to back it up other than your beliefs."

"You are constantly in my thoughts, Bree. I spend most of the time hoping I don't come back and find you've…" He moved back over to the door. "When Bobby stepped out of this door, I thought—it looked…"

"Don't even finish that or I'll use you for target practice." I leaned against the wall, struggling with my temper.

Kane turned and came over to me. "I will *always* come back, Breenna, until you tell me otherwise." He paused and I half wondered if he was waiting for me to tell him not to. "If you don't want me appearing whenever my heart can't take another day away from you, tell me now. Otherwise I will *always* find you."

My anger snuffed out like a flame under water. "You better." I stifled a yawn.

Pulling me into his arms he held me against his chest. "Lay down for a few hours, Kismet will make sure all of us know when they're moving." He kissed the top of my head. "He's an incredible beast, knowing enough to bring that damn hat to warn us."

I rubbed my cheek against his heartbeat. "I stopped trying to figure him out months ago."

"Get some rest. I'm going to be right outside the door."

"I doubt I'll sleep but I will stretch out for a minute."

~

"Bree, get up."

I jolted awake and opened my eyes, Bobby hovered over me.

"Get up, Kane's moving Tremor somewhere out of sight. He told me to tell you to hike your ass up that big tree out back and stay there until they're gone."

I sat up. "They're moving?"

He nodded. "Just having some coffee and getting ready to."

I looked out the door to see the sunlight was just starting to breach the darkness. "Okay." I got up and grabbed my hooded sweater and my harness of weapons. "Keep watch for two, I'm going around back to pee first." Scooping up a cup of water from the pail I drank it down quickly and went out the door. I didn't know why Kane wanted me up the tree, but since the moment I had been grabbed by him almost a year ago I'd learned he did know best in things like this.

Was I supposed to be the look-out or the sharp shooter? I wasn't sure, but at least I'd have the best view from the huge old Maple tree that grew behind the shack. I found it a little amusing that Kane had told me to climb the tree after the way he'd fretted when I shimmed up the last one to catch dinner. A hitch in my heart beat reminded me that things were serious enough that he wanted me out of sight *and* reach.

Bobby boosted me up to reach the first branch and then it was easy going after that, the large limbs were meant to be used for climbing. I kept going, glancing around every few branches to see if I had a good view of the entire area. When I finally decided I was high enough I straddled the wide arm of the tree and leaned back against the rough bark. Pulling the hood up over my head, I made sure all of my hair was tucked away so I wouldn't be a red beacon.

I had just settled when I spotted Kane moving quickly back in our direction, Kismet right on his heels. Bobby circled around the shack, checking to make sure nothing from inside was visible or left out and then he moved back into the trees to duck down behind one, knife ready in his hand. It occurred to me that I was the only one with a weapon of distance. Come to think of it I'd never seen Kane with any sort of weapon.

Kane paused beneath the tree and looked up at me. I couldn't see his eyes, but knew they were telling me to be safe and stay there until he said otherwise. I smiled down at him and then looked back towards the tree-line, watching.

When I looked back again, Kismet was moving over to lie down in the trees not far from Bobby, I wasn't sure but I thought he looked up at me once before he settled down. All the males were protecting me, which made me frown until I realized if it came down to it me with my, were watching out for them.

I couldn't see Kane, but knew he would be sitting somewhere in the open, just waiting. I barely had time to realize staying in the tree was going to get uncomfortable when there was movement from the tree-line. I leaned back to find a stable position that would hold, for a long time if I needed.

The first one came out of the trees and I recognized him by the hat he wore. The Captain that Kane was familiar with. Three more followed, all carrying jugs. My breath hitched, caught in my lungs. I hoped they were just after water and then would move along. As they went down to the river I kept a relaxed hold on the gun. My knives were useless at his distane, so gun it was.

When one of them turned, and stopped in mid-stride he said something I couldn't make out to the hat-wearer. The captain turned and looked towards the shack, I knew Kane was standing there in plain sight, not even attempting to hide.

"Kane?" He took a few steps towards the cabin,

motioning his men to go to the river.

"Captain." Kane's low voice replied.

"Didn't think I'd see you in these parts for a while." He reached his hand to the back of his pants. My hand flexed ready for what he hid there.

"Just stretching out for a few hours of rest before I move on."

One of the men whispered something to the Captain. He shook his head. "Kane is off limits—he gets a free pass." The man muttered and went back to the river. "Was it you that beat the shit out of two of my soldiers?"

"Those were soldiers? You must be accepting anyone now." Kane quipped in a sarcastic tone.

The man grinned. "Trainees."

Kane stepped out to where I could see him more. "I think you need to work on their training."

He shrugged. "I'm sure their stupidity taught them something."

"If they're stupid enough to harm young boys, then they get what they deserve."

The men came back from the river and stood behind their captain. "Which way are you heading, Kane?"

Kane raised his arm and pointed. "Down the river."

"Suits me fine." He said something over his shoulder to his men and then started walking back towards the trees. Just before he reached them he stopped and turned back to Kane. "Someday Ritter won't be in charge and then it's going to be you and me."

Kane crossed his arms over his chest and nodded once. "I'll see you then."

I watched the man with the hat walk backwards until he reached the bush with the others before turning. Kismet took off through the trees and went to stand by the edge of the path they had followed. He moved down onto his stomach and stayed there, watching and listening. Bobby moved slowly back towards the shack, glancing up at me as he went under the tree.

I stayed where I was, flicking my eyes over the trees along the path making sure they weren't going to double back. When Kismet got up and ran over to Kane, I knew they were gone. Breathing out a sigh of relief I tucked the gun back into its holster and turned to maneuver down the tree.

By the time I reach the last branch, Kane stood beneath me ready to help me down. Without straining he pulled me down into his arms in one swift movement. Carrying me, he headed back around the cabin. "Bobby went to get Tremor."

When he set me on the ground, I couldn't help glance back at the trees one more time. "Think they're going to keep moving?"

Kane nodded. "Yeah, they have an agenda."

"Do you know everyone, Kane?"

He shrugged.

"Who is Ritter?"

Turning he watched Bobby come out from the other line of trees. "The leader of the Red Bands," he answered quietly.

CHAPTER TWENTY-EIGHT

If I'd added up my tally marks right, it had been a little over a month since Kane had left me on the path of least traffic to go off to save the day again. The counting also reminded me that I had gotten a year older, not that age mattered out here in the slightest. As I was the only one in my quiet little world, I was both the youngest and had the most seniority, it really was the best of both worlds.

We'd kept going for most of that month, only stopping long enough to eat, rest and collect anything useful along the way. After the second week I felt too guilty to ride Tremor, as each day I added to his load with collected items, from flint stones, herbs and bark to a hand carved bowl we'd found along the way. I hunted every second day, stopping only for the hours it would take to scrape the hide and dehydrate the meat.

I had also killed my first and absolutely last deer. I'd taken the beautiful creature down with one well aimed throw when it wandered too close to our temporary camp. Before I could reach it my face was a river of tears. I think I cried the entire time I cleaned it and cured the meat. The hide hung over the growing tarp litter that Tremor pulled, drying in the warm sunlight. The meat was more than I could have possibly counted on from one animal. It had taken just a bit more than a day to dehydrate it all. Finally, I had to use the precious plastic bags Rosey had given me. I'd even sucked the air out, much like blowing up a balloon in reverse, as she had taught me so the meat would last into the months ahead.

To celebrate the arrival of my birthday and the distance we'd managed to cover in that short time, we set up camp for a longer stay in a small barn, next to the ruins of what was once a home. I'd spent at least a day checking every nook and cranny for stray animals, not unpacking anything until I was sure we were the only residents in the creaky small building. It wasn't my cave, but it would keep me dry and give me walls so I could rest properly for a few hours each night.

A few days after we set up house I discovered a small village only a few hours walk from where we were. I went there the next day with a few odd things to see if they did trade. My heart was giddy all the way home as I tested out my new boots. I didn't know where they had come from, but after spending many minutes deciding on a pair from the large table, I didn't care and generously rewarded them with most of my wares. The only thing that bothered me about this village was the way they looked at Tremor, I thought it was admiration for the beauty he was, but the goose bumps that covered my skin informed me they were looking at him like he was a meal or something equally useful. Tremor would not come along during any return visits to this place.

~

I argued with myself for three days. I didn't *need* that pretty metal tea pot I had seen on one of the trading tables. I thought I'd won the debate until I woke up and burned my hand trying to pour hot water into a cup. Maybe a pretty little tea-pot would be an allowable luxury after all.

Kismet pouted when I made him stay with Tremor and all of our belongings as I set off towards the village again. I decided on the walk that we really needed to be moving on soon. Many of the plants were moving past their prime and the fear of winter coming on too early nagged at me with each step. If we really hustled we could reach the caverns Kane had mentioned, in another month's travel time. I was dizzy thinking about setting up another winter home, until I remembered the work involved getting wood.

I practically skipped back across the field with my tea-pot clutched in my hand. Such a silly thing to be so excited about, but still something I would forgive myself for. Deciding on a short cut I headed out across a field of long grass. Not the wisest choice according to that demon named hind-sight.

As I tried to see my way over the long grass, the hair on the back of my neck stood up and I realized how utterly stupid my short-cut had been. I had trapped myself in a way I vowed never to do again. A noise came from behind and I spun to meet it with my knife in hand. This was the only time I didn't have my gun with me and I would never make that mistake again either. When the weeds moved again I took off through the long grass and headed in the direction I hoped brought me out into the open where I could see what I was up against. I made it one step out of the field when someone grabbed me from behind. Kicking and squirming I tried to get my hand free enough to use the weapon it held. Cloth was pulled over my head. Dropping the tea pot I grasped the material and pulled. More arms circled my legs as a hand shoved mine away from my face. I gasped once before everything went black.

~

Opening my eyes, I hissed out a breath, my head was pounding louder than thunder. Squinting I tried to look around but I was surrounded by pitch blackness. Trying to shift I realized my throbbing hands were tied tightly in front of me with a rope that stopped me from moving very far. I leaned back down and steadied my breathing, trying to hear any sounds around me. It took a lot of focus before it dawned on me that I could hear someone else breathing.

"Hello," my voice croaked. "Is anyone there?"

"Shh! Lower your voice."

They spoke so quietly I could barely hear them. It was a woman's voice. I shifted onto my side and tried to see where she was. "Can they hear us?"

I heard movement. "I don't know."

"Where are we?"

I could hear her breathing and moving around. "There were others but they're gone."

I shuffled to my knees and started trying to move towards her voice. "How long have you been here?"

Sitting there trying to look around, my heart began to pound. What could this mean? Who had me and why? The first thing that went through my mind was the mutant hunters had found me. My fear I was that I was about to be imprisoned with other survivors that were considered useful to the crooked leaders now controlling what was left of our country. I struggled against the ropes at my wrist, trying desperately to loosen their hold. Burns radiated up down into my hand, slowing me to stop and think it through.

Voices were suddenly close. Kneeling, I stilled and strained to hear what was being said, to see if I could figure out why I was here. The voices were muffled and hard to make understand. Definitely male though, that much I could be sure of. They came closer, almost as if they were standing right on the other side of the wall or door.

"She can't be valuable or they wouldn't have gotten her as easily as they did."

I frowned, hoping they weren't talking about me. Knowing this wasn't the time for injured pride I shook my head to clear it and moved towards where their voices were coming from.

"She's a bit on the small side, won't get much for a laborer."

I had to be the *she* they spoke of. My size pretty much cinched it.

"Why the hell did they go for her?"

There was a deep laugh. "gotta thing for redheads." was all I could make out in the loud snickering.

It was me. My heart was pounding in my chest, until I realized what they had said—they didn't think I was a survivor. Maybe I'd get out of this somehow.

~

It seemed like days as I lie there, occasionally saying something to the other woman. Each time she spoke it sounded like she was fading more and more. I tried to persuade her to talk more, to focus on something other than the rank darkness we were in. She tried for a while, but then would drift off and be silent for longer periods of time.

The first time I heard the bolt being undone, I shoved myself up and sat there waiting. Barely any light came in when they opened the door, telling me it was night. The man that entered also looked like he'd come downstairs, making me wonder if we were being kept in a cellar—which made the idea of calling out less likely to bring help.

The bowl of liquid he placed in my hands smelled greasy. I didn't say a word, just held it and waited for him to leave. When the taste hit my tongue I almost spit it out. It was like drinking oily salt water, there was no other flavor. It burned my throat on the way down and my stomach heaved when I swallowed it. With small sips I finished the bowl, not knowing how long it had been since I put something in my hollow belly or when I would be fed again.

Listening I could hear the woman trying to choke hers down as well. "Breathe through your nose when you swallow, it helps," I whispered.

A few minutes later my body felt like I had just eaten a large turkey dinner, that full sleepy feeling surrounded me. Briefly, before I succumbed to the sensation I wondered if they'd put something in the broth to keep us quiet and serene. My stomach hadn't growled and echoed into our silence since, so I had to feel a small bit of thanks for that.

~

The commotion brought me back to reality quickly. I strained to see what was going on, glancing towards the door to see if it was still night. It was lighter, but not much, so I guessed it was early dawn out there—or if I'd slept through the day, late evening.

No one came near me, but I could hear them moving around near the other woman. She made a muffled noise and then the men headed back towards the door. They carried her with them. I jerked at the rope, wincing as pains shot up my arms and right into my shoulders. Gasping, I leaned down onto my knees and watched helplessly as they dragged the other woman out and closed the door.

I was alone.

It wasn't that we'd had long discussions, but just knowing you weren't alone in the dark went a long way to ease the fear.

~

It felt like months, the hours dragged on. I'd listen carefully to the voices to try to figure out when the guards changed, but without ever seeing daylight or night I couldn't be sure if it was three times a day or only twice. My hands no longer throbbed; in fact I couldn't feel them at all.

I tried not to think about the woman I'd known only for that one day—or however long it really was, I tried not to think about Kismet and Tremor and what was happening to them without me to keep them safe. I drifted in and out of sleep, or maybe I was just numb, not feeling or sleeping at all.

When I stopped feeling thirsty, I knew I'd reached some sort of bridge. A person should always feel thirst to some degree I imagined. My stomach, was insistently reminding me that I hadn't had more than a few sips in the time I'd been here—I still didn't try to identify what the taste had been. With each second I lay there in the dark, I felt myself starting to accept not getting out of here.

My teeth hurt from trying to chew the cord around my wrists to free my hands. Why they only tied my hands I didn't know, was I a threat to the two men that were always outside the door? In my weakened state probably not much of one, unless they were afraid I'd flick dirt off the floor at them when they came in.

Jerking awake I stopped and listened, a wolf howled and tears rolled down my cheeks. I didn't think I had any fluid left inside me to come out. Would Kismet stick with Tremor? I lie there gasping through my tears wishing some nice and seemingly normal person would come across them and look out for them. Would that be asking too much? Rubbing my filth covered hands over my cheeks I tried to erase the tears along with the guilt that I had failed the two creatures I called friends.

Drifting off I thought of Bobby and hoped he made it to the mountains in one piece. As hard as I tried not to think about Kane, I did anyways. Would he know what happened to me or just wander around trying to pick up my trail and find where I'd settled. I wasn't going to be settling anywhere—I now admitted it.

Closing my eyes I rested my head back against the hard dirt floor and pictured Kane's silver eyes and that look he gave me when I annoyed him in some way. He'd carry on, as he had been doing before I met him and those he looked out for would forever be grateful.

~

My eyes popped open and it took me several seconds to remember where I was. My hip had pains shooting through it and I wanted to scream, but breathing took all the energy I had, there was none to spare for moaning out loud. The voices outside drifted within hearing and I strained to hear what they said. Was I being moved now? I fought to keep my eyes open to be aware when they did come inside. For half a second I could have sworn I heard Kane on the other side of the wall. I knew I was delirious now.

I listened some more, trying to keep my focus. What were they doing out there? I couldn't identify the sounds. Carrying something heavy maybe with all the grunting? I smirked alone in the dark; at least my imagination hadn't left me.

I heard a noise that rang so familiar I had to sit up, something had growled on the other side of the wall. In all the time they had kept me here I had not heard a dog or any noise that would lead me to believe there was one here. The growl was louder and a memory crawled down my spine. I had either lost all sense or Kismet was outside.

Struggling to my knees I knelt there with my head turned, listening carefully. More grunts preceded by the sound of fists hitting flesh. The feral growl of my companion sounded on the other side of the wood keeping me from him. I tried to call out to him, but I had no voice to use.

The sound of splintering wood crashed through the space I was in. A light blinded me, making me squint towards the door. I couldn't see who or what had caused the door to shatter and for a brief moment was stunned with fear. When fur rubbed over me, a tongue licked my face I knew Kismet had found me.

I tried to struggle to my feet, but I hadn't stood in all the time I'd been here and wasn't able to get my balance. A hand stopped me from landing face down in the dirt.

"I've got you, sweetheart."

It was Kane's voice. Sagging with relief and exhaustion I stopped trying to get up then felt myself being lifted into his arms. I'd never felt anything as good as that—ever. He held me against his chest as he freed my hands. I couldn't feel him with touch, but I still managed to wrap my arms around his neck.

"I've got you," he whispered in a rough voice against my ear. When he stood my stomach lurched, but there was nothing on this earth that would have made me ask to be put back down again. Fighting the bile rising in my throat I clung to him as he stepped out into the bright light.

A thousand knives felt like they were being poked into my eye sockets. Squeezing them shut I turned my face into his throat. Kismet growled loudly and I knew we weren't free yet. Another growl came from Kane's throat as he set me on the ground. I knelt there, clinging to Kismet who stood between whatever Kane was facing and me.

Peering through my lashes I could make out three other

silhouettes standing a few feet from Kane. My vision blurred when he moved, I could hear crunching that reminded me of bones snapping, but no one had moved as far as I could tell.

An inhuman sound came from Kane and Kismet pushed back against me. I could hear the gasps, but couldn't focus to see what caused them.

"Take one more step near her and you won't live to touch anything again," Kane growled.

His voice made the hair on the back of my neck stand up and it took no more than a heartbeat to fit all the pieces together. The bones snapping and his voice—he had changed. I remembered what he had told me to do if it ever happened, but I wasn't capable of making any kind of move even if I did want to leave, which I didn't.

When the sounds of flesh splitting started, I was able to focus if I just used one eye. Squinting I watched Kane, much larger than the man I knew fighting like a wild animal. One man was tossed through the air like he was no bigger than a small child. Kismet continued to snap and growl warnings, constantly pushing against me, keeping as close to me as possible.

The fighting was a blur to me. I stayed on the ground until the last one stopped moving. Kane stood with his back to me, and I could see the heaving as he struggled to catch his breath. Using Kizzy's neck as an anchor I forced my shaking legs to stand. One of the men struggled to stand up, swaying as he did. Kane took a step back towards me, but still didn't turn.

When he was within reach, I grasped the back of his jeans to keep myself upright. Moving stiffly, I stood beside him and placed my hand on his arm. My head was splitting from the light, but I was determined to keep my eyes open. Moving carefully I fought the dizziness and lifted my chin to look at him. His eyes were black and the face that was usually smooth was closer to that of a beast, his hair even seemed longer. He panted to catch his breath as he looked at me, jagged teeth filled his mouth. I could see hesitance in his dark eyes, but I refused to feed his fear. Gripping his arm tighter I leaned into him, almost losing my footing.

His arm wrapped around my waist and held me against him. I wanted to tell him it was alright, I wasn't afraid of this darker side but my voice was nothing more than a scratchy croak. Instead I stroked a hand over his huge chest hoping he'd still understand. I tried to swallow, "Home, Kane," was barely audible when it came out. The arm around me tightened enough for me to know he had heard me.

Lifting me up into his arms, he turned back towards the man trying to stay on his feet. "If you come after us—you die." Kane's voice was primal, an animalistic growl. "You tell Derek to give Ritter a message." His voice rumbled deep in his chest, vibrating against my cheek. "She's mine—if he crosses me on this one—I won't stop next time."

He didn't wait for a reply, just turned and began running with me held tight in his arms. The motion made me feel ill, but as long as he was taking me away from them I could have cared less.

CHAPTER TWENTY-NINE

My eyes popped open and the confusion set in—it was dark but the musty smell I'd been inhaling was gone. When I saw the flames I remembered what had happened. Kane. Turning I looked around for him, finally seeing him standing behind me looking off into the trees.

"Kane." My throat screamed at me for trying to say his name.

He spun immediately and moved towards me, Kismet right on his heels. "Don't try to talk." Picking up a small jug, he knelt down beside me. Lifting my head he held the jug to my mouth. "Try a sip to start."

The cool water hurt to swallow. I had no sooner swallowed it when I started coughing and thought for sure I was going to bring it back up again.

"Easy. It's going to take some time." Lowering the jug he leaned down and kissed my brow. "I'll make you some warm broth when we get back to your shelter—you won't be able to keep it down for the ride."

I was trying to sit up, trying to ask when something pushed into my hair from behind me. Looking up I found myself looking into a face I didn't think I'd ever see again. Tremor stood over me. A tear rolled down my face.

"Kismet found me, showed me where you'd been and

what path you'd taken—we'll discuss later why the hell you were wandering around a meadow alone— then he took me back to your stuff and we've been tracking you ever since." I tried again to sit up. "Relax. I left one of the people I trust from the village with your stuff."

I had to know. "How long…" I started coughing again.

Kane lifted me into his arms so I was upright. "From the time you left the village until now five days, almost six."

I closed my eyes, suddenly feeling tired again. What had felt like a month had only been five days.

~

I vaguely remember riding on Tremor, held tightly in Kane's arms, then reaching the little barn. I don't remember how many days I lay there, awake long enough to eat and drink only and then drifting off into a restless sleep, but Kane was there each time I opened my eyes. I only knew when it was night because he'd be beside me, holding me against him.

The first time I insisted on getting up, my head was pounding and my body felt disused and weak, but I was determined to get up and move on my own power. Kane supported me and let me pretend I was doing it on my own even when I would have landed on my face if his big hands hadn't been there to keep me upright. My wrists were marked with burns from the ropes, my hips with sores from being on the hard ground and not being able to move around but I was alive and other than a few pounds lighter, well enough.

I wanted to ask hundreds of questions, how they found me, how he knew the men that had held me, but my mind wouldn't stay focused enough to form the words so it would have to wait until I had a clear head. During the long hours of drifting in and out of consciousness I would think of what I could have done differently that day. Either my own overconfidence in my abilities or sheer giddiness over the teapot that I forgot to be aware, I didn't know. I would never leave Kismet behind unless I was armed with my gun, knives and anything else I could carry and conceal. I would also listen to that inner voice that everyone has as a child but blocks out as an adult, that warns you about dark eerie spaces and reminds you to always be able to see to leave.

~

The first morning that I could open my eyes without my head feeling like it was splitting wide open, I knew I had survived. One more notch in my timeline of continued existence was how I was looking at it from now on. Each day I'd survived since the very first moment that things began to change. I realized it had taken all of the events leading to this moment to. All I had to do was find the reason why and I'd be feeling more at ease with it.

Kane moved from the fire and my eyes widened when I saw what he was carrying. It was my tea-pot.

"Kismet found the spot they'd grabbed you," he smirked, "I thought if you'd risked your neck for this than I'd better bring it back with us." Setting it down beside me, he sat down and pulled me into his lap. "You took several years off my life by vanishing like that." He smiled even though his tone was dead serious.

"Mine too." I snuggled into his chest, feeling soothed by his heartbeat. "Kane, who is Derek?"

He stroked a hand up and down my back twice and then set me to sit beside him. "The Captain with *the* hat."

"How do you know him and Ritter?"

He was silent for several minutes, just kept touching me by running his hand up and down my arm as many emotions crossed his face. "The Red Bands have existed longer than most realize—they used to be the military. There was no need to retain the forces as they were, you can't defend when it's the planet declaring war. There have been so many miscues—it's hard to see where it all started. We weren't trained for that. " Leaning over he poured some tea into a cup and then handed it to me.

I took the cup and then watched him, not wanting to speak so he would continue.

"I used to be part of the military. Derek and Ritter were part of my team. We entered areas that people were leaving, trying to restore whatever and whomever we could."

I sipped the tea so I wouldn't ask the hundred questions filling my head.

"I was in charge," he continued quietly watching the fire rather than looking right at me. "When I got the orders to send two men into a questionable situation—strange deaths in a small village in some godforsaken third world country, I don't know the name of the place." Running his hand through his hair he paused and poured himself a cup as well. He didn't drink it, just looked into it as if it held the memories he was recalling. "I selected Ritter to go with me—we were the best trained, the strongest, the two who could find a way out of any situation." His silver eyes met mine in a brief glance before he looked back to the cup. "We got out believing we were unscathed—until we got home again."

A nerve ticked in his jaw as he sat there, rigid and tense. I wanted to reach out and comfort him, but wasn't sure how it would be interpreted so I remained where I sat, not speaking just listening.

"Ritter's whole family was wiped out by the virus—a new strand we brought back with us. My daughter fell ill before I did and then my wife…" Setting the cup down he stood up and paced away three strides before spinning back and stopping to look down at me. His eyes moved over me once, as if he contemplated continuing. "When I came out of the fever—I learned they were both gone and I lost it. That's when I found out how the virus affected me, I change into what you saw when I found you."

He waited as if expecting me to comment, I felt nothing negative despite the part he was ashamed of. When I didn't speak he continued.

"I destroyed my home and nearly my neighbor that came rushing over to help. I reported back to work, so did Ritter." He snorted, "we both found *comfort* in the structure of the military, it was what we knew.

I set the cup down and folded my legs beneath me,

giving him the time I sensed he needed to sort out his words. I couldn't be sure but felt I was being told a story that very few knew.

"Things started to change, the original organization was replaced, and the Red Band army was formed. Many left then and never looked back, taking their families to seek out something different. I stayed. I had no one to look out for any more—" He was restless and agitated, moving over to stir the fire even though I felt the warmth and didn't see a need. Still squatting down he stared into the flames. "We were sent to— *obtain*," he spat the word, "some people. Obtain was the order, but when we got there something wasn't right, it didn't mesh with our training. I tried to talk to Rit, telling him we weren't trained for this…"

Getting up again, he flung his arms in the air, aggravated. "I was not trained to harm unnecessarily!" Running his hands through his hair again he blew out a breath and spoke to the ground. "We fought. Both of us changing into something else—" Clenching his jaw, he paused.

I could see he was reliving that battle once more.

"I almost killed him—he lay there bleeding and unable to move. I watched him change back, to the man I had once respected, the same man that had hauled my ass out of shit as often as I'd done for him. We had fought and bled together—*together* for more years then I can count." Moving away from me he stood by the door and looked outside. "I left the service, or what it had become that day—warning him to never cross me again. I've been out here since."

I gave him the time he needed, the time I needed to process everything he'd said. In all the months I'd known him he had never said that many words at once. It wasn't just the words, it was the impact of everything said. I couldn't decide what he needed to hear. I know he was waiting for me to condemn him, to object in some way, but I couldn't find that inside me. "The Red Bands—they're collecting up mutants, survivors…" He leaned against the door, turning his body toward me as I spoke. "Do they know their leader is one?"

Kane chuckled quietly, surprising me. "Who better to strike the fear into a group of corrupted soldiers and thieves than a beast?"

I took that as a yes. In the delirium of the past few days, I'd had ideas. Whether I had the details worked out or not didn't matter, I had to share them. Now. It was the perfect solution—or at least a start. "The survivors have no one." He sent me a bewildered look. "They need a leader too, Kane." An odd smirk appeared on his face, as if he knew where I was going with this.

"I am not that man anymore."

I shrugged. "You're practically the president among them—us—you send aid where it's needed, negotiate for people, protect and rescue…"

Shaking his head, he walked over and dropped down to sit on his heels in front of me. "I think you need more time to recover, you're not thinking clearly."

Glaring at him, I continued, whether he agreed or not. "I know it's the truth. You're the obvious solution to so many problems and suffering. You build entire villages of survivors, Kane." He sighed but didn't interrupt me. "If you won't help, then find someone to do it. If the survivors banded together they could crush every single Red Band posse out there." I grinned. "Many of us have skills they wouldn't even know how to deal with. The people left on this planet need to be free to control their own destiny again. To not be afraid of their own species while they're trying to survive the battle with the earth." I snapped my mouth shut, and then just sat there watching him.

He signed loudly and then reached out and took my face in his large hands, cradling it between them. "I think you'd make a far better president than I ever could." Kissing my mouth softly he rested his forehead on mine. "Given the chance I think you alone could pull this off." As he released my face he sighed again. "I've been sending everyone I've been able to find to the mountains. The only way to stay safe is with sheer numbers alone and being somewhere safe."

Leaning back he studied me for a long moment. "*You* are the only person I haven't been able to convince to travel with others."

I looked outside at Tremor and then over to Kismet lying by the door. "I don't travel alone."

Chuckling, he got up and stood in front of me. "Something told me you were going to say that. I worry about you every second I'm not with you. I'm afraid for you, that something will happen to you, or to change you." He rubbed his jaw, looking at me. "I'd like to stay as long as I can." It wasn't really a question. I didn't respond. He held out his hand. "Come on, let's try a short walk today and see if your legs are better today."

I took his hand, I did want to see if I was getting better, but this discussion was not over.

CHAPTER THIRTY

I sat by the door to watch the sunset. My father said the sun could show you a world of information, if you knew what to look for. I was too young to realize I needed to listen then, because now I only thought it pretty and it would be back again in the morning.

It had now been two weeks since I'd been rescued and I was feeling more like myself. I'd decided that Tremor, Kismet and I would be moving again in the morning. Kane had stayed a few more days, but had left abruptly when one of the people he knew from the village had come to tell him something had happened in the South.

Despite his argument that he wasn't a leader any longer, he didn't do that job anymore, or couldn't band people together, he went to go see if he could help those in need. I didn't say a word to deter him from going, thinking of the times he'd arrived when I needed him, if someone had interfered, I wouldn't be here to stop him now.

He had tried convincing me to travel with a group leaving the village. I refused but promised that I would always travel with Kismet and have my weapons handy—that I would stop and camp near people looking for a new and safer life. Even though he didn't like it one bit, he still kissed me and told me he'd find me again before he jogged away.

Getting up, I went over to double check the packed litter, for at least the tenth time. The only thing left to pack was what we'd need until then. I had studied the map in Kane's handwriting hundreds of times now, studying the way, trying to think about the area he made me promise to avoid, even though I thought it would take weeks off the journey. It would be hard to ignore that part of my brain that was dying to know why he warned me away, but in all the time I'd known him he had yet to be wrong about anything out here.

As the sun set, I closed us in the little barn, a bit melancholy about leaving a walled shelter again. I hoped that once I reached the mountains, there would be a permanent place to call home. Tucking my knife under one side of my pillow and the gun under the other, I lay down to look over at Kismet. He sat beside the door looking at the litter. I smiled at the look he gave me, he knew we were heading out, if I wasn't mistaken he had as many mixed feelings as I did.

~

The first six days we walked, I was tired just from the traveling. I didn't want to admit it, but I wasn't fully recovered from my ordeal. The best I could do in these circumstances was to take short breaks when I needed rest. My stomach was still acting up when I ate, I decided it was meat causing the problem, I was better when I ate only fruit. I blamed that broth they fed me. I wanted to sleep more than before which worried me, I ignored it by forcing myself up early to head out before the day got too hot. Tremor and Kismet were, as always, tuned into me, staying close and not complaining when I stopped. I suspected my horse companion was happy for the breaks so he could eat again. He never seemed full, or maybe he was trying to stock up for winter.

The peak heat seemed to arrive when there were no trees for cover. Why that always seemed to happen, I didn't know, but I wasn't' going to suffer in silence. Off came my jeans and everything else except a thin cotton skirt, tank top and of course my boots. It was probably an odd sight, but I wasn't about to try barefoot and have to pull a chunk of something out of my feet. Without my feet our travels would end abruptly.

We pushed on across the open, none of us wanting to stop until we reached some shade again. Even my homemade harness for my gun was chafing and annoying me, but I wouldn't go without it again. When the sun would start to go down, we'd pick up the pace and push further forward or without the sweat rolling into our eyes. It was freezing on a few nights, which confirmed my skin was crispy fried. Our water was getting low, low enough that if we didn't find a new source soon, we wouldn't make it much further.

At dusk on the seventh day of travel, we stood on top of a hill to look down into a valley that stretched on for as far as we could see. Silhouetted in the setting sun was a large town, or at least the shell of what it once was. Beyond the town were trees. We didn't have a choice—spend two days in the sun to avoid it, or risk the town and use buildings to shade us as we traveled. I dug out my notebook with Kane's map and checked to see where we were on it. There was no valley and buildings marked. Either Kane had forgotten these or we'd strayed off his outline in the endless miles of open space we'd just covered. No way was I turning back to find the marker we missed on his sketch. A river and huge bridge, if I read it right was where we were supposed to be by now. Biting my lip I put the map away and looked back down at the trees on the other side. I didn't see any evidence of a river or a bridge.

Kismet sat beside me panting like he'd just run miles. I glanced down at him and then to the horse that looked, for the first time ever as if wanted to lie down and grab a nap. I made the decision that we'd figure out which direction to go later, and correct our course. We needed shelter and at least half a day's rest before we all collapsed from heat exhaustion. "Come on guys, let's go find a hotel."

As we headed into the town, my skin crawled, feeling like we were being watched. We followed a road, or what was left. Weeds had grown over the cracked and crumbling pavement, proving that nature prevailed over anything man would build. Buildings close to the road now were in piles of debris. The nearby trees were nothing but charred skeletons. Crumbled buildings, structures leaning on each other to stand—was I walking us into a trap?

Kismet walked a few feet in front of us, looking in all directions at once. The only sound that could be heard was Tremor's steps and the dragging of the litter behind him. That alone had me worried, there should be more sounds of —anything. A cat ran across the road, pausing to give us a startled look. I shook my head at Kizzy as his eyes asked if he could lay chase to it. Just the shocked look from the mangy coated creature eased some of my paranoia, it couldn't have seen many people recently to wonder what we were doing here. Either that or it was silently telling us to run like the wind.

My legs were complaining, feeling more lethargic as we went on. This seemed to happen around this time each day annoyed me more than I cared to admit. Pausing at an intersection, my eyes roamed over the rusted and deserted vehicles stopped mid-travel and abandoned when whatever had struck this place occurred. There wasn't enough damage for a big earthquake, or much ash to have been fire. Turning I assessed everything around us, then it dawned on me I was looking at the aftermath of a vicious tornado or tornadoes. The buildings outside of the trail we followed appeared to only be neglected. Obviously something else happened after the twister had ravished the town, but I wouldn't know what.

It wasn't uncommon for the few remaining after a disaster to pack up and move on to a safer location. We moved slowly, not wanting to rush back out into the open. What structures remained were blocking the sun well and the three of us were more than thankful for that.

As we crossed another street, I paused and looked at the building a half a block down. It had been a hospital. Now it stood in charred remnants, even though the buildings surrounding it had not been consumed by flames. Lowering my head I said a silent prayer for those that had been inside. It didn't take a genius to surmise that the inhabitants of the town had burned the virus victims during the peak of the outbreak. A small part of me hoped some had survived, but logic told me the blackened chains still holding a door closed made that nearly impossible.

Tugging on Tremor's lead a little rougher than necessary I hurried us past, not wanting to dwell on it any longer. We kept moving, numbed by the heat when a sound brought us to a sudden stop. It was water, running water. Pulling out my gun, I moved slowly towards the sound, Kismet right beside me. I stopped in front of a wall where I heard the sound, and took a deep breath to shake the droopy feeling. Chances were anyone still in this area wouldn't leave a water source unprotected—I wouldn't if I was left behind in this hollow, empty place.

I crouched low, moving to the end of the wall; Kismet crawled inches ahead of me. He stopped, ears forward seeking any sound I wouldn't hear. When he started moving again I took that as a good sign and was right on his tail as he rounded the corner. I cocked the gun and raised it to be ready to shoot anything necessary. Scanning the area quickly I couldn't detect anyone. Still not ready to accept we'd just found an oasis from the scorching heat, I turned slowly and looked for any spaces that a person could hide in.

In the center of the area was a water spout shooting straight in the air a good ten feet. Looking around, taking in everything in front of me I tried to figure out what this place had been. The water fell back into what could only be described as a well, but with a floor. Puzzled I went over and knelt by the edge of it, dipping my fingers into it and then sniffing. It was water but why it was spraying into the air with no power or pump I had no idea. Kismet came over and sniffed his way around the fountain before he started drinking it. I was going to go with his instincts and hope he knew what he was doing. Getting up I went back out to get Tremor.

The three of us stayed there until the sun started to set. I'd stood knee deep in the pooling water, not wanting to step out again in case it vanished and was only a mirage in this concrete desert. After studying the area further I could only come to the conclusion it had once been a gathering point in the small town, maybe a gallery or official building of some sort. Whatever it had been, I was happy the water hadn't dried up and was here when we needed it. Filling the last jug we had, I walked over and set it on the dry surface outside the raised edge. At least we'd have water for a while, once we forced ourselves to leave this place.

I was just stepping out when I heard what could only be a cough. Diving for the harness that lay safe in the dry area surrounding us, I pulled the gun out and the crouched down into the water and turned slowly. The coughing noise rang through the silence again. When a silhouette appeared along the far wall, I cocked the gun and aimed.

"I'm not…" they coughed again, and bent down to hold their middle. "I'm harmless," they gasped and then took a few steps into the open holding up their hands. A jug was in one hand, the other empty. "I just need…" Coughing again. I cringed at how painful it sounded. "Water." They took three stumbling steps, falling to their knees a few feet from the wet spray.

Kismet went over, crawling on his belly towards them. I stood my ground and waited for his assessment before making any move. He stopped beside them and sniffed. A shaking hand came up and hovered in front of his nose to let him smell. He did and when he licked it I knew we weren't in any danger.

Tucking the gun into the waist of the skirt, I stepped out of the water and went over to them. Grabbing one of the jugs I had set down I uncapped in and knelt down beside them. An older woman shoved her hair back from her face and offered me a smile.

"I didn't mean to frighten you," she whispered. I held the jug to her lips, with shaking hands she took it and sipped a few times. "I waited to see if you were going to go…"

"Are you alone?" I scanned the darkened areas around us as I asked.

Swallowing, she nodded. "Yes." She coughed again as she sat up, it sounded as bad, but she recovered faster this time. "I just have to get the water and get back." Pushing to her knees she handed the jug back to me and picked up her own. "I've been gone too long."

Frowning I looked back into the darkness. "Get back to where?"

A look of horror crossed her face as she realized the information she'd given away. I touched her shoulder, "It's okay, and we're not going to hurt anyone."

She looked over at Tremor and then to Kismet lying beside us. "You travel alone?"

I nodded quickly. "Yes, just my animals and I."

"You're braver than I am." She said quietly, her voice filled with remorse. "I couldn't leave with the others—we've been here alone for a long time."

"We?"

Leaning over the water she held the jug under the spray. "My daughter was sick when they were leaving…"

"They left you."

Capping the jug, she tried to stand then wobbled a few times. "Yes."

"Your daughter is alright?"

Lifting her head, she took on a defiant stance I had to admire. "She's a survivor."

I smiled and got up, taking her elbow to help her. "Me too."

A shocked looked appeared in her eyes. "I…"

"Mother?"

I jumped when the voice came out of the dark. Moving away, my hand hovered over the handle of the gun. Kismet jumped up.

"I'm fine Ellie, just waited too long and the coughing came back."

A tall girl came out of the dark and ran to her mother's side. "I told you I'd go when the sun set." Through her blonde hair she watched me as she helped her mother to her feet.

"You're a nightwalker." I stared at her when a puzzled look crossed both her mother and her face. "It's okay." I assured her. "I'm a survivor too." I stepped closer. "I'm Bree." I motioned to the large animal now looking over my shoulder. "This is Tremor and the fuzzy one is Kismet."

"He's a wolf," she whispered.

"Yeah, but he thinks he's a dog, so let's not tell him anything different." I smiled at the woman.

"I'm Ellie and this is my mother, Julie." She looked out into the dark. "We have to get back; it's not safe around here lately—not even at night." Julie started coughing again and doubled over from the deep biting sounds coming from her chest.

She didn't have to elaborate why, I knew the answer. Red Bands. "I'll help you." Turning I grabbed the jugs and moved over to strap them to the litter. "Help your mother up on Tremor, she can ride." I didn't know how far we were going, but I did know Julie wasn't well enough to be moving around. Grabbing my boots, I pulled them on and pulled the harness over my head. Sending me strange looks, Ellie helped her mom up onto Tremor, who behaved well and let them, thankfully.

I let Ellie lead Tremor as I followed along beside them moving through the streets. Kismet ran along the other side, keeping watch.

"How long have you been out here on your own?" Ellie asked as we rounded another corner.

"I guess it's been a year now."

There was a long drawn out silence. "We haven't seen anyone we wanted to in almost that long."

"Can you go in the sunlight at all?" It was something I'd wanted to ask each nightwalker I'd met.

She shook her head. "No. It's like having a migraine

and the flu all at once as soon as the rays hit me." She rubbed a hand down her mothers' leg. "We've tried a few times to go, but didn't get far."

I remembered the U-Haul trailer Jacob and Vince traveled in during the day. "Is it the fact of sunlight or can you move as long as it doesn't touch you directly?"

Turning she studied me for a moment. "We've tried covering all of me, but it didn't help all that much, I was too ill to keep moving."

"Hmm." My mind was sorting through ideas faster than I could process them. There had to be a way to get them somewhere safer, somewhere with people. I couldn't leave them here. I turned and looked at Tremor for a moment. "Is there anyone else here?"

An eerie feeling filled the moment. "No, they didn't survive."

My heart ached for the tone in those words. "I'm sorry."

"We're here." She reached up and helped the older woman down from Tremor. I stood back while she helped her mother through a large garage door, moving Tremor inside I was surprised when she went back and pulled the door closed and latched it. I didn't want to tell her that didn't offer much protection if someone wanted to get inside. Going over to the other side of the space, she slid some racks on wheels back and then bent down to grasp a rope on the floor, pulling up, she flipped up a trap door revealing stairs leading down. Her mother smiled at me and went down the stairs.

I went down and was surprised to find what looked like someone's living room set up in a cellar. It had all the comforts of home, with a footstool and small table beside a large overstuffed chair.

Ellie grinned at me. "It took months to drag all of this down here."

I nodded as I looked around. "I guess it would." Clothes hung all along the one wall, and what was stacked along the other shocked me, rows of canned goods.

The look must have been clear on my face. "They left almost everything behind, so the six of us left behind went shopping."

"What happened to the others?" My eyes moved over the blankets hung along the back of the wall, one was flipped up to reveal a mattress.

Julie sat in the chair and leaned her head back. "They were too old to for the trip, so we moved into one space together and tried to make a home." She pushed her graying hair back off her face. "We lost the last one a few months ago."

I moved back to the stairs. "I'm going to unhook Tremor and let him wander up there if that's okay."

Ellie looked from her mother to the stairs. "I have to close the hatch at dawn."

I nodded. "That's fine, we'll camp up there." I went up the stairs, trying to breathe through the emotions that were threatening to choke me. I couldn't leave these people here, alone and relatively defenseless. Going over I began to unhook the straps from the saddle. Kismet came over and whined at me softly. "I know boy, we'll figure something out."

I heard the footsteps behind me, glancing over my shoulder I smiled grimly at Ellie. "What's wrong with your mom?"

She knelt down and rubbed a hand over Kismet's head, much to his utter delight. "Bronchitis. We raided the drug store but what was left ran out months ago." She looked back over at the hatch. "It's getting worse."

I wasn't about to promise any miracles, I didn't know if what I could do worked on anything chronic as I'd only tried it on fresh injuries. "Feel like going out and doing some scouting with me?" She knew the town, and I needed to find a way to help them travel.

"What are you looking for?"

I shrugged. "I won't know until I find it." I set the litter down and folded the straps neatly over the top of. "We'll take the boys with us, unless you'd like to leave Kismet here for your mom."

She studied him. "He's really a wolf."

"Yes he is and also the best protector you could ever ask for."

"We'll leave him here to keep Mom company." She got up and went over to the stairs. I motioned to Kismet to follow. "I'll just go tell her we're going out."

~

We rode Tremor through the silent streets. I let Ellie sit in front after she confessed she had no knowledge of how to use a gun. When we found an old looted sporting goods store, I told her to stop. Puzzled she followed me inside.

"What are we doing, going fishing?"

I smirked and then frowned and wondered if nabbing a fishing rod wouldn't be such a bad idea. There wasn't much left but I found a few small tents and some other handy items buried in all the things left behind. A few fishing poles and line were added to the pile; along with a large duffel bag to haul it all back with us. When we moved into a small storage area, I knew what I was looking for and squatted down with my flashlight scanning the crushed piles of boxes and things scattered all over the place.

Moving over to a pile, I pushed some of it out of the way until the glint of gunmetal glared back at me in the light. Sure enough it was a small hand gun. Picking it up I weighed it in my hand and then began pushing more garbage out of the way. They'd have kept most of the ammo out front locked up, but surely they'd have had some stock in the back. Standing up, I moved the light to shine on the shelves that were covered with dust and cobwebs.

Taking a step my foot hit something and sent it skittering across the floor. Following the noise I spotted a single bullet spinning in the beam. Looking down at my feet, I knelt down to push the papers and cardboard out of the way. I had no real idea if the silver shells lying in the trash matched the hand gun, except to try one. Frowning I pulled the magazine out of the bottom of it and slid the round into it, it fit. Shoving the paper aside I picked up a small bag and emptied it onto the floor and started picking up the ammunition.

Ellie stood in the door not saying a word. I picked up all I could find, which was more than I expected from the bullets scattered across the floor.   Getting up, I smiled at her and held out the gun and bag. She took them without a word, probably thinking I was asking her to hold them. "I'll teach you how to use it later."

"Me?"

I grinned. "Yes. How you've survived this long without any sort of weapon to defend yourself I have no idea, but once we're moving you'll need it."

"Moving?" She paused, one hand on her hip, "maybe you missed the part where I mentioned I couldn't go out in the sun."

I nodded as I moved by her, hefting the duffle bag up over my shoulder and heading back to the hole in the wall. "No I caught that." I stopped and looked down at a package by my feet. It couldn't be—kneeling down I picked I up and dusted off the cover. It was a camping shower. I'd seen something like this once in an advertisement. You hung it from a tree or whatever and filled the bladder with water. Grinning I opened the duffle bag and stiffed it inside. A shower after all this time would be a treat, hot or cold.

Flipping the bag up onto the horn on Tremors saddle I glanced over my shoulder. "Somewhere in this town is the solution for you travel during the day, and we're going to find it."

She accepted the boost up into the saddle. "We are?" Holding the bag of ammo out in front of her face she studied it. "What exactly are we looking for? Maybe I know where it is."

I climbed up behind her and took out my gun again as I nudged Tremor's side. "Some kind of lightweight trailer that we can modify—at least that's the picture in my head right now."

She was quiet as we moved down the next street. "I know where there are some trailers and things, but none of them are small."

"Let's go look." Honestly I didn't know what I was thinking of trying. All I knew was I could not leave these two people alone here to struggle alone in such a dismal place. If I could find some way to move Ellie during the daytime, she could watch over us at night. I'd have to teach her how to fight and use a gun before I trusted her with my life while I slept. I wasn't planning on lengthy traveling companions or anything; I just wanted to get them to the safety of a village along the way.

I kept thinking of Micah, Jacob and even strange Vince—they would think Ellie was a treasure beyond compare. Nightwalker females weren't exactly common, and she represented a chance of them finding someone to love.

Ellie stopped Tremor outside a chain link fence that was now lying on the ground. Getting down, I started shaking the flashlight and looked around the yard on the other side. Remnants of bicycles lay scattered all around our feet. I climbed through a broken window to get inside while she stayed outside holding Tremor and keeping an eye out. Ellie had obviously encountered Red Bands sometime during her life, she was just too alert to danger to not have. I climbed over parts and pieces that meant nothing until I came to the storage garage at the back. Ellie had told me she'd seen trailers here. She hadn't been kidding, there were several in what I hoped was working order. I passed one that looked like the small one I had found and then given to the native family.

I was just about to give up and go back outside when I spotted a large box leaning against one corner. Going over to it I brushed off the layer of dust and then sneezed three times as a result. Shining the light on the picture on it I grinned. It was a three wheeled trailer with a canopy on it. The wheels were large, like on a bike so pulling it shouldn't be too difficult. Of course I didn't know how I was going to pull this and the litter, but we'd figure something out. When we got back I'd have to study Kane's map and see how close we were to another settlement and then just hope it was the sort of terrain that would make this possible. Regardless of all the kinks in my plan, I'd figure it out. I shoved at a door, trying to get it open wide enough to drag the box out. Pausing, I looked at the box, it was much bigger than I was. Shaking my head I went out through the door and navigated back around to get Ellie.

~

Julie came up out of the hatch when we closed the big door again. "I was beginning to worry."

Ellie helped me take the box from Tremor's back. "We had to walk back." She turned and grinned at her mother over her shoulder. "You're not going to believe some of the things Bree brought back."

I could hear the excitement in her voice. "We still need to do a bit more shopping, but I can wander tomorrow and see what I can find."

Julie looked at the box we stood over. "A trailer?"

Ellie nodded excitedly. "She may have found a way to get us out of here."

I hoped like hell she was right and I wasn't setting her up for disappointment. "If we can get you as far as the next settlement, I'm sure they'll have a better way to travel." I motioned to the box. "We can see about making this a bit bigger—but we'll have to limit the size or we'll never be able to pull it. "

Julie's mouth dropped as she pulled her daughter into her arms. Before she could say anything she started coughing again, this time hard enough she dropped down to her knees and folded over. Ellie stood there rubbing her back and not saying anything. I could see the thoughts in her head moving across her face, she didn't think her mom was going to make it much longer.

Knowing I may regret ever saying anything, I spoke

softly when the coughing fit had finished. "I may be able to do something about your condition, Julie."

Ellie's face lit up. "You have medicine?"

I grimaced, "no, not exactly." I started to explain what I could do when I realized how farfetched it would sound to people that hadn't been around many mutated survivors—which led to me talking about all of the people I'd met since coming out here. When I was done they both looked shell-shocked by the fountain of information I'd just poured out. They had honestly thought so few remained and that it was pointless to leave the town. They hadn't even thought that so many others would survive the virus, believing Ellie was a rarity that didn't exist anywhere else.

I shared some of the dehydrated meat with them and we talked about the places I'd seen and even of the map Kane had drawn for me. They knew of a bridge, not too far from where I'd traveled in the endless sun, so we made a plan to aim for it once we had everything ready. There was at least two days of preparations before we were ready to leave. And that was before testing the plan in my head to see if the trailer would protect Ellie from the sunlight.

I was nearly exhausted by the time we had a rough game plan to work with, but was still determined to try to use my mutated skill to see if I could help Julie. She sat in front of where I kneeled. "I honestly don't know if this will do anything. I've only ever used it on injuries and infection."

She smiled at me. "If it helps in any way, I'll be grateful."

"Is it going to hurt?" Ellie asked from where she knelt a few feet in front of her mother.

I recalled Kane's description. "I've been told it burns when it's working." I rubbed my hands together. I had no idea how to go about this so I pictured where I'd need to reach in order for this to work. Moving closer I placed my one hand on her back under her shirt, just above her shoulder blades and then when Ellie lifted the front of her shirt I rested my other hand opposite on the front. Closing my eyes

I took a deep calming breath and focused on my touch.

It took a few breaths before I felt any change in my hands and when the heat started I hoped that meant it was going to do something. Julie gasped and I smiled with my eyes still closed recognizing the sign from past experience. I kept my hands there until I felt a bead of sweat roll down my forehead, lifting them away I opened my eyes and balanced myself so I wouldn't tip over. I'd used more energy than I had thought.

Julie leaned forward onto her hands, panting softly. "I feel out of breath," she whispered.

Ellie looked from her mother to me. "Does that mean it did something?"

Wiping the sweat off my face, I slumped back against the front of the chair we sat near. "I can't' be sure. Any other time there's been blood or bruising to check to see if it did anything."

Julie chuckled quietly. "I feel light headed—as if my body is getting far too much oxygen all of a sudden." She grinned at me. "I think it did something, but we'll know when the next coughing fit hits."

Inside I hoped she wasn't just saying this to make her daughter, and me feel better. "I need to get some rest now."

Ellie jumped up and came over to me. "Are you alright? You look pale now."

I smiled as I pushed to my feet. "I'm okay, this always happens when I do that."

"You're a miracle from God." Julie said as she got up off the floor.

I laughed. "No, I'm a mutant survivor of the virus—but we'll go with your description for now."

Ellie motioned to the blankets hanging. "You can use my bed."

I looked back at the darkened area. "Actually if it's all the same I'd rather sleep up there with Tremor." She frowned. "I was recently abducted and I'd rather not sleep in a small dark space right now."

Julie gasped. "How did you get away?"

I knew a stupid looked crossed my face, one of those sappy ones. "A man named Kane broke me out." As I climbed the stairs I spoke over my shoulder. "With any luck you'll meet him soon enough. He'll be hot on my trail as soon as he's done helping some others."

CHAPTER THIRTY-ONE

Julie still coughed, but it wasn't as severe and she could breathe much easier. We discussed trying another session before we headed out, but she insisted we focus on getting things ready first.

For two days we worked together to get everything ready. We used pieces of thin plywood to make the sides taller and reattached the canvas on top. It was light enough that even Julie could pull it along without difficulties. Ellie was thrilled when we pulled it out into the hot sunlight and left her sitting there for what had to be an hour or more. She said it was warm, but she didn't mind because it had been so long since she felt the heat of day she'd didn't mind suffering through it at all. This wonderful revelation spurred all of us into working harder towards moving on.

I went back and got one of the smaller bike trailers, there was no way I was going to ask them to leave the canned food and so many other things behind. We made a harness so anyone of us could attach it and pull the little trailer. The day before we were to leave, I wandered about taking any treasures I thought would be useful or necessary. The grocery stores were all but empty, but I still managed to find a few things that were like winning a lottery. Shampoo, toothpaste, toothbrushes and laundry soap were the treasures I hoarded.

I had big plans for my portable shower and that shampoo. I'd even managed to find a few towels and sweaters in a small store. I even picked up one that I thought might fit Kane.

We set out a few hours before dawn, so Ellie could walk the first part as we headed towards the bridge. When the first rays of sunlight appeared, she got into the trailer and asked that we not leave her sitting anywhere to fry in the sun if we stopped. Yawning, she smiled at her mother and then closed the door.

I worried about Tremor pulling the litter with the trailer behind it, but he hadn't complained yet, so I hoped he was going to be okay with it if we hit rougher terrain. We plotted a course using the road as much as we could.

Julie told me not to worry about rough trails, when the sunlight was up she was dead to the world and wouldn't feel a thing. I had to compare that information to Vince thinking he was a vampire and it was eerie to think he had some of the facts right.

For a week we continued on, walking all day until the sun set. After a short break, I would ride Tremor while Julie rested in the trailer and Ellie pulled the smaller one. We'd spend a few more hours pushing towards our destination while the sun was down and the air was cooler. By the time we stopped for the night I was exhausted and thankful that Ellie had improved with her target practice because I dropped off into a dead sleep as soon as my body was stretched out. At some point I hoped I would begin to feel more like myself. Maybe I'd see if there were any healers or people with medical knowledge at the settlement. I couldn't keep up this pace for too much longer I thought, before losing myself in sleep again.

~

On the second week of our travels it was a little slower going as we traveled through the trees. I'd always taken for granted how Tremor had moved through the trees with ease, now that we had trailers to navigate among fallen branches and rocks it was more complicated.

We sat around the fire talking quietly about things we missed the most—a hot bath had the number one spot on the list—when a branch snapped in the darkness. Kismet was up beside me facing the source of the noise faster than we could stand. I had the gun out and cocked and aimed, Ellie right beside me doing the same a few seconds after that. Julie was behind us, staying low to the ground beside the trailer. I had the brief thought of teaching her some self-defense when I heard something that made my heart almost burst free from my chest.

"Easy, Red—last time I checked I wasn't bullet proof."

"Kane?" I stood up slowly, not believing what I heard.

He stepped out of the trees. "You know anyone else stupid enough to come up on armed women?"

I tucked the gun back into my harness as I skirted around the fire towards him. "I can't believe you're here." I practically jumped into his open arms.

He didn't even give the other two more than a quick glance before he picked me up and crushed my mouth in a heated kiss. Lifting his mouth from mine he smiled at me. "Maybe an introduction would be good."

"Oh." I slid down him and turned around. "This is Julie and her daughter Ellie. I found them in a town..."

"I don't remember leading you to any towns on the map."

I cleared my throat. "I got off track through that really big open area..."

"Hmm." He said in reply.

"Ladies, this is Kane." I grinned at Ellie who looked him over with wide eyes. I grabbed his hand and went and sat back down. "Ellie is a nightwalker and they've been trapped in that town not being able to travel, so it's a good thing I got lost."

He sat beside me and I knew he was taking in the trailers and everything about the two women that still sat there smiling at him. Kismet came over and put his head in his lap.

"Was everything okay when you got there?"

He turned to look at me, reaching with his free hand to run his fingertips down over the scar on my cheek. "I was too late to get some of them back, but the others are now on their way to safety."

I knew there was something he wasn't saying but I didn't want to push for any information that might break my heart.

"I came to find you." He gave me a look that was so serious I caught my breath. "They raided Maisy's village—" He grasped my hand. "Maisy was injured, but will recover. They got two of the boys and despite every attempt we couldn't find them."

I closed my eyes and took a deep breath running through the faces of everyone there. "Who?"

"The two I rescued— I don't know what the hell is so important about those two boys but they are determined to have them." He reached over and pulled me against his chest. "I'm going back to move all of them. They don't have enough protection to stay there now." Leaning down, he kissed the top of my head. "Tanner wanted to come with me to find you, but I convinced him to stay and help get everyone packed up."

I grinned. "What did he think I was going to do?"

Kane chuckled. "I think he just wanted to make sure you were okay—I told them about your little holiday."

I sighed. "That probably wasn't wise."

"Actually Tanner was pissed at me because I let you set out alone again."

"He is so sweet." Kane made a noise that didn't sound very positive. "What?"

He shook his head, his silver eyes burning into mine and I knew it was something he didn't want to say in front the other two. He continued to sit there looking at me and for a moment I just sat there falling into that look. With a gentle touch he ran his knuckles over my cheek and then exhaled and turned back towards the two looking at us from the other side of the fire. "Where are you heading?"

Julie grinned, "where ever Bree takes us. We didn't even

know settlements existed. Since everything changed we've stayed in the town trying to survive."

Kane listened as they told them their story, his hand stroking down my back through most of it. I was so distracted by his nearness I wasn't really listening. When he moved to stand I was startled back to reality. "I'm going to scout around us before we settle in for the night."

I got up. "I'll come with you." I took his hand and smiled at the women as we walked into the darkness.

~

We hadn't got far when he pulled me into his side. "How are you doing?"

I inhaled the scent of him. "I still get tired faster than I'd like, but over all I'm good."

"I've been half out of my mind worrying about you this time."

I grinned and looked up at him. "Only this time?"

"No." He answered abruptly. "I felt like a heathen climbing all over you the day before I left…" His arms tightened, "you've destroyed all of my resolve, not to mention my restraint."

I laughed against his chest. "Good."

In one fast move I found myself lifted off the ground and crushed against his body. He kissed me in a breathtaking way before his lifting his head to look down at me. "I don't know if I'll make it back before winter. You should stay at the settlement with Ellie and her mother until I return." He nuzzled into my throat nipping it gently with his teeth.

For a half a second I was ready to agree to anything as long as he was doing that. "I'll head to the caverns and wait out the winter for you there."

A low growl came from his throat. "I just want you safe, Bree, *why* do you fight that?"

Using my knees I gripped his sides and leaned back from him knowing he wouldn't let me fall. "I'm going to head to the caverns," I whispered and then watched him.

He closed his eyes and took a deep breath before

opening them. "You drive me insane—and I let you."

"I just want to keep moving. I don't know the reasons."

Huffing out a long breath, he rested his forehead on mine, his arms tightening. "I ran for close to two solid days to get to you this time…"

"I'm jealous."

He snorted, "I'm trained to keep moving regardless of pain or exhaustion —that's not the point I'm trying to make…"

I grabbed his face and kissed him before he could say any more. "I don't want words, Kane. Show me."

I found myself hoisted up his large body so I was straddling his waist. Stumbling over to a tree, he leaned my back against it and yanked at my shirt to lift it to my throat. The skirt was pushed up my body as he fumbled with the zipper in his jeans. The whole time his mouth didn't leave mine. He kissed me with such furry I was dizzy and if it hadn't been for his hold on me I would have slid boneless to the ground. With a groan he lifted his head and grasped my waist tight, lifting me higher against his body. I could feel the hard tip of his need for me just touching me and then as his eyes held mine he pushed into me as he moved my body down in one motion. Gasping, I huffed out a breath, already quivering inside.

Clenching his teeth, he lifted me up and slammed my body back down against his. I bit my lip to keep from crying out. "Kane," I moaned.

"You're…" he thrust hard into me again, "mine." His mouth crushed mine as I held on trying to find the rhythm when there wasn't one. His movement was wild and unsteady as he raced to bring us both to a point where all of it made sense.

~

When my feet finally touched the ground I had no feeling in my legs, my head was light and I panted for air.

Zipping up his pants, he pulled me back into his arms. "I should be shot for the way I treat you."

I giggled breathlessly. "I happen to *like* the way you treat me."

He smiled wide back at me. "You have no sense of self preservation."

"So you keep telling me."

He scooped me up into his arms and started to walk back in the direction of our camp. "I'll have to leave early— it's going to take a lot to move a group that large at once."

Resting my head on his shoulder I closed my eyes. "Tell everyone I said hello."

"I will." He stopped just before we moved back through the trees. "I may not be back before winter—get to the caverns if you can and I'll come for you."

I nodded, unable to say anything that wouldn't sound wrong in one way or another.

He set me back on my feet and led us back to the fire. Julie was already in bed for the night and Ellie was pulling on her boots to go walk the edge of the camp as she did at night.

~

Three days later I woke up with a start and looked around. It was bright and hot out already.

"Hey, you're finally awake. I was beginning to worry."

I focused in on Julie and then looked around. She had the rest of the camp packed up and ready to go. "You should have got me up."

She smiled. "You needed rest." Coming over she knelt down beside me. "I used to be a mid-wife's assistant before all of this began…" She gave me a soft look, "If I'm not mistaken you're going to have a baby."

It was so ridiculous I almost laughed, but didn't as an odd feeling came over me. "I doubt that." Sitting up, I flipped the blankets off my legs. "Why would you think that?"

Julie smirked. "You're tired and a little moody every now and then," standing up she picked up the blanket I abandoned and started to shake it out. "You have a glow to you one minute and then look green around the gills the next." Sending me a wide grin she began to fold up the blanket. "Only one thing in this world can do that to a body all at the same time."

"I haven't even had my period since the virus." I mumbled trying to sort through what she said inside my head.

"I know, neither has Ellie."

"I doubt getting pregnant is even possible—Kane's a survivor too."

She chortled softly. "You've told us about the young children with survivors—" she sent me a heated knowing look, "and your Kane is probably the most virile man I've ever set eyes on."

I felt my face flush. I couldn't argue any of that. "I'll see if the next camp has a healer and I guess we'll find out." With that I stumbled away to find a few moments of privacy. It was crazy really, to even think it might be a possibility. It was just the side effects of my kidnapping lagging a bit longer. It had to be.

~

The next morning we reached a small settlement. There was evidence of them packing to get ready to move. I had to wonder if Kane had been here when we weren't even questioned as we entered the camp area. They agreed to take Ellie and Julie with them, thankful for another set of eyes at night and hands to help during the day. I spent a few hours with Ellie practicing with the gun again—mostly drawing and aiming, we didn't dare waste ammunition— before I decided to get ready to go. I did go see the healer briefly before I set out again. I had mixed feelings about that. Feelings I would spend a week or more processing as I traveled.

I had one goal now, to reach the caverns and if I had to move all day and night I planned on doing it as quickly as possible.

CHAPTER THIRTY-TWO

I started to notice a spotty change in the leaves, and panic set in. According to the map I should have been at my destination. Winter wasn't going to wait much longer and I had a lot of work to prepare. For a few days I debated on moving non-stop, but I was too tired from the endless heat to try it.

When the rain started it made moving even slower, the ground was slick with mud and frustration was getting the best of me. When we were forced to pause under a heavy canopy of trees to wait out the rain, I wandered as far as I could to see what lie ahead on the next leg of our journey. The trees opened into a rock covered hill appearing to go on for miles. I didn't know if we'd be able to travel over that pulling the litter if the rain kept pounding into the ground. Turning to head back to the temporary camp, Kismet came out of the trees and flew by me. With a growl of frustration I went back to call him, but couldn't see him anywhere. I was not in the mood to go run through the rain to track him down so I stood there and waited for him to either come back or the rain to slow.

He yipped loud from where ever he was and I knelt down to scan along the rocks to see if I could find him. When his head popped up from between rocks, he looked excited. Frustrated, but still interested enough to see what he'd discovered this time I stepped out into the pelting water and worked my way up the flattest surface I could find. As he came into sight again I stopped so suddenly I almost tipped forward onto the rocks. Just behind him was an opening in the rock. Had he found a cave for us?

Tripping over the rest of the distance on the rock I ran into the opening and stood there. It was light enough I could see into it without a problem. It was huge from where I stood. Pulling out the gun I moved in slowly, not sure if I was about to disturb some animal's resting place or not. It dropped down gradually then leveled out into a very large area. There was a fire pit in the middle I wondered if we'd found someone else's home. Moving around the edge slowly I didn't see anything that signaled anyone had been here for a very long time.

I went back to the entrance and stepped out, looking down over the rocks for a smooth trail for Tremor. We'd stay here through the rain and then scout around a little further to see if there was where we could stay. Of course unless there was a hotel nearby, it wasn't going to get any more water and wind proof than this.

~

I had convinced myself that the healer was wrong, that I was just exhausted and still suffering from lack of food for that week in captivity. The third day in a row when I randomly threw up without much warning at all, then an hour or so later not feeling even slightly odd, I was halfway convinced. The final verdict came when I went to put on my jeans to go tree climbing—my jeans that had fit me a few weeks earlier refused to meet in the middle and zip up. There was no way I was just putting on weight from lounging about doing nothing. I was working my butt off getting wood and supplies for the winter.

I sat there in my cave and just looked at the wall. I was going to have a baby. It excited me to think it was even possible. Of course it scared the hell out of me too. I knew very little about pregnancy and caring for an infant. My knowledge was non-existent when it came to delivering a baby. I missed the internet like no other technology I'd known before. In a few keystrokes I could have had enough information to write a book.

For half the day I weighed the pros and cons of trying to make it to another village or settlement to be near help, but if the temperature fluctuations were any sort of indication I'd never make it before winter was here. I counted the marks that represented days at least twelve times trying to figure out how pregnant I was. Although not having had a period since I'd gotten the virus made that really hard to track. It had to have been after Kane found me because I'd been feeling fine up until that point. So that made me somewhere between three and four months—meaning I was going to be huge in the worst of winter and then having a baby in the wet part of spring.

I pondered Kane's map and wondered again how long it would take me to reach the base of the mountains. We were so close, able to actually see them in the horizon now. Instinct told me I wasn't going to make it so I went with that. What I had to do now was gather enough supplies and wood so that I wouldn't have to go too far when the snow was deep and I was too big to move with ease. The whole thing was overwhelming and it all sunk in when I was laying there looking at the fire. Kane had said he probably wouldn't make it back before winter began, but I still hoped. I had to wonder what he was going to think and feel about me having his child. Would he be happy or would it just dredge up emotions best left in the past with the death of his daughter.

I tried not to cry, much, when I thought about it all. Maybe it was the hormones my mother used to talk about, but tears came to me easier than they ever had in the past. I was going to be a mother and that whole thought clenched it for me. I fell asleep with my hand cradling my tummy, I couldn't feel anything yet but I knew that wouldn't last long.

~

The next month, when I wasn't throwing up or feeling like I was going to throw up, was spent hauling as much wood as I could find into the cave. Fate, in the form of a furry wolf, had shown me this large cave so I could store more in it. I used the first tall row I made to block the entrance off to create a wind block. I had enough tarps that if I could figure out a way I could make a curtain to block it off completely in the height of winter. Outside the cave entrance I piled more wood, hoping that by the time I needed it things would be thawing out and it would also serve as a snow fence to keep us sheltered.

Even though it made me want to throw up, I went back to hunting for animals with hides. I was going to need to make something I could wear when my belly expanded, not to mention I'd need something warm to put a baby in. Overall I kept myself busy so I wouldn't cower in the corner freaking out about doing this alone.

~

By the end of our next month in the cave, I had a small second fire pit set up that was burning low all the time, even on warm days, to dehydrate apples, meat and anything else I was able to find. On the furthest side away from any flame was the store of bundled dried grass, piled as high as I could reach. There would be no winter trips to find extra food for Tremor this year.

When I was too tired to move I'd sit and work on making a small cradle. With dried leaves and bark I made a soft basket and lined it with rabbit hides. It was definitely a labor of love as it took longer to form and make than anything else I'd done since I took off on my own.

Diapers had been days of thought and trial and error. Gone were the days of nice disposable nappies. Not that I agreed with the waste they created, but how is a girl supposed to make diapers out of nothing. In the end I had to dig out the needle and thread and made them out of my nice snuggly sheet. A luxury I traded for last spring, thinking how soft and warm it would be against my skin. Then again I guess that worked for a baby's bottom too. I'd hoped they could be absorbent and for waterproofing I worked at making a plastic wrap around that I could just pull up between the baby's legs and loosely tie. This part of the parenting was going to strictly be a trial and error learning process.

I had weird cravings for food my body hadn't had in a long time. Things like milk and chocolate—things I had no hope in finding anytime soon if ever, so to distract my body and console my taste buds I began experimenting with the dried berries I'd found. In the end I had created a sweet wild raspberry tea that seemed to tide over my sudden craving for sugars.

We were nearing the end of the third month in our little home when I began to feel the strong movements of the tiny being I sheltered inside me. I tried to write as much as I could when things happened so I could share them with Kane later on, if he wanted to know. My body seemed to change with each day and I wasn't sure how much longer I was going to have clothes I could adjust to wear. It must have been a sight when I went out of the cave to hunt. Shirts weren't a problem because I had those large enough to layer through the cold months, my pants still fit, up to my hips so that's where they sat tied in place by a loose belt that wouldn't cut off my circulation. I'd waddle around in Bobby's coat with my belly sticking out in front of me, the gun in the harness rested on top of the ever growing mound—yep I was a regular fashion don't for sure.

When the first snow began to fall I was out with Tremor and Kismet checking snares and keeping watch for any last minute plants or supplies I could add to our growing pantry. The huge fluffy flakes floated gracefully to the ground. It was beautiful even though in the back of my mind I knew once the charm wore off, winter would try to beat us down with frigid squalls and freezing temperatures. The baby moved as if it wanted to see the first snow-fall as well. I rubbed my hand over my tummy and soothed the squirming infant as best as I could.

When we climbed back up the small incline to the cave entrance, I turned around and looked out over the land. I watched for Kane, regardless of whatever reason I tried to convince myself not to. Winter was here and I needed him here too. I didn't know if I could do the rest of this on my own, even though logic smacked me saying I really didn't have a choice.

Kismet sat beside me, leaning against my leg in silent support. I rubbed the top of his head and kept looking into the distance. By morning we could be waist deep in snow, I couldn't know for sure so I stood there a little longer than I usually did, just taking in the scene and etching it to memory so when those long days of winter began to close in on me I'd have it to recall and look forward to.

That night I counted the marks and made a note of how long it had been since we'd seen anyone. It had been a long time. On the top of the page I had a separate count, more of a countdown and if I was anywhere close to the mark I only had roughly eight weeks until I would be having a baby. That fear that tried to swamp me kicked in right about then, as it did whenever I thought too much about the impending delivery. The what ifs' were enough to paralyze. Swallowing my fears I began to make a name list, trying out each one verbally and if it passed I wrote it down. After four of each male and female it occurred to me that I didn't even know Kane's last name. How devastating was that? I'd known him how long and been with him countless times and I didn't even know the man's last name? Exhaustion had me chuckling about it a few minutes later, not that last names were even needed out here. We had no mailing addresses to use or phone numbers to register, or paychecks or bills—yawning, I put the notebook away and went over to close the tarp over the entrance. Everything would be just fine I told myself as the animals watched me as I snuggled under my blankets and closed my eyes.

~

Everything was not fine, a few weeks after that. I

couldn't get comfortable, I constantly had to go to the bathroom, I couldn't sleep and I wanted to clean—which if you think about it is hard to do with dirt and stone as your dwelling. The worst thing was I wanted yogurt. With all of the odd things I was feeling and going through, that's what set me off in a temper. That I couldn't have something I didn't even like to eat. I decided any woman that did this more than once was completely insane and should have a psychological evaluation done immediately. Then I would get all weepy and regret thinking so harshly about something so wonderful and sit cradling my belly and cry myself to sleep.

I just wanted to hold my baby—outside of my body. Together we had mastered walking in the deep snow and ice fishing. Either this winter wasn't as cold as the last, or the extra blood pulsing through me kept me warmer—I wasn't sure but when too restless I would go outside and move around as much as I could.

That only lasted until the baby dropped lower then walking even a few steps was hard to do. I walked like those old cow pokes I'd watched on movies with my Dad, with my knees pointing out and slightly bent. Of course to counterbalance the bulge out front and the giant breasts I'd grown, I had to tip back at the same time.

Whoever said pregnant women were beautiful—was quite obviously blind and just trying to make his woman feel better.

When I reached the point where everything annoyed me, I had to wonder if all women went through this. I mean e-v-e-r-y-t-h-i-n-g. Kismet annoyed me, Tremor breathed too loud, the wind was irritating, the snow exasperating, even the fire got on my nerves when it crackled too much. I wasn't really hungry, although that wasn't shocking when I had no stomach left to put food in because it was flattened by the child inside me that was really too big to fit inside me.

I began to panic on how I was going to have this baby alone. I couldn't lie on my back, I wouldn't be able to see what was going on, not that I thought I wanted to but I knew

I had to. Where was Kane? Winter was long under-way, leaning more towards the end and he still hadn't found us. Had I found the wrong caverns? I didn't know. I tried several positions and it didn't seem to matter I had no flexibility in any of them.

By the tally marks I kept, the baby should be here by now if I'd calculated right. I began to wonder if I'd done the math wrong, which wouldn't be surprising when I couldn't recall much with the lack of sleep. This child did not like to be lying down and I wasn't allowed to either. Some nights I ended up sleeping half sitting up, so the baby would rest and I could find some peace.

When I was at the point where I didn't think I could possibly take any more I began to feel ill all over again. For a day and a half I felt nauseous and could only manage to stomach some weak broth. I was so tired I think I must have slept though half of it and by miracles the baby let me rest for once.

I woke up feeling like I had to go to the bathroom and groaned in frustration. Getting up was not the easiest feat at this point. Grumbling the whole time I struggled to my feet and took two steps towards the corner near the entrance. My stomach felt pinched and suddenly my feet were soaked.

My water had broken.

After all the thoughts I had to wanting this baby out now, I changed my mind in that instant and decided I didn't after all. Moving back towards the bed, more fluid ran down my legs. I stood there feeling nothing but that *eww* feeling you get when you're a mess. Kismet was at my feet immediately looking up at me with worry. I took the time to rub the top of his head and persuade him to go over by the door before I moved over to the little cradle to set it near the bed.

I'd been preparing for this moment for months, keeping spare blankets and sheets near the bed, water and towels, even a knife to cut the cord—thank goodness for movies or I would have missed that altogether. Now that it was time I was scared. When the first contraction hit, I almost dropped to my knees—forget scared, try terrified.

I removed my clothes and knelt down by the bed, pulling the spare blankets from the pile. I had thought enough ahead to keep the area where I sleep dry. Now all I had to do was wait. The next pain hit and I wondered just how long I would have to do this before something beyond the squeezing pains happened. I tried breathing and focusing like all the movies had said to do and discovered in that moment that the Hollywood version was pure crap and not at all helpful.

Finally something happened and how I didn't manage to throw up through it I still don't know. I was soaked with sweat and shivering at the same time while lying on my side propped up on a log I'd covered with a fur pelt. I felt like I should push so I did, but then it burned beyond any sensation I had ever felt and I sucked in a breath and held it.

Could that be normal? I wasn't sure. Relying once more on the movies I remembered when the doctors were yelling to push the woman was generally screaming at the same time and I now knew it wasn't with the joy of the moment. My whole abdomen clenched again and the pain ripped through me, I couldn't do this much longer so with having no other options I pushed myself up to lean on the log and pushed with every ounce of strength I had. The burning was incredible and then it just eased away. Panting I looked down and then half out of me was a messy little baby, arms flailing about. Forgetting the pain I pushed once more and reached to ease the baby down onto the soft padding beneath us. I crawled over with shaking legs and lie down to look at this tiny person. He was trying to open his eyes to look around. Using a piece of the blanket I wiped off his little face and was rewarded with an angry cry. I started crying and the rest from there was just a blubber-fest with me shaking and crying and the baby shaking and crying.

I managed to get him cleaned up and wrapped warmly and with weakened limbs I kind of put myself back together—and cleaned up the mess the best I could. A midwife I would never be, the whole of it made me feel like throwing up. Burrowing under the furs I held my baby in my arms and decided we both deserved a short rest after that ordeal.

A few hours later, I was walking around the cave on rubber legs, a towel tied between them, stoking up the fires and bringing fruit and water closer to the bed. Keenan was asleep in his cradle and looking like the most beautiful creation I had ever seen. Kismet was beside him keeping guard, and Tremor had moved over to keep an eye on the new companion. I was excited—beyond tired and for the rest of my life would be in awe of the entire thing. Wrapping a fur around me, I slipped on my boots and stepped just outside the tarps covering the entrance. The snow was falling in slow motion from the sky but the air seemed warmer. I looked into the distance and watched for a few minutes but when I saw no one I went back inside. I planned on staying in the furs for the next several days and resting whenever my son allowed.

CHAPTER THIRTY-THREE

As winter started to fade into spring once again, my days and nights were busy. The wood was down to the last row to keep the cave as warm as possible for Keenan. He was just close to a month old now and I could no longer remember what life had been like without him. I took him out with me a few times, constantly paranoid if I left him behind with his sitter Kizzy—although I was paranoid when I took him with me too. I'd made a pouch to strap to my chest so I could keep him close.

The only time we'd come close to other people were when a Red Band patrol was passing by. I was glad we were outside at the time so hiding was easier. I'd held my breath with one hand on my son and the other clutching my gun while the noisy men moved by us unsuspecting. That's when I realized it was time to get ready to move on again. The cave was too accessible without the snow and just about anyone walking the right path would see it. So I began to stock up on meat again, once we were on our way I wouldn't be dallying anywhere too in the open, not with Keenan to watch over.

I rushed back from checking the snares and peeked inside the tarp to see Kismet lying in front of the basket and the baby sound asleep. Breathing a sigh of relief I sat down outside the entrance just to take a few minutes to breathe in the fresh air. The snow was melting rapidly now, which meant the rains were going to start soon. I shivered remembering how much it rained last year, and traveling constantly wet.

A movement through the trees brought me to full alert, gun and knife in hands and ready. As the man came out of the trees my heart stopped. He limped but still moved toward me at a quick pace. It was Kane. As he moved closer the glasses came off and I could feel his eyes taking in every inch of me. At the bottom of the knoll he stopped and stood there.

"Are you going to shoot me?"

I remembered the gun in my hand and lowered it. "You're injured."

He moved a few steps up the incline, "healed, mostly."

"Mostly?"

A few more steps. "I fell and hurt my leg at the start of winter. I couldn't wait any longer to find you."

"You fell? Who were you rescuing?"

Smirking, he stepped in front of me. "A young family was trapped in a mud slide—they're fine." He reached out and took the hand that still held my knife and aimed it away from his body. "I know you might feel like stabbing me, but you'll feel guilty about it later."

I tucked the knife away. "I don't want to stab you, much." I stepped into his arms, "I thought you were never coming back."

Lifting me he looked into my eyes and then kissed each one of them. "They had to hold me down to stop me from coming sooner." Gently he kissed my lips.

I caught my breath and wrapped my arms around his neck. The reasons didn't matter now, it meant everything that he was finally here. I grasped two handfuls of his hair and held his head still while I kissed him with all of the pent up emotion I'd been holding in for months now. He growled in response attacking my mouth. Reaching around behind me he grasped the back of my thigh and hiked me up higher on his body and turned to take us into the cave.

I could feel the limp in his step and should have stopped to see if he was as healed as he said, but I couldn't. I knew I needed to stop and tell him my news but his mouth on mine was making my body heat, my heart speed up and my head was spinning. We deserved this reunion that had been denied for too long. I heard his pack hit the ground. I felt the cool wall against my back as his mouth moved down over my throat biting at the skin gently and all I could think was we had too many clothes on. As if reading my mind he yanked my jacket down my arms and started pulling my shirt out of my pants.

A waking cry echoed through the silence.

Kane stiffened and lifted his head. In slow motion he lowered me to the ground and stood there looking at me with black eyes, panting heavily.

Keenan cried out again. Smiling up at the bewildered look I was receiving I rubbed my hand over his chest and stepped around him. "I think your son wants an introduction," I said calmly as I walked over to the basket.

"Son?" his voice squeaked.

Reaching into the basket, I lifted up the squirming little bundle in the fur and turned back towards the man that looked to be frozen where he stood. "Yes." He took one stumbling step in our direction and then stopped again. "He's almost a month old—you were gone a long time." Kane still hadn't moved, he was in utter shock and it was the first time I had ever seen him unsure. I walked in his direction, with careful steps and smiling. My heart was stuck in my throat waiting for his reaction.

When I stood in front of him, I lifted the baby higher in my arms and looked up at the black swirling eyes. "This is Keenan."

"Keenan," he whispered on a breath, "my son?"

I grinned. "Yes he is definitely yours, looks just like you in fact." With that he finally looked away from me and at the small child looking right back at him.

"Is he—is he alright?"

I chuckled. "He is fine. He's demanding and likes to think he's in charge." I could see his hand shaking as he reached out and touched a finger to the soft baby cheek.

"I didn't know…" He frowned, "did you know the last time I saw you?"

I laughed quietly. "I didn't know until none of my clothes fit. I didn't think we could—"

Kane grinned around the shocked look on his face. "Obviously we can." Moving a little closer he looked down at the tiny man. "He's—amazing." I could hear the emotion in his voice.

Keenan started to squirm again, his face scrunching up. "He's hungry," I said with a smile on my face. Leaning down he kissed me quickly and then moved back so I could look after the baby. I sat down by the fire.

Kane stood a few feet away watching us intently. I waited for him to say more, because a thousand words were flying across his face while he observed the feeding child at my breast.

He sat down across the fire pit. "I am astound you did this alone. Why didn't you go to one of the camps so you weren't alone?"

I cuddled the baby close and looked over at the emotional man across from me. "By the time I figured it out, we wouldn't have had time before winter hit. So I worked like a dog to gather enough wood and supplies to get us through."

"I'm sorry I wasn't here."

I didn't have to look at him to know he blamed himself for me being alone. "How bad is your leg?"

He grunted and rubbed a hand over the lower part of his leg. "It will be fine."

I knew that answer like I knew my own name. It was not anywhere near fine. "I'll look at it once I get him settled down again." I moved to get up and he scrambled over beside me, helping me to my feet.

"He doesn't eat for long."

I smiled at the concern in his voice. "Don't let a little snack fool you, he's a little piggy and will wake up from his next nap starving and raising a ruckus until he gets what he wants."

Kane followed me over and watched as I bundled the baby back up and placed him in the basket. When I turned he was right there in front of me giving me an odd look. He took my face between shaking hands and kissed my mouth gently. "You destroy me, Breenna. I abandon you to go through all of this alone—you have every right to shoot me."

Clasping his wrists I looked up at his serious eyes and smiled at him. "If it did I would just have to turn around and heal you—rather counterproductive isn't it?" I patted his hands. "Now, let me see this *mostly* healed injury."

Reluctantly he let go of me and sat down. Working his boot off, he pulled at the pant leg.

"Take them off," I knelt down beside him.

He sent me a heated look. "If I take them off it's not going to be healing we're doing."

My heart skipped wild in my chest. "We'll do that too, right after I look at your leg."

With a grunt he leaned back and worked the pants off his body. I had to bite my lip to sit there and let him get both legs free. My ramped up hormones cooled quickly when I caught sight of the long reddened gash down his shin. "What did you do?"

He dropped back to look at the roof of the cave. "The bone came out through."

I gasped and glared at him. "Who looked after you?"

"Leif and Tanner." He cleared his throat, "Tanner practically tied me to the damn bed so I wouldn't get up too soon."

"Good, I owe him." I moved closer, rubbing my hands together.

"I think he's half in love with you," he added in a strange

voice.

I grinned and stopped long enough to look at him. "Well that's too bad for him. My heart belongs to a wild man with a heart of gold."

"His belongs to you," he looked at the basket, "and this little man now." Lifting his arms he dropped them over his eyes. "Hurry so I can touch you."

~

When I woke up a short while later I was sore and aching in a way that made me feel so loved I didn't care. Reaching out beside me, I found empty space. Sitting up I looked in the basket and found it empty to. My heart caught in my throat when I frantically looked around only to see Kane sitting by the fire with a fur wrapped around his waist holding Keenan in front of him. Keenan arms were moving around so I knew he was awake and oddly silent as they sat there sizing each other up. "How long has he been awake?" I couldn't believe I hadn't heard him.

"Not too long. We negotiated and agreed you could sleep for a while longer." He sent me an adoring look. "He's beautiful, Bree—you're amazing."

That weepy feeling threatened to overcome me, so I turned and rearranged the blanket around me to avoid answering for a moment longer. "I can't take all the blame."

Kane got up and moved back over towards me. "I think our agreement is about to come to a loud finish."

I could see the arms starting to flail around outside the furs.

Kneeling down beside me, he bent over and kissed me tenderly. "I didn't hurt you did I?"

I blushed. "Not in any sort of bad way."

Chuckling, he handed me the gasping baby that was starting to get wound up to make real noise. I lowered the blanket and guided the rooting infant to my breast.

"You take my breath away," Kane whispered in my ear as he lay down beside me propped up on one arm. "I would have made it back to you if my leg hadn't had other plans. I was in the mountains when it happened." With gentle fingers he touched the side of my neck, lingering over the bite scar he'd left behind. "I have a home for you, Bree—a cabin on the edge of a growing village." He kissed my shoulder, "I wanted a home for you, for us—that's why I was there." He made a strange noise in his throat. "I left your strange friend from the city with it watching it for me until I return." He shook his head. "He insisted on doing it."

I smiled. "He made it there, then." I signed in relief.

"Yes and many others as well—we were surprised when you didn't." He touched Keenan with a whispering touch. "Now I know why." Moving back he looked at me with so many emotions going through his mind his eyes were swirling between dark and silver. "I thought a lot about what we talked about—someone to lead the survivors." He grinned. "Although I still say you'd fit the part better than I would. You have your own group of followers already."

I touched the soft hair on our son's head. "What do you mean?"

"It seems you've touched many lives along the way. I've met a Jacob and talked to Micah—that can do nothing but sing praises of you. He actually claims a woman with flaming hair saved his hide from being fried—someday I'll ask about that one." He kissed my shoulder once more and watched his son. "Everyone from Maisy's is there and can't wait for you to arrive. The stories of the tiny red-headed woman with the wolf are endless."

He sat up and looked at me for a long moment. "I can't promise I'll always stay—I won't risk you or Keenan when things are bad—but I will promise I will always return." He clasped my hand between his two bigger ones. "I need you, Breenna. Say you'll come with me this time and live among those that need you."

I felt the tear rolling down my cheek and had no thought to wipe it away. "We can pack up tomorrow."

He pulled me into his arms, heedless of the squirming infant that was unhappy with the interruption of his meal and held us tightly as he kissed me over and over again.

~

I was nineteen when the world went crazy, nothing that was would ever be again.

I was twenty-four when I finally figured out that all things have to change, it's inevitable and wholly necessary for evolution. Living through the changes is where the challenge begins and those left standing are the ones to carve out the new path leading into the future.

ABOUT THE AUTHOR

Jacqueline Paige lives in Ontario in a small town that's part of the popular Georgian Triangle area.

She began her writing career in 2006 and since her first published works in 2009 she hasn't stopped. Jacqueline describes her writing as *all things paranormal*, which she has proven is her niche with stories of witches, ghosts, psychics and shifters now on the shelves.

When Jacqueline isn't lost in her writing, she spends time with her five children, most of whom are finally able to look after her instead of the other way around. Together they do random road trips, that usually end up with them lost, shopping trips where they push every button in the toy aisle, hiking when there's enough time to escape and bizarre things like creating new daring recipes in the kitchen. She's a grandmother to eight (so far) and looks forward to corrupting many more in the years to come.

Jacqueline also writes under the pseudonym of J. Risk

Jacqueline loves to hear from her readers, you can find her at

http://jacquelinepaige.com

Author note:

Did you enjoy reading one of my books?

If so, PLEASE help spread the word on social media. You can help by sharing on Facebook, tweet about it, post something on Instagram, Pinterest. Posting a review on your favorite book sites go a long way to help authors. With your help in keeping my books "out there", I can continue writing to keep those stories coming.

Writing and promoting can be very time consuming. I love talking to readers, but the hours spent on keeping so many social media outlets current can become overwhelming and time for writing pays the price. If you can take a few minutes to help, that would be awesome. Thank you!

By Jacqueline Paige

ANIMAL SENSES
1 *Heart*
2 *Scent*
3 *Passion*

MAGIC SEASONS ROMANCE
1 *Beltane Magic*
2 *Solstice Heat*
3 *Harvest Dreams*
4 *Autumn Dance*
5 *Winter Mist*

Dreams
Three steamy stories that started with a dream

Curses
Two tales of curses.

After the Silence
Volume 1 Bree

SINGLE TITLES
Solitary Witchling
Salvation
Café Serenity

<u>Writing As: J. Risk</u>

THE ALTEREALM SERIES
1 *The Huntress*
2 *The Seer*
3 *The Empath*
4 *The Witch*
5 *The Chronos*
6 *The Warrior*
7 *The Telepath*
8 *The Healer*
9 *The Kinetic* (coming soon)